FALKIRK COMMUNITY TRUST

30124 02518335 3

AF

D1336368

anno — 1369 — domina

altic sea

teutonia

lithuania

the golden horde

the sea of azof

the bavarian league

tyrolian highlands

the dalmation march

byzantium

the adriatic sea

elian gulf

venice

ariminum

rasenna

veii

thessalonica

aegean

the caghgrian isles

etrurian peninsula

salerno

taranto

gulf of taranto

messina gulf of taranto   the hande ... elen

messina

the three sicilies

ian sea

sea

Irenicon

AIDAN HARTE

Irenicon

Jo Fletcher
BOOKS

First published in Great Britain in 2012 by

Jo Fletcher Books
an imprint of Quercus
55 Baker Street
7th Floor, South Block
London
WC1U 8EW

Copyright © 2012 by Aidan Harte

The moral right of Aidan Harte to be
identified as the author of this work has been
asserted in accordance with the Copyright,
Designs and Patents Act, 1988.

All rights reserved. No part of this publication
may be reproduced or transmitted in any form
or by any means, electronic or mechanical,
including photocopy, recording, or any
information storage and retrieval system,
without permission in writing from the publisher.

A CIP catalogue record for this book is available
from the British Library

ISBN 978 0 85738 896 4 (HB)
ISBN 978 0 85738 897 1 (TPB)

This book is a work of ̇. characters,
businesses, organizaṫ ̇, places and events are
either the product of the author's imagination
or are used fictitiously. Any resemblance to
actual persons, liv̇ ̇ dead, events or
locales is entirely coincidental.

10 9 8 7

Typeset by Ellipsis Ḋ ̇ Limited, Glasgow

Printed and bound in Great Britain by
Clays Ltd, St Ives plc

Falkirk Council

GM

Askews & Holts	
AF	£18.99

To Bronagh

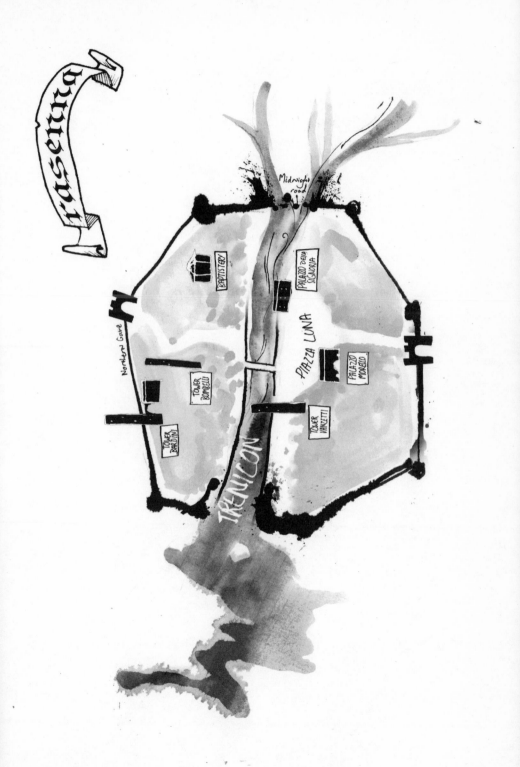

PART I:

ANNUNCIATION

And when the wise men returned with report of a new-born King of the Jews, Herod was exceeding wroth, and sent forth, and slew all the children in Bethlehem from two years old and under.

Amongst the lamentation of the mothers, the voice of Mary was heard in mourning. Her child, with the rest, was slain.

And behold, the angel of the Lord appeared to Joseph in a dream, saying, Arise, and flee into Egypt: for Herod will seek the Mother, to destroy her also.

Barabbas 2:1–13

CHAPTER 1

'Valerius?'

Madonna! Where *was* he?

If the boy got hurt, the Doc would mount her head on a stick next to the Bardini banner. Valerius might be a handful but the little *stronzo* was their only Contract this year. Besides, a dead Concordian would imperil all Rasenna. Sofia's dark eyes flashed with anger and she swore again: in her haste she had forgotten her banner. Being unarmed in Rasenna used to be merely careless. These days, it was suicidal.

Valerius ran down the sloping streets with his head in the air, pursued by his shadow made strangely large by the blood-washed light. Smashed roof-slates crunched underfoot like leaves in an autumn forest. He followed the trail of the topside battle as it moved downhill towards the river, focused on the jagged red slash of evening where the towers leaned towards each other across the emptiness.

The Concordian had the pale blond curls, soft skin and,

when he tried, the disarming innocence of a cherub. Now, scowling, he resembled something fallen and impious. Sofia, only five years older than Valerius, watched him like his mother. He had endured this ordeal since his arrival last Assumption, but to return to Concord unblooded? Ridiculous.

The hunt was practically the whole point of a year in Rasenna – that was what his father had paid for, not endless drills and lectures on banner technique. So when this chance came to sneak out, Valerius took it, vowing to get the General's money's worth. Two households in combat: what a story! This was Rasenna's real meat: raids and rogue bandieratori. He wasn't in real danger; this was still Bardini territory. Sofia wouldn't be far away.

He couldn't see the individuals leaping between rooftops, just the banners they wielded. Bardini black outnumbered Morello gold four to six, and the Morello were retreating – noisily. These boys weren't bandieratori, they were like him, just bored students looking for fun. So it was an unofficial raid, then; the gonfaloniere would never sanction such a pointless attack.

Valerius followed through one backstreet after another, concerned only with keeping up. A black flag vanished behind a corner. He turned it himself and saw nothing but swallows listlessly drifting on air rising from the empty streets.

No Morello, thankfully. No Bardini either. Valerius stopped to listen. The wall he leaned against was built around the ghost of an Etruscan arch, the gaps between its massive blocks stuffed with crude clay bricks, bulging like an old man's teeth.

He could hear the river now, but not the battle. He had been in Rasenna long enough to know that most raids ended 'wet'. How could so many raiders disperse so swiftly? It began to dawn on him that Bardini flags need not be wielded by Bardini.

How could Sofia be so irresponsible? He was the Bardini Contract, the Bardini's only Concordian student, and that made him an obvious target for the Morellos; he should be protected at all times. The General would hear of this.

'Keep calm, Concordian,' he rebuked himself, just as the General would have. He knew northern streets pretty well after a year, didn't he? Not like a Rasenneisi, not as lice know the cracks, but well enough. He looked for clues to his location. That ceramic Madonna, perched in a street-corner niche and drenched in blue-white glaze, that would orientate a Rasenneisi. The ghastly things all looked the same. The superstitions of Rasenna were not the answer; he would rely on Concordian logic. The raiders had led him down and south. If he followed the slope up he would eventually reach the shadow of Tower Bardini and safety.

He turned around. Now he had a plan it was easier to fight the urge to run for it. Yes: he was impressed with his courage, even if he did keep glancing overhead. If only his footsteps wouldn't echo so.

At last, something familiar: the unmistakable drunken

tilt of Tower Ghiberti – the Bardini workshop was close after all. Valerius' relieved laughter trailed off when a rooftop shadow moved. Another silhouette emerged on the neighbouring row. And another. Lining the tower tops, above and ahead of him. He counted seven, eight, nine – a decina – but forced himself to keeping walking. Whoever they were, they were interested in him alone. It was not a flattering sort of attention.

Behind him someone landed on the ground and he was torn between two bad choices, to turn defiantly, or to run.

'Walk.'

'Sofia! What are you doing?'

'Exceeding my brief. Doc said babysit. He didn't mention stopping you getting yourself killed.'

'I wouldn't be in danger if—'

'I said *keep walking*!'

He whipped his head round to continue the argument, but went suddenly mute. Anger enhanced the Contessa's beauty. Her dark eyes were wide and bright, her olive skin glowed like fire about to burn. She looked fabulous just before a fight.

'What do we do?' Valerius asked, his confidence returning.

Her wide-shouldered jacket was a bold red, in contrast with the earthy colours favoured by most bandieratori. She was not tall, but she held her head proudly. Below her large brow and sharp Scaligeri nose were the smiling lips that graced statues of cruel old Etruscans.

But she was not smiling now and her pointed chin jutted forward. 'You'll do as I say. I'm going to help these gentlemen get home. Give me your banner.'

'I don't have it,' Valerius whispered, losing hope again.

'*Madonna*. This is going to be embarrassing. I'm not exactly in peak condition.'

Valerius looked down at the sling on her arm. Without a single banner, against a decina, even Sofia . . .

'What do we do?'

'When I say run, run – *Run!*'

Sofia led the way through the maze of narrow alleys, not looking back or up. She knew by fleeting shadows over-head and loosened slates smashing around them how closely they were pursued. She skidded to a stop when they reached Piazzetta Fontana. The alley leading north was blocked by five young men. And now Valerius saw what Sofia already knew: they were not students. They were bandieratori. Their ruckus had been part of the decep-tion.

Sofia pushed Valerius into an alley on the right – it was barely a crack between two towers, but it led north.

'Run. Don't look back.'

He didn't argue.

She boldly stepped forward. 'You *bambini* must be lost in the woods. You're on the wrong side of the river.'

There was consternation as the southsiders saw who they had been chasing. 'What do we do?' asked one.

'Her flag's black. That makes her Bardini,' said the tallest boy with assurance.

'I don't know – if Gaetano—'

'Show some salt! There's one of her and lots of us. Haven't you heard who broke her arm?' The tall boy continued talking even as he approached her. 'She's hasn't even got a flag—'

Way too casual. Sofia was ready. She dodged his lunging banner and snatched it away in one movement and his jaw had no time to drop before she floored him with a neat parietal-tap. By the time she looked up the others had vanished, gone to get Valerius before she got them. Sofia returned to the narrow alley and vaulted *left-right-left* up between the walls.

Etrurians said that Rasenna's towers were different heights because not even the local masons could agree. But they made good climbing, and bandieratori jumped between towers as easily as civilians climbed stairways. The upper storeys were peppered with shallow brick-holes, invisible from the ground, which had originally supported scaffolding but which now allowed the fighters to scale what they couldn't jump.

With only one working arm, Sofia knew her climbing was awkward and inefficient. Even so, when she made topside she took a moment to catch her breath and scan the endless red roofs, feeling no need to hurry despite their head-start. This was her territory, and she knew every roof, every crumbling wall. They did not, and in the wan light of dusk they'd have to be cautious.

In the heat of the chase the boys let one of their number fall behind, and it wasn't long before Sofia caught up. His falling scream was cut off by the crash of broken slates.

Two down, out-classed on strange rooftops. Normally in this situation it would be each raider for themselves, but these three knew that their only hope of ever getting home was to regroup and turn and fight together. They were waiting on the next tower Sofia leapt for, and gave her no time to recover her balance. Two of them launched a noisy attack to make her retreat, while the third slipped behind. As Sofia dodged flags she was struck in the back of her knee.

'Ahh!' she cried as she landed on her back, sliding a little before halting herself. She had no time to rise before she felt a flag-stick prodding against her neck. She lay still before the pressure crushed her larynx.

'Beg your pardon, Contessa.'

Sofia ignored their giggling. She still had the advantage. She knew every tower bottom to top, their flags, the fastest routes, how old they were. She kicked her heel and a slate came loose, then several fell in its wake and the tower shed its skin with a shudder that drowned out the boys' shouts as they all slid and tumbled together. Sofia went over the side with the rest of them, but she reached out and grabbed the unseen flagpole. She didn't look down. No need.

She heard them land with the slates, breaking all together.

Sofia hauled herself onto the flayed rooftop, then climbed back down. She found Valerius waiting streetside with an amused expression on his face which, like his clothes, was splashed with blood. The boys' bodies lay where they'd fallen, perfectly arranged in a semi-circle around him as if hunting him even in death.

'Where's the rest?' she asked, more to herself than Valerius. She had been occupied, yet the others hadn't gone for the Concordian. Wasn't he the prize?

Valerius ignored her, more interested in rolling the corpses to see their last expressions.

'Show some respect!' she snapped. 'The dead are forgiven.'

'Sorry!'

'Come here,' she said, pulling Valerius towards her.

'Oh Sofia, I was frightened too!'

She pushed his embrace aside roughly. 'I'm checking for wounds, *cretino*!'

But no, none of the blood was his. Doc's charge was intact, the Contract secure. 'You got blooded, Valerius. Satisfied?'

It was a blade-sharp February, but this winter's night the alleys around the workshop were ablaze with torches. Groups of Bardini bandieratori gathered on the corners, banners up, tense and jumpy. Sofia nodded to a tall young man slouching against a wall, his hood pulled low. The other boys intended to keep darkness at bay with a constant uproar, but Mule contented himself with silence. A flat-faced boy, he had a drooping eyelid that suited his sleepy air. Nobody had ever called him stubborn, and that was enough in Rasenna to earn him his nickname.

'What's got so many flags out?'

'Burn-out,' he said. 'Ghiberti's.'

Sofia saw the ruse now and swore. 'We going over tonight?'

Mule shrugged. 'Check in with the Doc. He was worried about you.'

'He was worried about Payday here,' said Sofia, angrily pushing Valerius forward. 'Move it, will you?'

She led him to Tower Bardini. Black flags bobbed aimlessly around the base of its ladder. The single calm face in the crowd looked up. With no neck to speak of, the Doctor's bald head hardly broke the hill of his shoulders. He made no large gesture when he saw her, just raised his eyebrows. Sofia nodded back and pulled Valerius out from behind her. When he saw the Concordian, the Doctor paled.

Sofia patted Valerius' cheek and held up a blood-smeared hand. 'Don't worry, Doc. It's not his.'

'Are we safe now?' Valerius asked.

She nodded briefly, keeping her eye on the Doctor's reaction as he approached.

Valerius stepped forward and slapped her. 'Show *me* some respect!'

The Doctor leaned forward and grabbed Sofia's arm before she could strike back.

Valerius stuck a finger in her face. 'Noble or not, you're still just a Rasenneisi!'

The Doctor put his sturdy frame in between them. 'We apologise, my Lord. My ward forgot her place through her zeal to protect you.' His fingers tightened around her arm. 'Right, Sofia?'

'Right,' Sofia managed through clenched teeth.

Valerius looked sour for a moment, then nodded. 'Fine. I'm hungry after all that. Doctor?'

The Doctor released Sofia and bowed to Valerius. 'I shall await you.'

Valerius watched him leave, then turned, smiling, to Sofia, the guiltless cherub once more. 'I thank you for saving me, Contessa,' he said stiffly and then, lowering his voice, 'Look, sorry I had to do that. Concord's dignity—'

'Demands no less,' Sofia said. 'No apologies but mine are necessary, my Lord.'

'Oh, Sofia! Don't be so formal. Let's be friends again,' he said, and leaned forward to kiss her cheek.

She watched him scurry up the tower's ladder. Had he stayed, he would have recognised the glow surrounding her. It was not her throbbing arm that had made her angry – and not even Valerius; the Concordian was acting properly, in his own way. It was the Doc, and that she was party to his appeasement. Distrusting herself around either of them, she decided to retire to the Lion's Fountain. Mule and his brother were probably at the tavern already. The smoke of another burn-out tasted bad in every mouth. First, though, she grabbed a workshop flag. It wouldn't do for the Contessa to be caught unarmed twice in one day.

CHAPTER 2

Etruria was wrong: the Concordian Empire did possess a heart, of sorts. It was this unsleeping place of grease-pumping clockwork pistons. The final dome crowning the Molè Bernoulli had been dubbed the engine-room by ordinary engineers like Captain Giovanni, although ordinary engineers were rarely privileged to see it – or, indeed, to be personally briefed by the Apprentices. Giovanni did not rejoice to be so favoured, for he knew it was a curse.

Giovanni wore sober black like every other engineer. Only the Apprentices wore the long coloured vestments of the supplanted cardinals. Even so, the Third and Second Apprentices were shades in the darkness. Only the First Apprentice was entitled to wear the true colour, a red so vivid it seemed to emanate from a burning interior.

'Rasenna?' said Giovanni.

'You think the posting beneath you?'

'No, my Lord.'

'We are all heirs to Girolamo Bernoulli. You are not special.'

'I know that, my Lord.'

14

'Captain, I will not dissemble. You're a disappointment.' The First Apprentice raised his hands as if he had been interrupted, though Giovanni kept his head lowered, letting his unruly dark hair hide his eyes as he struggled to control the restless muscles of his broad face.

'You showed promise once. You performed a service that shall be remembered, once. Since then?'

'I follow orders.'

'Oh, you have an engineer's obedience, no one questions that. We question your enthusiasm.'

A man's voice behind Giovanni said, 'Rasenna's ambassador is waiting, my Lord.'

'Let him wait, General!' the First Apprentice snapped.

He was tall, and his sorrowful face had severe high cheeks and a tragic composure disturbed by neither joy nor wrath. He spread his arms, letting his long sleeves fall open, and looked on Giovanni. 'Captain, as different as they were, your father and grandfather had something in common: conviction. Show some. Be an engineer, or be a traitor. Do not be lukewarm. Nature abhors it. *We* abhor it.'

'Yes, my Lord.'

'We would advise you to make Rasenna fear you, but we suspect you are too lukewarm to do even that. We shall see to it.'

Giovanni looked up suddenly.

The First Apprentice was pleased to have pierced his feigned apathy. 'The Rasenneisi ambassador expects to deliver our message. He will *be* our message.'

'Please, my Lord, it's unnecessary—'

'I am the First Apprentice of Concord, Girolamo Bernoulli's *true* heir. Do not lecture me on necessity.'

'Forgive me,' Giovanni said quickly.

The First Apprentice nodded, though whether satisfied or just signalling silence, Giovanni could not tell.

'Rasenna no longer matters, but it appears destined always to stand in our way, if now only in a physical sense. Its position is key in the coming campaign. It must be ready before we send the Twelfth Legion south. You have the State's resources at your disposal. If cooperation requires soldiers, send for them.'

'That won't be—'

'Necessary?'

Giovanni looked down and said nothing.

'Well, we shall see. If we expected your work to be difficult, we would send someone who had our fullest confidence. Possibilities outweigh the certainties of this world, but some things we may count upon: towers fall, smoke rises and Rasenneisi quarrel. Use them. If you fail, it won't be your delicate conscience to suffer, but Rasenna. Send up the ambassador on your way out. We dismiss you.'

Giovanni didn't move. He was looking at his hands, remembering what deeds they'd done in Bernoulli's name.

'You may go, Captain,' the First Apprentice repeated.

'They've suffered enough,' Giovanni said quietly.

'Suffered enough?'

At the far end of the engine-room there was a screech

of chalk as the other Apprentices stopped their work.

'Suffered enough?' The First Apprentice repeated the queer word pairing, and his colleagues in the dark chuckled.

Giovanni lifted his eyes to meet the First Apprentice's – a small act taking great effort.

'Oh, Captain,' the First Apprentice said wistfully, 'there is no limit.'

It was a curiously unpleasant smile for an angel. The statue's colossal body glowed in the intersecting shafts of light. Bowing to read the Low-Etruscan motto inscribed in the base, the ambassador was covered by its shadow. '*Eadem mutata resurgo*,' he mumbled, and translated, 'Although changed, I shall arise the same.'

Valentino was pleased to display his erudition, if only to himself. He was far from home and did not belong. He had been abandoned in the great hall of soaring pillars. The pillar in the centre was thicker than the others, and made of glass that was dappled inside with pale green fugitive gleamings. Did every ambassador receive this treatment, or just Rasenna's? In their place he would do the same, so he could not resent it. Much.

He looked around while using his sleeve to rub the chains of office that stubbornly refused to shine. He was still glad his father had appointed him. The old fool had only agreed when persuaded that the prestige outweighed the danger. The problem as ever was money – another bad year, and Rasenna could not raise its tribute. Such fuss over such a small problem, with such an obvious solution. He would beg. The Empire had larger concerns than one insignificant town.

Valentino retreated from the colossus. In a gleaming breastplate he was pleased to find not some unremarkable boy looking back, but an elegant young diplomat. He passed a happy minute admiring his dignity, growing confident. Whatever they called themselves in their vulgar dialect, the Apprentices were Concord's élite just as the Morello were Rasenna's. Ultimately, they spoke the same language.

A distant large sound of great metal plates scraping off each other made Valentino scurry back into the shadow of the colossus. They would discover him there, lost in aesthetic reverence. His gaze was drawn up the column to a point of pure white in the distant darkness. The great dome seemed large as Heaven, and something was falling fast, emitting a whine that grew louder by the second. He yelped as the column began filling with water, the level rising to meet the star. The large coffin-shaped capsule cushioned on the water came to a stop. Valentino expected an Apprentice to emerge, not yet another engineer functionary, but he masked his annoyance with a smile and began his speech: 'Just admiring—'

The engineer broke free of the old soldier flanking him and grabbed Valentino's outstretched arm. 'Ride from Concord tonight,' he whispered fiercely.

'I don't understand—'

'Say you must return to Rasenna. An emergency. Say anything. You don't belong here.'

Valentino snatched his arm away. 'I came to see the Apprentices. I shall not leave before that meeting.'

A heavy hand on his shoulder. 'Ambassador,' the general said, 'the Apprentices are waiting. You have your orders, Captain. Give Doctor Bardini my regards.'

Giovanni looked on helplessly as the ambassador was led away. Valentino gave the colossus a parting glance, discerning too late that it was smiling derisively.

CHAPTER 3

The History of the Etrurian Peninsula
Volume III: The Bernoullian Re-Formation

FOREWORD

The Author's ambition in these volumes has been to narrate anew the most glorious chapter of our History, whilst avoiding, to speak plainly, the excessively reverential tone of recent scholarship which ignores, or more likely fails to see, the simple truth that our Re-Formation, like the Molè, was the work of many hands.[1]

An initial sketch of the main actor is necessary but be assured, Reader, the pivotal events here touched upon will be redrawn in later chapters from perspectives that other Historians, to bestow that noble title with perhaps unwarranted liberality, neglect.

---

[1] One example will suffice: 'All that is required to discover a new world is to sail until one runs out of water. Bernoulli did something immeasurably harder: he illuminated that sphere we stumbled over since Time began, before we had even seen the darkness.' Sycophantic drivel like this may keep Duke Spurius Lartius Cocles in print but it is not History.

CHAPTER 4

North of the trespassing river, dawn crept on cat-paws over Rasenna's briefly golden towers, clustering sheepishly in the long shadow of Tower Bardini. To one illiterate in the language of banners – in a word, *foreign* – Tower Bardini could only be recognised by the small orange trees on its roof. Every morning the Doctor sat there for an hour, tearing oranges in two and watching over Rasenna.

His half.

The older generation of Rasenneisi permitted themselves only essentials, so the Doctor's sleep was undisturbed by dreams. He had still passed the night brooding on Sofia's narrow escape, making careful plans and tearing them apart. He had raised Sofia like a daughter, but he remained clear-sighted: custody of the Scaligeri heir gave the Bardini what passed for legitimacy these days, a damp seat in the Signoria. Yesterday's target was not Valerius.

Scratching and stretching himself awake, the Doctor ambled down the wooden stair winding round the bare stone walls. A big man, and wide, he took his time in all things, confident in his strength if called upon. His thick arms and neck were covered with a downy thickness more like animal fur than hair. He wore wide, loose breeches tied up around the middle of his chest where his shirt opened, and over all wore a gown that had once been heavy; time had exhausted the colour too; it had once been the deepest of blues. The long sleeves were torn in places, but most of the time they covered his large callused hands which hung low when he walked, as if the knuckles carried some extra weight. His nose, broken and rebroken many times, was large and fleshy, and his cat's smile stretched wide across a heavy chin, dark with permanent stubble.

Every tower was drably similar inside, no matter what generous colours hung outside, and like a castle keep the door was never on the ground floor; a ladder was lowered for visitors. The Rasenneisi preoccupation with security told in other ways too: friendly families built towers close enough to be connected with rope webs but of course nothing as permanent as a bridge. Ropes could be cut. Alliances could break.

He knocked on the third-floor door. No answer. He glanced inside. His shrewd eyes hid behind a squint merry as an old pig's, and just as cruel. He slammed the door and with quickened pace, muttering curses, crossed the walkway to a plain wooden building, hearing laughter from below as he entered. The workshop was as low and wide as the towers were high and narrow – it contained a small army, so needed no such precautions.

The students were gathered in one corner of the long hall. Sofia's dark hair shone out in the midst of all those shaven heads. She had a firm hand on Mule's shoulder, and she was laughing too. The Doctor ignored the laughter, but he noticed both Mule's bandage and the rosy patch where an ear should be. He followed a trail of cherry drops in the wood chippings on the floor as he worked out what had happened.

'Morning, Doc! Mule volunteered to teach us first-aid.' There was laughter in Sofia's voice, but he caught the look she flashed him and returned an affirmative grunt.

She continued her story: 'So, I got home late – pretty drunk, I suppose, 'cause I crashed in the workshop. Just before dawn, I wake up to this horrific snoring – you can't imagine! Some drunk, I figure, napping on the Bardini doorstep–' Sofia stood with one arm on her hip, managing a good impression of a house-proud mama despite her sling. 'Of course, I'm outraged!'

The boys were rapt, and the Doctor knew that this was more than the respect commanded by her name. It was love. The Scaligeri inspired it effortlessly, and it had been their greatest asset – their enemies hated them for it. Sofia never braided her hair in complicated patterns, nor did she pluck her eyebrows, or apply perfumes, or powder her luminous olive skin. Though she dressed as other bandieratori did, doublet and hose, jacket and cap, she did not look boyish, yet she could show an arm without embarrassment or ceremony because one did not compare the Contessa to other girls. The Contessa was something apart, as far from the ordinary run of humanity as the statues in the alcoves.

This last year something had changed. She'd tried hiding in different ways – her fringe hanging over those dark bright eyes, the street-fighter's sun-muddied complexion, elbow and knuckle-scrapes proudly displayed – but it wasn't enough. A million other things said it: her belt, slung low on her hips, the tilt of her cap, the way she didn't sing any more. After a lifetime looking for weakness he always saw the things people tried to hide, and he knew the workshop saw it too. When had it happened? What moment? He guessed it happened the way spring turns to summer, the way fighters become killers. You only knew after the event.

'We'll see about this, I say—'

Mule interrupted, 'Last thing I remember was running down Purgatorio after Secondo, then I turned into Penitito and Secondo was gone—'

'I thought you were behind me,' Secondo snapped.

Sofia had never had to break a sweat, but the Borselinno brothers had become capodecini the hard way. They were equally tall and thin, and they started identical, but years of fighting had deformed each uniquely. Mule took life as he took this injury, with an easy laugh, but Secondo found disrespect where none was intended and had creased his young face with frowns and vexation. Even now he was holding himself stiffly above the general laughter.

The Doctor could see where the story was going. Purgatorio, Penitito – those streets were south of the Irenicon. After the burn-out, the Borselinno boys had taken the Midnight Road. Their bad intentions were good; a burn-out demanded reprisal.

The Doctor walked to the workshop door and opened it.

Sofia continued, 'Obviously some Morello hero got the drop on genius-boy, but what I can't figure out is how you can sleep nailed to a door.'

'They gagged me!' Mule said.

'You didn't think to *knock*?' She punched his arm before turning to her audience. 'So I yank open the door and scream, "You know what time it is?"' She paused for a moment, then, '*Riiipp!!*'

Mule was now helpless with laughter.

'There's blood spraying everywhere! I get a face-full. I ungagged this *deficiente*. He looks at me all innocent, and says, "What you wake me for? I was dreaming!"'

'I was!'

The Doctor tore the cold meat off the door then slammed it. '*Basta, bambini*. Story-time's over.'

The circle broke up and reassembled into classes. The intermediates had just gone from sticks to flags and it showed. The Doctor looked at Sofia, unsurprised to find her unsmiling now the audience had dispersed. The incident was nothing to laugh at – her performance had been for the novices. Boys needed to acquire a casual attitude to spilled blood.

The Doctor divided his bandieratori, those young men who needed no instruction, into sparring pairs, before discreetly approaching Mule. The injured fighter was sitting quietly on the stairs with a dazed smile.

'Want this back?'

'Naw, Doc. That was just my spare.'

'Wise up, Mule. Getting separated is apprentice stuff.'

Mule gave a noncommittal shrug.

The Doctor had enjoyed the performance, but there had been a lot of blood spilled on the doorstep. 'Go up to the tower and finish your nap.'

'Don't get any blood on my sheets,' Sofia sang as Mule went upstairs. 'I've a reputation to protect!'

As her students giggled, she called to Secondo, 'Keep an eye on this lot.'

'I'm going with you.'

'No one's going anywhere!' the Doctor barked. 'You're training.'

Secondo quickly wilted under his stare and retreated without protest. Sofia kept walking. The Doctor grabbed her good arm and pulled her out of earshot.

'It wouldn't have happened if I'd been with them, Doc.'

'Keep your voice down. I didn't train you to be a common street-fighter.'

'What's wrong with that? You're one.'

'Grow up. Someday soon you have to rule.'

'If Quintus Morello had his way, I'd be dead already. You think the south will suddenly pay homage when I turn seventeen? Right now, the Bardini name is in the mud, and Scaligeri is neck-deep with it.'

'You've inherited your grandfather's rhetorical skills at least,' he said patiently. 'So what does my bloodthirsty Contessa propose?'

'Nothing complicated. Cross the river. Crack some heads.'

The Doctor pushed her hard against the wall, slammed a fist down beside her face and glared.

'What's wrong with a good fight?' she said coolly, all music gone from her voice.

'The only good fight's one you can win.'

'What then? Do nothing?'

'Not nothing. We wait.'

She pushed the Doctor away and went to the door. 'You think I don't know you sent Mule and Secondo over?'

He looked back at his students until they went back to training, then said quietly, 'Don't question me, Sofia.'

'When I'm Contessa, I'll be in charge. How will I run Rasenna when you don't let me run my own life?'

'Your life's not yours to waste. I made a promise.'

'To a dead man!' Sofia slammed the door behind her.

The Doctor followed her out and shouted, 'Be back by evening. There's an emergency meeting of the Signoria.'

She didn't break her stride. 'There's always an emergency.'

The Doctor's anger was dulled by his bemused recognition of a family resemblance: for a Scaligeri not to carry high their head would have been grossly false, politic though feigned humility might have been. There are few things in life as truly ugly as conceit, or as common. Sofia's pride was the rarer kind, and it made her beautiful.

Back inside, the students were busy with their sets and pretending not to have heard. The Doctor pried his fingers separate to crack them. In repose they curled naturally into fists.

The young always hurry. Count Scaligeri once told him that everything had an appointed hour. Have patience, study, and come the hour you may succeed – if you've acquired sufficient skill. Thinking of Sofia's grandfather always cheered him, not in spite of the end, but because of it. To execute any act gracefully in this life was hard. To die well, hardest of all.

CHAPTER 5

The pristine morning light blended the Irenicon with its surroundings so perfectly that a stranger might be forgiven for assuming it had always been so, that the town had grown up around the river. No Rasenneisi would make that mistake though, and as the years flowed by, the town turned its back ever more determinedly on the river. To acknowledge the trespasser would be a betrayal of the dead, a form of collaboration.

In the days after the Wave, the water subsided a few braccia to reveal a few shattered structures that now stood like sentinels keeping futile watch on a no man's land. Those towers still occupied stood back from the river.

The young man wore good boots dirty from his travels. Under his dark hood and cloak his clothes were neat, even the patches where they had been torn. His equipment bag was heavy and he had carried it a long time. He left it down beside the base of the statue with care. The dun stone carving was long broken; all that remained were its paws – the perfect monument for the town left behind by History.

*

The Doctor walked up and down the toiling rows with eyes closed. The rhythm of banners slicing air when bandieratori fought was distinctive. One could tell how advanced apprentices were by the sounds of sticks clashing.

'Again.'

The hallowed *Art Bandiera* drill: the same set every day, every day the same. Do it a thousand times in the workshop until you fight like an old alley-cat – no plan, just the most efficient attack, decided and executed in the same moment. No second chance on the street.

'Again.'

They started young. When Rasenneisi were born, the question wasn't 'Boy or girl?' but 'Good grip?'

'Again.'

After an hour's review, he retired to the tower. A mournful sound as he climbed the ladder told him the creature he ventured to call Cat was waiting. Its mother had abandoned it without teaching it the most rudimentary skill of its species, so instead of purring, it had an ear-piercing whine for every occasion.

'Breakfast,' he grunted, throwing the severed head.

Like any old couple they lived together successfully by ignoring each other. Cat's best instinct was in judging whether the Doctor would tolerate its presence or was sufficiently angry to kick it. This morning it crept away hastily, gnawing the meat and shuddering with satisfaction.

The Doctor tore an orange in half and studied his flags.

Keeping Valerius alive was going to be tricky if he insisted on putting himself in harm's way. Secondly, their ambassador had not returned. Gonfaloniere Morello had been foolish to send his son to Concord, given its reputation. Would grief make a predictable rival unpredictable? Lastly, Concord had given notice of the imminent arrival of an engineer – a captain no less. His mission was unspecified.

Cat was not around to kick, so he rubbed the stubble of his head and chin with vehemence while looking at the surrounding town with suspicion. Rasenna had changed many times in many centuries, but in one thing it was constant: even when Etruria was known as Etrusca, Rasenna was quarrelsome. A century ago, Rasenna's population has expanded in step with its dominion. Most of the towers were built in that age of victory. The law forbidding new buildings higher than one hundred and one braccia was enacted to curb the rivalry even then plaguing Rasenna, and the Bardini had obeyed the letter of the law, all the while building on the 'healthy' northern hills (those too poor to live in the valley could scarcely afford debilitating indulgence). As a result, their tower of regulation height looked down on all the others.

The Bardini were proud to have risen high. Their workshop was the most famous school in a town famous for its martial artistry throughout Etruria. Talent was the reason the Scaligeri had winked at Bardini infractions. That age felt like a dream more than memory; it had ended the moment the Wave swept through Rasenna, when the low were made high and the high were swept away. Only a reputation was left and that, twenty years later, was almost forgotten too.

The Doctor's rueful gaze was drawn inevitably across the river to the handsome palazzo at the end of Piazza Luna's arc. Like the Bardini, the Morello had been far enough from Tower Scaligeri to escape the Wave. Their weakness had made them powerful in the new Rasenna, not a city, but the remains of one. The Weak had inherited the earth, as the Virgin predicted; he didn't think this was what She had actually had in mind.

While the Doctor studied his enemy he was himself under scrutiny.

Every tower in Rasenna flew a banner, but only the Vanzetti flew a multitude, advertising the family craft. Pedro was small for his age, small enough to be sitting comfortably in the window-frame of Tower Vanzetti. His mother had perished upon his early arrival into the world and he might have joined her had it not for his father's tireless care. Even now, Vettori Vanzetti could not be persuaded that Death was not waiting to steal his son away, and his fretting meant Pedro grew without ever losing his eggshell fragility. No amount of food would ever make this boy fat, but if Death had cast a cold eye he would have seen small hands gripping tightly to life.

Pedro did not believe that lacking physical stamina made him an invalid, or that expending his energies on books and mechanical instruments, things most Rasenneisi had no use for, was evidence of deficiency; he ignored such whispers, just as he ignored the heated conversation in the room behind him. His eager face was creased with the intense concentration it took to hold the device steady while focusing. Fresh washed wool smelled of home to Pedro, but weaving bored him – the final product was just a basic weapon. Yet the looms with their elaborately dancing parts had fascinated him since he could remember, and his father had come to rely on him to keep the hard-working machines going, though they ought to have been replaced a decade ago. Pedro not only kept them working, he made improvements, and on those rare occasions when nothing needed repair, he returned to his experiments.

Vettori's conversation with his old business partner was more fractious than usual – Fabbro Bombelli was diplomatic by nature as well as by trade. The men danced around it, but now their discussion gradually spiralled towards the familiar argument.

'We're the Small People,' Vettori said with his practised resignation, 'that's our fate.' He marked a length of new fabric with a chalk piece that then disappeared into his dusty leather waist-jacket. He had scissors, rulers, clips and sundry other tools cleverly secreted about his clothes, which were tight and trim as befitted a tailor.

'Who says we have to stay small?'

Vettori had returned to the loom. 'The men who decide.' His face was stretched and unlined, and his lips were careful and tight, as if emotion was another luxury they could not afford. His long, quick hands remained expressive of the generous man he had once been.

'They do.'

Fabbro Bombelli picked up the glass he'd perched on his generous belly and swirled it under his curlicue nose, looking sideways at Vettori. For every inch Fabbro gained round the middle, his old partner had contracted. Some great unseen weight seemed to hang from the tape round Vettori's shoulders, though it was not years but the manner in which he had spent them, curved over the rack, that had left him stooped in obeisance to the world, his head bowed so low that wearing a young man's neat beard looked like an old man's vanity. His loom jerked his limbs in tandem with its creaking parts, like a tired old puppet made to dance.

In the last decade demand had fallen until Vettori could no longer afford to employ carders and dyers – though still he wove, believing it the last thing he could do competently. He had once won his Woolsmen's respect by arguing on their behalf with the Signoria, and he still saw himself as the Small People's advocate, but talk which had once reflected healthy self-respect had become shrill, self-pitying. Years of defeat were stretching him thinner than the old thread he wove.

'You're really going to ask him?' Vettori asked.

'Won't be the first time I've asked.'

'Or the first time he's said no.'

'And I keep asking. What's the worst he can do?' said

Fabbro, running fingers though his beard, bright as white smoke. It separated out into two pluming cones, mirrored by the cloudy scuff encircling his bald and sunburnt skull. A portrait of respectability was an asset to maintain as judiciously as one weighed metal.

Vettori looked up pointedly from his work.

'All right, there's plenty,' Fabbro said quickly, 'but the Doc can't keep me – *us* – down forever. I've got money.'

'He'll say it's not about that,' Vettori said mildly.

Fabbro was not going to tolerate quibbles. 'I've got a right to sit in the Signoria, as much as Guercho Vaccarelli or any of those Family-heads who come knocking at midnight for loans I mustn't speak of. Maybe the Bombelli banner isn't as old as Bardini's or as pretty as Morello's, but we do well. People go to the Doc for his flag. They come to me to pay for it.'

'And you go to him when *you* need help. If you have a voice in the Signoria, you won't need him any more.'

'Well, he's pushing against the current.'

'Sure it's pushing that way? Why don't you wait till next year? The Scaligeri girl will be Contessa then, maybe she'll—'

'Bah! The Doc raised her. When she holds the mace it'll be another way to hide his hand. No. The time's now. I have a claim to a seat and a right. He can't fight progress.'

'He can do what he likes. The Small People can't fight the Families.'

'How would you know? Tried lately?'

Vettori slumped as if the frayed string had finally snapped. The loom ceased with indiscreet silence.

'Sorry,' Fabbro said quickly, 'I'm just— Not being able to use your people – it's frustrating. I've outgrown my shoes, but nobody will sell me a new pair.'

Vettori gave a thin laugh. 'Don't worry about it, Fabbro. You're right. You're the one who kept your business going, not me. What do I know?'

'You're just down on your luck.'

'Sure.' Vettori smiled, his lips tight.

Fabbro looked around for a distraction. He understood that old friends, like old ambitions, became embarrassing when you're poor. *Madonna!* What's that, Pedro?'

'It's what I needed the glass for, Signore Bombelli.' Pedro's maybe-machines were inhibited not only by a dearth of information; most remained sketches because the only material he had readily to hand was uncarded wool. On his last visit, Fabbro had brought his godson some Ariminumese glass as well as the usual descriptions of inventions Pedro so loved hearing about. By collating these stories and sifting through the layer of suspicion attached to all things Bernoullian Pedro learned *what* a particular machine did, and then he could tackle the larger question of *how?*

Now the merchant held the Magnifier to the light. His restless hands were always picking up things, appraising, weighing, costing – cost was more than a figure; it was merit enumerated, judgement every bit as just and severe as Heaven's, although God was not known to be open to negotiation.

He peered through.

'*Dio!* I can see across the river! You devised this?'

'I just copied it. The Morello's Contract this year is short-sighted. He has a pair of glass discs that let him see better. I just copied the design and doubled them up like this so I could see far.'

'Bah! A typical Vanzetti, too modest. That's not copying – that's *inventing*. To see a complete thing and understand its working, that's a gift.' Pedro blushed as Fabbro ruffled his hair. 'You remind me of your old man young.'

Vettori's head was bowed, and he was back at his loom. Fabbro downed the drink, smacked his lips loudly, then said what he'd come to say, quietly, 'If you need a small loan, Vettori, just ask. Of course, no interest for old friends.'

Vettori looked at Fabbro, contrasted the bright banners of the past with the grey and threadbare present, and set his jaw. 'Thank you for your concern, Signore Bombelli, but I didn't knock on your door.'

Fabbro saw that Vettori would go hungry before taking charity. He knew too that unless he regularly made the perilous crossing, their friendship would expire. Eager to avoid that day, and conscious of the sudden change in mood, he made his excuses.

With his back resolutely turned to the humiliating scene, Pedro continued scanning the northside until he came to a figure standing by the river. The young man was dressed in the black hood and short cloak of an engineer, but Pedro would have known he was foreign anyway – he was standing closer to the water than a Rasenneisi ever would.

Pedro was delighted when his father instructed him to escort Signore Bombelli to the Midnight Road. 'Wear a scarf, and wait until you can see he has crossed safely.'

He leapt down from his perch and flung on a long cassock. Like his father's, it also had a strange array of tools in hidden pockets. Pedro was always glad for an excuse to escape the stifling smell of wool and caution, but right now all he wanted to know was why this stranger was not afraid of the water.

CHAPTER 6

The moment the sun appeared Captain Giovanni threw off his dark hooded cloak, revealing a mane of untidy black hair covering a brow furrowed in thought as he studied the river. His eyes were dark, and his broad leonine face was dominated by a large, honest nose. An emaciated dog had limped after him since he arrived and now it sniffed at the bag cautiously, clearly expecting to be chased away. He let it be.

It was too early in the year for the northern mountains' snowmelt but the current was still powerfully fast and loud. He could see where the landslides had happened, of course, but there'd been little erosion of the banks after the initial Wave, which was typical of a forced river diversion: when they came, they came suddenly. These were the signs trained eyes detected, but it did not take an engineer to see this river was abnormal. Normal rivers do not flow uphill.

No wonder the Rasenneisi kept their distance. He knew the theory, and he had seen one other like it, but still it made him uneasy, like a thing from a story of omens and prodigies. From what he had heard, Rasenna was a town out of place too, still living in a time when it was some-where that mattered.

'Probably don't get many strangers, eh?'

The dog turned its head curiously. The flat Concordian accent sounded strange, almost toneless compared to the singing dialect it was used to. The engineer took a biscuit from the bag and threw it, and the dog snatched it out of the air, teeth clamping loudly.

'I guess they don't feed strays here either.' A soft smile spread over his face like the sun moving over rocks, soft-ening the deep shadows in between. While the dog barked and wagged its appreciation, Giovanni turned back to the river with the same stern look. He opened the bag fully. Everything inside fit neatly, with no wasted space. The dog studied the young man as he patiently searched; it was accustomed to intemperate passions – a Rasenneisi would either have chased it away or adopted it by now.

The engineer found the tool he needed and after adjusting the dials on the small glass rod, sank to the ground and crawled to the side of the bank. He'd dipped the rod into the water and was about to sink his whole hand in when the dog growled. Giovanni watched his flick-ering reflection carefully, then quickly stood as a shim-mering hand gushed from the water and swiped at where his face had been a moment ago. The water lost its shape and dropped back formlessly into the river, and as the dog barked again, Giovanni realised it was barking not at the creature, but at him – it had been *warning* him.

He frowned. His unkindly brow was at odds with his shepherd's eyes. Normally pseudonaiades moved sluggishly out of water, as awkward as men were in their world, but he guessed normal did not apply to a river not meant to be: a residue of the charge that had called up the Wave must still be present, though much depleted. As the errant partials tried to get home, so the water tended to stray – that was his theory, at least, and it was as good as the next when the pseudonaiades' very existence was so at odds with Bernoullian Wave Theory. Amongst so many imponderables one thing was certain: without a safe place to work, nothing could be built.

He searched his bag and took out a silver egg and a small belt strap. He unscrewed the narrow end of the egg, which remained connected by a fine wire, and slotted the tip into a notch in the belt. He found a small piece of old masonry by the bank to fasten the belt around, then, using the belt as a sling, he launched the lump of brick into the air while holding the egg tightly in his other hand. The brick splashed down thirty-five braccia away, half the river's breadth.

That was sufficient.

He rotated a second dial on the egg, its clockwork shuddered to life and it shot from his hand the moment he released it, skimming the water's surface until it reached the point where the brick had landed. There it stopped, vibrating and bobbing on the surface. He crouched and gingerly held his hand over the water once more and waited. The dog growled to see such folly.

Nothing happened.

The egg was a phased-current transmitter of his own design that induced density to a depth of three braccia, which in theory – and now in fact – repelled pseudo-naiades. He was pleased. Men immersed in this hostile water would still drown, of course, but this would prevent watery hands pulling them in – and it would also prevent Strays, a more serious concern.

Giovanni stood and pushed the hair back from his brow impatiently. Now, information. The glass rod was a Whistler; it calculated distance based on how long it took to hear its song echo. He repeated the procedure at five-braccia intervals along the uneven bank for the next hour, considering what Rasenna's Signoria would want to hear, and what he should tell them.

The dog tagged along.

Sofia had no destination; anywhere was fine as long as it was out of Tower Bardini's shadow. She needed distance from the Doc's hypocrisy. He was too smart to believe he could just hand over Rasenna to her as a birthday gift. Whoever ruled Rasenna had to be ready to fight for it, or they wouldn't rule for long. He only let himself be irrational when the subject was her.

She was not allowed to be involved in raids, but she

knew about them. True enough, some of the stories shocked her, but at least the Bardini didn't stoop to attacking family towers. She had learned to countenance the other violence, just as the Doc obviously had. It was for the greater good, and so for peace, for the Bardini and for her. Really, no excuse was necessary. It was enough to say: this is Rasenna.

Even without taking to the rooftops it was still easy to cross northern Rasenna quickly. The narrow interlocking paths winding downhill to the river overlooked each another, a tiered arrangement offering short cuts aplenty. The sorrowful chime of a bell made her notice she had reached the limits of Bardini territory and she hastily changed routes. Her last visit to the Baptistery was a fresh memory, and still painful.

The morning was dying when Sofia came to the abandoned towers before the river – the gauntlet, as it was known – and discovered the body at the entrance of an alley. There was nothing remarkable in a dead dog, but this animal had not starved to death: its fur was still wet. Local animals knew enough to avoid water, yet somehow, at a distance from the river, this dog had drowned.

'Signorina?'

Sofia looked around and saw a *Concordian* coming from the direction of the river. She instantly raised her flag. Her face showed hostility even as her body went taut, ready for fight or flight.

Keeping an eye on the alley, the engineer crept towards

her stealthily. He touched his lips. 'Shhh, Signorina, be careful.'

'Where's the buio?' she said with loud aggression.

At first Giovanni was confused, then he realised the term must be local dialect for the pseudonaiades, what the rest of Etruria called waterfolk. He explained, 'On its way back to the river it took fright. The dog chased it.'

Her eyes narrowed and a sharp crease divided her brow. 'Who the devil are you anyway?'

He was taken aback momentarily. 'My name is Giovanni.'

'A *dog* scared a buio? I don't think so.'

'Not the dog, a machine.'

'It scares them into our streets?' Sofia said, growing angry now. 'Why would you want to keep buio away from the river? It's where they belong.'

'I know. My machine is designed to protect people.'

'Great job so far, but I'll take it from here. Which way did it go?'

Giovanni pointed.

'*Cretino!*' Sofia smacked him on the head and ran in the direction of Tower Bardini.

Giovanni watched her go, blinking stupidly. In Concord women were demure, closeted creatures, to be admired from a distance, and most certainly never to be spoken to without an introduction – but whatever the local customs, something dangerous was wandering the streets and it was thanks to him. He cursed his carelessness for not

44

considering that a Stray might be loose before turning on the transmitter.

'Signorina, wait!'

There were too many streets to search for the buio before children found it – and young Rasenneisi delighted in risky games. Sofia stopped and listened; she could hear voices, catcalls, from the level above her. She climbed up and found them throwing rocks and shouting, herding the creature into a small alley. The children had made a game of it already, hitting the buio with their training sticks and retreating before it could launch itself at them in wave form. When the buio reformed as a pillar, another child would take the dare and leap in. Strays were as dumb as animals, but if they were kept too long from running water, they lost cohesion and dissolved into lifeless puddles – which was exactly what the children wanted to see.

'Get out of here!' Sofia grabbed one by the collar and kicked him in the arse. 'Leave it alone, little *stronzo*!'

The boy ran off bawling and the others pursued him, content with a new victim.

Sofia turned to face the buio as it reformed, like a tower rebuilding itself. It shuffled towards her. She wasn't worried until she took a step back and felt the alley wall at her back.

'Signorina! Don't make any sudden movements!' The Concordian was on the level above, brandishing a burning torch.

'What are you doing?'

45

'Saving you!' he said, leaping into the alley awkwardly, and spoiled the moment's heroism by dropping his torch. He kept his eye on the buio as he picked it up, and spoke over his shoulder, 'Now, very slowly, climb onto my shoulders and—'

Sofia nimbly vaulted up between the walls then sat looking down at him with a sweet smile. Giovanni looked more impressed by her acrobatics than the danger. 'How did you—?'

The sizzle as the buio advanced into his outstretched torch reminded him of his priorities.

'I'm a little confused. Is this part of the rescue? What happens next?'

'I was in this situation before. It'll attack.'

'Oh, so you're used to it.'

The children's sadism had vexed Sofia, but the chance to make a Concordian squirm, one she hadn't explicit orders to protect, was too rare to ignore. Her vague plan was to let the buio attack, then rescue him before he drowned.

Giovanni backed up against the wall. 'Signorina?'

'I'd help, but this arm,' Sofia said, showing her sling. 'Sorry!'

'Can you give me your flag?'

Sofia's smile faded. What kind of Concordian was he that he didn't realise she might be enjoying this? She felt a twinge of conscience. He *had* tried to save her life – ineptly, but he had tried. She was about to help when it

46

struck her that the buio had not attacked, and didn't look as if it was about to. It just stood there, neither advancing nor retreating.

'בֶּן מַיִם, הַנָּח לְעַלְמָה.'

Both Sofia and Giovanni looked at the alley's entrance, where an old woman had appeared. Sofia raised her flag and leapt down. 'You're not supposed to be here. These are our streets!'

The nun looked scornfully at Sofia before again speaking: 'בּוֹא וּלְךָ עַמִּי בְּאַחַת!'

It sounded like the Ebionite tongue but something about the tone made Giovanni's hair stand on end. Whatever it was, the buio obviously understood, for it slowly shuffled towards her. The old nun was a hardy one, with callused, rough hands, and wide, sturdy hips and a large bosom beneath a shapeless black habit. A chain of prayer beads hung from her belt like a mace.

Sofia glanced back at Giovanni, who looked surprised to be still alive.

'Where are they going?' he asked.

Sofia turned and saw the nun had gone. 'Come on! Let's see what that *strega* does with it – aren't you curious?'

'*Strega*? She saved me!'

'She should have asked permission.'

'Permission?'

'These are Bardini streets. Besides, I was about to. I was just having some fun.'

'You think she'll be all right?'

'Oh, she can take care of herself, that one,' Sofia said.

They walked in silence for a moment and Sofia glanced over shyly. Looking down at the foreigner in the alley she had noticed that he was no weakling. It was not bandier-atoro muscle, finely modelled and honed by daily prac-tise. His chest and upper arms had substance, but it was crudely carved bulk, like the farmers who came from the contato after harvest.

'Look, back there, I—' she began.

'That's all right. What's your name?' he said.

Sofia had hoped for anger, so she could respond in kind. Why did a Concordian care what a Rasenneisi was called?

'Honestly, I wouldn't have let it hurt you.'

'But you object to someone else preventing it?'

She gamely tried to take offence. 'Well, you've got a nerve, walking around Rasenna without permission, unan-nounced.'

Giovanni wondered how to respond politely. 'But I have permission – that's why they opened the gates to me. And I have been announced, so I understand. Your Signoria has been informed of my mission: I'm the engineer.'

'And I'm the Contessa. What mission?' She said it coolly, though she was fuming: yet another instance of the Doc's secrecy.

'The bridge?' said Giovanni uncertainly.

'There's no bridge in Rasenna.'

'Not yet there isn't. I'm here to build one.'

She stopped walking and for the first time really saw the engineer's uniform. 'You're going to bridge the Irenicon?'

'For Rasenna.'

'Let me get this straight: Concord sent you to bridge the river Concord itself sent twenty years ago? For *Rasenna*? Don't be patronising – Concord needs a bridge, and Rasenna happens to be where you need it.'

If she'd been looking for a reason to be offended, Giovanni saw she'd found it. Her reaction didn't bode well for his mission. 'My brief's very limited,' he said. 'They don't tell me why, they just tell me *what*.'

'I'm wondering how you intend to build this bridge without getting yourself and a whole lot of Rasenneisi killed. You had better talk to my guardian.'

'I'm supposed to report to your Signoria first.'

'My guardian is Doc Bardini. Is he in your brief? If he isn't, they left out something important.'

'General Luparelli mentioned him. Is he the gonfaloniere?'

'No, but he's part of the Signoria. If you're trying to get something done, you need him onside. Better idea than chasing buio into our streets.'

She sounded determined to pick a fight; was it personal, or simply that he was Concordian? He attempted to change the subject. 'What happened to your arm?'

'None of your business.'

The buio had stopped at the river, simultaneously drawn and repelled. The Reverend Mother was trying to coax it.

'Excuse me, Contessa. I need to tell her what's stopping it.'

'I'm not stopping you,' said Sofia, twirling her banner casually.

Giovanni introduced himself to the nun and, after thanking her, tried to explain what was keeping the buio from the river. 'The signal's too strong at this point,' he said, gesturing at the crystal rod. 'If you lead the creature away a few braccia, it falls off in strength.'

As Giovanni spoke, the Reverend Mother was studying him with interest. He could only guess that she had not seen many Concordians in her cloistered life. Stranger, though the buio was just a faceless column, he got the disquieting sense that it too was interested in him.

The nun thanked him and led the buio away.

Sofia walked over. 'Looks like you made an impression on the buio, Concord. Must be attracted to cold blood.'

'Signorina, my name is Giovanni. Have I done something to offend you?'

'Let me think – oh, where ever did that river come from? That's *inconvenient*. Never mind; I'm sure they'll bridge it presently. I'll just wait twenty years or so.'

'I'm just an engineer—'

'And who sent the Wave? The Cobblers' Guild?'

'I wasn't even born then!'

'Neither were you, Contessa,' the nun interrupted. 'Don't confuse blood with water under the bridge. He tried to save your life, didn't he?'

'Bit generous, but I suppose you could say that,' Sofia said evenly. 'Who asked for your advice anyway? Not me.'

'Not yet. But the offer stands.'

Sofia laughed hollowly.

The nun shrugged, and Sofia watched her, scowling, as she walked away. When she finally turned around, Giovanni's attention was on the far side of the river and the boy standing there.

Pedro was red-faced and out of breath; he had run back to the riverbank after seeing Fabbro Bombelli safe home. He didn't need his magnifier to know that the engineer could see him too: the foreigner was shouting and waving at him.

'I thought engineers were supposed to be smart. He can't hear you,' Sofia said.

'I just want his attention.' Giovanni took from his bag a bundled rope and another metallic contraption, a cone with two thin scallop shapes and a spring grip, like praying hands, on opposite sides. Completing the resemblance to a toy angel, it had a golden sheen and was crowned by a small hoop.

'Well, I should be going,' Sofia said, very casually.

He didn't look up. 'Goodbye, Contessa.'

He unrolled the scroll he had been jotting measurements in all morning and tore off a corner to scribble on. He pried the angel's 'hands' apart and placed the note in between.

Sofia studied the stranger as he worked, reminding herself that this was the real enemy. He might be a clumsy climber, but his thick fingers were dexterous and efficient. The Concordians they trained in the workshops were soft sons of soft fathers, but the engineers were a different breed. They had not inherited their authority; they had taken it.

When Giovanni glanced up, she was still standing there. He held out the rope. 'Want to help?'

'Not unless you tell me what you're doing.'

'Making a temporary rope-bridge. How else am I going to get across to the Signoria?'

'The Midnight Road, of course.'

'Excuse me?'

'The ruins of the old town wall. Enough still stands to jump across.'

Giovanni looked down at his measurements. 'Sounds like the long way round.' He was looking at her again. 'Will you help me?'

Sofia was surprised. Rasenneisi made do, and Concordians took what they needed. *Nobody* asked for help. She took the rope and slowly knotted it round the broken statue's base while Giovanni skilfully tied the other end to the angel's bottom half.

After consulting his notes on the river's breadth he began winding the halo. 'Tied off?' he asked.

'Madonna, wait!' she said, then, 'All right, now.'

The angel shot up into the air and she laughed despite herself.

As the contraption hovered across the river, Pedro laughed too. He'd heard descriptions of mechanical carrier pigeons – *annunciators*, they called them – but he'd never imagined he'd get to see one.

Suddenly his smile vanished. He looked around. If he could see it, so could other southsiders, and Virgin help anyone the Morello saw associating with civilians or, worse, northsiders. But it was early yet and no one else was around. Most people avoided the river anyway, preferring to imagine it – and Rasenna's other half – did not exist. He knew his father would warn him to avoid entanglements with strangers, but he *had* to know how the contraption worked.

As it passed the halfway point, the wings' rhythm slowed and it started to descend. It was going to undershoot. Bracing himself on the remains of a wall, Pedro caught it before it fell into the water.

The note was written in a small precise hand. *Please help*, it said. *Tie rope off, rotate halo 25 times, face north & release. GB*

'What's he doing?' said Giovanni.

Sofia squinted. 'Did you think flags were just weapons?

He's Signalling. It's how we primitives communicate between towers.'

Giovanni ignored the sarcasm. 'You can read it?'

'Of course. He says, "Why should I?" Cheeky little—'

Giovanni brightened. 'Can you answer for me?'

'And say what?'

'Tell him I want to build a bridge.'

Sofia waved the message and read the reply: '"Is that an order?".' She laughed and explained with a shrug, 'Southsiders . . .'

Giovanni frowned, attempting to employ the logic he'd studied for so long. He knew he had authority to give orders – all Etruria had learned to fear Concord, and thus to comply with its agents. He didn't know if the Contessa was a typical Rasenneisi – she didn't seem a typical anything – but she was not being in the least cooperative. It would be illogical if the towns that had suffered most were the least afraid, yet. Giovanni just *knew* that the boy would baulk at an order, and that wasn't logical either.

'Tell him I'd consider it a favour.'

She chuckled sceptically as she signalled back.

After a moment, she said, 'Well, fancy that! In return, he wants to know how the angel works.'

'Tell him it's a deal.'

Sofia relayed the message, then said, 'I've got to go tell the Doc what's up. There's an emergency Signoria meeting this evening. Guess you're the emergency.'

He smiled. 'This should be ready when you return.'

'I'll believe that when I see it.'

'Trust me,' he said.

Typical Concordian presumption . . . Strangely, she did.

CHAPTER 7

Girolamo Bernoulli's origins are, inevitably, surrounded by the clutter of legend. None dared broach the subject after the Re-Formation, and he never discussed them. The folk-tales agree with each other as rarely as they match the historical record, and that occasional scholar courageous enough to eschew hagiography's siren song is obliged to discard these several picturesque versions.[2]

The Engineers emerged in the last decades of the thirteenth century from a controversy soon forgotten[3], and the stage was

---

[2] In one charming version the babe floats down the Irenicon in a basket, rejected by mother and river both. Others have it that he had no human master; an Angel taught him the Divine Masonry. Predictably, many southern versions replace this Angelic instructor with an erudite Demon.

[3] As elaborated in Volume II, from a trivial theological disagreement came schism. A reforming branch of the Curia proposed that the *Original Sin* was not Seeking Forbidden Knowledge but *Murder*. In the heat of the controversy, the *Empiricists* (as they became known) went further: no knowledge was forbidden. After the Heresy trials the surviving *Empiricists* resigned themselves to the study of Nature. Within a single generation the Engineers' ecclesial origins were forgotten.

clear for an actor of genius. The innocent lad we meet in the early thirteen twenties, dazzling the Curia's preeminent Natural Philosophers with his mathematical gifts, is all but unrecognisable. While the man was solitary and secretive, the boy was noted for his friendships with the great theological and philosophical minds of the day. He cultivated many masters.[4]

---

[4] That generation's fate is a question for another History. Most of his first champions denounced him eventually: Plagiarist, Heretic, Tyrant and so on. In turn the Inquisition denounced many of them, while others were simply discredited. After the Re-Formation there was small appetite for Theology.

CHAPTER 8

Before the Wave overturned Rasenna, the city was already upside down, its poor packed into high towers looking down on the nobility in their thick-walled palazzi. There was one exception, in the heart of old Rasenna, where the palazzi clustered around Tower Scaligeri like worshippers praying to an idol. The family name derived from the dizzying stairway to the tower's only entrance on its uppermost floor.

The Morello family grew up on the southern periphery of the centre of power. They were the Bardini's only real rivals in *Art Banderia*, but they were ambitious to be more than mere soldiers, and on the back of their growing wealth they gilded the scales of their Dragon crest and descended from their towers to a palazzo more suited to their rising status. Their abandoned towers went to poorer cousins, bodyguards for the new palazzo, betraying an insecurity that names of longer standing and surer footing had outgrown.

This was obvious to those Rasenneisi who remembered life before the Wave, but there were few of those left. To everyone else, Palazzo Morello was simply the finest building in Rasenna, and Lord Morello the city's first citizen – excepting, of course, the Contessa, the last of the Scaligeri.

Gaetano Morello was a broad-shouldered youth combining strength with restless agility, as balanced as a good sword should be. So why did he never feel sure of his footing in his father's study? It was a refined, high-ceilinged chamber of wood with too much varnish lined with scrolls with too much ink, and he hated it.

Gaetano knew his father was waiting for him to go. The old man's jealous fingers were fondling the seal on his ring, fearful even of those of his own blood. Gaetano did not shout, nor pound the desk with his fist. He did something more foolish: he attempted reason. 'Say what you must in the Signoria, it doesn't matter anyway, but afterwards we should make terms,' he said quietly.

'What for?'

Gaetano groaned and put his hands on his head, shaven, like every bandieratoro's. He was still beardless, and his dark brows framed gentle, sincere and now pleading eyes. 'If we stop now, we can consolidate. If we keep pushing, Doc will push back.'

Those very martial qualities that made Gaetano a leader on the streets as well as in the workshop somehow disqualified him from being taken seriously in his father's study. Ordinarily, he didn't care – he'd never envied Valentino's influence – but now, when their father's unrealistic ambition was making more bloodshed inevitable, he wished for just a portion of his brother's glib verbal facility.

Quintus Morello pushed back his chair with a beleaguered air, retreated to the window and sighed, 'I miss Valentino, don't you?'

Valentino's mischievous counsel would only acerbate their problems, but suggesting that would be a complete waste of time. 'I do, Father. His delay is strange.'

'Stranger still that he hasn't written to explain.' As usual, Quintus Morello's attention was fixed upon Tower Bardini. The old man was a contradiction. The hair that had once curled up like a tower-fire at night was now greying, and just as his pale skin became more wine-blotched, so the expensive gonfaloniere robes faded to the colours of wilting autumn. But he was still a Morello, descended from fearless bandieratori, and such blood would never be water. He had the bearing of a patrician; his brow was noble, his nose Grecian – but beneath these assets, his face crumpled into sceptical lip and timid chin.

'Gaetano, everywhere I look I see Bardini reversals,' he said. 'You say it's different on the streets, but look! There is the smoke of another burn-out, proof writ large that we are winning. What do you see that I cannot?'

'We're winning because Bardini hasn't struck back.'

'Because he can't,' Quintus said blithely.

'Because he's strong enough to wait!' Gaetano took a breath and regained his composure. 'The bridge will let them use that strength. If it goes ahead, we are undone. If you let this become a war, we lose, either way – they beat us, or Concord makes us an example to enforce peace.'

'Perhaps.'

Gaetano watched his arguments running aground against wilful blindness. His father had never stooped to study the *Art Banderia*, even though it was the means by which the Morello had risen. Gaetano had been taught by an uncle he promptly succeeded as workshop maestro. History had repeated itself in Quintus' sons: while Gaetano dutifully trained the Morello bandieratori, Valentino pursued politics and power.

That was the real reason Quintus missed Valentino. Deciding was difficult. It was easier to let his sons fight it out and then choose a middle path.

Quintus lifted his chin and straightened his neck against the tall collar, as he always did when he had to exercise authority. 'I will,' he announced with gravity, 'see what comes from the meeting.'

Gaetano sighed. This ambiguous commitment was obviously the best he could hope for.

A strangely smiling servant opened the door suddenly, and Quintus became suddenly lordly. 'How dare you enter here without knocking?' he barked. 'I should have you—' He stopped suddenly. 'Why the devil are you grinning, man?'

'Your Lordship's son has returned!'

'At last!' cried Quintus, and flew past Gaetano to the door. Draped still in his ambassador's cloak, Valentino Morello climbed the stairway slowly. In the great hall below, servants and bandieratori alike looked on in disbelief as his father and brother simultaneously backed away. The young man was much changed. His hair, once dark and neatly coiffed, had grown long and wild, and was streaked with white. His pallid skin stretched insubstantially over a bruised skeleton.

Quintus strove to fill the uncomfortable silence with babble. 'What timing! Arriving the very hour you're most needed, Valentino. The prospect of victory makes Gaetano nervous. Could you credit it? He counsels me to make peace with the Doctor.'

Valentino ignored Gaetano. 'Father, I have seen the future in our enemy's face. If we do not pacify Rasenna, Concord will do it for us. With fire.'

'I am so glad to have you back!' Quintus exclaimed, drawing his elder son into the room. 'Gaetano, that will be all.'

As the door slammed behind him, Gaetano felt the small influence he'd built in the last few weeks collapse like a burning tower, but as he walked down the steps to join his bandieratori he discovered he felt unburdened, not disappointed. He did not belong in that room. Servitude was more congenial for a sword. 'Back to your sets!' he shouted, clapping his hands.

Quintus quickly released Valentino from an awkward embrace. 'Barely there at all, Son. You've left the better part behind in Concord!'

'I have just been exhumed.'

Quintus choose to treat this as a joke. 'We shall fatten you up as we talk. The Signoria meets in an hour.'

Valentino's face was ashen, like the faces of the damned in the murals of Hell's torment, though he did not grimace or weep like those doomed souls. His smile was that of one who had retreated from flesh too far to find the way back to the common symmetry.

'I may accompany you?' he asked.

'Of course – you must tell us all of Concord's answer.'

For an instant Valentino's courtier smile warped into a bestial snarl before he mastered himself. 'I must show you,' he whispered.

CHAPTER 9

The condottieri rode through the north gate, knowing that eyes were watching from every window of every tower, though this pair would have been noticed even if Rasenneisi were more accustomed to strangers – each man and his horse, draped in the same gaudy patterns, looked and moved like one great beast.

Condottieri did not pretend to chivalry, and when knights of Europa said mercenaries *were* beasts, condottieri laughed at their deluded hypocrisy; obviously they were all beasts together.

After a while the steep-winding streets so confused the condottieri that they dismounted, allowing the faces behind the dark windows better study. The first was a big fellow, arranged in a dignified, sensible hierarchy: broad chest and shoulders supporting a stout neck and manfully frowning face, capped with a squared-off, proudly plumed helmet. Like his piebald charger he was groomed fastidiously and his armour caught bolts of light that fell between towers and sent them shimmering back blindingly.

The other was skinny, and ragged like a scarecrow, a

poorly got-together specimen beside his colleague, yet quicker in most respects, and certainly quicker to smile, which made him the mob's first target. All condottieri were tanned by life in the saddle but the darkness of this man's skin must have originated in the peninsula's southern extreme, perhaps even further. His armour was older than his partner's, or perhaps just less well-polished, and it was softened by a floral-patterned green kerchief that wound around his long neck like ivy.

'We're under attack!' he cried as young beggars squeezed out of impossibly narrow crevasses and dropped from unbelievably high windows. He scattered coins, but that only left a gap for the next bombardment, making their progress slow. They were relieved to finally find a particularly tall tower draped with black banners and the crest depicting two flags crossed in front of a charging hog, emblazoned with the robust motto:

Who Shall Divide Us?

'Thank the Virgin,' the Scarecrow laughed, 'this must be Tower Bardini. I'm almost out of ammunition.'

The Doctor was watching from the workshop entrance while Sofia told him about this morning's events. In her excitement, their quarrel was quite forgotten. Sofia was not easily impressed, but this young engineer had apparently managed it, and the Doctor was curious to meet him.

'Call off your hounds, Signor!' a voice called out.

'Don't tell me a condottiere doesn't know the quickest way to break a siege?' he responded.

The Scarecrow sighed, 'I thought as much,' and threw his purse to one of the beggars. 'Boy! Yours – if you can keep it!'

The luckless child bolted with his fellows in fast pursuit. As the men tied up their horses, the Doctor whispered to Sofia, 'I'd rather a certain Concordian did not see us fraternise with these gentlemen.'

'I'll get him out of the workshop.'

'Then send for Guercho. I need to confer before the meeting.'

Sofia looked at the strangers. 'Why are they dressed like that? We're not at war, yet.' There was almost a family resemblance between her and the Doctor, as she stood with arms crossed and studied the strangers with a cool distance.

'It's to advertise their profession.'

'What do they want?' she said with distaste.

'Gainful employment, I fear. I'll show them the view first.'

The Doctor waved her off and advanced with a smile and a bow. 'Gentlemen, welcome. Doctor Bardini, at your service.'

The Scarecrow gave a neat bow. 'My name's Colonel Levi, this is Colonel Scarpelli.'

Scarpelli removed his plumed helmet to reveal a neat but old-fashioned bowl-cut, like some militant monk of a century ago. He did not bow, and if the Doctor was offended, he hid it well.

'Would you prefer to talk privately or have you time to take a tour of the workshop?'

'How about it, Levi? I know I've always wanted to see how tough Rasenneisi really are.'

The Doctor looked up at Scarpelli with a bland smile and recognised a killer. The condottiere towered over him by more than a braccia, and his arms were sculpted muscle. He was balanced – and ready, too.

Levi laughingly interrupted the face-off. 'Perhaps later, Doctor. First, let's talk.'

As the Doctor led the way up the endless stairway, Levi systematically complimented Rasenna's history, architecture, food, women and fighters until Scarpelli interrupted, 'It's true then? You train Concordians?'

The Doctor turned on the step. 'I do.'

In the moment's silence, Levi became aware how high they'd climbed and how far they could fall and laughed. 'I'm sure you have your reasons.'

The Doctor ignored him. 'Whatever your opinion of engineers, Colonel Scarpelli, you will agree they are sensible. Forgive my crudity, but the Guild use their nobility like a stud-farm. Blue blood means nothing to them, but it's respected by the scum who make up the infantry. Officer selection is competitive, so Families who can afford it send their boys here.'

'I don't doubt Concord's policy is sensible. I merely ask how you stomach training the enemy.'

The Doctor nearly smiled. 'Rasenna's not important

enough to have enemies any more. If one must be a servant, is it not better to be a useful one?'

Scarpelli looked stony-faced at the Doctor.

'A sensible attitude,' said Levi.

The Doctor grunted, as indifferent to flattery as antagonism, and continued up.

Levi hung back and whispered, '*Madonna*, Scarpelli! If you can't be polite, behave.'

The other spat, 'Why are we here? It's pointless begging from beggars.'

Cat was waiting on the roof for the strangers. As Levi admired the view, it rubbed against his legs with a friendly whine, hoping for a bribe. For a rude soldier he was indecorously handsome, though hardly any part of him matched together; no painter ever painted a knight with such an unserious smile.

'Enough shadow-boxing,' said the Doctor.

'John Acuto sends his regards,' said Levi.

'Please return mine. I've long followed the exploits of the Hawk's Company. All Etruria has.'

'You know of his quarrel with Concord these last few years?'

'Men rarely admire their employer for long. I'm only surprised they haven't reconciled.'

'It's no tiff,' Levi replied seriously.

The Doctor shrugged. 'I spend much time up here. When you can't see details, you concentrate on important things.

A condottiere who wants a raise picks a fight with the city employing him. If that doesn't work, he starts working for its enemies.'

Levi chuckled. 'War is salary negotiation by other means? Doctor, you make us sound cynical.'

Scarpelli interrupted, 'It's a mark of condottieri professionalism to remain neutral.'

'This is different?' said the Doctor.

'This is personal.'

'If you say so. But come, it hardly matters what I think. You didn't come to hear second-hand gossip.'

Levi agreed, considering how to put it politely.

The Doctor didn't flinch when Scarpelli drew his sword.

'This sword's for hire, Bardini.'

'I have soldiers.'

'You need an army.'

'A freelance army,' said Levi hastily. 'Respectfully, we offer our services.'

The Doctor smiled. 'A Contract? Then this is a question for our government, not a citizen.'

Levi said, 'We have been frank with you, Doctor. Do likewise, I beg you. It's John Acuto's business to know who to talk to.'

The Doctor looked at them seriously. 'I'll carry your offer to the Signoria if you prefer, but Rasenna has never dealt with condottieri and,' he jabbed a thumb to his chest, 'as long as it listens to my advice, it never will.'

Scarpelli grunted disgustedly and re-sheathed his sword.

Levi tilted his head at a certain angle the Doctor recognised.

'Perhaps,' he began, 'if we make a donation to your workshop, you could represent our case in a summer light?'

'I appreciate the offer, but again I must refuse. Condottieri are not in Rasenna's interests, and so not in mine. What need have we of an army? We lost our war twenty years ago. I wish you success in yours, but we cannot be part of it.'

Scarpelli didn't bother concealing his irritation. 'I thought Rasenneisi were supposed to be passionate, but you're as sensible as an engineer. We're wasting time, Levi.'

'Doctor, you said you train Concordians,' Levi said. 'How many?'

'This year, just one. There's another in a workshop across the river.'

'Formerly there were more?'

'Many more,' the Doctor said cautiously. 'Concord seems to have changed its policy.'

'And now they are building a bridge here,'

'You're well informed, Colonel Levi,' said the Doctor. 'Why don't you make your point?'

'What if the bridge is the first step in a permanent garrison?'

'And now you reveal the limits of your information. The temperament of Rasenna is such that it cannot be garrisoned. Concord sent a podesta to govern us once; he soon left. They've learned since we don't need a garrison or podesta to keep us obedient. Our own quarrels keep us divided.'

'Which suits you,' said Scarpelli.

'I will unite Rasenna, one day, Virgin willing. Until then, half is better than none. If we took up your offer, Concord would destroy us along with you.'

'When Rasenna's value stops being its workshops and starts being its location, neutrality may be both impossible and imprudent,' said Levi. 'To go south, any army has to go through Rasenna, but why bother building a permanent bridge unless to lay permanent claim to the south?'

The Doctor shrugged hopelessly, as if such things were beyond him.

Scarpelli said, 'Let's go, Levi. I told John Acuto Rasenna was out of salt.'

Cat leapt away from Levi, agitated by the rising tension. As it ran between Scarpelli's legs he kicked it away, all the while holding the Doctor's eye.

The Doctor smiled. 'I'm sorry to disappoint you after you've come so far. Perhaps that workshop tour will make up for it.'

The boys stood in four lines, each boy paired off. At the end stood Sofia.

'*Avanti!*'

The swooping banners and clashing sticks was deafening rain.

'*Contrario!*' Sofia roared.

The same exchange repeated with roles reversed, attackers now defending in the same well-drilled rhythm. She walked between rows, adjusting students' posture, feet and grip, correcting flaws with quick demonstrations.

'You teach girls as well as Concordians?' With no prospect of a Contract, Scarpelli was being more blatantly rude.

'She's the one teaching,' Levi observed.

'Must gall to sell yourself so cheap, Doctor.'

The Doctor smiled at Scarpelli. 'Actually we're rather expensive. But what, pray tell, is the difference between us? John Acuto may not be Etrurian, but *you* are.'

Scarpelli reddened, and the Doctor knew he had made a hit – so, a condottiere who wants to be a knight.

Scarpelli covered embarrassment with anger. 'Yes, my loyalty's for sale. I'm sensible, like you.'

The Doctor just smiled as he called Sofia.

'You're being rude,' Levi whispered.

Scarpelli spat on the floor chippings. 'So what? This baby-tyrant isn't buying what we're selling.'

'Colonel! You wanted to see how tough Rasenneisi are?' Not waiting for an answer, he threw Scarpelli a combat banner. Sofia stepped forward.

Scarpelli looked at the flag contemptuously and dropped it. 'In the real world, soldiers fight with steel.'

The students began to take an interest. A civilian might not know what throwing down another's banner meant, but even Scarpelli could sense the sudden change in the air.

'Use your sword then,' the Doctor said coldly.

'This is absurd. I won't attack a girl with her arm in a sling!'

The Doctor stood close to Levi.

'Doctor . . .'

'Relax. I'm sure a condottiere can defend himself.'

Scarpelli put his hand on his sword, but got no further. Sofia jabbed him just below the diaphragm, partially winding him. A boy laughed as Scarpelli stumbled. The condottiere blushed violently and pulled out his sword.

The Doc wanted a show. Sofia let the sword-strokes pass close by her body, keeping her flag low, luring him on.

Scarpelli was red-faced and already getting tired. She glanced at the Doctor. He nodded and her flag went up. Scarpelli stabbed desperately and struck nothing, then a pole crunched into his nose, followed by a bruising rap on his knuckles. He dropped his sword. Flag strokes above him, in front of his face – where was she?

'Boo!' Sofia whispered, and kicked his feet out from behind. Quickly propping the end of her banner on the floor, she jammed her knee into Scarpelli's back. He struggled to stop his own weight strangling him.

Levi's hand went for his sword and found the Doctor's hand resting lightly on his. 'You'll just embarrass yourself. That's all Signorina Scaligeri is doing to your colleague.'

'Scaligeri?' said Levi. 'Of the—?'

'My ward,' said the Doctor.

He walked over to Scarpelli. 'See? It's easy to disarm the weak. For years, Concord has kept our leash loose, and we have been sensible. But struggle' – Sofia jerked the pole – 'and we die! Get it?'

Scarpelli gargled affirmatively. The Doctor nodded and Sofia released him. The condottiere rolled on the floor, gasping, and the circle broke up.

The Doctor turned to Levi. 'Should I swap a leash for a noose?'

'I apologise for my colleague's poor manners,' Levi slipped into dialect, 'but John Acuto's war on Concord is real. By Herod's Sword I swear. Acuto's son died in the belly of the Beast.'

'Should I risk my town for that? You seem less of a fool than your friend. You think your Company can win a pitched battle against a Concordian legion? Believe me, you can't. I trained Concord's generals.'

Like Scarpelli, Levi had known this mission was a long shot. Now he wondered if the forthcoming campaign was too. 'Thank you for your hospitality, Doctor. You've made your position clear. I understand you cannot risk Contessa Scaligeri's inheritance.'

'This isn't Rasenna's war.'

'It isn't the Hawk's Company's war either. It's Etruria's. For everyone's sake, Concord has to be stopped.'

The Doctor extended a hand. 'They've already won.'

CHAPTER 10

The condottieri left without delay. The Hawk's Company mustered shortly in the south and John Acuto must know which towns had rallied, which had not.

As they left, Guercho Vaccarelli arrived in answer to the Doctor's summons. He wheezed and creaked as he walked, reminding Sofia of the ravaged towers by the river. The old man's eyes were weak; his young daughter Isabella, a pretty girl with cheeks spattered with freckles, usually accompanied him, but today he leaned upon someone else.

'Signorina Scaligeri, you look like your mother more every day!' The inlaid discs in Bombelli's sleeves jingled musically as he kissed her hand. Torn clothes were common in Rasenna, but the slits in Fabbro's fur-lined jerkin were high fashion, not accident, designed to display the expensive silk chemise underneath. When visiting old friends like Vettori, Fabbro dressed down. When visiting the Doctor, he dressed up.

'Thanks,' Sofia said flatly. 'Look, come back tomorrow. The Doc's preparing for the meeting.'

'That's why I came! Doctor!'

The Doctor eyed Fabbro coolly, nodded briefly, then turned to embrace the old man. 'Signore Vaccarelli, how is your Family?'

After exchanging pleasantries, he blandly regarded his uninvited guest. 'Bombelli. What do you want?'

'To help, Doctor. Let me accompany you to the Signoria.'

'Certainly – come along. We're about to set out.'

'I mean, *sit* with you, Doctor.'

'Sofia, show Signore Vaccarelli round the workshop,' the Doctor said, putting his arm round the merchant. Then, 'Fabbro, haven't we discussed this before? What could be so urgent that you must tell the Signoria?'

'Business.'

'Your business is none of their business,' he said with a kindly smile. 'Nobody stops you making money.'

'I have employees in all the towers you watch over, but' – for a moment he hesitated – 'that's only half the town! It's like trying to eat with one hand tied behind my back. There's money across the river too.'

The Doctor took his arm away and started rubbing his chin. 'Ah,' he said, 'Fabbro, I respect you. You look after your tower and do well—'

'I can do better with a whole town, working with Vettori Vanzetti again—'

'Vanzetti doesn't have weavers any more.'

'He could get them.'

'How would they cross the river? What with the

buio and the raiding?' The Doctor waved his hands in the air to convey the immensity of the complications he foresaw.

'I can solve problems like that – and the more I make, the more you can tax me!' Fabbro had rehearsed this conversation, considering every objection.

'Only the Signoria has the authority to tax. You make *donations* to my workshop.'

'Yes. *Donations*. Fine.'

'And what if Morello is jealous?'

'I'll give him one,' Fabbro said impatiently.

'Problematic,' the Doctor said.

But Fabbro was too excited to stop. 'We can find a way around, surely—'

'If this is all you have to say, then let me speak to the Signoria on your behalf.'

'I can speak for myself.'

'But will they listen? You know I don't look down on new men, but Quintus Morello, some of the older Families, they see the money you make and—'

'Does my money smell? Does it hurt people? What's so noble about fighting all the time?'

'Nothing, but it makes us dangerous folk to cross.'

Fabbro saw finally the line he had crossed. His hands dropped impotently and his chin sank towards his chest. 'I understand. My money's good. My name is the problem.'

'No, no!' The Doctor grabbed the man's arms, embraced

and kissed him. 'The point is you have me! *I* will be your champion.'

As Fabbro left, he saw the Doctor return to Guercho Vaccarelli with a warm smile. The deference was especially galling because he knew Vaccarelli was broke. He himself had given the old man loans he would never see paid back. But that didn't matter, because Vaccarelli was noble. It didn't matter how rich you became if you were unlucky enough to be born one of the Small People. At times like this, Fabbro understood why his old friend Vettori had given up a long time ago. Doc Bardini was not the one pushing against the current.

CHAPTER 11

An hour later the Doctor led his allies south. An uneasy peace held amongst the heads of the northside towers, but these old fighters all recognised Bardini authority. Young Valerius insisted on coming along – the truce observed while the Signoria sat was a great chance to see Rasenna's other half. The Concordian had recovered from yesterday enough to begin bragging of the adventure, much to Sofia's annoyance. It was downhill all the way but Signore Vaccarelli set the group's pace, so it was late afternoon by the time they reached the river and found Giovanni's rope-bridge in place.

'Where is he?' said Valerius, impatient to see his newly arrived countryman.

Sofia shot him a disdainful look, wondering the same thing. She saw him then – on the other bank, talking with the southside boy – and at almost the same moment, Giovanni waved. He bounded onto the bridge (it was just three taut ropes, one to walk across, the others for balance) and made his way across.

When he came within earshot, Sofia called, 'You said you'd be waiting.'

'Sorry. Pedro kept me,' he said, leaping down.

'Pedro? You made a new friend.'

Hearing the playfulness in her voice, Valerius frowned, regarding Giovanni with hostility, and a sense of familiarity that was odd because Concordian nobles and engineers rarely mixed.

'He had many questions,' said Giovanni.

'He's not the only one. Captain, my guardian.'

Giovanni bowed. 'Pleased to meet you, Doctor Bardini. General Luparelli sends his regards.'

'Ah! Nice to be remembered by an old student. This is the general's son, Valerius.'

'Did Father have any word for me?'

Giovanni began awkwardly, 'I'm afraid he didn't mention—'

'No matter,' Valerius said blithely. 'This bridge doesn't look much, Captain. How do we know we won't end sleeping with the buio?'

'It's temporary, but sound. Care to try it?'

The Doctor climbed up without hesitation and shouted to the others, 'What are you waiting for?'

The northsiders had assurance of safe passage, but nothing could make them *feel* safe south of the Irenicon. When they reached land, flags went up and they traversed the empty expanse of Piazza Luna like explorers in a hostile land where every looming tower held enemies, not countrymen.

Only the Doctor was unperturbed, walking as if he had merely chosen an unusual route for his evening passeggiata. Adopting the role of host, he led Giovanni towards an antique temple-like palazzo sitting precariously on the piazza's crumbling edge. The building he grandly described as the Rasenneisi Senate was supported, laboriously, by an uneven row of stone pillars of pale green, like sodden old breadsticks.

The Palazzo della Signoria's remoteness from the centre of old Rasenna showed how little the Scaligeri had paid attention to the collective voice of other towers; it was also the reason it had survived the Wave – survived, though not escaped: to reach the Speakers' Chamber, the men had to wade through a braccia of stagnant water. The mildew encasing the outer hall's pillars like tired ivy and the way the pillars were doubled in the inky cold water made normally unimaginative men see the Speakers' Chamber as an ancient, mottled crypt within a winter forest, a crypt wherein the quick petitioned the unheeding dead. Sitting in their sodden shoes, they yearned to adjourn even before they had begun, and now meetings were called only in crisis, so loathed was the Chamber.

Giovanni glanced at the old Rasenneisi crest on the door as they entered. Gold leaf was peeling from the crudely carved Lion and the red was barely visible. He felt ashamed that his country left vanquished enemies alive only from the neck up, with enough blood to generate income, but not a drop more.

As they came to the Chamber door the Doctor whispered, 'Captain, know that people will say things in here intending the opposite. If you need help – and I think you will – come and see me. I'm a good friend.'

Giovanni had sensed tension talking to the boy and the Contessa. Like this rotting palazzo, Rasenna was on a precipice, and contrary to the Apprentices' recommendation, he believed he must maintain independence if he was to accomplish his mission. He said nothing, but pulled his sleeve from the Doctor's grasp.

Amused, the Doctor let him go ahead. 'Keep an eye on the wolf cub,' he whispered to Sofia.

She took Valerius' arm. 'Come along, *principino*. The town-fathers tend to express themselves undiplomatically.'

Valerius laughed. 'About Concord? Now I really want in.'

To the left of the Chamber door were three high steps leading to a small landing where a bust of Sofia's grandfather stood sentry. Above Count Scaligeri's sage portrait hung a swarm of family crests, a chequered field of faded green, scarlet and yellow, overrun by creatures fantastic as griffins, mundane as swine. They belonged to Rasenna's *Families*, those whose rarefied blood entitled them to sit in the Signoria and made them eligible to be elected gonfaloniere. This niche had become a shabby shrine to old Rasenna, a reminder of how many once-great towers were fallen. Sofia led Valerius here, just far enough from the Speakers' Chamber to prevent eavesdropping.

She was surprised, pleasantly, to find Gaetano Morello

waiting there too. She guessed the stout, happy, pale-haired boy with him was the Morello's Contract this year; just like her, Gaetano had been relegated to babysitting. She marched over with a lop-sided grin, twirling her flag around her arm.

'Well, well.'

Gaetano smiled. 'Contessa.'

'If it isn't the terror of Rasenna.'

'Don't start.'

'So, what's the next stage of the Morello master plan, Tano? Overthrow the Apprentices?'

'All right, get it out of your system. How come you haven't been making a nuisance of yourself lately?'

Sofia leaned against the wall. 'The usual. Doc's got me on the leash.'

'We should trade places. I think I got demoted to foot soldier this morning.'

Sofia laughed. 'Your brother returned in one piece?'

'Not quite,' said Gaetano, glancing at his student. The boy was placidly cleaning a set of glass-ringed discs. 'Never mind that. Allow me to—'

The boy perched the glasses on his nose and interrupted, 'Contessa! The renown of your noble name precedes you, but of your beauty I heard not a whisper! Count Marcus Marius Messallinus, at your service.'

Sofia smiled at the round little boy, bursting with old-fashioned chivalry. 'Pleasure. Don't listen to a word Tano tells you. The Morello fight like girls.'

*

The notary's ink-stained spidery fingers drifted over the leather cover of the Rasenneisi Signoria's Book of Minutiae and Procedure. Like him it was a yellowing relic, and he loved it. He opened it with the light touch of devotion. So long had it been since the last session that a dust cloud escaped. He inhaled with relish and let the rest settle upon him as he looked around the Speakers' Chamber.

On his right, the heads of southern Families encircled this year's gonfaloniere, speaking in whispers. The notary wondered if Quintus Morello appreciated the irony of being gonfaloniere of a town that no longer possessed a banner. Doubtful, he decided and, sighing more profoundly, he turned to his left where Bardini's unruly and noisy allies lounged. A reluctant parliamentarian, the Doctor sat towards the back, spoke only when called upon, and even then under protest.

The notary's family were not artisans or fighters: they were literate. That skill was little valued today, but there had been a golden age when Rasenna's swift heralds had daily ridden forth carrying Count Scaligeri's words – strong words elegantly inscribed – to all Etruria. Then his family had carried their humpbacks as proudly as other families carried banners. That age was gone.

The Doctor was early. Today was certainly unusual. The assembly watched as he led the Concordian engineer to the centre. While the seated areas were covered, the Speakers' circle was open to the elements, the shattered dome creating an accidental but perfect spotlight for orators. The notary was disappointed at the hush caused by the foreigner's arrival. He particularly enjoyed banging his gavel.

The Doctor effortlessly took the Speakers' mace from the notary and set his sights on Quintus Morello, as if preparing to hurl the dense metal orb. He gave the gonfaloniere a nod before handing it to Giovanni.

Sofia and Gaetano ignored their Concordian charges while they caught up. They hadn't spoken for months, since the escalation, and both were relieved that it was still possible.

'Does every Concordian have a genealogy instead of a surname?' Sofia said.

'All except engineers, I suppose. Speaking of which—?'

'He's all right. Got salt, for a Concordian.'

'I wasn't asking what he's like. Why's he here?'

'As if you don't know.'

'I don't,' Gaetano protested.

She wanted to believe him. It would be a relief if her old friend was kept from intrigue or, still better, avoided it.

'He's going to build a bridge, Tano.'

Gaetano whistled. '*Madonna!*'

Sofia nodded.

They were silent, thinking what it meant, for Rasenna, for them; they had always avoided each other on the streets – with a real bridge, that wouldn't be possible.

'Remember when I used to come over here?'

Gaetano smiled. 'Sure – you used to beat me up.'

'Just to make you chase me.'

They laughed together, reminiscing about crossing the rooftops, not hunting, just running for the fun of it, innocent of the arguments below. When Gaetano's uncle died, all that stopped and Gaetano became workshop maestro. Sofia knew from her closeness to the Doctor what power does: it stunts; to be constant is to be static. Gaetano remained that boy on the roof, catching his breath, while she ran further every year.

'We have to grow up sometime,' Sofia said with a smile she did not feel.

The Concordian boys were engaged in a dance of their own. Deciding who had higher status was complicated and Valerius took the steps more seriously than his rival. He circled warily, probing Marcus' defence with small talk about cousins and titles.

'I've heard of everyone, but I've never heard of you. You can't be anyone important.'

Marcus laughed. 'That's reasonable, I suppose. Well, what matter? We're all nobodies now.'

'Speak for yourself. My father's General of the Twelfth Legion.'

'Really? That is impressive!'

'We Luparelli have adapted to the times.'

'He studied in Rasenna too? That's why I was sent here too, to get a good posting.'

Valerius drew himself up. 'May the best men win.'

'No need to be like that. There *are* twelve legions.'

'Child, *everything* is a competition.'

Having enjoyed a genteel upbringing, Marcus had no idea how to deal with this extraordinarily aggressive boy. He decided it was best to agree. 'Undoubtedly. I just meant that we nobles are in it together, since the engineers took over, if you follow.'

'You're preposterous. If circumstances change, the best Families change with them; the best always rise.'

Valerius thought of his year in Rasenna as a career step; for Marcus it was an extended holiday, full of rough camaraderie and daily drama. What did the nobility's irrelevance matter? That race was run and lost before he'd even been born.

'I suppose there's no point asking if you know who this engineer is?'

Marcus was relieved to change the subject. 'I heard he's here to build a bridge,' he said in a conspiratorial whisper.

'Bah, everyone knows that! I'll write to Father. One thing's certain, he can't be any good.'

'But he *is* a captain. Must have done something to earn that rank.'

'And something worse to be sent here.'

'What's wrong with Rasenna? I like Rasenna.'

'It's a fine place to learn fighting. But for an engineer, it's relegation. Punishment. For incompetence, insubordination, who knows what.' He suddenly looked over his shoulder. Gaetano had succeeded in making Sofia laugh. She never acted *that* way – like a girl – with the boys of workshop Bardini; certainly not with him. When Valerius turned back, he saw Marcus had begun polishing that ridiculous glass contraption again.

He smiled his cherub's smile. 'I've never seen eye-pieces up close before,' he said in a friendly way.

As evening drew on and torches were lit around the Chamber, faces already angry took on a demonic hue and the milling whisperers threw monstrous shadows.

Fearing he would blunder, Giovanni had made a note of what he needed to say – and for a horrible moment he thought he'd lost it. He found it and looked down at the swimming text in despair. Then, with heart hammering in his chest, he looked up and began to speak. 'Men of Rasenna, thank you for this audience. I am Captain Giovanni of the Engineers Guild. My task is to bridge the Irenicon.'

He waited for the whispers to subside, then went on, 'I will complete my survey this week and then provide details of the material and men I need. Based on a cursory examination, I shall confirm to Concord that the allocated time is sufficient. Concordian machines make it possible to build a bridge by summer's end, but Rasenna's men will make it happen. I propose taking an equal number from north and south. I leave my initial notes, with approximate costs and quantities, for the Signoria to study.' He felt that he was speaking too loudly but carried on, 'Concord expects your cooperation. My task is to bridge the Irenicon – it is your task too. Thank you.'

He folded his note slowly before looking back up into the impassive faces of the cynical and prematurely old men and he remembered Pedro's first question this morning. *Was it a request or an order?*

He cleared his throat. 'More than just cooperation, I ask your support. I say this bridge is for all Rasenna knowing that you have reason to doubt me. Until today, you have only seen Natural Philosophy's destructive power. I pray you, see today as I do – a new beginning for Rasenna and Concord, an opportunity to heal our discord.'

The faces were still hostile, but now looking towards their respective leaders.

'Thank you, uh, again,' he finished.

Quintus Morello stood. 'Thank you, Captain. This is indeed a new era. As gonfaloniere, I pray your example inspires Rasenna to put aside our own divisions. May the Virgin grant success!'

The applause surprised and embarrassed Giovanni. He bowed to the assembly, gave the mace and estimates to the notary and, blushing furiously, went towards the door.

In the outer chamber, Sofia was watching the Concordians play their game of status. The games she'd played with Gaetano had been more innocent, and yet more dangerous.

She remembered the day she had blundered into a crow's nest on the eaves of Tower Ferruccio. When the outraged mother crow attacked, she lost her footing and began sliding down the tiles – she still woke sometimes from nightmares where she kept sliding – but Gaetano had caught her, and she had kissed him and slapped him, and then run home in a cloud of giddy laughter. Everything was easier back then.

The Chamber door burst open suddenly and the engineer stepped into the water. He was wiping his brow dazedly, then blushed when he saw them looking at him. He nodded stiffly before wading out to the piazza.

Sofia caught Gaetano's sceptical look. 'Really. He's all right.'

A tinkle of smashed glass brought their attention immediately back to the Concordians.

'Damn it, Valerius! What did you do?'

'Are you all right, Marcus?' said Gaetano.

'I won't be able to see now!' Marcus cried.

'You little *stronzo!*' said Gaetano, grabbing Valerius and slamming him against the wall. Several crests fell and smashed.

'Get your hands off me!' screamed Valerius.

'Hands off, Tano!' The end of Sofia's flag-stick lightly touched Gaetano's temple.

'All right, all right—' He let go and backed away, dragging Marcus with him.

'I can't see!'

'I'll make sure he's punished,' she said.

'Do that.'

Valerius laughed. '*Idiota!* She can't punish me!'

Sofia stuck Valerius in the stomach. He doubled over and gasped, 'Why did you do that?' He sounded genuinely shocked.

She held her stick under his chin. 'Say it again. I dare you.'

Gaetano pulled her away. 'Sofia, he's right. Anything done to him, Rasenna gets back tenfold. Let's just keep them separate.'

Sofia had to leave or she'd do something she'd regret. Outside, amidst the slender-columned loggia adjoining the palazzo, she found the engineer glumly regarding the river.

'What's the matter with you?' Then she saw: someone had cut the rope-bridge. While he had been speaking inside about reconciliation, somebody was sabotaging it before it had even begun.

The applause ended the moment the engineer left the room. Quintus Morello crossed the floor, snatched the estimates from the notary and crumpled them into a ball. 'Let's hope the buio take him for a tour of old Rasenna.'

Cheers and laughter from the southern benches while across the floor, the Doctor leaned forward and whispered to Guercho Vaccarelli.

The old man took the mace and fixed his one functioning eye on Quintus. 'Levity?' he spat, 'at this hour, Gonfaloniere? If our extension was refused, and we gather it was . . .' He spoke in whistling gasps, and when breath was exhausted he left sentences suspended in midair while his dusty lungs recovered a second wind.

'We have not come to that point on the agenda,' the notary interrupted, glancing at the ambassador. Valentino sat quietly beside his father, his slender frame still draped in his cloak, his face as blank as the empty sky above the old man.

Guercho Vaccarelli caught his breath and continued, 'If there is no extension, I say, then Rasenna faces greater demands than ever: tribute for last year *and* the year to come! This is no time for levity or partisanship, not in this house, not on the streets.'

A southerner jeered, 'You liked it when you were winning!'

The old man ignored the interruption and raised a shaking finger of admonition. 'Concord will pay for the bridge. It brings employment and commerce to profit our merchants, and to we who tax them. It is a means to pay our debt. Who knows another? Before displaying your considerable patriotism, my Lords, consider one more point.'

'Hurry up!' Boos erupted from the southside and the notary hammered his gavel, shouting for order.

'Defaulting has strained relations with the Empire. What if we add defiance to our sins? You are all tower-owners.

When a tenant defaults, you throw him out. But when he insults you, you throw him out of a window.'

Property owners both sides of the Chamber laughed in recognition.

The old man was not smiling. 'Concord has a strategic reason to build this bridge. Is it to help Rasenna? Or is it a provocation to goad us into rebellion?' He waited a moment before loudly answering himself, 'It is neither! We are not that important. The reason is simple: before Concord looks to Europa, it must secure its rear. It must bring to heel the last free cities of Etruria.'

'The Doctor's visitors revealed all this?' Quintus Morello interrupted with exaggerated surprise.

The notary piped up, 'Lord Morello, the condottieri are a separate order of business.'

Vaccarelli was unfazed. 'Gonfaloniere, it's obvious to anyone who troubles to study a map. Concord needs a bridge to campaign south, but there is no reason to build it in permanent stone except to send a message, to the south and us, that *this* is the new order. As we own our towers, they own us. If the bridge is unfinished in five months' time, they will pause long enough to complete it, and when they leave there will be a bridge and no Rasenna. Our role as playground for Concordian pups comes to an end. A sword hangs over us. We can be Concord's vassal and live, or her enemy and die.'

The old man proffered the mace challengingly. 'Gonfaloniere?'

Quintus Morello waited for Vaccarelli to take his seat before speaking in tones of barely contained rage. 'Friends, do not be deceived by arguments of expedience. Concord's Wave made us eunuchs! This bridge is another assault, more insidious, for it comes gift-wrapped. If it was indeed Trojans who founded Rasenna, should we emulate their valour, or their credulity? The Doctor – excuse me, *Signore Vaccarelli* – paints a dark picture. Is it really so dark, or is it coloured by ambition? Does he hope to win Concord's favour by bending over at every opportunity?'

As every other southsider dutifully cheered his father's words, Valentino stared at Doctor Bardini. There was something impressive about the old street-fighter. He had not troubled to put his name in the election purse for years. What would be the point?

In the ebbing light, Quintus Morello's faded red robes had become finally colourless and his voice had reached that unpleasant pitch that meant he was getting to the point. 'Are we children, to be scared by rumour? I remind the northside that Rasenna is a republic, where *all* the people have a voice. Or am I not your elected gonfaloniere?'

Riotous cheers answered his question. The Doctor whispered in Vaccarelli's ear again. 'The northern towers recognise the gonfaloniere's authority,' the old man answered.

After the roars died down, Morello announced proudly,

'Very well. As uncontested Gonfaloniere of Rasenna, I *approve* this bridge–' He paused for effect.

'–on the condition that the engineer lodge in a south-side tower, under *Morello* protection.'

Guercho Vaccarelli turned and whispered with the Doctor for a while and then, looking a little puzzled, croaked, 'No objection.'

Valentino would have admired such coolness once, but the Beast had taught him better. Yes, the Doctor played more skilfully than Quintus, but the game itself was ignoble – the two worms were vying for a dung heap.

The notary moved to the second order of business and, scratching himself like a flea-ridden dog, the Doctor wandered into the circle, carrying the mace and a deferential manner, and said, 'Friends, you know me as a plain-spoken man. There's been talk that this morning's visitors came by invitation, to propose a new southern league. It's a wonderful story, but the truth is more mundane. The condottieri were merely passing through, and they were curious enough about *Art Banderia* to ask for a workshop tour.'

When the Doctor went to return the mace, Quintus called out, 'Anything else?'

'Now that I think of it, Gonfaloniere, we did discuss a hypothetical situation.' He scratched his chin. 'It's embarrassing to repeat it, but they invited me to speculate on whether Rasenna would hire condottieri. I said it would not – it was but idle conversation; I am glad they wasted a citizen's time and not the Signoria's. Entertaining such guests officially would be difficult to explain to Concord, should they hear of it.'

Morello harrumphed. 'Why should Rasenna not employ condottieri? It is our right—'

The Doctor nodded. 'As is suicide.' He added, as an afterthought, 'Though it's rarely a wise course.'

He dropped his abstracted air abruptly. 'Etruria has no use for condottieri. The towns that employ them have been bankrupted or betrayed often enough that they see their foolishness. The last such army in Etruria is led by John Acuto, who fights for whoever he can bully into employing him. As my esteemed colleague mentioned, Concord's Twelfth marches south this summer – not a few squadrons, not a patchwork of allies fighting with the aid of one Concordian engineer, but an entire legion. That is the end of John Acuto, and Rasenna too, if we join them.'

'In short, you told those mercenaries you were happy to be a slave.'

The Doctor smiled good-naturedly. 'Much eloquence is spilled on the subject of freedom – its splendour, its nobility, its necessity. I only ask, Gonfaloniere, what is its use? We are slaves of time, of hunger, of passion, and yet we make no complaint. We are rarely slaves of reason in Rasenna; of those chains we are unfortunately emancipated. We are too weak to win more freedom, but perhaps wise enough to keep the little we have.'

The Doctor handed back the mace to a barrage of cheers and insults. Before vitriol turned violent, the notary squealed, 'Next order of business! Ambassador Morello, please.'

The young man stood. A hush descended. When Valentino had left to seek the extension, he had been mocked for his youth. Now every eye was locked upon him. He reached the circle, shrugged aside the cloak and cried, 'Here is Concord's answer!'

As shock rippled through the chamber, Valentino's gaze was nailed on one man. The Doctor remained expressionless.

A northsider broke the silence. 'No extension then?'

'A small reduction,' the Doctor said.

The southside benches erupted with anger, but Valentino dropped the mace with a bang, bringing sudden silence.

'I am a warning of the price of disobedience.' He raised his remaining hand. 'But Concord misjudges us! I would sooner cut off this hand too than cast away my honour. Rasenneisi' – Valentino pointed his stump at the Doctor – 'this man is a traitor!'

With surprising haste, old man Vaccarelli leapt to his feet. 'Slander! Slander, I say! Notary, remove this boy.'

Red-faced, Quintus Morello stood. His men's flags rose with him. 'Everyone, be seated. As you value your lives, molest none of my house.'

Bardini and Morello affiliates shouted at each other,

then crowded onto the floor. In the crush, Valentino found himself back to back with his father.

The Doctor was amused that a boy who left Rasenna before ever wielding a flag himself had returned militant. Whatever tortures he had been subjected to, he had left more than flesh behind in Concord. Quintus Morello was the perfect rival, weak, irresolute and predictable; what if this son took charge?

With a tired grunt, he stood. He let the shouting dwindle before he spoke. 'Brothers, anyone who bleeds for Rasenna has earned my respect and your attention.'

It was enough to restore order. Everyone returned to their side of the chamber as the other Signoria members looked upon Valentino Morello with mingled curiosity and annoyance.

Valentino spoke calmly. 'The Doctor's analysis is essentially correct. The Concordians mean to be paid. They'll plunder the south to feed their war machine. Rasenna has no riches to lose, but we still have our pride.' He turned slightly. 'Perhaps, that's where we differ, Doctor. I ask how we can hold onto our honour, not what price we ask for it.'

The mace lay where it had fallen. Instead of the usual shouting, boos and threats, there was unbearably taut silence. Hastily the notary adjourned.

When Sofia said they must go home the old way, the Doctor sounded unconcerned by the sabotage. His catlike grin spread over his wide face as he said, 'It went well.'

He had told her that he desired one thing from the meeting only, and the rest was theatre, and that had happened: the bridge was going ahead. Come what may.

CHAPTER 12

Unwilling to be a mere parchment-engineer, Bernoulli made his name by mapping the so-called 'hydra', Etruria's river system. Because of his youth, his first building project was a renovation. The Etruscan bridge connecting the old city walls to the mainland was straining under the rising population. Unimpressed by its antiquity, Bernoulli considered bolstering inadequate structures not only folly but immoral.

His alternative proposal, an audacious one-span bridge, was controversial. Surveyors, masons and engineers of the day insisted that such a structure would not support its own weight, let alone the city's traffic. Bernoulli found an influential advocate in the Patrician Senator Postumus Tremellius Felix,[5] whose forceful arguments convinced the Curia. The old bridge was demolished and speedily replaced with a bridge immediately recognised as an architectural marvel. Bernoulli was never questioned again, at least in matters of technique.

---

[5] The Author's father.

CHAPTER 13

Giovanni was given a floor in a Morello tower that, although unfurnished and rather strange-smelling, suited his needs. An open space with good light was all he needed for drawing. After getting settled, he climbed the stairs. The trapdoor opened before he had the chance to knock.

'*Dio*, you take a long time to unpack!' Pedro motioned him up with impatience. 'Come up and meet my father.'

When Giovanni saw the wool crammed into every corner he realised what his room had been used for. Vettori Vanzetti rose from his loom. 'Captain, Pedro has told me all about you. He's wanted to interrogate an engineer since he was old enough to put two words together.'

'My door will always be open.'

'You might live to regret that,' said Pedro with a grin.

'I'll take my chances.'

As the men spoke, Pedro went back to repairing a loom. Noting Vettori's fresh black eye, Giovanni guessed he had not volunteered for the job.

'What do you need, Captain?'

'Answers, to start with. You've construction experience?'

'Not much.'

'Quintus Morello recommended you as foreman. Why?'

'I can't speak for my betters, Captain, but I used to run a small business. People know me, northsiders too, and trust me, as far as that goes.'

'Concord will pay for your equipment, however it got damaged.'

'None of the crew can accept money. We're all in debt to Morello or Bardini. Our money is their money. My loom, I broke it myself. That's how I got this shiner too. I'll help you, Captain, but if you don't want an accident-prone crew, please don't ask questions.'

'I am not here to cause trouble.'

'Simply by being here you will.'

The two men stared at each other in silence.

'He's all right, Papa.'

'What do you need, Captain?' Vettori repeated.

Giovanni knew it would take more than his son's word to satisfy Vettori. He stuck to practicalities. 'Stone. Wood. Iron.'

He cut and pinned paper to the wall to make one large sheet and drew his plans while Pedro watched over his shoulder. It had been a long time since he had felt any enthusiasm for his work. The bridge was a tool. Even if the Apprentices planned to use it for war, the bridge itself would be innocent. Perhaps he could be too. His window looked out to the piazza and the river beyond and he saw it as it could be: a graceful symphony of material, a lithe shape belying hidden tensions – the contest of strength between design and matter, and the pressures they must bear: of gravity, load and environment. The first was simple to calculate, the second was a variable, and in time he would come to understand the third.

The charcoal snapped. He caught his breath. There were other contests, warring bone warring muscle. It was with him always.

Gubbio.

Always, though he'd done his duty. Always, though the Guild said that geometry was innocent, that guilt was atavism, that sin did not exist. There was no Right and Wrong, only correct and incorrect. For the hundredth – the thousandth – time he wished he believed the dogma.

Vettori warned his son not to be distracting, but Giovanni needed an assistant and curiosity was the prime quality of a good one. Vettori, overhearing the engineer's explanations to the unending questions, noticed he spoke to Pedro not as a child or a Rasenneisi but as a colleague, and he watched as Pedro responded with growing confidence, absorbing the barrage of new ideas Vettori himself found so alien.

Discussing logistics, Giovanni was pleased to find Vettori rational, fair, and far too cautious – these were the qualities of a good foreman.

*

Before the week ended, Giovanni's plans had the gonfaloniere's seal. The Signoria's indifference suited him. He did not need assistance, and he dreaded interference.

Scaffolding was the first priority. Two decades with no building had allowed the forests outside the walls to regenerate. Time had also erased any evidence of previous visitors, and Giovanni could imagine himself the first man to walk there.

He broke a branch off and peeled back the bark. 'You don't know how lucky you are, having this life outside your walls, near enough that you can smell it. Touch it.'

Vettori watched the Concordian moving softly between the trees. 'Aye,' he said evenly, 'it's peaceful.'

'It's more than that: it's alive. The land around Concord has been barren for years.'

Vettori didn't respond, unsure of his ground. Normally, the engineer talked fast, and only about practicalities; and normally Concordians boasted of the things they *had*, things that others lacked.

'When they started diverting rivers, the trees stopped growing. We were woodsmen once, but you can't plant in dust. All the scaffolding for the Molè's nave had to be imported – that's why Bernoulli built the domes without any.' Giovanni pulled off another branch. 'He wanted to prove even Nature couldn't hold him back.'

'What are you looking for?' asked Vettori.

'Quality' – he stripped another in the same way – 'consistency.'

Vettori waited. It was irrational, perhaps, but he felt patriotically concerned that the wood would meet the engineer's standards. 'Well?'

'It's good. Who owns it?'

'Morello,' Vettori told him, 'and Bardini owns the quarries on the north.'

'Think they'll give me a good deal since I'm buying wholesale?'

'Sorry, Captain. They'll both gouge you for every soldi they can.'

'I won't quibble. Concord has deep pockets. I suppose it's good the Families agree on something. I expect iron will be more problematic.'

Vettori smiled. 'I know a northsider who eats problems for breakfast.'

They crossed the river on the east side, where the Wave had smashed though the town walls on its way out. It was a risky journey, leaping from one uneven pillar to another. Vettori was far from athletic but he was a still a Rasenneisi; Giovanni found himself clinging to the wet rocks his guide had leapt between without a second thought.

'Why's it called the Midnight Road anyway? It can't be used solely by assassins,' Giovanni shouted over the water's roar.

Vettori looked back incredulously. 'Why else cross over?'

Giovanni, taken aback, had no response. Since the

Signoria meeting he'd brooded on the consequences of reuniting this turbulent town. He saw someone standing on the north bank and shouted, 'Seems we're expected.'

'Spotted, more like. Every riverside tower is a look-out for raiders.'

Sofia leaned nonchalantly on her flag and called, '*Madonna*, I've never seen such clumsy climbing. I'm surprised you haven't broken something yet.'

'Is that how you broke your arm?'

'Still none of your business, Captain. What *is* your business northside?'

'I'm meeting a merchant to discuss supplies.'

'Fabbro Bombelli, Contessa,' Vettori stuttered.

'Fine. Follow me. I don't know what lies those southsiders have told you, Captain, but it's not safe for Concordians to walk the streets unescorted.'

'I'm not a soldier, I'm an engineer.'

'What's the difference?'

Vettori was visibly relieved to reach the merchant's tower. The door burst open and Giovanni saw a short, well-fed, well-dressed man sliding down the ladder with surprising grace for someone with so white a beard.

'Vettori! Just as I am about to come to you, you come to me. Hello, Captain! Pleased to know you. You'll never guess, just this morning another friend suggested I help out with your famous bridge. Naturally, I was delighted.'

Giovanni caught Fabbro's shrewd glance at Vettori's black

eye and wasn't surprised when he asked, 'You'll be working on it too, my friend?' He clapped his hands and cried, 'Vanzetti and Bombelli, together again! Captain, may you never have sons as cruel as mine! The scoundrels mock me, telling me you have the power to keep the buio at bay!'

While Giovanni explained how the eggs worked, Fabbro tilted his head appraisingly. He looked upon business opportunities with almost motherly affection and, though he did not understand the technology, he saw the possibilities at once. 'Let me understand: we can unload barges without endangering the operators? But this is marvellous – my sons are honest!'

'You're forgetting the wall,' Vettori interjected, 'what's left of it.'

'We'll knock it down,' Giovanni said. 'With a real bridge, you won't need it.'

The very notion left Vettori speechless, but Fabbro's nimble mind had already leaped into a future where river traffic was not feared but welcomed. 'Knock it down. How simple. This will make delivering your iron a trifle, Captain. Tell me exactly what you need and Bombelli and sons will look after the rest.'

After Giovanni had gone over his requirements, he turned to Vettori. 'You can go back now. I need to speak with Doctor Bardini.'

Vettori looked sheepish and Sofia looked suspicious. 'Why?' she demanded.

'He's in charge, isn't he?'

Sofia picked up her flag. 'Go home, Vanzetti. I'll see the Concordian gets back in one piece.'

When Vettori had left, Giovanni caught up to her. 'I didn't mean to be rude, Signorina. I just meant— Well, you *are* under his protection, aren't you?'

Giovanni thought she wasn't going to answer until she turned on him. 'The Signoria sits at *my* pleasure. I'm not some ordinary Rasenneisi; I am the Contessa Scaligeri!'

'We don't make such distinctions in Concord.'

'How wonderfully modern. Keep up, will you?'

Giovanni followed through quick-turning streets with difficulty, annoyed with himself for glibly repeating Guild dogma. He had reviewed their last meeting several times; imagining ways he could have done better – now this! What was it about wanting to make a good impression that ensured you didn't?

The Doctor greeted him from the steps of the workshop like an old friend. 'Captain, come in!'

'Doctor, I need help.'

The Doctor looked for Sofia, but she was already dragging Valerius from the pillar he was lurking behind. It wouldn't do for Concord to hear second-hand of any arrangements the Bardini might make with the engineer.

'What's *he* want, Sofia?' Valerius said, sulky at having been removed from his vantage point.

'If you paid as much attention to your studies as you

do to gossip, you might be half the soldier your father's expecting to collect.' As she led him away, she glanced over her shoulder. She was curious too.

'I'm impressed that you've come so soon. You're a fast learner, Captain. And Sofia tells me you've got some salt in a tight corner.'

'I got the impression she hated me.'

'She hates *Concord*. In time, she'll see you have many good qualities. Knowing when you need friends, for example. How can I help?'

'Keep your feud away from my bridge.'

The Doctor's smile didn't falter. 'What do you mean?'

'You know very well: neither Vettori Vanzetti or Fabbro Bombelli were given a choice in working for me.'

'Vanzetti's a southsider.'

'I already told Quintus Morello I don't want my crew intimidated.'

The Doctor smiled a little wider. 'And how did our sage gonfaloniere respond?'

'He said he didn't know what I was talking about.'

'Ah, you're simply confused by our provincial ways. Fabbro Bombelli asked me, as a friend, whether he should get involved, and I told him exactly what I told the Signoria: Concord wants a bridge, so Concord will get a bridge. It's in Rasenna's best interest to cooperate.'

'Maybe you don't listen to others in the Signoria. I came to build a bridge *for* Rasenna.'

'Then, if you'll forgive me for saying so, you've misunderstood your mission. Not that it matters whether you pick it up or not, Concord holds the rod.'

'You're still not listening, Doctor. You're talking small-town politics. A crew needs peace to get anything done, and if you and Quintus Morello disrupt that, there's going to be discord and delays.'

'And what I'm saying, Captain, is that discord's inevitable. We're not like other towns—' He broke off and laughed. 'But you'll come to see that. I'll stay away, since you ask, but don't think I'll let that dreamer take advantage. He agreed in the Signoria for form's sake. He imagines he can stop the bridge and still avoid Concord's wrath.'

'You know better?'

'I was a boy the first time Concord punished Rasenna. For years I dreamed about it.' The Doctor looked away. 'Don't misunderstand, I'm as ambitious as Morello, but I don't put faith in dreams. The only constant in Etruria is Concord's strength.'

Giovanni followed the Doctor's gaze. At the other end of the workshop Sofia was instructing the students.

'And my ambition is not for myself. If you won't take my help, at least take my advice. Like it or not, you're a conqueror. Act like one. Strength is all Rasenneisi understand. Whatever you are, don't be lukewarm. It's no good to anybody.'

'I came to build a bridge for Rasenna,' Giovanni repeated stubbornly.

'Then you're just another dreamer.' The Doctor sighed and turned. 'Sofia, take the Captain home. I no longer guarantee his safety.'

On the way back, Giovanni was quiet and thoughtful. Sofia had assumed the engineer had come seeking Bardini protection – everybody folded to the Families eventually – but the Doctor's abrupt dismissal suggested otherwise.

'Get what you wanted?' she asked casually.

'I said what I wanted. I don't know if he heard.'

'What do you want?'

He realised he could easily appear rude again if he didn't frame his reply carefully. After a moment he said, 'I don't want to interfere with Rasenneisi politics, but I have a mission. I need both Families to keep their quarrel off the bridge.'

She frowned. 'Look, you mean well—'

'But?'

'You're not a Rasenneisi, Captain. What you want might not be possible.'

There was no arguing the point; he could see that. He said, 'I saw you in the workshop, by the way. I'm no judge but you look very skilful.'

She shrugged. 'I have to be.'

'But won't you inherit all this at seventeen?'

'It's not that simple,' she started. 'Engineers know about maps, right? Well, you only need maps when you're going somewhere. I found one in my mother's trousseau when

I was seven. I didn't know what it was until Doc told me. Don't laugh, but I couldn't find Rasenna until he showed me the crease where the map was folded. There we were, worn away.' They could hear the river now. 'I realised then that being Contessa was something I couldn't count on; I'd have to be a bandieratoro too. I practised harder than anyone in the workshop until—'

'—you were the best,' he finished for her.

She blushed, realising it sounded like pride. 'So who taught you?'

'Every engineer studies with the Guild.'

'I meant, was your father an engineer?'

'Yes, I come from a line of men with machine-grease instead of blood.'

They reached the river. Giovanni looked at it like a bandieratoro sizing up an opponent.

He caught her staring. 'Contessa, you say you're Scaligeri, not Bardini, but from what I've heard, the Morello don't see a distinction. And I can see why the Doctor might not want them to.' Even as he finished, he realised he'd done it again.

'And I keep reminding you to mind your own business! You think you can drive a wedge between me and Doc? Divide and conquer, eh?'

'I'm not a conqueror—'

'We'll see,' she said turning away. 'Mind you don't break your neck getting back.'

*

Giovanni returned to the tower feeling like his efforts had been disastrous, yet when Vettori heard he'd stood up for the Small People, he started working with gratitude and gusto.

While masons puzzled over Giovanni's templates, Fabbro engaged in voluminous correspondence, searching Europa for the quantities of metal needed. Giovanni sketched the machines that would allow building to proceed at a Concordian pace. Pedro, working with everyone, was soon making informed suggestions as well as following orders, and looking less assistant than engineer.

When the site was finally marked out, the masons were reassured that the buried town centre's silt shroud would be undisturbed. It was better that their ancestors slept ignorant of their children's poverty.

CHAPTER 14

After exhausting the great libraries of the Curia,[6] Bernoulli wrote a list of questions touching on fields as diverse as Anatomy and Physics. Answering these questions would require new mathematics, new methods, new machines and great audacity. He was undaunted. Though he famously left unanswered one question,[7] his *Dialogue with Myself* is a thorough dissection of Nature that contradicts much Classical authority. This theoretically undercut Clerical authority but the Cardinals either failed to notice or found such rarefied theory harmless. Here Bernoulli elucidates, somewhat poetically, his observations on Time:

> *The greater the Engineer the further he sees. The Method is to foresee Modes of Collapse. The corollary to the Method is that a Structure is not a composition of Stone or Steel.*

---

[6] He consumed facts 'like a pig, eating all that was put before him', according to contemporary diarist and wit, Ciuto Brandini (Born 1304 – Executed 1348).

[7] '*Pace* Pythagoras, material proof of Perfection, $X^3 + Y^3 = Z^3$, possible?' Since it was found scribbled in a proof margin, most scholars consider it a whimsy rather than a question proper.

It is an infinity of uncreated Worlds. Each stroke of the Engineer's pen creates the World anew[8].

---

[8] Two decades were to pass before the Most Holy Inquisition made their jaundiced interpretation of this passage the centrepiece of Bernoulli's trial for heresy.

CHAPTER 15

Dogged application of two infinite resources, Concord's money and Bombelli's persistence, ensured supplies arrived the morning before they were scheduled to begin. Giovanni left Tower Vanzetti with his nose buried in various plans, double-checking contingencies and measurements, oblivious to the shadow overhead. As he turned a corner, the shadow dropped in front of him and he fell back, scattering his plans.

Sofia deftly caught them and handed them back.

'Thank you!' he stammered.

'Sure I'm not a courteous assassin?'

'Should I cry for help?'

'You could try,' said Sofia dryly. 'Don't worry, you're safe with me.'

'But you're a northsider.'

'And proud. Your point?'

'This isn't the northside.'

'The truce was extended. And, as I keep telling you, I'm Contessa – you might not make distinctions, but Rasenneisi do. Southsiders pay rent to Morello, but they're still loyal to Scaligeri.' She took his silence for scepticism. 'You'll see!'

Giovanni wondered if all Rasenneisi were as change-able as Etrurian weather; had she forgiven their quarrel, or just forgotten it?

'So, big day. Nervous?'

'Why should I be?'

'Oh, little things like half your crew harbouring *vendette* against the other half?'

'I get the feeling you don't want a bridge.'

'Perceptive.'

'The Doctor wants it.'

'Who knows what he wants . . .'

He heard anger in her voice and assumed he had he blundered again, but Sofia was simply tired of being treated like hired help. The Doctor had told her to shadow the engineer after his last visit, but he wouldn't tell her more.

'Perhaps I'm overlooking something obvious, but surely the river makes life difficult?' he said, choosing his words carefully.

'You should have considered that before sending it,' she shot back.

'That wasn't me personally – and it was another time. Rasenna was belligerent.'

'Some of us still are.'

'I've noticed – but I still don't understand whether you really object to the bridge, or just to Concord?'

'Why not both?'

'You can't simultaneously object to being divided and to being united – that's a contradiction!'

'Well, you're not from around here.'

They were fast approaching Piazza Luna, where Vanzetti was assembling the crew.

'Thank you for your company, Signorina.'

'It's "Contessa" to you – and don't thank me, thank the Doc.'

They passed out of the alley's shadows to find the usually empty piazza thronging with two hundred men, all milling about in front of the town fathers who were standing stiffly, lined up in the Signoria loggia. On seeing the Contessa, all of the crew, southsiders too, doffed their hats.

'Told you so,' whispered Sofia, with a proudly jutting chin as they circled the crowd of tall and shoulder-sturdy men. 'What's so funny?' she added.

'Vettori calls these men the Small People.'

They call themselves Woolsmen these days, but they knew construction; their fathers erected these towers, and many more. Can you handle them, Captain?'

'We'll soon find out. Have a good day, Contessa.'

'Go to hell, Captain,' said Sofia walking up to the loggia where the Doctor waited with the rest. She glanced over her shoulder. 'But until then, good day to you too.'

Vettori said the men were ready to begin, but Giovanni wanted to address them first.

'Rasenneisi, I'm here today for the same reason you are – to build a bridge.' A room full of politicians had daunted him, but now he spoke with assurance. 'Signore Vanzetti is overseer. Signore Bombelli, his second. You'll have noticed small engines along the surface of the water. They keep pseudonaiades – the buio – from breaking the surface.' He raised his voice, so all could hear. 'You'll be safe while working – but fall in, and you'll drown all the same.'

'So put your harness on before you start!' Pedro interrupted.

'My apprentice, Pedro, will be around during the day to check. He can help you read plans if I am elsewhere.'

Fabbro grinned as Vettori failed to hide a big proud smile.

To those with no experience with Concordian machinery, the schedule looked impossible – it is one thing to hear of miracles, another to be expected to perform them – but by the time the engineer had finished speaking, few doubted his conviction. Like the Etruscans before them, Concordians were bridge-builders, and that was the reason the Empire had expanded so swiftly, despite the topography of Etruria: a narrow peninsula so river-riddled that some foreign cartographers described it as an archipelago.

A pale, wiry northsider raised his hand. He introduced himself as Little Frog and was dressed the part in an ill-fitting green worker's tunic, his long legs painted moss-yellow by old hose ventilated with rips and large feet entombed in hand-me-down boots.

Giovanni waited. He had been expecting interruptions.

'No objection to your contraptions, Captain,' Frog said with an amiable drawl, 'but we're starting with a prayer, ain't we?'

Giovanni could see the boy was not making trouble; the concern was genuine.

'He means a sacrifice,' Vettori whispered. 'Tower builders use a pigeon. I brought one, just in case . . .'

Giovanni turned swiftly back to the crowd. 'There'll be no prayers and no sacrifices. This is a modern building site. We make do with stone and iron and each other's strength.'

Older builders grumbled until another argument broke out. A short, sweaty dour southsider pointed at Fabbro, spat, and announced, 'I don't work for Bardini.'

'You know him?' Fabbro whispered.

Vettori nodded. 'Unfortunately.'

'Bandieratoro?'

'No, that'd take salt. Hog Galati is just a low-life *cafone* whose idea of work is betting on cockfights.' Vettori shook his head angrily and added, 'His children eat tripe.'

'Signor, you work for me, not Bardini.'

'Oh,' said Hog with a quick grin. 'You work for Morello then.' His face was framed by black hair that curled into improbable ringlets stiff with grease.

He was answered by the shout, 'Bardini!', in turn answered by another, 'Morello!'

In the loggia's shade, Quintus Morello chuckled. The Doctor knew he expected the project to flounder. 'Don't worry, Gonfaloniere. He'll rein them in. Or do you want my men to restore order?'

'Try it, Bardini. The truce holds so long as you stay off this bridge.'

Sofia and Gaetano Morello exchanged a glance. She gripped her banner and prayed the engineer would do something, and quickly.

'Listen, please!' Giovanni held up his hands. 'I am *no one's* man. On my site, you are no one's either.'

Tower owners frowned as one, a rare display of unity.

'Thought this was a ground-breaking,' said Hog, 'not a wind-breaking.'

But the idea that a man might *not* belong to another was singular enough to restore order.

'I came to build a bridge, that's all. Your quarrels don't concern me. Leave them off my site and pick them up at the end of the day. The bridge is no man's land.'

CHAPTER 16

Even before the first day was over Giovanni fully understood how exceptional Pedro was. To ordinary Rasenneisi, Concordian technology was alien. Most inventions are refinements of old technology, but Bernoulli's were different: not just new concepts, but applied in an inspired fashion, and so for the workmen, every little thing was difficult to begin with. Only after grasping this did Giovanni make progress by explaining first principles.

Another temporary bridge was built, this one with chains, less vulnerable to sabotage. The chains doubled as pulleys for a small platform to carry men and materials quickly from one bank to the other. Though it was looking unlikely that the framework of the arches would be completed before the stone arrived, there had been no quarrels; and that, Vettori assured him, constituted success. Giovanni slept without the dark dreams that had plagued his nights since Gubbio.

Next morning he waited patiently but in vain to be ambushed at the same corner. He was walking on disappointedly when he felt a tap on his shoulder.

'They won't be waiting where you expect them.'

'Contessa! You really think I'm in danger of assassination?'

'I think you're doing better than the Families expected.'

'Glad to disappoint.'

'I'm glad you didn't have a blessing.'

'I presume your disagreement with the Sisterhood isn't theology-based.'

'You really want to know how I broke my arm?'

'Only because you don't want to tell me,' he said, playing along.

Sofia prided herself on being a good storyteller, and for a moment considered how best to begin, though it wasn't hard. The memory was still raw . . .

The Borselinno brothers were flanking her, and seven more boys brought up the rear. Bardini bandieratori were heroes to northside children but mothers pulled them inside when they saw a decina approaching. When flags come out, fights break out: for Rasenneisi women, the maxim was a fact of life.

It was fun to hear the alarm, to see men of unaffiliated towers keep their flags lowered, to see the young bulls nod and make way. But Sofia knew this was a game with purpose, it sent a simple message to every family, affiliated or not: rent due.

The Bardini owned towers, though not nearly as many as the Morello, but this was different: this was rent of the streets, and the sight of a Bardini decina on parade was a reminder of who owned them. The only thing spoiling the fun was knowing this was business the Doc wanted her involved in.

'How's that?' Giovanni broke in.

Sofia looked cross at the interruption. 'He doesn't want me fighting in an *unofficial* capacity. The Borselinno weren't there to protect me – they were to make sure I didn't exceed orders.'

'Which were what? Just to be seen?'

'Shut up and let me tell the story! The Borselinno turned on their heels at the sight of the Baptistery, but I kept walking.'

'They didn't notice you were gone?'

'They were concentrating so hard on their war-stories I'm surprised they found their way home. Now, *zitto!*'

The Baptistery, a squat octagonal gate-tower, guarded the cloister. It was richer in design and ornament than any tower, but the real difference was that its large green doors were always open. Some might call it hospitable. To Rasenneisi, it was provocative.

She steeled herself and entered the airy darkness that was pierced only by the light entering the door behind the central baptismal font. She was immediately aware of the scent of incense, and something else – more elusive, as if time beat with a slower rhythm here, each second dragging out a little longer. Such peace was strange to Sofia.

The Doc rarely spoke of old Rasenna, but the other survivors of his generation never tired telling tales of former glories, like the Cathedral bell that tolled then for fish, and now for buio. Far older than the Cathedral, the Baptistery had been built by Rasenna's founders, the Etruscans or Trojans, whichever lie one chose to believe.

She hadn't come to admire the iconography, but as she let her eyes adjust to the darkness they fell upon one treasure then another. From the middle of the vaulted ceiling an ornate Herod's Sword hung tip-down, reflecting darkly in the Holy Water of the font, where infants became the Innocents murdered with the Christ, if one so chose to believe. Sofia had put such things behind her, but even so she dipped her hand in and made the Sign of the Sword before going into the small courtyard.

As incense gently surrendered to the scent of living lilies, silence yielded to doves cooing. In the centre of the garden, an old woman was quietly pruning an orange tree.

Sofia leaned her flag against the door's arch and strode over. 'Reverend Mother, please forgive this intrusion.'

The nun, who evidently had not heard Sofia's approach, dropped her shears in shock and they stuck in the ground beside her sandals. 'My child,' she exclaimed, 'I *dreamed* you would come this very hour.'

Suppressing her smile, Sofia nodded solemnly.

The nun gestured to a small table as evidence. 'I had a novice prepare refreshments for us. Would you like a glass of water, *amore*?' said the old lady, shuffling over.

Sofia glanced up at the surrounding windows, but they were empty. Their privacy was complete. 'No, thank you. I've come to ask your advice.'

''Course you would. Lovely water. Just the thing. Here you go, drink up.'

Smiling, Sofia reached to take the glass – then punched her in the face.

'You *what?*'

'I punched her in the face,' said Sofia.

'That's what I thought you said.'

'Just wait till you hear what happened next . . .'

The old lady staggered back, dropping the glass, and Sofia followed up with a low sweeping kick. The nun crashed to the ground; at the same moment, the glass shattered.

'Didn't *dream* of that, huh?' Sofia leapt back. 'Bardini *own* the northside. *Everybody* has to pay. Sisters too.' Her heart was pounding. This would show Doc – and whoever listened to him – that she didn't need babysitting.

Flat on her back, the nun chuckled. She poked a finger into her jaw, then spat out a tooth. 'Is that it?'

'Don't get up!' Sofia said, trying not to sound worried.

'I assume this visit is unofficial? I don't remember the Doc being *that* stupid.'

It was all wrong: that punch would have knocked out any bandieratoro, but the nun was perfectly lucid.

Sofia grabbed the bottle and smashed it against the table. 'I'm warning you!'

'Let's see what you've got, then.' The nun twisted her legs, pivoting on her back, then sprang up, and before Sofia could move the bottle was knocked from her grip with a quick, accurate kick. She backed away hastily, but the old lady moved faster, pirouetting lightly on her feet, and before Sofia could react, she'd been punched in the stomach once, twice, three times. They only felt like taps, yet her whole body convulsed – and they were impossible to block, because it was impossible to see the next one coming. Sofia realised that the nun was using her sleeves just like a bandieratoro used his banner: to conceal, to distract.

Sofia let herself fall backwards. Her hands touched the ground as her legs left it.

The nun, seeing her somersaulting towards the door, sprang weightlessly into the air. Sofia snatched her flag away a second before the nun's masonry-shattering kick landed. Panicked birds flew into the sky.

She defended herself, but it was hopeless; the nun patiently advanced with sweeping blows that passed by her face, closer and closer, her sharp nails just in front of her exposed throat. She was toying with her, studying her technique, exactly how the Doc tested the workshop novices. Even if she was fast enough, the nun was too close to let her use her flag. With the next blow, Sofia let herself fall and roll.

'You're too old to fight like a girl,' the nun said patronisingly.

Sofia knew she'd been overconfident; the blood on her tongue was evidence of that. A feather drifted by her face. She glanced up at the courtyard roof and leapt. For a moment, it felt possible – then a claw gripped her ankle.

'Enough of this nonsense,' said the nun, pulling her down. 'It's time for my nap.' She grabbed Sofia's wrist gently and turned it. Sofia winced, and dropped her flag. She shot a knee up, but the nun tilted her body away. Sofia leaned back too, grabbing the fallen shears and—

'Enough, I said!' and the nun slapped the shears out of her hands. Calmly, with an almost leisurely pace, she stepped behind Sofia, still holding her wrist, and pushed on the elbow until—

'*Ahhh!*'

She heard cooing in the warm, numb darkness – then, like a fire catching alight, pain that wrenched her eyes open.

The old nun smiled down at her. 'Ah, you're back. I was just thinking how you've grown, Sofia, since the day I baptised you.'

She pulled her up. 'Well, you know the way now. The door is always open,' she said and returned to pruning, 'Come back if you need more advice.'

'And that was over a month ago,' Sofia finished her story, finding herself a little shaken reliving it. 'The Doc set my arm, said it'll be good as new when it heals. He hates the Sisterhood more than me, but the nuns do everything beautifully, he said, even bone-breaking.'

'Wasn't he angry?' said Giovanni, less surprised at the story than the catch in her normally confident voice.

'He didn't give me the lecture I was expecting, just shook his head and scratched his chin a lot. He's like that, never tells you what he's thinking. And it's funny, up till that day, I thought he was Rasenna's best fighter.'

Giovanni shook his head. 'Is that true, that she named you?'

'How do I know? Even if it is, how could that old *zoccola* recognise me? The Sisterhood have acted like the rest of Rasenna doesn't exist for years.'

'Maybe she knew you were coming, like she said.'

'And let me get the first one in? Aren't engineers supposed to be rational? Or did you miss that day in school?'

'Rationality means following evidence wherever it leads.'

They walked on in silence until Sofia said, 'You think I got what I deserved.'

Giovanni became engrossed in his plans.

'Tell me. I won't get mad.'

'Do you do that type of thing, threaten people for the Doctor, often?'

Forgetting her promise, Sofia snapped, 'That's the natural order of things, isn't it? Concord doesn't use love poetry to wrest tribute from bankrupt towns, does it?'

'That doesn't make it right. Will the Small People accept you as Contessa?'

'You saw yesterday what they think of me. Besides, I don't need permission, it's my right. You might have broken your nobles' banners, but we still carry ours. Certain families are born to rule, others to follow. That's the way it is.'

'Why? Has it proved efficient?'

'This isn't Concord; we don't aspire to efficiency. Rasenna's problem is the Morello. If they showed proper respect to Scaligeri—'

'What do the Scaligeri have to do with it? The Morello quarrel's with the Bardini—'

'—and Doc's loyal to the Scaligeri. I don't like what you're implying. Concord's no different.'

'Since the engineers took over our nobles don't—'

'Your Re-Formation was the same thing that's been happening in Rasenna for the past decade: a power struggle. The engineers gelded the old aristocracy and now *they're* the aristocracy.'

'You misunderstand: the Guild has no institutionalised privilege. Promotion and advancement are based on merit.'

'Didn't you say you came from an engineering family?'

'Of course, some families have an aptitude—'

'—just as previously the criteria were martial skills. All that's changed is the criteria for exclusion. Concord, Rasenna, wherever: there's still one group who rule and Small People who serve.'

They had come to Piazza Luna, and Giovanni did something she hadn't expected: he agreed. Taken aback, she became almost conciliatory. 'Don't get me wrong – I don't object to it, here or there. Like I said, it's natural. Certain people are born with a higher destiny.'

'You believe that?'

'I do. The only thing I disagree with Doc about is how he takes the long way around. When I'm in charge, the Morello – or anyone who gets in my way – had better watch out!'

They parted as before:

'Have a good day, Contessa.'

'Go to hell, Captain.'

Sofia stopped midway over the chain-bridge to look at the river underneath. A permanent bridge still seemed as impossible as a tower built on clouds, but when she looked back and studied the man who was committed to building it, she knew that, impossible or not, he would do it.

In Piazza Luna, a shanty-town of workshops for carpenters, masons and smiths had sprung up overnight.

The workmen were quick studies, and Giovanni was surprised at their readiness to adopt the labour-saving devices other Etrurian towns had shunned. Gradually he began to realise the important difference: no other town had been so completely defeated as Rasenna. Traditional techniques were cause for shame, not pride.

The first week's progress was impressive. Pile-driven

stakes outlined cofferdams where abutments would be planted even deeper for stability. He envisaged a structure with a long central arch, elegantly bracketed with two lower and shorter arches, a subtle gradient rising from each bank.

Giovanni was everywhere, solving technical problems almost before they arose. He knew it was vital to have the cofferdams drained before the spring rains, and he knew the men would test each other, so whenever confrontation came he did not shy away but stood there, arms crossed and head slightly lowered as he listened to both parties, and then deciding matters with certainty. He did not draw his authority from distant Concord, or from the ever-watching Signoria. It came from another place.

And then came a problem engineering could not solve.

'This side, it's lagging. Why?'

Vettori was evasive, but by now Giovanni recognised the resignation with which Rasenneisi met certain realities.

'I hate to say this' – Vettori looked down at his feet – 'but it's because the crew here is an even split. On the other side, it's mostly southsiders. The northsiders over there are cutting stone, away from the rest. They don't have to mix.'

'You're telling me we make more progress on the other side with fewer people?'

Vettori called to one of the workers, 'Galati, any reason why you're just sitting there looking stupid?'

Hog looked up casually and spat. 'Got no nails, boss.'

'Nails, anyone?' Vettori asked.

Hog wasn't the least abashed as several hands went up. With a strangely vain gesture he ran a hand though his lank black curls.

'What do you recommend?' said Giovanni quietly.

'This is Rasenna.' Vettori regarded Hog coldly. 'Put a crow's head on a stick.'

'Fire him?'

'And make sure the Signoria hear why. Morello won't let Bardini break Hog's legs, but he'll tolerate a beating. Then re-divide the crew.'

'It's divided according to the crafts they know!'

'Which would work if this *was* no man's land and not—'

'I know! You don't have to say it.'

Rasenna: when things fell, they didn't blame gravity – they said, 'Rasenna!' and walked away. It explained everything. Giovanni had come to know Vettori as a reasonable man, a good father, yet here he was, calmly recommending throwing a man to the Doctor. He stared hard at the river flowing under his feet. He'd drown under logistics while they squabbled like children. Building sites have a thousand tests of competence, of leadership, every day, but this was different. This was the noise of a fight brewing. Vettori was right, an example was needed. An image assailed him: a crow's beak caked in blood; a boy bathing his face and smiling like a cat.

'That would be an example,' he agreed. 'Not the right one, though.'

'What else can we do?' asked Vettori impatiently.

'Work together. If it takes longer, so be it.'

'I guess Rome wasn't burned in a day,' Vettori said, sceptical, but impressed at the engineer's stubbornness.

'I'll make up the difference today; I'm a decent carpenter,' said Giovanni, walking over and taking a place beside Hog.

After an awkward silence, Hog spat and got to work.

By day's end, Giovanni was exhausted. There'd been no fights yet, but at close of play the men gravitated north and south like armies lining up.

CHAPTER 17

Fabbro was frequently off-site sourcing materials, and when the first barges docked, he struck up conversations with their captains, but Vettori didn't complain. Luck had reunited them, and he was conscious that he'd done little to keep their partnership alive over the years, while Fabbro had been tenacious.

Escorting Giovanni to and from the bridge, Sofia noticed Fabbro's absence too, and told the Doctor.

'Bombelli's got plenty of sons. Tell him to delegate.'

The Doctor grinned. 'Why throw away an opportunity?' He wrote to remind the gonfaloniere that the truce stipulated they each had a man on-site at all times.

Sofia couldn't understand why the Doctor picked Secondo Borselinno to take Fabbro's place. Secondo had been agitating for payback since the ear incident.

'You said the bridge is an opportunity, Doc,' she started.

'Yes, and Secondo will help things along. Trust me.'

Sofia knew Doc too well for that. She decided to avoid the bridge while Secondo was on it until she knew what Doc was after. The truce was fragile enough.

Giovanni didn't understand the Doctor's methods either. 'A straight line is shortest.'

Vettori shrugged. 'Not in Rasenna.' He was frustrated with Fabbro for giving the Doctor an excuse to interfere, but he quickly saw that if it hadn't been that, it would just have been something else. 'Don't fight it, Captain,' he advised, 'in the interests of safety.'

The Doctor's man proved to be not just useless but divisive. Secondo didn't know construction, nor did he care to learn, but he arbitrarily decided that the southsiders were working too slow and wasting money. It was pointless to argue. Secondo had other goals in mind.

Towards the end of the second week, the rains got heavier. Seeing clouds coming in from the north, Giovanni ordered the carpenters working on the floating platforms to come in while the storm lasted. They reached the bank just as the central platform broke loose. It was left hanging by a corner.

'Thank the Virgin no one was on it,' said Vettori.

'That raft is worth something,' Secondo shouted.

'Don't be stupid, it's too dangerous!'

'What did you call me?' Secondo grabbed Vettori by his collar. 'I don't take that from a Morello stooge.'

'Let him go,' Giovanni said.

Secondo pushed Vettori away and glared at the engineer.

Giovanni had to shout to make himself heard over the

wind. 'Concord's got deep pockets. We can replace equipment, but Rasenna can't spare men.'

Secondo gave Giovanni a slow blink, shook his head disgustedly and turned back to the river.

The crew huddled into the craftsmen's tents in Piazza Luna and as lightning dispelled the gathering gloom for an instant Giovanni looked over them. By now he knew every face. The boy who asked for a sacrifice on the first day wasn't amongst them.

'Where's Little Frog?'

'Secondo was talking to him,' said a voice.

'Where's he now?'

When no one answered, Giovanni ran out into the slashing rain, cursing.

Secondo was crouched on the bottom level of the abutment, holding his combat banner into the darkness. On the other end, Little Frog crawled towards the wildly bobbing platform.

'Get back in!' Giovanni cried.

Frog looked back uncertainly, as Secondo shouted that he almost had it.

'I don't give a damn! Come back – that's an order!'

Frog crawled back to the abutment—

—just as the platform broke free, pulling with it the section he'd been on a moment ago.

Secondo had the decency to look embarrassed as Pedro took the shivering boy back to the tent. Everyone inside watched Giovanni berating Secondo outside in the rain.

'Take your banner and get the hell off my site!'

'The Doc'll hear about this.'

'So? I'm not frightened.'

The Captain surely did not understand: Secondo was more than a bandieratoro: Bardini capodecini intimidated even seasoned fighters. The crew waited to see what Secondo would do.

None of them understood why he backed down and, after a lull in the storm, slunk back north.

After Giovanni sent everyone home for the day, he stayed in the tent. Frog, shivering in a towel, was trying to drink a glass of spirits he'd been given.

'It's my fault,' the engineer said. 'The platforms should have been secured better.'

Frog's hands trembled, but he shook his head firmly. 'Nothing you could have done. The river hates us. What can you expect from something the Devil set loose?'

Giovanni looked back at the Irenicon, seeing it like a Rasenneisi: something impious, unnatural, unwelcome. The wind pulled up sheets of spray, ghosts that briefly soared before they were torn apart by other winds.

'Quitting?' he said quietly.

Warily, Frog looked up. Giovanni knew he was debating the most prudent lie to tell a Concordian. He was surprised to hear the truth.

'Yes. Tonight's my last night in Rasenna and I'm going to get drunk!' The boy held up his glass. '*Cincin!*'

'You're going to join the Hawk's Company, right?'

Frog, pale already, became paler. 'Who told you?'

'No one. If I wasn't Concordian, I'd fight us too.'

Frog laughed and handed Giovanni the glass while he drank from the bottle. 'Then let's drink to being someone else!'

CHAPTER 18

The same drooping lips had supped for years in the Lion's Fountain, a simple and charmless establishment that was little more than a few tables scattered around a square under the frugal light of a few charred torches and the more generous donation of the moon. A counter kept the patrons away from the bottles. Crammed into the constrained piazzetta was the usual mix of students and Woolsmen, each convinced they toiled for the other's leisure, a nightly test whether lions and lambs could lie together.

Rasenna might be poor, but it was a profitable place to own a tavern. Young men required to be careless with their lives became first intemperate and finally reckless; publicans became rich.

Valerius cheerfully joined bandieratori in patriotic toasts of 'Death to Concord!', indifferent to the hostile glares he provoked.

He clinked Mule Borselinno's glass. 'How's the ear?'

'What?'

'How's the ear?'

'Speak into the other side, can't hear this side. My ear.'

Drunk already, Frog ordered another round, and after that: 'One more!' Inspired by drink, he attempted a farewell speech: 'As the Virgin's my witness, before I go, I'm going cross that river and—'

He fell backwards, bringing a dozen drinks with him and lay laughing, his green legs and boots waving in the air.

'I think the Morello can sleep soundly,' said Sofia, raising her glass. 'Froggy, we'll miss you. Don't be a hero tonight. Just get some sleep.'

'I'll come back for you, Contessa, when I'm a famous condottiere with my own company!'

'And I'll wait for you, *amore*. To the scourge of Concord, *salute!*'

Sofia drank, then looking at Frog seriously, pulled aside her scarf to reveal a Herod's Sword. 'This was my mother's. It'll keep you safe.'

Valerius tried to interrupt the moment. 'Sing us a song, Contessa!

'"The River's Song",' shouted Mule.

'No, something lively!'

She dismissed them all. 'Sing for yourselves. I don't sing any more!'

Valerius watched Frog receive a parting kiss, followed by a playful slap and a final admonishment.

Sofia knew it was even money that he would stay; lots of boys had 'last nights' and next morning thought better of it, or went on drunken raids and next morning were dead. Yet year by year, more boys left town, more towers emptied.

There were more toasts to future knightly deeds, more drinks and counterfeit joy. When night erupted the chill air filled with curses and the crowd, sensing that they were celebrating the town's slow death by blood-loss, became irritable.

Sofia took a bottle and left, uninterested in joining the brawl she smelled brewing. Valerius crept after her. Since he'd effectively blinded the other Concordian boy, Sofia had been cold, still training him and guarding him, but no more than that. But Valerius was drunk. He grabbed her shoulder. 'Contessa! Can't we be friends again?'

She spun round and slapped his hand away. 'Touch me again, I'll snap your pencil-neck!'

'Is *that* why you're sore with me? Look, I'm sorry I hit you – I'm an ass. May I walk you home?'

'Drop dead. I'm not going home.' She might be too drunk to be polite, but still Sofia remembered practicalities. 'Get one of the Borselinno to bring you home or you'll end up gutted in an alley.'

Valerius slunk back to the party, trying not to be noticed. Mule slapped him on the back. 'Don't worry, lad. You're not the first.' He winked his good eye and raised an empty glass: 'To the Contessa!'

Valerius burned crimson with humiliation. To be usurped by engineers was painful; to be mocked by inferiors, unbearable. But a fight broke out and the crowd's attentions moved on.

Valerius quietly nursed his drink, watching the drunken Rasenneisi claw at each other, retreating into comforting fantasies of revenge: on his father for sending him here, on the engineers, on Rasenna, Bardini and Morello, and Sofia – they could all drown together. With lighter spirits, he toasted the heroes: '*Cincin!*'

Sofia needed to clear her head, but the alley air was stubbornly stagnant despite the wind, and there was always the chance of bumping into couples tussling, amorously or violently. She drained the bottle, threw it over her shoulder and vaulted up the walls.

Topside, a cold wind swept off the Irenicon, waking her like a splash of water on the face. She wrapped her scarf tighter and looked south. Sometimes, when she forgot the duty to hate it, the river's solemn beauty could startle.

Earlier that evening, Secondo had stormed into the workshop to tell the Doctor about the accident, along with his theory that Captain Giovanni was conspiring against them. Frog's rather different version of events surprised her. She wasn't naïve enough to believe the engineer cared; it was obviously about control – and a happy crew was a productive crew – but it was far better than the standard brutalist tactics. There was no doubt about it, he was different.

Sofia skipped onto the roof of a higher tower and sat smiling on its gable; it was pleasant to think of families inside, soundly sleeping, oblivious to night visitors. Then she caught sight of light shining from the narrow windows of Tower Vaccarelli; evidently somebody else was awake, probably old Guercho, writing more windy oratory.

She looked over the rooftops, rust-bleached in the moonlight, and imagined other nights and better times, chasing Gaetano, him chasing her: children, innocent of simmering feuds soon to boil over. She did not feel young any more. Once, she had looked forward to turning seventeen, but lately she only worried about the responsibility it would bring.

She yawned, and caught an acrid smell on the air. She leapt up, her head spinning – that light in the window!

She crossed the rooftops dangerously fast. Up close, she could see the lower storeys of Tower Vaccarelli, already burning. A window on the fifth floor was open. She paused to wrap her scarf more firmly around her face, then dived. She landed inside, rolling, her knife out of her belt before she'd even stopped.

A masked man looked up in the act of pulling a dagger from Guercho Vaccarelli's chest. He picked up his torch and came for her; Sofia had no time to rise before the blow came. She blocked it with her forearm. As she flinched from the sparks, the man kicked her in the chest. When she fell back, her scarf came open.

Figuring she'd only get one chance to strike from this position, she feigned unconsciousness. When she finally opened her eyes, he'd turned his back on her and was climbing to the sixth floor. She swore and threw her knife without aiming. It grazed the back of his neck, a flesh-wound, but painful, she hoped.

Sofia was about to give chase when she heard a cry from below. '*Cazzo!*' she swore again, and bounded down to the third storey. Towers would crack and crumble before they burned, but they quickly became ovens for those trapped inside.

The family chamber was in disarray, and smoke was already rising. In the centre there was a mound, covered by the family banner. Several feet stuck out pathetically.

Sofia, shuddering, pulled it back.

Donna Vaccarelli was lying dead with her sons. Their throats were cut, and they were sprawled as if they were still trying to defend her, even in death. They were just boys, but good fighting stock. A knife against three flags! Whoever the southsider was, he could fight.

Sofia heard a shifting sound from the pile of blankets in the corner. She pulled the knife from Donna Vaccarelli's chest and crept towards the noise.

The little girl leapt at her with a feral scream, but Sofia caught her by the wrist and held it until she dropped her knife.

'*Isabella!*' she shouted, 'you know me, don't you?'

Tears and soot smeared the girl's freckled cheeks. At last she mumbled, 'Contessa?'

Sofia lifted her up. 'Come with me now,' she said, keeping the child's face buried in her shoulder. Her tangled black curls stank of smoke already. 'They're just sleeping.'

'They're dead,' the little girl said with chilling calm.

Sofia considered her next move. Up or down? Jumping from the second floor to the ground was their best bet, damn the height, damn the heat.

She climbed down the next flight of steps. The centre of the floor was smouldering; the room below must be an inferno. She pressed Isabella tighter to her shoulder, trying to protect her from the smoke that was filling the great room. She kicked at the door, and when nothing gave, she put the little girl down, telling her to wait, and ran at it with her shoulder.

The pain from her broken arm was intense but she willed herself to ignore it. They had blocked the door, so this was no ordinary raid, it was planned. Somebody had marked the Vaccarelli family to burn tonight.

'We're going to die too, aren't we?' Isabella said as Sofia lifted her in her arms again.

'Someone will see the flames and help,' Sofia said, but that wasn't true either. They'd raided on a night when everyone was too drunk to notice.

CcraaAK!

Sofia flung herself to the wall as the burning beam just missed them and crashed though the weakened floor, starting a general collapse. She dived for the stairs and started running up as everything else fell into the fire below. With more air to burn, the flames suddenly grew higher.

She put Isabella down on the fourth-floor steps.

'Don't leave me!' the little girl cried, looking terrified.

Sofia slapped her, hard, so it stung. 'Listen, Isabella, I lied. No one's coming – it's just you and me, understand? If we panic, we die, and if you die, who'll avenge your family?'

The child stopped crying.

'That's more like it. Now, I can't move as fast carrying you, so if I get into trouble, you'll have to start climbing yourself. You need to jump from the top floor to the nearest tower. You can do that, can't you?'

She nodded, calm now.

'Ready?' said Sofia, looking up, calculating.

Suddenly the girl broke free and ran down the stairs into the smoke.

'No, Isabella! They're all dead!' Sofia cried, but a moment later the girl had returned.

'Ready,' she whispered. She had a bundle under her arm: the Vaccarelli banner.

They reached the fifth floor, but the window was blocked by burning debris. Below it, old Vaccarelli's body was smouldering black. Sofia prayed the masked man wasn't waiting on the floor above; she could hardly walk now, let alone fight. But when they climbed up they found the upper part of the stairs being eaten away by flames, and a hole in the roof where beams had fallen in. The bastard had tried to cook them from both ends.

Halfway up, the stair began to crumble. Sofia hoisted Isabella through the gap, then leapt after her. Thankfully, there was little to burn on the top storey. The night sky beckoned tantalisingly through a skylight. Sofia looked around, and saw a locker in the corner, about the right height. She pushed it as close to the hole in the centre as she could get, and praying the floor would hold long enough, lifted Isabella onto it before clambering up awkwardly after her.

She was breathing smoke now, and gasping. 'Get on my shoulder and jump,' she rasped.

'You'll follow me?' Isabella said anxiously.

'Yes – hurry!' She doubted she could even stay on her feet much longer.

Isabella crawled onto her shoulders and sprang up through the flames and into the night.

'Thank you, *Madonna*,' Sofia said, sinking to her knees.

There was a loud creak: the floor, sagging beneath the locker's weight. *This is it,* she thought.

'Contessa!'

She looked up, and saw the Vaccarelli banner being lowered towards her.

'It's tied off!' the little girl cried. 'Hurry!'

The rain sizzled on the ruins of Tower Vaccarelli. A column of bitter smoke rose with the morning sun, another black spectacle for Quintus Morello's satisfaction.

Giovanni had worked through the night, oblivious to events across the river. He set out to work with a smile, expecting to be accosted at any turn, and he was looking for her overhead when he finally noticed the smoke. He broke into a run, fearing for the craftsmen's tents in

Piazza Luna, but as he got closer, he saw the column originated across the river. A northside tower had burned –
that was why Sofia hadn't appeared. He felt a stab of
dismay, *What if—?*

Yet if the smoke had nothing to do with the bridge,
why were his foremen waiting and looking so grim?

'Turn back,' Fabbro said. 'There's no need for you to see
this.'

Giovanni ignored him and pushed past. 'An accident?'

He caught the import of Fabbro's glance. 'Maybe not
an accident, Captain. Don't get involved.'

'I'm already involved,' he said, and elbowed his way
through the Woolsmen, hardly seeing them. The crowd
thinned out on the gangway leading to the first cofferdam.
The pump had been smashed and Giovanni could see the
pile-driver, suspended over the pit as normal, except for
the body that was lying on the gangway underneath. A
boy's body, legs in ripped green hose, feet in clumsy old
boots. The head would have been directly under the pile
. . . but there was no head. Flies buzzed greedily around
the red mess pouring from the neck. It had been Frog's
last night in Rasenna, after all.

'We have to get this drained,' Giovanni said, pulling off
his shirt.

'Captain, someone else can do this,' said Fabbro.

Giovanni turned on him fiercely. 'It's *my* responsibility.
It's *my* bridge!'

*

The Baptistery door was open, as always. The Doctor received the news so impassively that Sofia knew he had anticipated Guercho Vaccarelli's murder; he had, after all, used the old man as a mouthpiece for years. Guercho's other task, plainly, was a lightning-rod.

Sofia's task was to find a home for his daughter.

The Reverend Mother appeared just as she was about to knock. 'Bit old to leave on the doorstep, don't you think?'

'You think it's funny? We lost another tower, and she lost her family last night. Or didn't you dream that?'

The little girl hid behind Sofia.

'Don't worry, Isabella. She's not a witch, just ugly.'

'I'll protect her.' The nun took her hand. 'Hello, Isabella. I remember you too.'

By midday the puddles had dried up under a burning sun. On her way back from the Baptistery, Sofia went by the bridge. Men were pacing on the bank instead of working. She pushed her way to the pit and saw him working in a kind of frenzy, waist-deep in bloody water. Before he looked up, she backed away—

—and walked, then ran, back to workshop Bardini. Vaccarelli and Little Frog were Rasenneisi; they expected this end. The engineer was blooded now for dreaming anyone could live differently. Welcome to Rasenna.

She burst into the workshop. 'Bandieratori, flags up!'

CHAPTER 19

'Are we really going across?' Valerius said.

Decini assembled with bandieratori at their heads. They grew loud with the intoxication of wrath.

'*We* are. You're not,' said Sofia.

'No one's going anywhere. Flags down!'

Sofia, and everyone else, looked up. The Doctor stood calmly in the stairway.

'Doc, we're getting it from all angles! We've got to hit back!'

'We wait.'

'For more bodies? More burn-outs? How many will it take?'

He went back upstairs without responding. A raid had been imminent, but he said the word and flags dropped. For all the affection the borgata had for Sofia, she had no chance of persuading them. She was not Contessa yet.

The Doctor sat placidly in his usual spot by the low table in the shade of the orange tree.

'The hour is now, Doc.'

'The hour's when I say it is. I'm head of this Family, and you're still my ward. I'm not planning a raid, and if I were, you would not be part of it.'

'Why not?'

'Because you have to rule one day!'

'You didn't see Isabella's family,' she cried, trying to swallow the hitch in her voice. 'They were *butchered*.'

He looked at her. 'What if a time comes when we must do likewise?'

'We're strong, Doc – we don't have to go sneaking around at night, burning towers. We could cross the river today, fight it out and win.'

'You're too old for fairy-tales, Sofia. In a civil war, no one wins. I want you to understand that, because you'll look back one day and want to know why I kept you away from' – he scowled – 'the things I have to do. When we push our enemies to the wall, we have to go all the way. Are you ready for that?'

'I'm ready to fight!'

'The thing about being a Scaligeri is you don't *have* to fight. Don't throw that away because of one night's excitement. Fight *smart*, not mad. Making the bridge the focus puts us on the side of Concord. Let the Empire do the heavy lifting.'

'The engineer won't be drawn into our quarrels.'

'We'll see about that.'

Sofia sighed disgustedly and began to descend, then stopped. 'You've said "wait" for as long as I remember. The hour *is* now, but you're too used to waiting to recognise it.'

As she went downstairs, the Doctor stood shouted after her, 'Don't do anything stupid.'

He picked another orange and looked down at the river, smiling. Red streaked away from the bridge like a comet's tail. Things were moving along nicely.

It was evening before Giovanni had emptied the last bucket into the river; in the end the blood was thoroughly diluted with mud. Utterly spent, he had to be helped out of the pit. He'd learned something down there. It wasn't his bridge any more, it was Rasenna's.

He went to redraw a schedule where every day was precious. Hours later, a light was still burning in a window of Tower Vanzetti. As the night's black tide drew over Rasenna, the storm waited, nursing one last tantrum before it expired.

Addled by too little sleep, too many figures, Pedro walked to the window to stretch his legs. He picked up the magnifier, remembering how superficial his understanding had been when he made it. The bridge would probably look even more like some great beast's skeleton in the dark.

After a moment, he said, 'Captain?'

'What? I need to finish this before dawn.'

'I don't think you do,' Pedro said, handing him the magnifier.

Through the lashing rain, Giovanni saw it. It was a boy,

most of one anyway. The clothes covering its limbs and trunk were blood-red, daubed with black. It was standing by the riverbank, looking around Piazza Luna, although what or how it *saw* was a mystery, for the thing had no head.

'*Madonna*, what is it?'

They took turns watching the spectre's aimless wandering. It seemed to be getting its bearings, but stayed close to the bridge, as if it did not want to abandon that one surety. Then at last—

'It's going north.'

But not by the chain-bridge. It staggered drunkenly across the river's surface, and wherever its boots stepped, blood blossomed for a moment before being torn away by the current.

Giovanni rubbed his eyes, hoping the vision was just some leftover nightmare, but he knew full well he wasn't asleep. This *was* happening.

He wondered at how calm Pedro was being and returned to the idea he had since coming here; if a person could be unreasonable, a family perhaps, could a whole town? If certain altitudes inhibit respiration, might sufficient density of lunacy inhibit reason, permit prodigies, break rules supposed to be unbreakable?

Or was Concord to blame? Did Girolamo Bernoulli break something in Nature when he sent the river?

'Tell Vettori to keep the crew away,' Giovanni said, grabbing his hood.

'They know, Captain. Nobody's going to come to work.'

And, sure enough, one by one the windows of every riverside tower were being bolted shut.

Wrapped in her flag, Sofia kept a lonesome watch in the abandoned embankment tower she'd stationed herself in. Doc wouldn't sanction reprisal, but she'd be damned before allowing raids to become nightly occurrences, though it wasn't likely anyone would venture out on a night like this. She was thinking of her warm bed back in Tower Bardini when she saw *it* walking from the river to the land as if there was no difference.

After taking a few steps on land, the spectre stopped, seeming to lose its resolve and direction. Sofia suppressed her dread, reminding herself that she was the front line; she was the Contessa. She shook herself awake and climbed down.

'Who are you?' she said softly.

It took a hesitant step forward and she recognised, with shock, the chain around its neck stump. The Herod's Sword that had failed to protect Little Frog.

'Damn, why are you haunting me? Didn't I tell you to be careful?'

After a few steps away from the river and its influence, it remembered its destination. She stood aside as it marched up the sloping streets.

'Contessa!' Someone was coming across the chain bridge.

Sofia raised her flag. 'Who goes there?'

'Are you all right?' said Giovanni. 'Did you see it?

'It's Little Frog!'

'That makes no sense.'

'I guess nobody told him – *it* – that. Whatever it is, it's on Bardini streets.'

Giovanni followed her, marvelling that at a time like this all she could think about territory.

'Maybe he was right,' said Sofia, 'about that blessing,'

'You think that's why he's roaming the streets?' he said doubtfully.

'It's not that complicated. Frog was Rasenneisi. He wants to know why the Bardini haven't gone south to revenge him. Hell, I want to know too.'

'The Doctor wouldn't allow it?'

She didn't reply and he understood. 'And you disagree?' He had to run to keep up with her, and shouted to be heard over the wind, 'Contessa, I was neck-deep in blood this morning.'

'I don't expect a civilian to understand.'

They followed the creature at a distance. It wasn't difficult: it left a trail of bloody footprints and moved slowly, drunkenly lurching through the empty streets. It stopped in the Piazzetta Fontana, illuminated when the exhausted storm unveiled the dead man's eye in the sky.

'This is where we gave Frog his send-off,' Sofia whispered.

'You think he's thirsty?'

She gave him a look.

'I wasn't joking! They say ghosts don't know they're dead, don't they?'

'Pretty superstitious for an engineer.'

'All I know is what my eyes tell me, and that's an unquiet spirit!'

'Brilliant deduction, Captain.'

'Thanks. I can't believe I'm saying this, but maybe the nun *can* help?'

'Help how?' she said angrily.

'Keep it down! I don't know, an exorcism, maybe?'

'That woman has no business on Bardini streets and I'll be dammed before I invite her to shake her beads at this thing. There's nothing to be afraid of. Look—'

Sofia leapt out of the alley and walked boldly towards the creature with her flag down.

'Hey, Froggy. What's the matter, my friend?'

Somehow the spectre heard or sensed her, for it turned with the same blind lumbering movement.

'Are you lost?'

It swung; she dodged and brought her flag up, jabbing into the thing's sternum. But her stick didn't meet bone; it just sank in and came out bloody.

'What the—?' She hadn't hit it *that* hard.

'Sofia, look out!'

She dropped low as it swung again and rolled out of reach. It turned to follow and cracked open where she had punctured it, falling apart like water spraying from a broken glass.

Sofia was on her back as the blood flowed towards her, *searching* for her, hungrily. Giovanni pulled her out of its path and the pool stopped, then ran together, leaving dry a space for two footprints, then rushing in to form boots, then legs and the rest, stopping at the neck.

'Did you see that?' said Sofia.

'I don't think it's Frog . . .'

'It's a buio, *idiota!*'

'That's even more irrational. Why's it shaped like a human?'

'Who cares? We need to get it home.'

'You can't fight water with flags— Hold on, where's it going now?'

'Tower Bardini. All right, damn it, let's go and disturb the nun's beauty sleep. See if she's got any lethal prayers up her sleeves.'

They met her coming from the Baptistery.

'I got tired of waiting for you. I was—'

'Expecting us? Not this again,' said Sofia. 'I knew this was a bad idea.'

'How can I help?' the Reverend Mother said.

It was close to dawn. They found it standing in front of Tower Bardini, looking up, if something without eyes can look, at the Doctor leaning out of a second-storey window.

'How long's it been standing there, Doc?' Sofia shouted.

'A while.' He was breakfasting on orange segments, and didn't look too worried.

'He wants to find out what he paid his taxes for. Don't let conscience ruin your appetite.'

'I won't. Under control?'

'No thanks to you,' she mumbled.

'Fine morning, Sister,' the Doctor said with a half-salute. It was not returned.

'Well, I'm going back to bed. Call me if you need anything,' he said, and went inside.

The nun approached the creature. 'Poor boy.'

'It's not a ghost, Sister.'

'I know. It's the water the boy bled in.'

'How can you tell?' asked Giovanni.

'I've contemplated Water since I was a girl, Captain. I've learned a thing or two. I can see the things people hide from themselves' – she glanced back up at Tower Bardini, – 'and everyone else. Concordians think they can cut Nature open with a scalpel. Some things are learned only by going inside yourself.'

'That's wonderful, Sister,' Sofia interrupted, 'but why did it try to kill me? Frog was my friend.'

'Because it's only part Frog.'

Giovanni wasn't satisfied. 'But it's *impossible*. The transmitter on the river surface stops buio—'

'But this buio believes it's human.'

'That doesn't matter! Natural Philosophy isn't contingent on belief!'

'Bah, Concordians! Always think they know reality.' She smiled then, and said, 'Belief can change the world; and if you doubt it, I'll prove it.'

The Reverend Mother stood very close to the creature. 'Little Frog,' she said, 'בּוֹשָׁל תֵּע הָעִיגֶה. אוֹב.'

Their shadows stretched behind them as they followed the nun and the creature. The creature's shadow quivered like water in a glass, shot through by light. The night's storm had retreated, pursued by ghosts of misty drizzle.

The sun was peeping behind the towers when their strange procession reached the embankment, though the streets remained empty and windows remained tightly closed.

The creature stopped.

'He's afraid,' the Reverend Mother said.

'You blame him? This is where Frog's head was caved in.'

'He said the river hates us.'

'This isn't Frog, Giovanni.'

'It thinks it is. And if he still wants to leave Rasenna, I can help.' The Reverend Mother took a step towards the creature.

'Sister, don't get too close.'

'There's no danger, Captain. Today's not my day to die. Or yours.'

Sofia and Giovanni watched and held their breath as she reached out and touched the creature's hand.

'It doesn't know what it is. I have to show it.'

It snatched its hand away suddenly and stepped back. The buio became transparent, then reformed. It raised its hands and left bloody prints hanging in the air where its face should have been. The misty rain around it took on a red hue. Frog's face materialised for a moment; he looked grateful.

'*I know*,' she said.

The hand vanished as the creature changed from boy to buio, then collapsed into a puddle of nervously shimmering water which rushed off the bridge's limits.

It bloomed briefly in the water, then was taken.

'He's at peace,' the nun said, sighing deeply, suddenly unsteady on her feet.

Giovanni reached out to help, but she drew back. 'I'm fine. It's just— The river is so powerful – you can't open yourself to it without getting some back.'

Sofia knelt where the puddle had been and picked up the chain.

The nun watched her. 'Anything else you need from me, Contessa?'

'No, the buio's gone. You can go too.'

Giovanni escorted the old lady home, and apologised for Sofia.

She laughed. 'The Contessa doesn't care for me.'

'You *did* break her arm, Sister.'

'Yes, unfortunate, that. Yet I think she would have forgiven me if she had won.'

'She's proud,' he said, smiling to himself.

'The Doctor taught her to act like someone apart, and so she is, but not as he thinks. He's taught her to rule Rasenna as it is now. When a child wants a thing, it takes it, whatever the consequences.'

'She's fearless.'

'*Children* are fearless. They believe they are immortal. It never lasts. We must face fear and overcome it, or surrender to it.'

They stood in the Baptistery's doorway where they could feel the spice-bloated air of the cool darkness.

'Can Rasenna change?' Giovanni asked after a moment.

'It must, or must die. The street tells us to ignore fear; that's why we've torn ourselves apart ever since your people showed us how cheap life is. That's all she knows too. But when she finds someone to love and the fear that comes with it, oh, Virgin help her!'

'Fear?'

'Certainly. Fear of dropping one's flag; fear of losing love; fear of being rejected; fear of being unworthy: the beast has many forms. Sofia must grow up or drown in it. She'll need your help, Giovanni. You came to Rasenna to make up for the past, and you can.'

He looked away. *Impossible, how could she know?* Yet he'd seen other impossible things tonight. 'How?' he asked.

'Fight for her when the hour comes,' she said, then went inside.

She watched the engineer walk away and called out, 'You can come out now, Lucia.'

The novice, a long-limbed girl younger than Sofia, emerged from behind the font.

'Get to bed,' the nun growled. 'Remember your vows!'

Rasenna was still locked up in her towers when Giovanni returned to the bridge. The sun tinted the river a blood-less yellow, washing away the night's sadness. The nun said Rasenna must change or perish, but that didn't help today, or tomorrow. If the bridge was not ready for Luparelli's army, Rasenna would pay. No use trying to rise above the conflict. Like it or not, he was waist-deep.

He could throw his tools away if he sent for reinforce-ments – the crew would never trust him again. The other option was to play the game like a Rasenneisi, climb back into the pit, ready to get dirty. Sofia was right about one thing, prayers were worthless at a time like this. But as he walked to Tower Bardini, he prayed she would under-stand.

CHAPTER 20

The greatest irony of the Second Italic War is that Rasenna's early success persuaded Concord to use its greatest – and as then, unused – asset. Bernoulli was not yet twenty when the Curia founded the Engineers' Guild in Thirteen and Twenty-Eight and appointed him First Engineer[9]. He set to work with enthusiasm, though keener perhaps to apply principles discovered in his anatomical studies than to bolster Concord's ailing war effort.

Unlike previous anatomists, Bernoulli was unhindered by the Curia's traditional prohibitions: they forbade only dissecting corpses. If his technique of 'wet dissection' required immense numbers of experimental subjects, the resulting data was also immense[10]. He created engines with the moving joints and suppleness of living

---

[9] Already universally lauded as a second Daedalus, had just been made Chief Architect of St Eco's Cathedral. A decade would pass before it acquired its current title.

[10] The morphological changes occurring post-mortem make corpses inefficient for anatomical study, but, ever practical, when subjects expired he used them for 'harmonic' experiments. It is unlikely, however, that these attempts to find 'Divine Music' to animate the inanimate produced anything but ghastly smells from his student quarters.

flesh and, with them, turned the course of the war. The Guild's real importance, as we shall see, is not how it hastened the inevitable decline of Rasenna, but how it brought about the unthinkable: the end of the Curia.

CHAPTER 21

Mule laughed as the Doctor disarmed his brother with a tap on the wrist.

'Secondo, how many times? Hold that thing correctly! Too loose and you're not in control. Too tight and you'll lack flow. Now tell me, Mule, how long is your stick?'

'Ask Maddalena Bombelli,' Secondo sniggered.

The Doctor ignored him. 'Hold it straight. What point will it reach? Here?' He pointed in the air, then again, 'Or here?'

Mule shrugged. '*Merda—*'

'Practise, the knowledge will come. *Avanti!*'

The Borselinno came for him with sincerity. Full-contact training was what gave Bardini's black flag its snap. After a few passes, the Doctor suddenly knelt to simultaneously snatch their flags.

'Less bad, but still bad. What was your mistake?'

'Let you get too close,' said Secondo breathlessly.

'Didn't hit you?' offered Mule.

'Those are just the effects, caused by lousy priorities! Concentrate on the *man*. Your flag is to distract *me* – if you let it distract *you*, you've lost before you begin. A bandietoro must learn to be still as the world moves, or he's lost. Secondo, you're not listening.'

'Look who's here—'

'Captain!' the Doctor cried joyfully.

He threw the brothers their practise sticks and if he noticed the blood on Giovanni's clothes, he didn't show it. 'This is overdue; I won't count last night a proper visit. Come and see my wonderful view!'

Behind the slender rooftops, the Irenicon shone white in the crisp morning light. The Doctor sat at the low table by the orange tree.

'I see why you like it up here,' said Giovanni. 'You see all Rasenna.'

'The other reason is that Rasenna sees me. Ever wonder why nothing bad happens in Baptisteries? Sinning's harder when God's watching.' He poured the tea. 'I saw you in the pit the other day. Horrible business, but I was impressed. You're not afraid to get your hands dirty.'

'When I have to. It shouldn't have happened.'

There was a silence. Giovanni took a drink.

'Why don't you ask what you came to ask, Captain?'

'One of my crew was murdered.'

'No, one of *my* crew was murdered. Frog was a north-sider. Lie to me, but don't lie to yourself. You're here because of your bridge.'

'Sofia was right. I should have come to you before the

Signoria. Undiplomatic perhaps, but it would have prevented this.' He gestured to his bloodstained clothes.

'You sound like a Rasenneisi.'

'I'm learning. I haven't mentioned the delay in my reports to the Apprentices yet, but the pilings should be sunk before the melt-water comes. I'll miss my chance unless the saboteurs are stopped.'

'And brought to justice?' the Doctor asked innocently. 'Who do you believe responsible?'

'Stopped, I said. Morello, obviously,' Giovanni said with growing exasperation.

'Why not tell the Signoria?'

'It's ineffective, as you've made it. I want Bardini colours over the bridge.'

'You say it like a simple thing. It may mean—'

'I know what Protection means! That's why I came to you. You're more dangerous than Morello.'

'I'm blushing, Captain! I accept. Consider me your trusted ally!'

'That's a problem, Doctor, trusting you.'

He rubbed his chin for a while. 'I'll think of something to make it easier.'

The Concordian stood. 'Thank you for the tea.'

'Surely you won't leave with threatening me?'

'I wish my country loved peace, but we know it does not. It will go hard for Rasenna if I am delayed. I want to avoid more blood.'

'I believe you, Captain.'

After he left, the Doctor watched the river for a while. He held a knife in one hand. His grin, the lively spark in his eyes, all expression, drained gradually from his face. His breathing slowed to the in and out of a tide.

The Doctor was leaning over the side, his back to her. There was a small yellow box on the table.

'I want you to guard the bridge.'

She yawned. 'I've been keeping an eye.'

'I know, but I want you to be seen doing it. I want Bardini flags flying over the bridge in an hour.'

'We said we wouldn't get involved! Giovanni doesn't want—'

'He came here this morning to invite me.'

'I don't believe you.'

The Doctor handed her the box. She noticed his little finger was bandaged. 'Been hearing that lots lately. Tell him this represents how seriously I take Concord's friendship.'

She opened it to find a silk handkerchief wrapped around something bloody. 'What's this?'

'A declaration of loyalty, in terms Concordians understand. To protect their bridge, we're ready to spill blood. I thought you'd be happy – you finally get to throw your weight around. Take a decina with you.'

'Why upset the truce?'

'Sofia, I give you what you want and you question it – and you wonder why I can't trust you? The first rule is obedience.'

Sofia turned away in anger as the Doctor scratched his chin and murmured, 'Quintus Morello understands now that the bridge is key to your secure reign. That's why he wants to stop it.'

'Then why did you insist on Secondo as overseer? He did nothing but cause trouble till the engineer sent him home.'

'Because Quintus Morello's brain moves slowly, and the crew was splitting at the seams. Nothing brings people together like a common enemy; until Morello was ready to act it was necessary to be that enemy.'

'You weren't surprised by Frog's murder.'

Now he looked at her, his eyes snapping. 'How dare you! If I'd known, I'd have stopped it.' He turned and looked back at the bridge.

'But you knew *something* would happen, and then the engineer would come calling. You sit up here and weave plots when it shouldn't be complicated. Yesterday, we should have gone to war. Now, instead of doing something real, we're going watch a construction site. And when it's finished, what then?'

He walked over to her until they were face to face and said, 'What then? That's the hour we march over. That's why we need the bridge, Sofia. We're stronger, but as long as the Irenicon divides us we can't use that strength. It's obvious, and Quintus can't avoid seeing that every day the bridge gets longer, his end gets closer. I mourn the dead, but I rejoice at what's coming; you're too young to know the virtue of patience. We'll strike, but we want a clean kill when we do. And until then—'

Sofia grimaced. 'I know: we wait. Fine, I'll watch the bridge while our allies get slaughtered and you stay safe in your tower. I hope the hour comes before they burn it down.'

Sofia went down to the ground-floor kitchen to make breakfast. As she cooked, Cat repeatedly attempted to infiltrate the larder until she lost patience and hurled a plate at it. She had grown up fending for herself; the Doctor wanted her to be independent, just like Cat. *That* Doc, the one who didn't meddle like other parents, Sofia loved. There was another – watchful, secretive and unendingly patient – that she was coming to hate.

She heard Valerius enter – his heavy footsteps were unmistakeable – but kept her back turned. He helped himself to the last drop of broth, then sat opposite her. 'Why so glum?'

She was giving serious thought to feeding Cat Doc's finger.

'Ah, I think I know. I could tell my father about the escalation if you like? Citizens of the Empire shouldn't live under the shadow of civil discord.'

'I'm not in the mood for Imperial propaganda this morning.'

'Don't be like that, Sofia. I can help. Concordians know politics like Rasenneisi know fighting; I see what's happening. The Bardini aren't the power they were.'

171

'Bardini run Rasenna.'

'For the moment, maybe. What about that burn-out the other night? That makes how many this month?'

Sofia pointed a fork at him. 'Study *Art Banderia* as closely as you study politics and maybe you'll be capable of holding a flag properly before we're rid of you.'

'*Madonna!* I only wanted to sympathise! If I'd known you were so touchy I wouldn't have bothered.'

She stabbed a ham slice. His prying annoyed her less than his presumption – eating in Tower Bardini instead of the workshop, aping Rasenneisi dialect – and since when did Concordians call on the Virgin?

Valerius tried a different tack. 'What about the accident on the bridge? That's insult enough to Concord. My father—'

'Enough!' Sofia pushed her plate back and stood. 'I don't care about your bridge. I care about my friend who died on it. Bardini fight our own battles. Shove your family connections up your—'

'I beg your pardon—' Valerius attempted to stand, but Sofia pushed him back.

'Concord encourages our feuds to keep our nails sharp,' she said, glaring at him. 'And who are you kidding anyway? Engineers run Concord; nobles are the help! Your blood's blue enough to bleed for the Empire, but that's all it's good for.'

'Sofia! I'm a *guest*!'

'You're no more a guest than the bridge is a gift.' She

sat back down, still glaring, taking savage bites of her bread.

After a prudent minute, he tried again – he couldn't help himself. 'Small People at Concord's helm gall me too. The Scaligeri and the Luparelli – we're both noble families under their thumb—'

'We've nothing in common!' Sofia threw down her fork. 'Excuse me, your Lordship, I've been appointed guard-dog on your paesani's bridge.'

Before the door slammed, Cat was on the table finishing her meal, leaving Valerius to ask in dismay, 'What did I say?'

Sofia assembled her men, who wondered at the cause of her sudden anger. It wasn't Valerius, she had accepted the rules of that game a long time ago; nor was it Doc's machinations. At the bridge, she saw the foremen talking to the engineer. He had told her he was no one's man and like an idiot she had believed that things could be different. How quickly he'd learned the rules. How quickly he'd adapted.

It was early, but Hog Galati was already covered in sweat. He hadn't started working yet; the sweat was stale. The Morello wouldn't stand for it, he opined to anyone who'd listen. 'That's why the Captain didn't use a bird for the opening prayer. He wanted to sacrifice one of us. We're building a real Concordian bridge now, boys.'

Hog spotted the Bardini bandieratori as soon as they arrived. He dropped his hammer and asked loudly, 'Why is *that* here?'

Vettori said, 'Keep working – and show some respect. That's your future Contessa.'

Hog spat and went back to his half-hearted hammering.

'Captain, this is a problem,' Vettori said in an undertone.

Giovanni looked up from the stone delivery he was examining. Other southsiders had noticed Sofia and her men too. She wasn't trying to be inconspicuous.

'What else can I do?' he asked his foreman.

Vettori knew the strain Giovanni was under, but he started, 'Well, the Bardini and the Morello—'

'I *know* how it works!' the engineer interrupted. 'You think Rasenna is unique? Every town Concord's conquered is overrun by borgati – that's how we prefer it. I wanted to keep colours off the bridge, but I have to make my deadline. Black flags will be bad for morale, but more murder would be worse.'

Vettori shook his head sadly. 'Captain, in a town like this there's going to be killing whichever way, and now that you've reached out to Bardini—'

'Doc's only interested in helping himself,' Fabbro finished.

Giovanni saw Sofia walking towards their huddled conference and dropped his voice. 'I see that, but what other choice is there?'

Fabbro shrugged nervously.

Vettori put an arm on Giovanni's shoulder. 'If that's the way it is, that's the way it is. I'll explain it to the south-siders. They won't be happy but—'

'Let's just keep an eye on it,' Fabbro forced a smile, 'and hope the Virgin does likewise.'

'Thank you,' Giovanni said sincerely.

The two men went back to work, leaving him alone with Sofia. She thrust the box at him.

'Little gift. Hope you like it.'

He opened it warily, lifted the cloth, flinched and dropped it.

'Compliments of Doc.'

'Sofia, I'm sorry.'

'Don't waste lies on me, Concordian.'

'I mean it.'

'You say plenty you don't mean. This bridge is no man's land, remember that?'

'You saw what happened to Frog!'

'If it wasn't him, it would have been someone else. Morello was baiting you, and you, *cretino*, you took it. When you made the Doc back off I thought you had some salt, but that was just your opening move, wasn't it? You figured it was what the Small People wanted to see.'

'Please, keep your voice down.'

'No – I take orders from Doc, that's why I'm here,

remember? You ran to him the moment your schedule was threatened.'

'I had to do something!'

Sofia pointed to the Woolsmen around Hog.

'See all those friendly southsiders? This is a Bardini bridge now, whether you've realised it yet, and the Morello are obliged to respond.'

'I'm sorry to involve you in this.'

'You think you're sorry now? Just wait – oh look, here comes the welcoming committee. Maybe you won't have to.'

Gaetano Morello was marching across Piazza Luna, a decina of his own in tow.

Before Sofia went to head him off, she looked back. 'I really thought you were different,' she said bitterly.

Gaetano's decina didn't step onto the bridge. That would be a provocation too far.

'Look. The engineer's got a pet Rasenneisi already.'

She ignored the taunt. 'Who came over the night Tower Vaccarelli burned?'

'That's not why we're here. By the terms of truce, you can't be here.'

'I'll give you the benefit of the doubt, Tano. This time. Tell your father and brother that they crossed a line.'

'I'm not your messenger. If you've got something to say, cross and take your chances.'

'Maybe I will.'

They looked into each other's eyes. It was unfair but

undeniable: the day had come and now they were set against each other – by Gaetano's father, by the Doc, by the engineer and his damned bridge – and there was nothing left but to voice but the formalities:

'Stay away.'

'Try stopping me.'

CHAPTER 22

The southsiders filing in under the black flags the next morning felt like prisoners, a feeling Sofia's decina did everything to enhance.

Even before noon came, Giovanni tried again to apologise.

'You don't get to say that. I know how precise engineers are: you don't make mistakes, you take calculated risks. When being nice to the natives didn't work you didn't think twice, just moved straight onto your contingency plan.'

'It's not like that – *I'm* not like that.'

'Because you're *different*? That's what all Concordians think. It's how they breed you!'

'If the bridge isn't finished on time, the Apprentices will blame Rasenna,' he said, desperate to make her understand.

She laughed dryly. 'There's that rod again.'

Neighbouring towers were used to the third floor of Vanzetti's being lit up into the early hours but tonight, its usually tranquil working atmosphere was absent.

Giovanni swore softly as his quill blotted.

'You all right, Captain?'

'Fine, Pedro. Fine.'

He threw the worn-out feather down on the plans and groaned. 'I messed up, didn't I?'

'There's no right answer in this situation.'

'Bardini was the wrong answer. How much worse will he make it, that's the question.'

The boy shrugged. 'Who knows?'

'I do – the Apprentices told me before I came here, once killing starts, there's no limit.' He suddenly walked away from the table. 'I had to do something!'

'But you were!' Pedro held up a new design. 'Listen, the Families can't do this! They only know how to tear things down. You can't beat them at that game.'

Giovanni was surprised, hearing an echo of Sofia's accusations.

'Sorry, Pedro. I let you down too. The Doctor told me strength's all Rasenneisi understand, and I believed him.'

'Morello says that too – it's the only thing they've got to offer. They want us as incapable of learning as they are – but we Rasenneisi *can* understand other things when we get the chance. Since you came, I've learned enough to know that another life is possible.'

Giovanni paced back to the window, taking Pedro's consolation as reproach. 'And, damn it, I've thrown it away.' He saw the northern towers' reflection in the river. 'And now Sofia's involved.'

'The Contessa?' Pedro laughed cynically. 'If she's part of the Bardini borgata, she's part of the problem.'

'But *she's* not a Bardini, is she, Pedro. And you know what's funny? I told her she had to show people the distinction between Scaligeri and Bardini. I told her it's how you act that matters. *Madonna*, I've been a fool. Can I fix it?'

'Doc Bardini and Quintus Morello would say no. My father would say Small People can't stand against the Signoria.'

'What do you say, Pedro?'

'I think we can do better.'

Giovanni nodded slowly. 'Let's get back to work then.'

Pedro looked at him. 'There is one thing you *can* fix tonight.'

Sofia awoke from the same dream, about the Baptistery and *that* day. It was still dark and her bed chamber was silent, no shadows looming, yet instinct *had* woken her and she knew better than to ignore it. She held her breath and let her eyes adjust to the darkness as her fingers searched.

There! A whirring, and movement at the tower window, a glimmer of moonlight on gold. She rolled onto the stone floor and grabbed her flag. The dark shape hovered outside, the size of a bird, though it didn't move like one. She crept towards it, keeping her flag up. The whirring tempo slowed and the shape began to drop.

She dropped her flag, thrust her arm out the window and grabbed it before it fell. It was the annunciator, and there was a note between its 'hands'.

She read it, then looked over the balcony.

'I should drop this on your head!' she said, wanting to shout, but trying to keep her voice to a whisper.

'Then I'll be back tomorrow with another,' said Giovanni, pale in the moonlight, and smiling.

'Will you shut up? You'll wake the Doc.'

She quickly pulled on hose under her linen night rail. 'Stay there, I'm coming down.'

The moonlight was bright enough to light her way, but Sofia had done this a thousand times and needed no guide. She stopped at the second-floor window. She could see Valerius' blond curls on his pillow and hear his snoring. He always woke up later than the other students and for once she was thankful for his sloth.

Giovanni watched her descend. It reminded him of the controlled falling of a cat. She landed soundlessly in front of him.

'Have you gone crazy?' she hissed, looking around at the shuttered windows of the surrounding dark towers. 'You can't show up in the middle of the night and send notes through my balcony. I'm the Contessa Scaligeri! Towers have ears and eyes and tongues!'

'You care what people think?'

'I'm still mad at you, remember? Doc's got me watching

your bridge, but I finished work hours ago. Keep it up and we recommence hostilities.'

'Sofia, I made a terrible mistake. I'm sorry. I came here as an engineer, not a conqueror, and I do believe in my mission: I think the bridge will bring Rasenna together and I didn't want anything to delay that. We saw Frog – whatever it was – rise up. It might not have scared you but it scared me! And I saw more innocents being sacrificed because I'm not leader enough to stop it. I forgot what I promised the crew, and you. I acted like any engineer would in any other town, but this *isn't* any other town. It's different – it's the edge of things.'

'All right, stop blathering. So you messed up: you're not a liar, just a *deficiente*. The crew'll come round too. Whatever happens, my men won't make the first move. Satisfied?'

'Contessa, you have my gratitude,' said Giovanni with a courtly bow.

'Oh, *Madonna*. Do you have any idea how this looks? Get the hell back to Tower Vanzetti, will you? I'll see you tomorrow.'

'Thank you!'

'Go!'

Sofia clambered back up, keeping her eye on the Doctor's top-floor window. She didn't check on Valerius again.

She got back to her chamber and laughed. '*Idiota*,' she whispered, crumpling up the note. She put the angel on the windowsill and got back into bed. After a moment, she threw the sheets back and found the note in the corner. She flattened it out, refolded it and placed it back in the angel's hands.

'*Idiota*,' she repeated, smiling in the dark.

CHAPTER 23

The weeks of spring melted into one long pitiless day of summer.

The Doctor said he'd remove Sofia's splint soon. Though he trusted his web of stratagems to protect them, she feared the imminent war would be a storm, coming suddenly and at no one's convenience. She spent evenings in the workshop becoming dexterous with her left hand, horribly conscious of how vulnerable she would be in a real fight.

So far she had not kept her promise to visit Isabella. She told herself practise was more important – told herself it wasn't fear that kept her from the Baptistery – but her dreams, deaf to these excuses, returned her repeatedly to the garden to refight the fight: *that whirlwind of sleeves around her, that leisurely final snap.* She practised.

Vettori passed Fabbro on the bridge and they shared a look of dread, that the bridge, having tasted blood, might thirst for more.

The midday sun hung stubbornly immobile, pouring

molten heat on the water and on the land and on the men who moved over it, scheming and fighting and toiling. The no man's land between the river and the northern towers, abandoned since the Wave, was all hustle and bustle: a fire fed by men, material and machinery.

Sofia was sitting on her usual perch between the broken statue's paws, fanning herself with her cap, pondering, once more, the nun's uncanny technique. Her reflections were brought to a sudden stop by a sudden awareness that something was out of place.

She'd been around fighters all her life and she was attuned to the bitter reek of a brewing quarrel. Tools slipped from sweaty hands of heat-drunk workers shoulder-bumping against one another, with no apologies voiced, nor even curses.

Yet there was another spirit moving too. Since Giovanni's apology, she made sure her men behaved discreetly. She compared his method to the Doctor's as he went from station to station, exchanging quiet words with his foremen, meeting questions, suggestions and obstructionism from the crew with the same composed intelligence. The Doctor might grunt opaque Etruscan proverbs if pressed, but he remained impatient and distrustful of words, a teacher who preferred students to fight for their epiphanies.

Experienced masons, carpenters and smiths who thought themselves entitled to professional informality were disappointed and intimidated by the engineer's detachment. The Woolsmen were used to being spoken down to; they appreciated his impartiality.

The Bernoullian Re-Formation was traditionally dismissed as an ungodly rebellion, but the engineer spoke of the new mathematics, of action and reaction, balance and tension, with a preacher's conviction, and they were surprised at the commonsense of his hierarchy of verifiable principles. Consistent, if not beautiful.

Firm foundations rose from cofferdams, defying the rushing waters. The wooden template was complete; a skeleton prophecy of the bridge's eventual silhouette. It grew like a body disintegrating in reverse: dry bone became covered in muscle, blood unclotted and pumped once more, dust to flesh.

Two spirits; which would triumph? Gut told her that Rasenna always choose blood, and to confirm this black instinct, she caught Hog Galati's malicious stare directed not at the engineer but her. He met her stare and turned aside and spat before going back to work.

Sofia grabbed her flag – and then stopped, realising in that moment what was out of place.

'You must be distracted.'

She spun around to find Giovanni standing there awkwardly. 'Didn't think I'd be able to sneak up on you,' he admitted.

'I was thinking.'

'Me too. You first.'

Sofia glanced around to see if any of her men were

nearby, then held up her splint. 'When this comes off I'm going back to the Baptistery.'

When Giovanni looked at her with despairing exasperation, she laughed. 'Not for a rematch! I'm going to ask her to teach me.'

'I thought you hated her,' he said sceptically. 'And anyway, you can fight already.'

'Not like her.'

'Think she'll have you?'

'I have a strange feeling she's waiting for me to ask.'

'Doesn't the Doctor know Water Style? I got the impression he knows the Reverend Mother.'

'He told me once that Water Style was ineffective, and besides, nobody knew it any more.'

'Why would he lie about that?'

Sofia looked around again. 'I come into my inheritance in a few months. I need to be ready. Doc won't let me— Well, he won't give me certain responsibilities even though I'm his best student. And lately we can't agree on anything.'

'You can't agree to differ? He cares for you, I think.'

'This is Rasenna. He was fine with me being Contessa when it was years away, but I'm not a little girl any more. If he's got used to being Number One I can't just wait to be given power. I have to be able to take it.'

'But how can she train you without him knowing?'

'He'll think I'm here, watching over you. Bringing me to the next point: I should go. I'm not helping.' She stopped. 'What's funny?'

'That's what *I* wanted to say, but I couldn't think of a nice way to put it.'

Sofia picked up her flag and said, 'I'll check in every day, and I'll keep the rest of them watching from a distance. Doc just wants to see black flags.'

As Giovanni watched her leave, Vettori came up to him, smiling. '*Bravo!* You finally told her to go.'

'She suggested it.'

Vettori looked sceptical.

'She didn't bring black flags to the bridge, I did. Bardini came at my invitation, but I still feel . . .'

'Manipulated?' Vettori suggested. 'Now you know how the Small People feel. Don't be upset; that's how the Families stay powerful.'

Giovanni looked in the direction Sofia had gone. 'That's not how she'll rule.'

Vettori squinted into the sun. 'If she gets to.'

'The Small People still revere the Scaligeri.'

'That makes her useful, today. Tomorrow, it'll make her a rival. She's a pawn, just like the rest of us and, once Bardini or Morello get the upper hand, she's disposable.' He saw Giovanni's reaction and shrugged. 'Things could be worse, Captain.'

'That's not success. I remember the day I made that rope-bridge with Pedro. It was easy, Vettori. With so many men, shouldn't this be easier? Instead, our problems are multiplying. You know these men – what's keeping them apart?'

'Hate's a hard habit to break, Captain. Things happened

over the years that can't be forgotten just because the Families say "work together".'

'Was it like this when you ran your workshop?'

Vettori shook his head. 'No, I was too small to compare – and all my people came from the south.'

'But what did you do?'

'I gave them a share. When I made money, they made money. When you own something, you fight for it. That's the thing: the northsiders think it's theirs and the south-siders resent it.' Vettori looked around at the men from both north and southside. 'What can you do? We can't all own it.'

That night, Giovanni burned through a dozen candles studying old maps of Rasenna. Next morning, he found Pedro alone on the bridge. It was the feast day of Saint Daniel; for once Giovanni was grateful for the congested sacred calendar that was playing Hell with his schedule.

'How's the crane coming?' he asked with a grin.

Pedro pulled the toggle and the engine spluttered to life and rolled along the track. A second lever rotated the segmented neck. 'Perfect day for a test-run. Anything in mind?'

Since there was no work on the bridge, Sofia and her bandieratori were back in the workshop. With a gentle touch, the Doctor unwound the sling and moved her arm at the elbow. 'How's that?'

'Good,' she said, flexing it.

He looked thoughtful and said offhandedly, 'By the way, where's Valerius?'

Sofia shrugged. He'd taken to sneaking out alone, looking for attention, presumably. 'If he wants to get himself killed, let him. All part of growing up, right?'

'You're supposed to be looking after him. Try the arm,' he grunted.

She did a few clumsy flag combinations.

'It's fine, just weak. In a day or two I'll be ready to spar.'

'You think your enemies will wait?' the Doctor said, looking around the workshop, then, 'Mule, banner up.'

Sofia set her jaw firm. The Doc was making a point. She wanted to fight? So he'd make her fight.

Fine. She wasn't worried. She had been able to beat Mule since she was twelve. He had terrible defence; all she had to do was wait for a big obvious attack and see where he left himself exposed . . .

Nevertheless, Mule managed to do better than usual, landing several blows before she put him down with a careful attack that took advantage of his weaker eye.

The Doctor was stern. 'What's on your mind? It's certainly not the fight you're in. Secondo, you're next.'

Normally she wouldn't be worried, but Doc was right: she wasn't focused. Secondo lacked Mule's courage, but he was more dangerous: he had enough cunning to change tactics when necessary. He fought smart, made her work her weak arm. Kept up the pressure and—

'*Ugggh!*'

Sofia recovered, and picked up her flag again. A crowd of students was gathering. She ignored them, telling herself this was just practise.

Thinking he was winning, Secondo became obvious as Mule. She lowered her flag, inviting an attack, and he thrust his stick behind an obvious flourish. She dived for it and Secondo fell back with a cowardly yelp. A quick blow to the knee and he tumbled to the ground, groaning.

The Doctor didn't congratulate her. 'Wake up. Daydreaming makes you fight like a novice in the workshop. On the street, it'll get you killed.'

Before she could retort, the door burst open.

'Doc!' Valerius called loudly so everyone would look, 'you've *got* to see what the engineer's done!'

The Doctor led him away so he wouldn't distract the students more than he already had, and Sofia watched his expression change from annoyance to anger.

'He did *what*?' Doc grabbed a flag and went to the door with Valerius.

When Sofia followed he shouted, 'Where do you think you're going?'

'With you.'

'You can't even focus in the workshop. Practise until you can.'

He slammed the door in her reddening face, leaving the students staring at her. *Publically undermined. Again.*

It felt like a gut punch.

'Well, you heard,' she said, flattening all emotion from her voice. 'We need practise.'

Rasenna looked on as the Lion was lowered into place on the bridge's southside.

Using old plans and estimating the impact of the Wave, Giovanni had correctly triangulated the likely position of the first of the old town's mascots. Pedro fished the first sculpture up with the crane. The native stone's earthy grey had turned mottled green underwater, yet the accumulated filth and weathering somehow accentuated its dignity. The crew cheered as it was set down.

'*Madonna*, he's ready to roar!' Fabbro laughed, stopping abruptly when he saw the Doctor.

'Captain, have you gone mad?' the Doctor whispered fiercely.

'No,' said Giovanni, 'but I've stopped being lukewarm. This bridge belongs to Rasenna. The Lions are one of the few things people have in common.'

'Don't be facetious. The banner of Rasenna is outlawed by Concord. The Mascots only remained because no one could see them. Put it back.'

Giovanni refused to back down. 'I'm responsible for this *and* the civil war that'll happen if Rasenna isn't united when it's complete.'

'*Dreamer!*' The Doctor used the word as an insult. 'We risk far worse offending Concord! Put it back.'

'It's staying,' Sofia said loudly.

The Doctor turned and found her standing with the crew.

'Girl, be obedient,' he growled.

'How dare you! I am the Contessa Scaligeri. I don't take orders, I give them.'

The Doctor checked if Valerius was in earshot, then stepped forward and whispered, 'And what if one of the Concordians mentions this in a letter home, Contessa? What about when General Luparelli comes? You don't think he'll notice?'

'No – you've spent too long in your tower. Just look around! See what it means to them.'

The Doctor turned his back on Sofia's angry stare. He walked up to the Lion, lightly touching it. 'The others remain where they are, Captain.'

'Very well.'

'Explain to the Apprentices in your next report that you did it without the Signoria's sanction and with my reservations.'

'Very well.'

The Doctor seized his arm. 'Captain, you mean well. You see ragged flags and want to return our pride – but pride led us here!' He released him suddenly and turned north. 'Contessa.'

'Doctor,' she said, apparently unruffled, even though she felt the ground shifting beneath her feet. The bridge was the future of her reign, he said, but when Giovanni tried to make it part of Rasenna, he objected. He'd left her no choice but to hide a dagger behind her banner too.

Sofia only remembered the smell of incense. The last time she'd been here she'd been too apprehensive to pay attention to her surroundings. In a dark niche, the Madonna of Rasenna held the infant Saviour's body in one arm; in the other, a cluster of miniature towers. Her face was kind, but she was still a Rasenneisi: one of her delicate feet was crushing a serpent's head.

The Baptistery roof was a mosaic depicting the Virgin showing Saint Barabbos the keys of Heaven. He and the Prophets would languish in *Limbus Patrium* until the Second Coming, or so went the story.

The font bore closer inspection too, if she'd truly been baptised in it. Its five faces were decorated with paintings, composed in gold, black and red, showing the traditional Stages of the Virgin's life: the Annunciation, the Nativity, the Error, the Substitution and the Assumption.

Familiarity had dulled the tale's strangeness. From a distance, it was just a record of madness and hysteria: a grieving mother who called herself a virgin, and her murdered child, God, preaching of a Kingdom to come, until the Etruscans grew fearful of sedition. Her Apostles claimed She escaped crucifixion and bodily corruption by ascending to Heaven.

The virgin who conceived a saviour who could not even

save Himself – it was truly an odd story – was it odd enough to be true?

The Doctor had not raised her with a shining example of observance – he recognised no obligations, religious or otherwise, unless they profited him – but these tales were in the air in Rasenna, and the blood.

Her reverie was broken by the sound of footsteps. 'Contessa, are you here to see Isabella? She'll be pleased.'

'No. Yes. I mean—' Sofia stood to attention. 'I apologise for attacking you, Sister.'

'No harm done. To me anyway.'

'Well, it was impolite.'

There was a strained silence until the Reverend Mother said, 'Why don't you ask what you came here to ask?'

'Will you teach me?'

'I'll think about it. Anything else?'

The crowd was still on the bridge when Sofia returned.

'I don't know if this is a good idea,' said Giovanni.

'Are you a pagan?' the nun enquired.

'I'm an engineer.'

'Then be rational! What harm can an old woman do?' she said, striding onto the bridge and pulling up her sleeves. 'I only wish you'd called me earlier.' She stopped abruptly at a certain point in the middle of the bridge. 'Here. Let us pray,'

The crew knelt as one.

'The river has been much offended: driven from its

natural course, made party to murder, by Concordians *and* Rasenneisi. This bridge will divide the river, just as the Wave divided us. Forgive us, *Madonna*, all trespasses. The hour is late and the Lord is not refused. He cannot be diverted, though He suffers Himself to be delayed. Like a river, History pushes through all obstacles; if the Lord's will is diverted in one age then It will be made manifest in another. Therefore be patient, the Kingdom is at hand. The Lion awaits its brothers. Until they come, he will not wait alone. The Virgin, who has always protected Rasenna, now protects Rasenna Bridge!'

'Amen!' the crew agreed.

The nun nodded. 'Less bad. Assist me, my child.' As Sofia helped her to her feet, she whispered, 'We'll start the day after tomorrow. You must bring two things . . .'

CHAPTER 24

The wind's howling made it impossible to hear other footsteps, and until that moment Marcus Marius Messallinus
had not really missed his spectacles. Losing them was a
good excuse to skip the training intended to give his military career a head-start. The young Concordian saw no
reason to apply himself; modern generals didn't lead so
much as point the machines in the right direction.

Gaetano would never have allowed Marcus to venture
alone from Palazzo Morello, but after all, Gaetano might
well be part of the plot. Marcus had only learned of the
conspiracy today. In the excitement of the bridge ceremony, someone had dropped a note in his hood:

If you love Concord, be in Piazza Luna at Midnight –
A fellow Patriot.

What Marcus lacked in drive, he made up for in imagination. Clearly, his counterpart in the Bardini workshop
had put aside rivalry to enlist his help.

He waited in the empty piazza until bells rang out across
the river. He had bright visions of himself and Valerius,
friends tested by battle, returning to Concord in triumph,

to be congratulated by the First Apprentice. On the twelfth chime, a figure gestured on the far side of the piazza. Yes, Valerius was shrewd! If the two heroes were seen, it would alert the plotters.

An hour later he was lost in the dark, twisting back streets, and seriously worried. A strange thought was gnawing him ever more insistently. Perhaps this 'patriot' was a Rasenneisi. It had simply never occurred to Marcus that one could be loyal to a place that spawned schismatics so prodigiously – but why not? If he had learned nothing else in his time here, it was that Rasenna and contradiction were no strangers. Was it true, though? Had some Rasenneisi murderer lured him from safety this night? Wait, was that someone up ahead, at the mouth of that alley?

'Valerius?'

He felt a chill that had nothing to do with the wind. He'd overheard stories of the headless northsider; if one ghost had risen, might not another? How many Rasenneisi had Concord drowned all those years ago? How many yearned to share their tombs? He dropped his flag and ran.

The boy had been ensconced in Palazzo Morello for the last year and his knowledge of the streets was poor at the best of times; in the darkness, it was even worse. But if he could find his way back to Piazza Luna, he could get to Palazzo Morello and safety.

Had he seen that Madonna statue before? That mural? It was pointless, they all looked the same; in trying to retrace his steps, he'd just got himself even more lost. The harsh sound of cloth ripping made him jump and he called out tentatively, 'Hello?'

There was no answer – then a glint of gold, his flag, torn from its stick! By who? By what?

It danced on the wind, then, animated surely by vengeful spirits of old Rasenna, flew towards him.

The blood pounding in his ears was louder that the screaming wind. Marcus ran round corner after corner, but every time he looked back it was closer. He turned into a narrow alley and stopped.

It was a dead end where two towers leaned into each other.

'Oh *Madonna*, help me!' he cried. He turned and—

Nothing. It was gone.

After a moment, he stuck his head out of the alley. That Madonna, painted like a doll, he recognised it! This must be Via Purgatorio, east of Piazza Luna.

In his haste, he stumbled, and cracked his head on stone. He pulled himself up in a daze and saw it—

'I'm sorry! I'm sorry!'

Gold covered him, trapped him, struggle as he might. The weight on his chest was holding him down, hands on his neck were strangling him – he couldn't escape, couldn't breathe—

The fabric invaded his mouth, a thousand raging corpses teaching him how they had drowned . . .

*

As breakfast was served in the lonely luxury of Palazzo Morello, Gaetano's men were searching every tower south of the river. He just prayed Marcus hadn't been dumb enough to cross the bridge. Bardini would eat him alive.

'Oh, he'll turn up, Gaetano!' His father had been unbearably garrulous since the engineer's behaviour on the bridge. The Doctor's Concordian turned out to be insufficiently loyal to Concord; what a great joke.

'Don't you realise what could happen if—?'

'Oh Gaetano, *tranquillo*. The boy's just hiding in a tower. Have a drink. Your brother's never understood politics, has he?'

Valentino smiled.

Quintus kept going, 'Either our water is potent enough to breed faction in an engineer's heart, or the fellow was eccentric to begin with.'

'Perhaps that's why they gave him this job,' Valentino suggested, amused at his father's heroic self-deception. The old fool had made a policy of popular gestures, but his patriotism was a pose made safe by the Doctor's pragmatic balancing act. They'd performed this ritualistic dance so long that Quintus had forgotten he was being led.

A bandieratoro entered and whispered something to Gaetano.

Valentino noticed his sudden loss of colour. 'What is it?'

Gaetano looked at him suspiciously. 'They found Marcus' body by the Lion, under a golden banner.'

Quintus Morello spat out his drink. 'Our flag!'

He followed Gaetano out in a stupor, leaving Valentino alone with his thoughts and the dozing Donna Morello.

The only thing that upset the dance was disagreement about who should lead. The bridge would change everything, and his father was too frightened to acknowledge that Morello power had waned. Gaetano suspected it; the Doctor knew it. Valentino had another ambition entirely: to see the dancers destroy each other, and let the world burn afterwards. They had sent him to the Beast. All were guilty, all must be punished.

With threat of murder abroad, Valerius was safely under guard in Tower Bardini when the emergency Signoria meeting began.

The gonfaloniere was haranguing the Doctor. 'You all know – the *assassin* knows – that Concord will hold the Contract-holder as responsible as the assassin. But this assassin has miscalculated: this crime endangers *every* tower in Rasenna!'

Gaetano and Sofia sat next to the respective heads of their families, a silent signal of violent expectations.

The Doctor, grieving for Guercho Vaccarelli at last, took the mace. 'Why would I provoke Concord?' he asked. 'How could I possibly imagine they would smite my enemy and leave my tower standing? War will not make such nice distinctions: if no one is guilty, all are guilty. If war comes, all suffer. Call me a scoundrel, a murderer, but please, not a fool. Why would I suddenly change my policy, which has ever been one of conciliation and realism?'

'Because we are winning!' Quintus spat.

'Order!' said the notary.

'The murder of Marcus Marius Messallinus can, more plausibly, be blamed on a reckless unknown provocateur.'

No one doubted whom the Doctor suspected: Valentino sat at Quintus' other side, nursing his stump like a peevish baby.

When the notary's gavel failed to curb the din, the Doctor knelt and pounded the mace on the ground. 'If you cannot be civil, be rational,' he said. 'Gonfaloniere, I fear war more than hot words. I swear by Herod's Sword, my hand is not in this. When General Luparelli comes to collect tribute, there will be repercussions, yes, but we will bear them together. For my part, the truce stands. No raids, no retaliation.'

Sofia stared disbelievingly at the Doctor as he returned the mace. The Morello murdered their own student and he begged for peace? *Shameful.*

In the strained silence Gaetano whispered to his father.

Valentino surprised everyone by leaping up. 'Are you such fools to be twice deceived?' he cried. 'He seeks to escort us to the scaffold! You're a marked man, Bardini!'

At that, every flag went up. Sofia's planted bandiera-tori surrounded the Doctor as Gaetano's men poured into the Speakers' circle.

Sofia stood between them, her flag lowered. 'Stand down. I am your Contessa.'

Gaetano lowered his flag slightly.

'Not yet, girl!' Quintus shouted. 'You don't have a voice in this Chamber until then, and you can't shield a murderer. When you rule, you'll rule at Concord's pleasure, as I do.'

'You heard my guardian. Bardini aren't behind this. Look to your own house. And see you keep the truce.'

The Doctor looked on proudly as Sofia turned her back the Morello. 'Let's go,' she said.

They waded out of the palazzo with gold flags shadowing them as far the Lion and crossed the scaffolding to the north-side in single file. Anticipating this outcome, the Doctor had the entire borgata waiting for their arrival.

Sofia stared back at Gaetano, separated by the river and a bridge which, despite everything, remained no man's land yet.

CHAPTER 25

Night fell impartially on both sides of the Irenicon, a crushing black weight bringing fear and darkness, but no respite. Rasenneisi woke gasping like drowning men, their chests too narrow for hearts beating too fast. The claustrophobic air between the banks, between towers, was pregnant with violence to come. From river windows hidden watchers spied for interlopers who never came.

It was dark yet when Sofia went down to the pantry to steal a glass. She crept from Tower Bardini into seldom-used back alleys, taking a winding route. Just before sunrise she entered the Baptistery.

The pigeons' murmuring dispelled tensions lingering from yesterday. As before the Reverend Mother waited in the enclosed garden, but this time she was not alone. The nun took the glass, examined it solemnly, then handed it to the novice. 'Put it in the chapel, Lucia.'

Sofia gave her a cursory look. Just as it was a bandieratoro's business to know every tower his side of the Irenicon, it was the Contessa's to know all the families who inhabited them. This girl with an uncharitable jaw was a stranger to her, obviously then a southsider – presumably another orphan taken in by the Sisters. She was pale, skinny, breakable, like most.

'Now let's see if you brought the second thing I asked: an open mind. First, your stance. Make it stable.'

'Like this?'

The nun palm-tapped her chest and Sofia found herself on her back looking up at clouds.

'You could have just said no.'

'Ah, but would you have listened? I know you better than you think, child.'

Sofia adjusted her stance.

'Did you come with the Doctor's permission this time?'

'The Contessa,' Sofia said frostily, 'does not require permission.'

'I see. Where does he think you are?'

'Guarding the bridge,' Sofia said grudgingly. 'The engineer knows where to find me.' She didn't like discussing Bardini business in front of the southside girl. She changed the subject. 'What about Isabella? Has she told you who burned her tower?'

'If you didn't recognise the raider, you can be sure she didn't. Besides, we don't remind her of that night. I'm surprised you don't ask if she is better.'

After a moment, Sofia muttered, 'Well, is she?'

'Lucia looks after the other girls.'

The novice had just returned, and after throwing Sofia

a quick dart of disdain, said shortly, 'She's sleeping,' and continued her exercise with imperious serenity. Sofia wasn't surprised by her impression that the novice despised her. The girl was a southsider. Reason enough. She looked her over again and recognised a common Rasenneisi deformity: the girl had suffered, and responded by growing sharp. The severe line of the novice's mouth and the narrow focus of her eyes marred her austere beauty.

'Isabella couldn't sleep at all at first,' the nun said. 'All she talked about was revenge.'

Sofia smiled. 'She's a Rasenneisi.'

'I told you, Sister,' Lucia interrupted, 'she's just a thug.'

'Hey, I'm right here,' Sofia said indignantly. 'If you've got something to say, say it to my face.'

'Lucia, that's enough. Contessa, a man who managed to be both philosopher and saint said a city is people connected by love of something – that can be God, or money, or any other thing. If Rasenna is united only by the capacity to hate, the same thing which keeps it apart, then your inheritance is doomed.'

'That's nice, Sister,' Sofia said, scowling at Lucia, 'but this thug came to learn Water Style, not listen to fairy-tales.'

'Bah!' The Reverend Mother slapped her shoulders. 'Back straight!'

She adjusted her stance again. 'So Isabella can sleep now?'

'Yes. I calmed her down with another fairy-tale – how Water Style came to be. Do you want to hear it?'

'Do I have a choice?'

'Ignorant girl. Imitate my movements as closely as you can.'

The nun fell languidly into a succession of elegant stances, which Lucia copied with such grace that Sofia was embarrassed. The movement was so subtle that she couldn't tell where one position stopped and the next started.

Stopping occasionally to correct Sofia's grosser infelicities, the nun began her tale.

'Long ago, before Christ was born and died, Rasenna and Concord were the twin capitals of Etrusca, allies in a war against the growing power of Rome. Rasenna's bandieratori kept the legions back for years, but finally the Romans reached the city walls. It was only a matter of time before the siege overwhelmed Rasenna, and her sister, Concord would be next.

'In Concord one morning, a young maid was sitting by the river where her beloved, a knight of Rasenna, had said goodbye to her. She prayed that he would be returned to her before night fell that day. God heard her prayer.

'The next morning found the young maid once more by the river, now washing the blood from her beloved's body with her tears. The maid fell to her knees in the water and entreated God for help, promising both cities' eternal obedience in return. It was not God who heard her despairing prayer this time, but the river. But we rarely recognise our prayers when they are answered. A faceless angel rose from the water, and she attacked it, but could not land a blow. Its movements were as quick and powerful as a waterfall in spring.'

'Angel? Sounds like a buio,' Sofia said.

'Before the Wave, water did not seek to drown men any more than fire seeks to burn.'

'If you say so.'

'The maid knew she was defeated. She begged the angel to teach her or kill her. And the angel said—'

'This is so stupid. Buio can't speak.'

'The angel said it could not teach her to fight, for it did not know how. Instead, it taught her what Men call prophecy, which is really understanding Time's flow, and when the angel left her, the maid realised she could fight like Water. As the Etruscan Empire spread, the knowledge spread too, and bound its cities closer. The legions were turned back and after Rome was burned, there was peace in Etrusca.'

'Nice story,' said Sofia. 'I see how it put Isabella to sleep. But seriously, Concord and Rasenna as allies? A bit far-fetched.'

'Nothing is parted that was not once whole.'

'Then Concordians know Water Style?'

'For a time it flourished, but after the Empire fell, it declined in both cities. It is a difficult art; one can have a school of *Art Banderia*, but Water Style cannot be codified any more than a river can stop flowing. Rasenna put its faith in the *Art Banderia*, Concord in Natural Philosophy.

Rasenna, led by your family, was dominant for many years and then—'

'And then Bernoulli came,' said Sofia, 'and we lost.'

'But perhaps *Concord* did not win. When you are as old as I am, you begin to see Time repeating itself.'

'That's called senility, Sister.'

'Ignorant girl. Move this way . . .'

Rasenna woke that morning with the feeling it had been spared some awful punishment. Perched on the pier where Sofia usually sat, Giovanni watched the men coming to work giving the Lion an affectionate pat as they passed.

He had a good feeling for the day, which sure enough passed fluidly. His crew had acquired that rare economy of movement and speech he'd seen in the workshops.

Giovanni stopped Pedro as he ran by. 'Good catch with the wood. We'd have lost days if that batch had been used.'

Pedro stammered thanks and changed the subject. 'Something odd, Captain. I don't know if it means anything. Yesterevening I set the eggs recharging, but this morning they were flat.'

'Someone turned them on in the night?'

'Seems unlikely, doesn't it? How many Rasenneisi know how to work them?'

Giovanni furrowed his brow and ran his fingers through his hair, messing it further. 'Maybe we should post better security. Who knows how long the truce will hold?'

'Fabbro said he'd look after it.'

'Good, thank you.' He smiled, thinking how Pedro's competence was growing daily, and how appalled the Apprentices
would be at the thought of a Rasenneisi engineer.

Concord now seemed strange to him. He remembered
the lofty bridges and aqueducts, the broad empty streets,
the Academy and, overshadowing and mocking all other
human endeavours, the Molè. Details of the dark white
city were clear, but like stained-glass facets which somehow
never coalesced into a full memory.

Was it another Engineers' Guild mind-trick? They took
your name and replaced it with number and rank. They
took your family and replaced it with – what? The Guild
itself. Comforting as it would be, it would be another sin
to pretend his past wasn't his.

Fabbro disturbed Giovanni's meditation with a hearty
clap on the back. 'You were right, boss! They don't love
each other, but we won't have to split the crew up. Typical
Rasenneisi, though, they need an enemy, so now they're
grumbling about the Signoria.'

'They have a right.'

'Oh, *Madonna*, not so loud, Captain! You sound like
Vettori! Ask me what's the secret of long life.'

'Signore Bombelli, pray tell, what is the secret—?'

'Be apolitical,' Fabbro said, tapping his nose, 'like condottiere.'

'I'm a Concordian engineer, remember? We do the
impossible and never think of the consequences. By the
way, you're here at odd hours, aren't you?'

'Well, not really. I—'

'Have you seen anything out of the ordinary?'

'No, no – actually, maybe. Yes, now that you mention it, Captain, I was working late with my sons last night, down on the embankment—'

'Yes?'

'—and someone crossed over from the south. I shouted "Stop", but they didn't.'

'That's it?'

'Like I said, it was dark.'

Giovanni was as puzzled by Fabbro's evasiveness as his story, but he let it be. He had trouble enough without looking for more.

Sofia splashed her face in the font before going back into the garden. Bandieratori had to be in excellent condition, yet the morning's lesson had exercised muscles she didn't even know about.

Unimpressed, the Reverend Mother criticised her many bad habits – and even worse, *too much style!* 'When you do something, do it,' she told Sofia. 'Why think? Only necessary is necessary.'

Now she waited for Sofia in the small chapel that adjoined the garden, almost hidden behind the row of lush orange trees. Inside, the chapel had bare walls, a wooden floor and no furniture other than a low table with a terracotta jug and the glass Sofia had brought. In spite of its homely austerity, it was a welcoming place. A large stained-glass window on the wall facing Sofia bathed everything in a warm yellow light. It had colder colours too, emeralds and cerulean blues, but they changed, moment to moment.

The Reverend Mother sat below it, in front of the table. When Sofia settled herself in cross-legged imitation and looked into the light, she immediately felt her tiredness lift. Some artful craftsman of old Rasenna had fancifully depicted the Virgin as a well-to-do Etrurian housewife whose embroidery had been interrupted by a most unexpected visitor.

Our Lady of Obedient Domesticity bowed in submission to God's will. Flowers shot up wherever the angel trod – must be a nuisance, Sofia imagined. The angel had an androgynous sort of beauty, a youthful but wise face, and a slight smile played on his lips. Perhaps he'd forgotten the pain his gift would bring, or perhaps he smiled in spite of the knowledge, knowing the gift's worth was greater.

'Behold the handmaid of the Lord.' Every Etrurian child knew the humble words with which the Virgin had accepted her role as God-bearer. Sofia smiled to think that once she had believed it too. Now that she knew the world, it strained credulity: who would willingly accept such pain? Perhaps that was why the angel smiled – the housewife had no idea what she was buying into.

After clearing her throat, the nun took a set of beads from her sleeve.

Sofia groaned. '*Madonna!* We're not praying now, are we?'

'No, I just like to keep my hands busy.' She poured water to the top of the glass. 'Oh! I don't know about you but all that exercise gives me quite a thirst!' She drank the water down without taking a breath, her gullet bobbing mechanically.

Sofia watched in silent horror, swearing to herself she'd never get *that* old.

The nun slammed the empty glass down, wiped her mouth and poured another. 'Yaaaahh! Didn't realise I was so parched!' And again she drank it in one go.

When she carelessly emptied the rest of the jug into the glass, Sofia blurted, 'What about me?'

'Oh, did you want a drink?' The nun held out the glass and smiled.

You sadistic old cow, thought Sofia as she reached for it.

The nun placed the glass on the table. 'You, ungracious child, do not have to pray. Instead, perform this simple task while *I* pray: contemplate the water. When I finish praying, you may drink.'

'Contemplate. The. Water.'

'Yes.'

Sofia strove to mask her irritation better, and thanked the Virgin that no one except one very old, very mad nun could see her now.

The old woman looked asleep, but the click of her busy bead-counting fingers and the low, constant drone of her prayer resounded eerily in the small room. It was neither speech nor song; the humming had something of that tone she had spoken to the Little Frog ghost with.

Sofia took a deep breath. No point arguing with an *ubazze*; that would be crazy in itself. But when she tried to concentrate on the water, it wasn't easy. Water, she saw for the first time, was always moving. There were little pieces of matter whirling around the world within; Sofia saw beads of moisture as the glass perspired, felt it drying on her own body, saw it on the old lady's upper lip, drops of sweat creeping though the small forest of hairs. The morning's exercise had brought new clarity, as well as aching muscles.

The coloured light poured through the window, through the Virgin and into the water and shattered into stars swimming on the table, on the walls and her. The particles in the colours and in the water were all moved by the same unheard, unfelt wind.

The water the nun had spilled gradually seeped to the edge of the table and held in precarious tension over the precipice. Sofia watched breathlessly as a single drop began to creep down the side of the glass. The light shook with terror; the world trembled as it reached the bottom, racing towards the end and crashing; the puddle broke its bonds and the Wave came.

In the water everything tumbled, buio and people together. In Tower Scaligeri, the old Count floats away from his desk; in the liquid space around him the ink spreads and steals out of the window like a fragment of night escaping dawn. Above the sunken tower, a man comes down from a liquid sky. The buio rush for the invader, but he swims on towards them, his face becoming finally clear.

She tried warning Giovanni, but found she had no voice to scream, no air to breathe. She was drowning.

The glass shattered on the floor. The old woman had dropped it.

'Hey, my water!' Sofia cried.

'*My* water! I told you it was your reward for contemplation and instead, you took a nap – so no water for you!' The nun sprang to her feet. 'The Doctor thinks you're guarding the bridge? Then go. There's trouble.'

Sofia had to physically untie her legs. 'How do you know?'

'You slept. I contemplated Water. *Go!*'

The keystone was ready at last. The massive piece was bound with thick ropes and restrained by wooden stays as Pedro chiselled the date.

'Rings like a bell,' he commented, standing back to examine his work, his foot resting on the rope. Suddenly a heavy chain crashed against the stays. As it swung back, he ducked and shouted, 'Shut it off!' at the crane operator.

'What? Speak up!' Hog shouted back.

The keystone hit the river with a splash heard by

everyone on the site. Whipping after it, the rope tightened around Pedro's leg.

Giovanni was conferring with the masons on the platform below the central arch. He turned in time to see Pedro flying past. He ripped an egg from the water and climbed the rope ladder.

Everyone was frozen, watching Vettori grappling with Hog in the crane's cockpit. Giovanni pulled Vettori away.

'He's a traitor!' Vettori cried.

'*Madonna*, forgive me,' Hog wailed.

'Hog, I know you didn't mean to hurt Pedro.' Giovanni looped his safety harness around the crane. 'Help me now.'

'What can I do?'

Giovanni unscrewed the buoyant half of the egg. 'After I dive, count three, then release the chain, as far as it'll go. Then start retracting it, half-speed. Understand?'

Hog nodded. 'What if you can't find him?'

'I'll find him.'

When Sofia arrived she saw her decina keeping out of the way. They were better at causing havoc than dealing with it. She pushed into the centre of the crowd to see Vettori, kneeling and staring with terrible intensity at the water.

'The Captain dived in,' said someone.

'Killed rescuing a corpse,' another tutted. 'Stupid.'

Sofia felt a dark pit open at her feet. He couldn't have

– and yet she *knew* it was true; she'd already *seen* him diving in her dream in the Baptistery.

The rope shuddered. A hand broke the surface.

'Giovanni!' she cried.

'Vettori, he's got him!' said Fabbro.

Giovanni said, 'Take him first.'

The lifeless boy was lifted from hand to hand up to the light. Giovanni shouted, 'He needs the Doctor!'

Sofia threw down her flag. 'No time. He's breathed water; lay him down.' She brought her hands together like a club on his chest, once, twice . . .

The crew waited, Hog weeping. Vettori prayed. Sofia listened, and then thumped again, once—

—and Pedro convulsed in a coughing fit. Sofia helped him turn over and patted him on the back, helping him to spit out the water.

'Stand back. Give him air!' someone shouted.

Vettori smacked Hog to the ground and stood over him, brandishing the chisel.

Fabbro restrained Vettori. 'He was trying to hurt the bridge, not Pedro.'

'But why?' Giovanni demanded, climbing the ladder.

'He said he'd take my hands!' Hog was shattered, tears and drool mixing with blood pouring from his nose. 'He showed me his stump and said he'd leave me with two. What could I do? Who'd feed my boys?'

'You'd kill my child to save yours?' Vettori raised the chisel.

'I swear, Vanzetti, on Herod's Sword, I would never—'

Hog caught sight of Pedro, white and trembling on the deck, and pulled his shirt open. 'Oh, kill me now!'

'Fabbro, let Vettori go,' said Sofia. 'This is Rasenna. It's his right.'

Giovanni looked around and saw she was right. Every one of them knew how this would end.

'So do it, Vanzetti,' said Sophia. It's exactly what they want.'

'Who?' sobbed Vettori.

'The Signoria. Don't you know how scared they are of this? These men aren't southsiders and northsiders any more. They're Rasenneisi.'

'What do you care? You're Bardini.'

'My name is *Scaligeri*. I want a town worth inheriting. The Bardini and Morello feud is theirs. This bridge is yours. They can't have it unless you give it to them.'

Giovanni said, 'Make a choice.'

Hog flinched and closed his eyes. When he heard the chisel drop, he opened them to see Vettori cradling Pedro.

Giovanni looked for Sofia to thank her, but she had already gone to visit her cousins, and she had taken her flag.

CHAPTER 26

Quintus' sons ate in silence, disturbed only by Donna Morello's snoring in her stew, which was always served lukewarm because of her impromptu siestas.

There was a clamour outside, and an unconscious guard came through the door, closely followed by Sofia, choke-holding another. She kicked the door shut and slammed the guard against it.

'You dirty son of a bitch.'

'Pay no heed, Mother. Cousin Scaligeri is upset,' said Valentino. 'Correct me if I'm mistaken, but isn't there a truce in effect?'

Sofia kicked his chair out. His chin slammed on the table and he fell to the ground, moaning, 'Mow! My tonugu! Gaetamo!'

Gaetano finished cutting his steak before looking up. 'This should be entertaining.'

She stood over him. 'Your "accident" nearly killed Vanzetti's boy.'

Valentino touched his bloodstained lip. 'So?'

'A *child*! A southsider!'

Valentino remained impassive as he slowly reached for the nearest weapon to hand. 'If he's on the bridge, he's one of yours.'

'The engineer almost died too! Do you even *care* about the consequence?'

'What shall I say, better luck next time?'

'There's not going to be a next time,' she said, grabbing Valentino's wrist and making him release the fork.

Gaetano's knife flew by Sofia's face, landing between the shrewd eyes of the Dragon in the family crest. 'Sofia, I'd happily let you carve him up but Father would be put out.'

'Relax, Tano. Me and Tino are just talking.'

She suddenly stuck the fork in his hand, pinning it to the crest.

'*AhHHHH ahah oww!*'

'Something to remember, next time you feel like burning a tower.'

Gaetano had raised his flag. 'Contessa, I warned you.'

'No, *I* warn *you*: keep this dog on a leash or I'll put him down.'

'Sofia!' Gaetano called, but she was gone. He sat down again pensively.

'*Oooohhhhohahaha,*' Valentino's moan became a laugh. 'You think she'll pop round often once the bridge's finished? I must say, her manners are rather—'

'Father obviously didn't order Marcus killed. Did you?' Gaetano asked.

'No. Did you?'

'I wish I could believe you.'

'It's the truth. Perhaps Mother found him in the wine cellar. Um, I seem to have run out of hands. Little help here?'

Gaetano went on eating.

'She accused me of tower burning,' Valentino said, 'but I've never gone raiding in my life.' He smiled when Gaetano shot him an aggressive look.

'She doesn't really *know* you, does she?'

'The Doctor hides Family business from her.'

'Silly of him. I dare say she's almost as good a fighter as you.'

'Better,' Gaetano said, with a small smile.

'You still *like* her, don't you?' Valentino laughed. 'You think she likes you? I see: forbidden fruit, and all that.'

Gaetano took Valentino's plate and tipped the contents onto his own. 'You're finished with this steak, right?'

Perhaps the rosy clouds behind Tower Bardini augured better weather to come. When the day's work finished and northsiders wished southsiders good evening, Giovanni knew that something had changed. Vettori had passed up his right to revenge, unthinkably, and that single act had bound the crew tighter than any symbol could.

The Contessa herself said it was *their* bridge, silencing the cynics who presumed her coronation would be simply an exchange of yokes. The notion of a Contessa who stood up for them was profoundly strange, profoundly inspiring.

He was watching the southsiders spilling into Piazza Luna when he saw her – coming from Palazzo Morello – flushed but happy.

He waited till she was in earshot. 'Not a diplomatic mission, I presume?'

'No, but it made me feel better.'

'Thanks for speaking to Vettori,' he said.

'Doc won't be happy. A southsider publically killing another southsider? He would have loved that.'

'You said you only disagreed with his tactics.'

'*Madonna*, I did, didn't I? I've been asking myself recently what kind of leader I'll be.' She blushed slightly, laughing to cover her embarrassment. 'Don't get a big head but it's partially because of you.'

'Me!'

'They told you to build a bridge. No one told you to worry what we madmen do afterwards. You worry anyway.'

'I have my reasons.'

He was uneasy, and she guessed where he was going. 'Look – I know you've been posted to other towns. War is war.'

'Sofia, you said that certain people are born with a higher destiny. Do you still believe that?'

She shrugged. 'It suited me once to think of Rasenna as my divine right. I'm Contessa, but maybe that's just luck. Maybe nothing's *meant* to be. The Sisterhood said that Rasenna would defeat Concord, just like the Prophets said a virgin's son would save the world. Rasenna was flooded, and Christ was murdered in his crib. Bad average, if you believe in destiny. Prophecies are just dreams people want to happen. I bet buio have prophecies too. It doesn't make them real.'

'Just because something hasn't happened yet doesn't mean it can't. Don't laugh, but I thought I was sent here to make up for things I've done. I thought the bridge was the answer. It is, partially, but there's something else.'

'Sounds like you swallowed too much water, Captain.'

Giovanni watched her go, troubled. He tried to concentrate on the work ahead, but it was impossible – as impossible as what had happened down there.

It was like a half-remembered dream.

He found Pedro tethered to the stone. The swarming buio pulled back as he swam closer, but while untying Pedro he dropped the transmitter. Instead of attacking, the buio floated there. He *heard* them in his mind, speaking a strange language. He only remembered one word: *Iscanno*.

At the other end of the bridge, the foremen made use of the evening lull to take stock.

Fabbro caught the direction of Vettori's glance. 'He's not like any Concordian I've ever met either.'

'Or any Rasenneisi. He's not afraid of buio.'

'That's the courage of youth. Speaking of which, how's Pedro?'

'Shaken up, naturally. But good. And no, I didn't fire Hog.'

Fabbro became suddenly interested in the hem of his jacket. 'What do you make of this?'

'You don't have to change the subject, Fabbro. I know I nearly lost control. I'm not proud of it.'

'No, really, I want your professional opinion.'

Vettori took the proffered material. 'It's good, but that stitching . . .' He shrugged, a doctor with a bleak diagnosis.

'I got it through an agent from Burgundy. You could do better?'

'Fabbro, don't take offence!'

'None taken. Could you?'

'Yes,' Vettori said, cautiously.

'That's what I thought. Last night we smuggled in a shipment of wool.'

Vettori hurriedly looked around to see no one was within earshot. 'You're crazy!'

'Well, they can't come over land! Borders mean bribes, and too many borders means no profit. I turned on the eggs to keep away buio while my sons unloaded.'

'So that's what you've been up to – *Madonna*, if the Concordians catch you trading with Europans they'd hang you! That, or the Signoria will kill you with taxes.'

'Bah! They're all too busy fighting to worry about my business. The wool comes from a monastery on the Anglish Isles and bad stitching or no, it sells for a good price.'

'Congratulations,' Vettori said awkwardly. He was happy for Fabbro, but he had trouble making ends meet.

'I'm not bragging, Vettori! I'm saying I'd double profits if I could bypass Burgundy. It's cheaper to order raw wool instead of finished goods. I know you could get weavers, but what about carders and dyers?'

'Hang on, I didn't agree to anything.'

Fabbro went back to examining his jacket.

'I could organise it,' said Vettori slowly.

'Good! And, since I'm taking most risk, we'll divide the profits sixty-forty.'

'Say fifty-fifty, since I'm doing most of the work and you've got a deal.' Vettori turned back to his stock list nonchalantly.

Fabbro was amused at his efforts to be casual. 'Deal.'

'Sofia Scaligeri invaded my home?'

Gaetano kept eating while Valentino glared at him. He had finally managed to pull himself free.

'Yes, Father, your *Contessa-to-be*. Like she owned the place. Suppose she does, in one sense.'

Quintus pulled the knife from the crest. 'Well, Gaetano? A Bardini bandieratoro walks into my palazzo and not one of your bandieratori tries to stop her?'

'She's the Contessa!'

'Think, Father,' said Valentino, 'if it's like this now, how'll it be when the bridge is finished?'

'We won't let that happen,' Quintus said haughtily.

'*Cretino!*' Valentino slammed his fist on the table, then winced at the pain. 'It's come too far for that.'

Quintus slumped. 'What can we do?'

'Face facts first. The bridge is coming, and when that bitch becomes Contessa, we won't be the highest-ranking family in Rasenna any more. We need to try a new flag while we still can.'

'Tell me – I'll do it,' Quintus pleaded.

Valentino recognised that Quintus was finally desperate enough to listen to him. He glanced at Gaetano, then said, 'Write to the Doctor. Tell him we don't want the bridge to bring civil war, and therefore we propose a settlement. Say you'll support Sofia Scaligeri as Contessa and, as a measure of your sincerity, you propose a union to consecrate the peace, that she marry your eldest son—'

Gaetano stood. 'Shut your poisonous mouth—'

Quintus remained slumped. 'What will that get us?'

'Father! For once, please listen to me,' said Gaetano. 'Sofia – the Contessa – should choose her own husband.'

'The Doctor would allow that?' said Valentino. '*Please.* Father, he sent her here to show you he can spit in your face with impunity.'

'That's not true!'

Valentino whirled on Quintus, crying, 'Father, you *know* it makes sense. Bardini's promised to shoulder responsibility for the dead Concordian. He's lying, but this obliges him to mean it. What's more, it's statesmanlike. Think! You'll be Rasenna's peacemaker.'

'Will he agree?'

'Whatever else, the Doctor's practical. For Rasenna to accept his ward she needs to *appear* impartial, at least to begin with.'

Quintus struggled to keep up. 'You believe peace is possible, Valentino?'

Valentino's body began to tremble, then rock; his mouth opened, but nothing came out: he was laughing, though he didn't make a sound. He shut his mouth with a snap. 'No!' he said after a moment, 'there must be war! But without the Doctor, Sofia Scaligeri is just a girl, and, without her, the Bardini are pretentious upstarts we'll slap down, then cut down.'

'I won't be party to this.'

'If Gaetano's not interested, you can put me forward,' said Valentino diffidently.

Gaetano pushed his chair back with blazing eyes. 'No!'

'Then you'll—?'

'If I have to, yes, I'll do it, but—'

'I shall draft a letter this very night!' Elated at the prospect of finally besting the Doctor, Quintus skipped all the way upstairs.

Valentino watched him go with a derisive smile.

'Valentino,' Gaetano said quietly, 'please, don't do this.'

'If I can keep him resolute, it's done. Remember what we used to dream of when we were growing up, Tano? You'd be workshop maestro like Uncle and I'd be gonfaloniere like Father. Becoming ambassador to Concord was the first step. Remember? You're the one who convinced Father to send me.'

'I thought it was the first step – you wanted it!'

'And thanks to you, I got it. Now you'll get what you've always wanted. See how you like it.'

CHAPTER 27

Over a decade of war Rasenna's initial advantages, its extensive alliances, its genius for violence, came to naught thanks to the organised intelligence of the Engineers' Guild. Many commentators have overlooked the far-reaching consequences of this, Bernoulli's so-called Revolution of Efficiency[11]. The military overhaul meant, in essence, that Generals shared command with senior Engineers[12]. By the last decade of the conflict, the Generals' authority was so nominal that those who died were not replaced. Concord's civil authority was thereby surrounded even as its final victory appeared imminent[13].

Rasenna was isolated, her allies defeated by siege-craft or bribery. Though Concord's victory was assured, the reckless impatience of

---

[11] A set of reforms pushed through the Senate by Bernoulli's obliging patron, Senator Tremellius.
[12] Drawn from Bernoulli's inner circle, the brilliant young men known as the Apprentices.
[13] By unhappy coincidence, eight Generals died in the last decade of the war. The four remaining were purged in Forty-Eight. Our current Generals' limited tactical authority makes them pale beside these predecessors.

Senator Tremellius' faction almost undid it. These professed hawks took to ending their bellicose speeches with the mantra: *Rasenna must be destroyed*. Repetition seems to have dulled the Senate's wits for in the summer of Thirteen and Forty, it endorsed a premature and disastrous offensive.

CHAPTER 28

'Focus!' the Reverend Mother said, 'you're daydreaming.'

'And you sound like the Doc sometimes.'

Sofia was recalling with amusement Giovanni's notions of Fate's plan for him. Guilt truly was the victor's luxury. People came to Rasenna to commit sins, not atone for them.

Another dry, monotonous morning. She yearned to swing a banner in the workshop, but instead, she dutifully marched to the chapel where a new pitcher and glass were laid out. The nun's eyes were closed so, instead of 'contemplating' water she wouldn't get to drink, Sofia studied the window.

This afternoon Our Lady of Chronic Dehydration didn't look full of grace, she looked weary. At the end of a long day of housework, some winged *coglione* swans in to dump another chore on her. Thanks a lot, what did your last handmaid die of?

CRASH!

Sofia woke to the sound of breaking glass.

'Until tomorrow,' the Reverend Mother said serenely.

*

231

'Until tomorrow.' Vettori waved to the men passing the Lion, then turned back apprehensively.

Fabbro shook his head. 'It won't do.'

Vettori snapped the garment back and studied it. 'Is it the cross-stitch? I can assure you—'

Fabbro chuckled. 'It's too fine! We can't keep up this standard, surely?'

'Vanzetti have weaved for generations,' Vettori affirmed proudly. 'Of course we can keep it up! The question is, can you sell it?'

'Sell it? Yes! And for more than those Frankish rags retail. You must explain how you make such vivid colours.'

'Pedro experimented with the dyes.'

'Inventive as ever, that boy. He's recovered, then?'

'Yes, and with his help, I'll finish the rest in a month.'

'If I send this example, they'll trust us with a bigger order.'

'Slow down, Fabbro: for that, I'd have to make more looms, rent more space. I don't have—'

'I have money, enough for that.'

'That's not the only issue,' he said, and looked north. 'An attic business smuggling in small loads can be kept secret, but—'

'If it's worth doing, it's worth doing big. So word gets out—'

Vettori crossed his arms starchily. 'So word gets out – and what then, protection?'

'Feed the wolf, he'll keep coming back.' Fabbro beat his

belly like a drum as he thought it out. 'And part of the service will be wrecking equipment and product on the "wrong" side of the river.'

'Even if we ask them not to?'

'Nobles taking orders from the Small People? Vettori, the idea!'

After another day's training, Sofia once more contemplated the window. That conceited angel was oblivious to Our Lady of Artful Subterfuge's scheme.

The nun finished praying and began to stretch. Sofia's hand shot out and grabbed—

—nothing. She hadn't seen the nun move, yet—

CRASH!

That sound was becoming tediously familiar.

Next day, she affected indifference to the proceedings, until the second the glass dropped. The nun caught Sofia's hand in midair.

CRASH!

SMASH!

BASH!

tinkle . . .

As Fabbro walked Vettori home, he remarked how vulnerable he would have felt, crossing Piazza Luna in the old days.

'I've been thinking about the thing,' Vettori interrupted. 'Be honest, old friend, will the Signoria really let us import and export without interfering?'

'Certainly not.'

Vettori took a deep breath. 'Then I'm sorry. I can't get involved. I've my son to think of.'

'I've got seven!'

'You're used to risk – how can I invest in equipment that'll be destroyed to prove I need protection?'

'Vettori, all I know about business is if you don't risk anything, you don't get anything. It comes to this: If you let a man steal from you, he owns you, but pay him for what you want and you own him. Stay frightened and you're a slave. Now, here we are!'

As Fabbro reached for the door handle, a snub-nosed dragon with its tail entwined around its neck, Vettori realised whose palazzo this was. 'What the hell are you doing?' he asked.

Fabbro put a finger to his lips as the door opened. He slipped a coin to the servant, who led them through a courtyard of practising bandieratori, their gold flags shimmering like windswept corn, and up the stairs at the back. Fabbro whispered, 'Since the Wave, Rasenna's only export is violence. And the Signoria has a monopoly.'

The door of the study opened to reveal Valentino Morello, dictating a letter over his father's shoulder. The gonfaloniere looked up eagerly, relieved to escape his son's attention, if only momentarily.

Bowing neatly, Fabbro said, 'Gonfaloniere, we need protection.'

'How serendipitous!' Quintus exclaimed. 'No need to

propose union when Bardini's own people come to us, eh?'

Valentino looked them over coldly, saying nothing. Vettori doubted this wolf could be satisfied with scraps.

CHAPTER 29

She made a habit of stopping by after training, so she could later report on progress to Doc. And, if she spoke only to the engineer, why, who better to talk to?

'Then you're on schedule?' She tried imagining the bridge a year from now. The Irenicon would be as much a part of Rasenna as its towers.

'No – ahead of it.' He spoke without modesty or pride. Sofia had grown up in a town defined by what it had lost. Now, thanks to him, the Wave's shadow was retreating.

'Where do you go when it's finished?'

'Wherever they send me – if I finish ahead of time here I am to conduct mineralogical surveys. We like to know everything we can extract from our subjects.'

'Oh . . .'

'I have a different plan. Look' – he pointed – 'that's not a river, it's a herd of wild horses, and with the right expertise, Rasenna could harness them together. Whisper it, Contessa, but Pedro Vanzetti and some others working on the bridge have real talent.'

It took her a moment to understand. 'A Rasenneisi

Engineers' Guild? If you're feeling suicidal you could just dive into the Irenicon. They'll label you traitor—'

'Let them!' he said with vehemence. 'I won't be the first.'

'Maybe not, but countries are like families: you don't get to choose.'

'Engineers don't have families,' he said quietly. 'We're not supposed to, anyway . . .'

She didn't expect him to continue, but—

'A few years after the Wave there was a plot against Girolamo Bernoulli.'

'I didn't know that.'

'It's not part of our glorious history. The plan was discovered, but Bernoulli let it go ahead, to draw out the conspirators. The Nobility were involved, of course, but also some engineers who felt the Re-Formation had veered off-course. My father was executed in the purge.'

Sofia touched his shoulder and heard herself say, 'My father was murdered too.'

He looked at her strangely, and said, 'I'm sorry.'

'Everyone says my grandfather was special, but he drowned like everyone else. My father survived. He and the Doc were like brothers – our families had always been close. Ten years after the flood – Rasenna wasn't as bad then – there was still traffic across the river, and friendships were possible. My father wasn't the politician my grandfather had been, but he tried. He married Quintus Morello's sister.' She kept her eyes on the river and added with bitter humour, 'Building a bridge, I suppose. When I came into the world my mother left it, and the alliance died with her. Morello wore black with my father, feigned friendship, and waited.'

'For what?'

'The Hour, I suppose. It's my first memory – I don't know what that says about me.' She laughed softly. 'I was three, maybe four? The cart-burning commemorates the capture of Concord's carroccio at Montaperti.' She laughed. 'Ancient history is all we've got! Anyway, that year, Morello organised a spectacular show – sweets, entertainment, music, the lot. I loved to sing. Even the lowering clouds couldn't dampen the crowd's sprits. When the cart – it's shaped like a lantern – was pushed out of Palazzo Morello over the cobblestones, I remember worrying it would tumble. Across the river, the Baptistery bell rang. Quintus Morello was waiting on the steps of the Palazzo della Signoria – of course, he knew what was going to happen.'

Giovanni followed her glance to the Signoria's silent, empty loggia.

'There was a high-pitched squeal that ended with a loud bang. Fireworks shot up, beating out a rhythm, and people clapped along with the explosions. There was another big bang, and a flock of pigeons flew up from the palazzo, and everyone applauded as if he'd arranged that too! The Signoria was hidden behind coloured smoke and lit from underneath – it looked hellish, and I started crying. Papa just laughed, and he lifted me onto his shoulders so I could see better. The rhythm of the explosions grew faster, then, with a funny little pop, a miniature Morello banner unfurled from the lantern's spire. Everybody laughed; it was nicely done. The Doc would have understood, but my father was no fighter. He just clapped along with the crowd.'

'You don't have to tell me this,' he said softly.

'I want you to know who I am!' She glared at him fiercely. 'When the show ended, it began raining – more immaculate planning; he'd even organised the elements to suit his needs! I sang the Virgin's hymn along with the choir as Morello servants distributed red umbrellas, and when they were opened, gold confetti rained down. I remember my father shielding my eyes from the spokes. I remember peeking out between his fingers; the umbrellas were like a rolling sea.'

She gave a short sad laugh. 'It was beautiful. When the choir began their procession to the river, we followed. I saw a man standing ahead of us, and the crowd parted and moved around him – there was time to warn Papa. I kept singing.'

She looked at the river for a long time.

'You see, holding me like that, his ribs were exposed. He let me down gently. It was like sinking under a red sea. The crowd moved on and I stood there, holding the umbrella. His blood spread over the cobblestones. I thought it was searching for me, but really it was just flowing down the slope to the river. Then the wind got stronger and I cried when it took my umbrella. I was too weak!

'The Doc came looking for me. Eventually he found me, still standing there on the cobbles. He brought me up, but not soft like a noble, not weak like Papa.'

'I'm sorry, Sofia.' His voice was gentle. 'That's horrible.'

Her voice was hard. 'That's Rasenna. The one bold act of Morello's life, but he didn't have the salt to follow through and kill me. He never expected a commoner to oppose him, but the Doc remembered his promise to the old Count.'

She stood abruptly. 'It's late. Doc'll be waiting.'

'Sofia, wait!'

But she had gone. She would not let him see her cry.

Later, in the warmth of Tower Bardini, Sofia went to sleep looking at the annunciator, still surprised that she had dropped her flag the way she had. Like her senses, her dreams had grown more intense, more *real,* in the last few weeks and, for the first time in years, she dreamed of her father's murder. No matter how she ran from the spreading blood, it followed, sentient like a buio, until finally darkness swallowed her.

She left the tower with another stolen glass and as usual glanced back to see if she was watched. The day's first sunlight was glinting off the angel on her balcony. Valerius' window was dark, as always.

*

Today. If Giovanni could harness the river, if northsiders and southsiders could be civil, if a virgin could conceive, surely she could reach the glass before this doddering crone? Sofia's attention narrowed to that single object. Her universe was the glass.

Who cared how Our Lady of Hopeless Causes was feeling? The miracle of God made flesh was trivial compared to that glass of that water on that table.

CRASH!

'*Cazzo!*' Sofia swore.

The Reverend Mother opened her eyes sleepily. 'I'm sorry, I think I dozed off.'

She seemed not to have moved. The broken glass said otherwise. 'Why are you standing? I haven't dismissed you.'

'I quit! Every day we do the same thing. Am I making progress? No. Have I learned anything? No.'

The nun pointed to the shattered glass. 'Is this not progress?' She leaned closer to the broken shards. 'Yes, very impressive.'

'You're crazy! Why didn't I see it till now?'

'Fine, go – but clean up your mess first.'

'*You* spilled it, *you* clean it up!' She didn't care that she sounded like a petulant little girl.

The nun closed her eyes. 'I did not spill it. Goodbye, Sofia.' She resumed her prayer.

'All right then,' Sofia said, interrupting her droning, 'so who spilled it?'

The nun opened her eyes and looked at Sofia. 'You did.'

'What are you talking about? I didn't touch it—'

Presently the nun opened her eyes. Sofia was sitting once more.

'Good. I keep my glassware in the same closet as the mop. Lucia will direct you.'

Five minutes later, Sofia was watching a glass filled with water with a new absorption. The nun turned the glass upside down, so fast that she almost missed it, pressing its rim down tight on the table. No water had spilled.

'What happens when I remove the glass?'

'Nothing – the water will spill,' said Sofia.

'You are the contents of this glass. Why do you not spill?' The Reverend Mother slowly lifted the glass away. 'I too am water.'

Sofia stared. The liquid did not spill. Its surface was still moulded to the shape of the absent glass.

She held her breath. If she let it go, the world would collapse.

The Reverend Mother placed the empty glass on the table, then held her hands to each side of the column of water. 'Faith is the reason,' she said. 'We live in a world we see only darkly, Sofia. Learning to see it all is the next stage in your training. You are ready.'

As she spoke, she moved her hands, and the water moved with her. She pulled them back as if dropping a great weight, and the water splashed into the glass once more. 'You were born with great power – and I do not mean your name. You came here to learn to fight, and that is well, for a great and terrible battle is coming. But before that battle, you must pass into a darkness that cannot be fought, and to reach the light, you will need faith.'

The coloured light pierced the glass, as before. The particles floated in the water, as before, circulating somewhat faster perhaps. Sofia felt like she was tumbling with them. Had she seen what she had seen?

The nun got up slowly, like an ordinary old woman. 'Why are you waiting? You've been thirsty a long time. Drink! We've finally emptied your mind of illusions. Tomorrow we start filling it with truth.'

CHAPTER 30

Uncertain what to do without her, Sofia's decina went to report the unscheduled docking to the Borselinno. Secondo raised his flag and led them back to the bridge. Mule stayed behind; he had an intuition of where Sofia might be.

Giovanni confronted Secondo at the river. 'I told you to stay away.'

'It's nothing to do with you, Concordian.' Secondo pushed by him, telling his men to hang back.

'You've no right – the bridge isn't complete!' Giovanni was about to follow when Fabbro pulled him aside.

On the southside, Gaetano Morello had arrived. He too left his bandieratori off the bridge as he stepped onto it. Workers parted, making a path for the capodecini. Flags up, focused on each other, neither noticed Vettori waiting in the middle.

'We defend this barge,' Gaetano shouted.

'Like hell you do, Morello. The shipments are under Bardini Protection.'

'Now, just hold on,' said Vettori, trying to keep them apart.

'Gentlemen,' Fabbro ran between them, 'let me explain—'

As soon as they understood the merchant had sought both Families' Protection, they turned on him.

Fabbro was implacable. 'My dear boys, this is but *part* of a delivery. I have large orders to meet. The work requires the skills of both north and south, so I sought shelter of two great houses, north and south. Was that wrong? Our need for security is genuine – as, I trust, is your Protection?' He smiled, as if anything else was highly improbable.

'I will pay for Protection,' he continued, 'just as I pay my taxes. I don't interfere with Signoria business, but without my money, how will it pay the tribute?'

There was no answer.

'Gentlemen, quarrels cost more than we can afford. Please, lower your banners.'

'I don't take orders from tradesmen,' Gaetano said.

'Go home then! Let your masters decide if Rasenna should survive, and what price we must pay for that favour,' Fabbro said.

Mule brought Sofia from the Baptistery in time to see the standoff.

'We were looking for you,' said Secondo angrily.

'I'm here now.'

'What should we do?' whispered Mule.

She answered him loudly. 'Signore Bombelli is right. If we can't pay tribute, we won't have a town left to fight over. Lower your flags.'

'Is that an order, Contessa?' Gaetano said.

'This isn't the time to show me what a hero you are.'

'Doc won't like this,' said Secondo.

'Who's the Scaligeri heir, me or him? I'll answer to Bardini. What do you say, Tano?

'I'll take it to my father.'

Giovanni wondered whether it was Fabbro and Sofia's words, or the unprecedented spectacle of united angry Woolsmen that made the borgati retreat.

'Where have all the glasses gone?'

Cooking *l'ampra dotto* usually calmed the Doctor, but this evening he was livid. 'How did things get to be such a mess?' He took a few bites, then threw his fork down. '*Shared* protection? This really stumps us – if we fight, we lose the Small People. Bombelli's a wily one: he's balanced us against one another. And Morello went for it! That's the difficulty when your opponent is a fool, sometimes they make the right move without knowing it.'

He raised his wineglass. 'When you're Contessa, Sofia, I wish you intelligent enemies.'

'Thanks!' She took a sip herself, and said, 'Have you ever considered that protecting the Small People *is* in our interest?'

The Doctor couldn't disguise his frustration. 'A couple of months ago you were thirsting for southside blood – now you're the friend of the working man?' he growled. '*I* wouldn't be bleeding wind now if you'd watched the bridge like I told you.'

'I've kept my flag down so as not to antagonise the southsiders.'

'I didn't tell you to do that! And where are you, if you're not on the bridge? Not the workshop anyway.'

'You've got the Borselinno.'

'And they idolise you, Sofia – all the students do. In a few weeks the Twelfth comes, and you come into your inheritance. The hour's at hand. I hope to do it neatly, but flags blow where the wind takes them. If things go awry, I need every student at their peak.'

'Sorry,' she said, finally sounding a little contrite. 'I've just been thinking a lot lately. I guess I'm nervous about becoming Contessa,' she said, studying his reaction.

'I'm behind you every step,' Doc said. 'Eat up now.' And he refilled her wineglass.

Sofia went early to bed and the Doctor climbed the tower with a heavier tread than usual. He'd spent a lifetime learning how to look for weakness, and he saw the things people hid, from themselves, from others. What was she hiding from him?

CHAPTER 31

Sofia should have noticed her shadow trailed by another, but her mind was elsewhere that morning. She felt guilty deceiving Doc, about asking herself if she could side against him when, just months ago, the question was unthinkable. Before Giovanni came, Doc's way was her way; her only complaint was being excluded.

Things were different now. She'd grown accustomed to the pace of the Nuns' quarter. Every day was a crisis in Bardini streets: grief in the morning turned into revenge by nightfall. It was the way the Doc preferred it. 'When the world is off-balance, it takes a small nudge to spin it your way,' he always said.

The Reverend Mother was waiting in the garden, Lucia too, and for once the novice looked happy to see her.

'Today you will show me what you've learned,' said the nun. 'Force your opponent out of the square. You will attack, Sofia, Lucia will defend, then the reverse. *Avanti!*'

This is more like it! Sofia thought, and launched herself gleefully at the novice.

Lucia sidestepped and gently pushed Sofia as she passed. She found herself face-down on the edge of the square. She was unhurt, though her cheeks were burning. She leapt up and attacked again, more carefully this time.

Still the novice parried every one of her blows.

'*Contrario!*'

Sofia hadn't a moment to catch her breath before being pushed to the edge, again and again. She was flailing about like a beginner; her opponent might have been arranging flowers.

She tried to get close but somehow Lucia got behind her. It only took a gentle push and—

'*Uggg!*'

She picked herself up. '*Cazzo!*'

'What just happened?' the Reverend Mother said.

Sofia, walking back into the square, scowled at the nun's facetiousness. 'I got beat.'

'How? What were the last six moves you made?'

'*Madonna*, I don't know. She went low, I blocked? Then she went high . . .'

'Show me.'

'You can't analyse fighting like an engineer; that's not how it works. It's instinctual.'

'Instincts are important; yours are excellent. You're naturally fast, naturally supple and naturally aggressive – and those instincts are the only reason you are still standing. Lucia is exceptionally adept. Imagine what you could be with her level of control combined with your own natural talent.'

'I'm in control.'

'You think so?' The Reverend Mother chuckled. 'Lucia, show me the last set.'

'Yes, Sister.' The novice began to recreate the fight, move for move, exactly as it had happened.

'Now: slower.'

And that became the pace of the morning: the brutal attack became a dance, elegant and poised, and now Sofia recognised moves she had practised for the last month, combined and adapted to the need of the moment.

'Now, go back to the first stance, Lucia.'

The dance unwound backwards; only a pigeon passing overhead reassured Sofia that Time was marching forward as normal. As though she were reading her thoughts, the Reverend Mother said, 'You think Time is immutable, that the past is gone and the future is a wall you can never punch through.'

'Is there any other type of wall?'

'Hush, child! These are illusions. Realise that Time is fluid, and if you train your mind to feel that flow, you can use it. The current still carries you, but every move you make carries it too. Your speed and strength are constrained by your flesh, but matter no longer matters when you have fluidity. Even skill is unimportant when you move with Time's flow.'

'Great – so no more practise?'

The nun smiled sourly. 'Skill is the means to attain understanding. Lucia, same combination.'

'Let's see if a thug can learn,' said the novice with a smirk.

Sofia limped to the bridge, musing on the lesson. So Water Style was more than a way to fight – but if the Sisterhood could see the future, why hadn't they warned Rasenna about the Wave? Perhaps that was the reason Doc distrusted them.

She found the bridge crew lined up as if for a fight.

'Crane malfunction,' Giovanni greeted her with a smile, 'so we're moving stone the unfashionable way.'

Sofia tapped Pedro's shoulder. 'Take a break, kid.'

'You sure, Contessa?'

'Don't think a girl can handle it? Relax. And call me Sofia, I'm not Contessa yet.'

Curiosity abated as the evening went on and she held her own. Giovanni talked about progress at first, then asked, 'And yours? How's your Water Style?'

'We've just started,' Sofia said, grimacing.

'I'm still amazed that she agreed to teach you. The night Frog – whatever it was – returned, she told me the last thing Rasenna needed was more fighting.'

'Who knows why an *ubazze* does anything? Maybe she thinks we'll be friends – all I know is she's making me suffer: for every hour we train, there's three of meditation—'

'Sofia, look,' said Giovanni quietly, breaking her flow.

Sofia grabbed her flag. 'Maybe he's come to surrender.'

Gaetano Morello was standing by the Lion, watching them.

'Since when do you need a flag to talk to me?' he said as she walked over to him.

'I see you forgot your friends today.'

'Fine, be that way.' He scowled. 'You're getting pretty friendly with that Concordian.'

'What business is that of yours?'

'Well, you're supposed to be Rasenna's Contessa—'

'I said what business is that of yours?'

His shoulders sagged. 'None, I suppose. I'm sorry.'

'All right, all right, don't start blubbing.'

'Sofia, things are getting out of control.'

'You're telling me?'

'I want you to know this wasn't my idea. I said I wanted no part of it, but after yesterday . . .' He handed her a letter. 'It's for the Doctor.'

Sofia was perturbed that her old friend couldn't meet her eye – whatever his limitations, he had never lacked for courage before. 'What is this?' she asked.

'I had nothing to do with it,' he repeated.

'I get it: you're just the messenger boy.'

'Sofia, why be like that? You know I've never done anything to hurt you. I'm not my father. I'm not my brother.'

'Sorry, Tano,' she said, 'I'm just— Like you said, things are out of control.'

'All right.'

'All right.'

'Well, see you around,' he said quietly, and turned and walked across Piazza Luna, trailing his flag behind him.

The Dragon on the letter's seal stared at her. She was about to pull it open when Gaetano looked over his shoulder with such an expression – of warning, of regret, of hope – that it convinced her to deliver the letter immediately. It must be important.

'What's on your mind? It's clearly not the fight you're in,' the nun scolded.

Sofia was wondering about the Morello letter. After the Doc had read it, he just scratched his chin. When he noticed her still standing there, he offered her an orange. She had turned on her heels in a fury.

Now she said defensively, 'I'm making progress!'

The nun grunted, but it was true, Sofia had done better that day. Lucia still dominated their sets, but lately Sofia hadn't embarrassed herself. Even as she sought to emulate Lucia's control she was testing it. The modest penitent girl belonged to Rasenna as well as God, and Sofia thought there must be a place where prayer had no purchase; if there was, she did not recognise it because she was seeking hot-hate, sudden squalls, joyous short-lived rage.

'Somehow, child, you are. It shows self-control to meet something stronger and not give into fear.'

'Thank you, Sister.'

'You're welcome. Proceed.'

Sofia took up the pitcher and poured.

'Now, show me your faith. You are the contents of the glass.' She began to pray. The surface of the glass stirred as if a breeze flowed over it. Slowly, the water bulged from the centre. The small swelling grew slowly until a bead of water pulled away and hovered just above the rippling surface. The nun's drone dropped to a deeper tone; she was shaking with effort.

And, somehow, Sofia felt its weight too.

'Don't try to help!' the nun gasped.

'I didn't!'

'Child, you think I can't sense your ambition? It's large enough to fill this room. You must learn to see beyond appearances.'

The bead floated higher.

'All water is one. The drop is not separate from the water in the glass, or the ocean. If you are not ready, you can drown in it. Controlling even this much is a lifetime's work. Lucia cannot do it, and you've seen her level of self-control. Yet two days ago, you moved the whole glass with your mind.'

Sofia wasn't listening; she was entranced by the drop. She could *feel* the power. 'I can take it!'

'No—!'

Suddenly Sofia felt herself sucked up in a great wind. The current stopped and reversed with the speed of a great weight dropping. The glass exploded.

She came to with the nun clucking over her. 'Why must the young assume they know everything?'

'What happened?' she groaned.

The nun pointed to the wall; the plaster had crumbled where her body had smashed into it.

'You pushed. Water pushed back.'

'Gaetano didn't say?'

'He just said it wasn't his idea, three times. What is it?'

The letter was on his lap. Doc stood up, handed it to Sofia, plucked an orange and sat on the edge of the tower, waiting.

She suddenly cast it away like something infectious.

'It could work.'

'Doc, I'm a *woman*! I've answered to you since I was a girl; I *won't* be a docile bride waiting on another man.'

'Don't be irrational,' he said irritably. 'You'll still be Contessa; Gaetano would merely be consort.'

'You can't make me!'

'It wouldn't be for long.'

'I don't care if it's for a day!' Sofia shouted, then stopped short. 'What do you mean?'

'Morello's panicking – about the bridge, about the assassination of their Contract—' He caught her look. 'For the last time, I've no idea who killed the boy. But this will make him relax. I *need* him relaxed.'

She left, shouting, 'I *won't* do it!'

He didn't bother knocking on her chamber door. She was on the balcony, looking down towards the bridge.

'Damn it, Sofia. Talk to me!'

'I can't take a vow knowing you're going to break it. I can't believe Gaetano agreed to it, but he's not my enemy. Whatever you're planning, I won't be party to it.'

'You wanted to finish Morello for good!'

Sofia spun around. 'And I was *wrong*! Don't you see, there's no end if we keep fighting each other?'

'Noble sentiments; where do they spring from, I wonder?' He picked the angel from the windowsill. She wanted to snatch it back, but affected indifference.

'This isn't about an old friend. It's about a new one. You've been acting inappropriately.'

'Who dared say that?'

Instead of answering her, the Doctor read the angel's note. He glared as he crushed it in his fist.

'It was that little *stronzo*, wasn't it?'

'If it wasn't Valerius, it would be somebody else. All Rasenna's eyes are on the bridge, and still you rolled up your sleeves like a common labourer yesterday.'

'And now southsiders accept me as one of them!'

'Precisely! But Sofia, you are *not* one of them! This tower's protected you for the thirteen years since Morello killed your father.'

'And now you want me to marry his son!'

'A means to an end! All these years I've safeguarded

your reign. Obey me in this one last little thing and you need never listen to me again.'

'*Little thing?*' She was almost incandescent. 'How *dare* you, Bardini? You've taken advantage of being my guardian too long. The word of a Scaligeri is not something I soil lightly.'

'I wish you'd have the same care with your name.'

'What's that supposed to mean?'

'Open your eyes, Sofia! You're a girl, he's Concordian. People talk.'

'Let them talk!'

'Let them talk? Let them talk?' he said murderously, 'I will not!'

He leaned out of the window and flung down the angel. It smashed into stone, leaving just crushed metal and scattered screws. Keeping his back turned as he stopped at the door, he said softly, 'You'll do as I say while you stay in this tower. I'll keep my promise to your grandfather, with or without your approval.'

When the door slammed, she ran to the balcony. The angel was just a mess of springs and cogs and fragile devastated beauty.

CHAPTER 32

Count Scaligeri inflicted on Concord its greatest defeat at Montaperti. After the rout, the Senate expected Senator Tremellius' prompt resignation and suicide; instead he pronounced himself vindicated – surely *now* it was obvious to all that Rasenna must be destroyed? And just as obvious, where arms had failed that they must deploy a stronger weapon.

Girolamo Bernoulli was invited to address the Senate, a signal honour for a commoner. His speech began modestly enough:

> *Senators, I am no orator. If I speak plainly, allow me the indulgence due any novice. Regardless of my words, I remain in your hands a dumb tool, to be utilised as you will. You employ my engines in Concord's glorious cause. I would say a few words about my Method, if I may.*

The young Engineer's self-effacing tone drew appreciative murmurs from the Senators. He continued:

> *I make each part separately, taking great pains. I choose the purest ores, and combine them precisely to create strong alloys, equal to the pressures of the worlds in which I encase them. My Lords, my profession obliges me to see not only further than you, but more clearly, so I must tell you that*

Concord is not like a well-made machine. Our Creator, in His wisdom, chose to leave the mean and base material mixed with the better. Is it wise to test our weak alloy in War? Take care that, striking hard, we do not forge our Enemy's metal, weak like ours, into something stronger. The Engineer may for a time surpass his materials, but finally Nature will have her due. Think on what poor material you are before acting.

Imagine a commoner, arguing for peace by questioning the quality of Concord's assembled Nobility; I need not report how unprecedented this was, how unpopular[14], how embarrassed Senator Tremellius was, or how Bernoulli's arguments were shouted down; but I must tell you what happened next, when he was made to act.

---

[14] Unpopular in the Senate; this voicing of intellectual independence changed the way the Guild saw itself and becomes, in hindsight, one of the early intimations of the reforming spirit of Forty-Six. Afterwards Bernoulli decided never again to bow to intellectual inferiors. As ever, he planned patiently.

CHAPTER 33

'My guardian instructs me to communicate that, in principle, he is not averse to the gonfaloniere's proposal and is prepared to discuss terms.' Sofia handed over the letter, a replica of the first but for the Boar in place of the Dragon.

'Very well.' Gaetano gave a military nod.

'Tano?'

'Yes?'

When he spun around, she slapped him. 'You *knew* what it said!'

He stepped back, but kept his flag down.

She followed him into Piazza Luna. 'You made *me* carry it!'

'*Tranquillo*, Sofia!'

'I feel sick. You think I want that?'

'Be rational, girl, for once in your life! When the bridge opens, you think the streets will flood with brotherly love? They'll be flooded all right – unless we act, and now. The Small People look to us for an example.'

She laughed bitterly. 'You still believe that? *We're* the reason for this mess.'

'Excuse me for not having an outside perspective.'

'What's that supposed to mean?'

'Nothing. Look, for good or ill, the Families are in charge. If we go to war, Rasenna follows our banners and the river will run red, towers will tumble. I don't want to force you against your heart, but I don't see another way. I'm your friend – I'll always be your friend – but if it's a choice between diplomacy and killing, I choose diplomacy.'

'*Diplomacy?* This is a tactical manoeuvre conceived by your father – or more likely, your brother. Do they love peace? They want me in a cage of pretty dresses and servants while they run riot over the north. I know that.' Sofia took a breath and said quietly, 'And the Doc knows it too. Please, don't do this.'

Gaetano whispered in turn, 'You don't think I know that? I may not have my father's ear, but I am his arm.' He held up the letter. 'And however nice his reply, I'm not naïve enough to trust the Doctor either.'

She didn't contradict him.

'I know he'd never give you away if he couldn't get you back. I know your borgata is stronger. I know Doc's been holding back so he can deliver a death-blow. But Sofia, I trust *us*! That's why I gave *you* the letter, so I could propose a real alliance – call it that, instead of marriage. We used to whisper about it when we were little, don't you remember? Teaming up, stopping the fighting? Well, here's our chance! Fight for Rasenna, with me – we're as guilty as them if we don't. So, will you? Will you be my ally?'

Sofia kissed him. 'Tano, I don't love you.'

He swore and raised his banner to strike.

She didn't flinch.

He lowered his weapon and gave that same constrained martial nod. 'Thanks to your Concordian friend, Rasenna's coming together, so their way, or our way, it's happening.' He held up the letter. 'And you can let them rip it apart again, or you can put duty above your feelings and bind it for ever.'

'I don't care what Doc's letter says. I'm not marrying you, or anyone else,' she said, knowing he couldn't hear her, and that there was nothing more to say.

He watched her walk away, back into the engineer's arms. Was this fidelity's reward? He'd been raised in intrigue; he knew what to call it.

Betrayal.

As hard as that first week of full-contact sparring had been, Sofia realised, as the training went on, that Lucia had been holding back. Still, she managed to defend herself and, after another week, actually land a blow. It was sufficient to keep her motivated.

'So, can you see the future or what?'

'It's not that simple. We can't choose what's shown to us. We merely stay aware of Time's current, and hear echoes others are deaf to, and when the current shifts, we see possibilities.'

'Impressively vague. Prove it: what's my future? Will I be married like a fairy-tale princepessa?'

'I told you, we see only ripples. It is said adepts experience the whole current before death but for us, usually, it's just a feeling – it's not much, but an intuition about what an opponent will do next can mean the difference between victory and defeat.'

The sun, low over the river, threw the crew's shadows across Piazza Luna as they headed home.

On the bridge's north side, Giovanni waved to Sofia. 'Just doing a final check.'

'Me too.'

'We're fine,' he said, waiting till she came nearer to continue, 'the Morello haven't interfered lately.'

'They're keeping a low profile because if they behave, they get me. I come with a hell of a dowry.'

'I heard about the proposal,' he said, crouching to examine the balustrade, either very preoccupied or trying hard to give that impression.

'I'm not going to be bought and sold like that.'

He looked up suddenly. 'You *don't* want to marry Gaetano?'

'I never do anything I'm told to.'

'Well, that seems to be level,' he said, not hiding his smile very well. 'All good here, I should be—'

'Walking home? I'll escort you.'

'I'm not in danger any more.'

'I just want to walk with you' – she raised her voice – 'if that's all right with you, Captain?'

'Oh,' he said, getting flushed, 'I'd be delighted.'

'*Avanti!*'

The bandieratori circled. Gaetano waited a moment, let his focus sharpen, then took a step back and, keeping his eyes on the front two, jabbed his stick backwards where it connected with the face of the third.

'You could have taken me if you'd coordinated. Now, I've got a chance.'

'Do you really?'

Gaetano looked up to the second floor. Valentino stood in the door of their father's study, smiling sympathetically.

'Don't let me interrupt,' he said, descending the stairs.

That was impossible; Gaetano's choleric younger brother intimidated the students more than he ever could.

'So, Bardini accepted our proposal, but the Contessa refuses to dance?'

'Shut up.'

Valentino paced around the training square, oblivious of the twirling banners around him. 'Unless! Ah, here's a thought—'

Parrying the attacks of the two students in front, Gaetano received a side-jab from the third. He dropped his flag and grabbed the one who'd got lucky, pulling him into his fist. That left two.

He whipped around and parried their joint attack while sliding a foot under his own fallen flag. He kicked it into the air and caught it, twirling each flag until they balanced.

'Unless?' he grunted.

Valentino sauntered between the nervous bandieratori. 'Unless the Contessa likes forbidden fruit as well.'

Gaetano roared and went for the last two. They struck back, too fast, off-balance. He rotated his stick, caught them in the chest together and pushed them off their feet.

'But unlike you, she gets to taste one.'

Gaetano swung, but pulled up short.

Valentino laughed. 'I'm not afraid. That's what the Concordians taught me. Train with these boys all you like. You need to be ready up here' – he tapped Gaetano's forehead – 'for what's coming.'

'And what's that?'

Valentino went back upstairs, shaking his head with exaggerated grief. 'War, Brother. War.'

'Flags up, boys,' Gaetano said.

Sofia and Giovanni walked south in easy silence. The evening retained the day's heat yet, with no whisper of impending autumn's funeral march. In the once-deserted piazza, Rasenneisi mingled around the workers' food-stalls. The life that appeared with the bridge came so easily that it went at first unnoticed, like the passing away of summer.

They walked from the piazza through narrow streets

lined by towers – and they too were different, as overhead neighbours leaned from windows exchanging worries: the legion, the tribute, the prospect of peace and, of course, the bridge, which one neighbour called a godsend, while another cursed it. That was another difference: silence may be better than whispers, but argument out loud is better yet.

The expiring sun painted dark towers blinding white and Sofia had to squint to see beyond the shimmering cobblestones in the heat. White-glowing seed-heads from the surrounding contato floated lazily through the streets like bubbles in a slow-moving stream. She imagined the street was the drowned heart of old Rasenna; that that was the reason they walked so slowly.

The first Giovanni knew something was wrong was when Sofia raised her flag. He looked up and saw shut windows, heard the silence.

'Let's go.'

There was no point trying to get back to the bridge; they were nearer to Tower Vanzetti now.

She turned a corner to find five bandieratori waiting, all masked but one.

'Stay behind me.'

'Should we run?' he said.

'I don't turn my back to pigs like these. Who sent you, Tano?'

'No one.'

''Course they did. You're just too dumb to know it.'

Gaetano held back as four gold flags went forward. Sofia tried at first to defend *and* keep an eye on him, but that was impossible so she focused on bringing the flags down efficiently. When she turned back, Gaetano thrust a threatening flag towards her with one hand; his other held a knife to Giovanni's throat.

'*Idiota!* You can't kill a Concordian engineer. The consequences—'

'Damn them! I should have done this months ago!'

There was no talking to him; he'd come to kill – nor was there any way to reach him in time, or stop him fast enough if she did.

In a moment, Giovanni would die.

And that too was impossible; there was no way she'd let that happen. And believing that, Sofia saw that the *time* it took to cross the *distance* didn't matter. She just had to get to the point where she could stop Gaetano, even if she had to move faster than a blade could cut air.

She watched the moisture drops in her exhalation, then inhaled and

moved

Gaetano's body slammed against the wall. Sofia stood several braccia from where she was a moment ago. The blade clanged noisily as it struck the ground.

'Giovanni, come on!' Sofia shouted.

'How did you—?'

'No idea, but I feel drunk.'

'Tower Vanzetti's back there.'

'First place they'll look.'

'Where then? I can't climb like you.'

Her curse echoed in the narrow streets. She had never realised how constraining those streets could be.

'The bridge will be guarded too. Where's the last place anyone would look for a Concordian?'

Gaetano's men searched fruitlessly for hours before returning to Palazzo Morello. Quintus had panicked when Valentino revealed Gaetano's likely intentions; a second dead Concordian – an engineer – would seal their fate irrevocably.

'How could you be so *reckless*?'

Gaetano took his admonishment in sullen silence; he could scarcely explain it to himself.

Inside the Palazzo della Signoria, Giovanni picked up the Speaker's mace, feeling its weight. 'I can't go back to Tower Vanzetti?'

'Not tonight,' Sofia said, 'not until Quintus Morello gets a leash on Tano.' She paced between the rows as if she had lost something important there.

Giovanni put the mace back. 'He cares for you, doesn't he?'

'That's how Love looks in Rasenna, exactly like Hate. I hate this town.'

'Why don't we leave?'

'And go where? Ride south and join a Company?' she

said in exasperation. 'Would you fight paesani?'

'I'd fight for Rasenna.'

'Oh stop!' Sofia snapped, 'just stop. This is just *dreaming* – that's all Gaetano and I did when we were children and now look at us, all grown up and can't be enemies, can't be friends.'

She sat down in the Doctor's usual chair. 'There's nowhere to go, nowhere you could escape your country or I could escape my name. You can't understand what it means to be a Scaligeri . . .'

'It's your decision,' he said quietly. 'You're the one who's going to have to live with it.'

Everyone else told her what to do; they all wanted her for something. She never had to think what the right decision was, just do the opposite. He was asking her to decide for herself, and that was scarier than any approaching army.

She left after an hour, ordering him to stay hidden until she got back. 'If they find you, they'll kill you,' she repeated, sombrely. 'I'll figure something out.'

She knew there'd be no waiting this one out, however. Gaetano was a Rasenneisi, new to love but well-practised in hate. He'd keep coming until one of them was dead. Unless she thought of something, Giovanni wouldn't live to see his bridge open.

Lucia wiped the blood from her nose and bowed low, and, for the first time, with respect.

After she left, Sofia said casually, 'Less bad?'

'I'd go as far to say good.' The nun studied her. 'You're different somehow.'

'I think I used Water Style last night. I was attacked. It was strange—'

'Strange that you needed it; you're already a match for any Rasenneisi.'

'One of them had Giovanni, and a knife—'

'And you were frightened?'

'I—'

'And, best of all, for another!' She sounded almost excited.

'You act like getting ambushed was a good thing.'

'You care for him?'

'Sister, if a second Concordian is killed, an engineer especially, Rasenna's going to be in serious trouble.'

'Perhaps more than care . . .'

'Perhaps you're getting imaginative in your old age.'

'As you like. Whatever the spur, it was the fear you've been avoiding. This is a start. We must go further.'

'Can't we spar for a little longer? I'm finally getting good at this.'

'You still don't understand that fighting is secondary, do you? No matter. I'll show you.'

When she closed her eyes, she could hear the nun warning against haste, but she wasn't sure if it was real or imagination. The twilight was pleasant; she felt as if she was floating in warm water.

'I can reach your mind because you are near. You cannot stay on the surface and learn.'

Reluctantly, Sofia swum down until she could feel the Water's coldness, its immensity, its power. She could hear the nun's voice still, but now it was distant.

'Yesterday, you felt dizzy, yes? That was Water, pushing back. Fear pushes back too. You must learn to go towards it, and that means seeing it as it truly is. You must go

down

Sofia went deeper into the pit; water so chill should freeze, but it just drained strength and speed from her limbs. She could not hear the nun, but realised she was not alone – death was a breath away. This was the furthest point one could be from life and yet live.

In the darkness below, the water became, impossibly, still colder; there was *something* there – not *in* the darkness; it *was* darkness. Fear, the Dark Ancient, boiling furiously like a black sun, took shape. She felt paralysing ice obstruct her blood's flow, dead bone fingers enfolding her timidly beating heart and squeezing.

It was when she decided to flee that she heard it – a voice, calling from behind the Darkness. It wasn't the Reverend Mother's, but a young woman's; it was music, a song, but not a siren's.

Sofia.

Before she could answer, the Darkness felt her presence and reached out. Its cold tentacles touched her flesh and she was back in that moment: Giovanni had a knife at his neck, and this time she *knew* she would never reach him in time. It was too hard, too far, too dark.

A voice, small, distant and weak: *Sofia, wake up!*

The Reverend Mother pulled her back. She was in chapel. And safe.

'*Madonna!*' The nun's face was ashen. 'I'm sorry, child, you were not ready. It's just there's so little time left.'

Sofia heart was beating as if she'd been in a fight. 'What was it? A buio?'

'More – and less – than that. There is a power that connects man and buio, land and water. We see one face of it every day in Nature, but the dark face prefers to hide. It is in you, in all of us, and we nourish it with doubt and despair, with hate. It is the sum of a life lived in fear, and one day, you must face it again.'

'It almost killed me!'

'It impedes your progress. If you dive deep enough you leave behind History and reach the infinity of what might have been and might yet be. Giovanni's machine may restrain buio but when I was a girl, water needed no restraint. Because Man is fallen, we made the buio fall; bit by bit we will corrupt the whole world, until all is rotten and mad, or until things are set right.' She sighed. 'Rest, child. Tomorrow, we go deeper.'

Sofia was still shaken by her vision. She stopped at the

doorway. 'The world is the world. How can I change it?'

'Your life's only worth something if you give it away,' the nun said.

Sofia heard, and knew what she must do.

CHAPTER 34

When Sofia told Giovanni he could safely return to work, she did not mention the price. If being a leader meant anything, it meant sacrifice.

'I'll marry Gaetano.'

The Doctor was surprised to see her on the rooftop. They hadn't spoken since he had made her deliver his response.

He smiled. 'Then we shall have peace.'

'Doc, I know your peace. All this time I wanted to be just another Bardini, and you wouldn't let me. I understand why now, but you have to let me be my own woman. I won't be Morello's, either. I need you to promise you'll give this alliance a real chance.' She did not mention the other reason.

'You're growing up, Sofia. It's hard to let go.' He rubbed his chin. 'I promise!'

That morning, she practised with passion. She even pushed Lucia out of the square a few times.

The nun remarked on her improvement during meditation. 'Lucia's my best student,' she said, watching

Sofia, 'and she's studied for years, but you can already defeat her.'

'Which fight were you watching? She still wins most times.'

The nun chuckled. 'Ah, but you've been holding back, haven't you? You could beat her – you could even beat me, if a lack of faith didn't restrain you. You've embraced hate for so long that now you're its prisoner.'

'I came here to learn fighting, not be converted. What's faith got to do with anything?'

'That's what it takes to drop your flag. Lucia has it. Do you know how she came to be here? Her family were killed in a raid, just like Isabella's.'

'But she's a southsider.'

The nun let her realise the implication.

Sofia's hand went to her dagger. 'If that were true, she would have killed me on the first day. I couldn't have stopped her.'

'Is it so unbelievable?'

'Bardini don't hide in shadow like Morello. We're fighters, not butchers.'

'You've let yourself be sheltered from the truth.'

Sofia snatched up the glass and threw it. 'Liar!'

The nun avoided it effortlessly but it smashed the window, and harsh daylight invaded the chapel.

'I only went along with this nonsense to learn Water Style!' Sofia kicked the table at the nun.

The old lady moved gracefully out of the way, then went

on the attack. 'Foolish girl. You hide your skill, but you cannot conceal your thoughts.'

Sofia blocked a barrage of kicks, backing out of the chapel to get some space. The nun didn't let up, advancing on her, whirling her sleeves like before.

'The Doc's right: you're either traitors who knew the Wave was coming, or liars who didn't.' This time, Sofia wasn't distracted by the nun's sleeves; she dodged and then grabbed one, pulled the old woman forward and kicked, hard. The nun staggered and grabbed a branch to prevent herself falling.

'I know what Doctor Bardini thinks of me! When your father died, he refused to let me teach you Water Style. So I waited. I know how proud the Scaligeri are; the only way you'd submit to learning was if I beat you.'

'That's why you broke my arm?'

'Reverend Mother!'

Sofia turned. Lucia had appeared at the entrance of the Baptistery, drawn by the noise.

'Here's your little acolyte; why do you need me? You remind me of the Doc, you know that? I'm sick of being manipulated by old men and old women.'

'Stay back, Lucia,' the nun said. 'Let's see what she really knows.'

'I'll show you!' Sofia focused as they traded punches. The nun was still superior, but she wasn't toying with Sofia any more.

'If you saw this coming, why did you teach me?'

'You'll have to understand that yourself.'

'Have I hurt your feelings?'

'No, I'm just not going to be around much longer.'

The nun suddenly stepped around Sofia's arms and planted two fists into her torso. Sofia flew back and landed just outside the square.

The nun did not press her advantage.

'The sooner, the better,' Sofia spat. She pushed Lucia out of her way. 'Both of you, stay out of Bardini territory. Stay away from *me*.'

Sofia watched the deal done from an abandoned tower. So many torches were assembled on the bridge that it looked like a great shining hourglass.

While their masters stood face to face, discussing terms and making great display of their amity, Morello and Bardini bandieratori waited on the banks for a war-cry that never came.

In the shadows, Sofia's face burned with shame. Every man in Rasenna could hear them trading her like livestock, haggling over the price. The deal was done; only the exchange of goods remained. The Doctor spat on his hand. Morello overcame his fastidiousness and shook it. War asks only blood; Peace demands sacrifices more brutal.

'What were those lights on the bridge last night, another shipment?'

Fabbro and Vettori looked at each other. After they told

him, Giovanni went straight to the Baptistery. His foremen seemed to think the deal was the best thing for Rasenna: even if the Small People north and south were content to live and work together, they'd have no choice but to follow if the Families went to war.

'Signorina Scaligeri understands the choice she's making. And it's about time,' Fabbro said vehemently. 'Why should the Small People make every sacrifice?'

The nun was in the enclosed garden with a younger novice, performing a kind of slow-moving dance together.

'Sister, they're making Sofia marry! I think she's doing it to protect me. It's wrong. I thought you could—' Giovanni stopped as the Reverend Mother turned around. 'How did you get that black eye? Oh—'

'This is nothing,' she mumbled. 'I had a brother once.'

'You asked me once before if I would fight for her. Well, I'm ready to do whatever it takes.'

'You'll get your chance. She will not marry.'

'How do you know—?'

'How do you know your bridge will bear an army marching over it? Because you have studied such things. I too have studied. It's hard to describe things that are shifting, but Sofia's destiny is even stranger than yours.'

'I need more than that!'

She glanced at the girl. 'Go into the chapel, Isabella. I'll follow shortly. Captain, imagine a line, curved like a wave. It could be a man's life, or a town's, or a nation's. Now imagine a second line, rising when the first falls, a reflection – the intervals can be minutes or centuries. When they intersect, wonderful or dreadful things happen. One thousand, three hundred years ago, Christ was born, and His birth intersected with the reign of a wicked and jealous king. If the currents had met a year earlier, or a year later, the child might have escaped the sword. What kind of man would He have become? His Mother spread the Word, but She could never do what He was meant to, and so we remain unredeemed. Bernoulli ensnared the buio with a song of absolute power. Their first sin, like Man's, was murder.'

'But the first sin was—'

'A lie, to justify the Curia's ignorance. Engineers have committed many sins, but seeking knowledge was never one. God wants us to understand His creation. All sins are forgivable but for murder; after Cain slew his brother, paradise was lost. Now we have tainted the water. Murdered, murderer and Messiah, the same person. Man and buio, fallen together, together we must be redeemed.'

'But the Christ did die—'

'At the wrong time! *The choice must be understood!* That is what makes a sacrifice.'

'Sister, what has this to do with me or Sofia?'

Her head hung heavy with age. 'Time has a direction, just like a river. In the flood of centuries, there are moments when History can change course.'

He looked down. 'What if you're wrong? If one of us is not—'

'We are none of us what we seem. Our nature is hidden to us until the hour comes.'

'How will I know when that is?'

'You'll know. The earth itself will shake.'

As the hot season ended, a storm rose up in northern Etruria. With the indifferent hunger of locusts, the Twelfth Legion crossed down the peninsula. Towns paid tribute, and in return Concord brought not Justice, but Law, a thing like Nature's violence: containing no hate, no love and no mercy. Feuding factions made peace and prayed together till the storm passed.

All sought shelter, the good and the wicked together. Some were passed over, some perished. And the storm moved on, on towards Rasenna.

CHAPTER 35

Though we are more concerned with the Wave itself than the Philosophy that created it, it would distort our subject to ignore his sublime calculation[15]. In an age disfigured by War, its beauty is too seldom mentioned.

Bernoulli's maps were a boon for Concord's soldiers, but that was accidental; Bernoulli had surveyed Etruria's plentiful rivers to learn their secrets. And learn he did, discovering that apparently random undulations were no such thing: as rivers travel from source to sea, friction causes erosion which causes winding, even as land-tilt, gravity and momentum carry them forward. This contest between order and disorder was governed by a certain ratio[16].

From the hour of this discovery, Bernoulli's study changed course

---

[15] As less conscientious commentators have seen fit to do. Conscious that he is a relic of an obsolete pedagogy, the present Author proceeds with gratitude for his Masters' patient explanation, and the need-less caution that any errors are his own.

[16] A ratio of extreme and mean i.e. the *Golden Section* of the *Etruscans*. Before this discovery, Bernoulli dismissed Clerical reverence of Classical authority as 'ancestor worship'. He soon began studying the *Disciplina Etrusca*.

too, to focus on all things governed by Chance[17]. The Curia's inconsistent mathematicians thought and taught that Perfect Numbers
occurred as randomly as the stars fret Heaven, but Bernoulli soon
proved that they were governed by the same ratio that governed
his rivers. He appears to have found religious significance in the
fact that every Perfect Number has a negative twin, 'a fallen angel'
for ever seeking its reflection's annihilation[18].

So by happenstance foundations were laid. Likewise, Bernoulli's
earlier work on Harmonics, Number-theory and Time proved a vital
springboard for the leap from Wave Theory to Wave Technology,
a happy confluence that no one, the unworldly young boy least of
all, predicted[19].

Unleashing the Wave would be simple enough now that he had
a unifying system. The remaining problem, he told the Senate, was
how not to destroy Concord along with Rasenna, and after seven
years' toil this last minor inconvenience was surmounted.

---

[17] Luca Pacioli, our first First Apprentice (served 1353-1357), commented
on 'this drive to unify in Bernoulli's thought, strategy and adminis-
tration. His method was to find in separate truths, one larger.'

[18] This research prompted private misgivings, with Bernoulli noting
in the margins of his *Disciplina Etrusca*, 'I have plucked the Tree of
Knowledge bare; the great Spiral is now visible and, with it, the great
Secret: the War between Order and Chaos is *itself* the cause of Beauty.
I have built a Tower tall enough to spy on His design, and for that
am damned.'

[19] *Did the Wave will itself into being*, he wondered in later life. *Did it
cast a shadow on the Past as well as Future?* The question, variously
phrased, appears often in his last notebooks.

The Wave struck Rasenna, dividing her for ever, and the example of that great city brought low was sufficient to shatter the Southern League[20]. Yet for Senator Tremellius and his party there would be no laurels; while the Engineers succeeded in controlling most of the Wave's physical effects, the Senators took the brunt of the political storm unleashed in Concord.

---

[20] We live with the unexplained side-effects to this day. After two decades of research, the pseudonaiades, colloquially known as water-folk, or *buio*, remain a mystery, a subject where even the use of the word *creation* is contentious. Were they created, or were they freed? Whatever the truth, after the more dreadful example of Gubbio, a dread of unweaving other hidden bonds of reality prompted the moratorium enforced to this day.

CHAPTER 36

For good or ill, the week promised to be eventful. Tomorrow there would be celebrations as the bridge opened. The day after, the Concordians would interrupt their march south to collect Rasenna's tribute. On the third day, Sofia would turn seventeen, come into her inheritance and marry, to share that inheritance with a new husband.

Many pitied the Contessa, but few doubted the union was necessary to prevent war in the imminently-to-be-united town. For Sofia, it was simply a sentence of death, and a uniquely cruel sentence, for not only could she see the scaffold being assembled from the tower, she must participate in its assembly.

Fabbro's wife, the imposing Donna Bombelli, led the invasion of Tower Bardini. Her army of giggling matrons, who'd come to prepare Sofia's bridal clothes and trousseau, repeatedly said the dress, one of her late mother's, hardly worn, became her splendidly. The overdress was of deep burgundy velvet and sewn with pearls and lavish gold trimmings; the underslip was a bright poppy-red, the same colour as the impractically long sleeves dangling almost to the ground which obliged her to clasp her hands, as though praying.

The high waist, just below her bosom, accentuated the womanly shape she had made such efforts to conceal in recent years, as did the neckline, cut low and wide, the type of coy bait an ordinary girl would display for a husband. Sofia wore her Herod's Sword to distract from the expanse of skin. The high collar, which accentuated the gracious tower of her neck, was set with jewels. She would get used to the discomfort, the matrons insisted, as they washed and powdered every inch of her exposed skin till she resembled a porcelain Madonna: Our Lady of Dynastic Marriage.

Her hair – they'd insisted she let it grow for the last month – was pulled tight to flaunt her unlined brow, and then wrapped laboriously in a crépine that would keep its shape, 'No matter how vigorously you dance!'

She endured the tittering matrons' innuendos with growing impatience. She was, of course, forbidden a glimpse of *the other dress*. Her wedding gown promised to be an even more elaborate prison. Her new, coddled, life was a reduction in every sense. She had misunderstood the terms of the Contract: she was merely Rasenna's proxy: the town itself was being married.

Her mood was foul when Donna Bombelli finally let her see herself in the long mirror. 'Aren't you pretty, *amore*?'

She couldn't speak. The woman staring back was noble and beautiful and strong, the ideal Contessa she had carried in her heart as a motherless girl. It was immaterial how – or if – Giovanni remembered her after this, but somehow it blunted her grief to think this was how he would see her last.

The opening fell on the Feast of the Assumption, so it was only correct that Our Lady of Rasenna, garlanded in roses, was the first to cross. The Sisterhood, much reduced, like every Rasenneisi institution, carried the old statue from the Baptistery and chanted the Virgin's Hymn, followed by excited northsiders pressing round to pin notes on the Madonna, who was bearing the hopes of every Rasenneisi that day.

She saw him in the throng of southsiders crammed into Piazza Luna waiting for the procession. There was no point weeping or fighting, so she blushed and played the docile Madonna they'd made her. To be Contessa was to be first, first to suffer; you carry the town, it carries you. When a sacrifice is needed, you are the well-fed lamb ready for the occasion. Your life is not your own.

When the hymn ended, the Reverend Mother untied the flags and cried, 'In the name of the Virgin, I declare Rasenna Bridge open!'

The crowd cheered as the procession took on a carnival pace, pouring into the Piazza.

Giovanni was caught in the crush as the Madonna approached. After fighting his way out he found himself next to—

'Sofia?'

Now he saw her as Rasenneisi had always seen her: a Scaligeri, something more than a person.

'You look like a Contessa,' he said, smiling calmly, though he wanted to grab her and steal her away. 'Shouldn't you be with the Doctor?'

'Probably, but I'm still your bodyguard, remember?' Her smile didn't reach her glistening eyes.

'I know why you're doing this,' he whispered. 'You don't—'

'But I do! And who knows, some good may come of it.'

There was nothing he could do. He pointed at the Madonna. 'What did you wish for?'

'Don't heathens know how wishes work? That's between us girls.' She joked to distract him from the truth, that all this joy came at the price of hers.

The procession slowed in front of the Palazzo della Signoria and as Quintus Morello called for attention she had to admit he wore the full regalia of gonfaloniere with patrician dignity. Beside Quintus stood the Doctor, and between them was a small chest filled with dull silver coins.

'Many of Rasenna, and I am one,' Quintus started, 'predicted this bridge would bring only discord, but I look around today and see before me no northsiders, no southsiders, but Rasenneisi all. Today I see citizens in congress, friends united, families made whole: a town ready to know itself once more! Concord's army will pass through and have this tribute tomorrow only because Rasenna is united today. Tomorrow, we may disagree, but we feud no longer; that is yesterday. Today, I extend another bridge, the hand of friendship, to my friend Doctor Bardini.'

They shook hands and then together dropped a final soldi into the tribute-chest, to the sound of applause and cheers.

Once the Madonna was installed in the loggia, the carnival proper began: Rasenneisi mingled: cousins who had never before met embraced; bandieratori who'd only interacted in street-battles bought drinks and toasted each other's health. Thanks to the bridge, foreigners were not the rarity they had been; there were even novelty acts, juggling and tumbling to triple-time galliards to entertain the boisterous throng.

Sofia pushed into the crowd surrounding the puppet show, and when the engineer was accosted by crewmembers offering congratulations, she kept a tight grip on his hand; they would not be separated today.

'Congratulations, Captain,' said the Doctor over the hoots and laughter.

Sofia stiffened, but she did not release Giovanni's hand. The tension between her and the Doctor, renewed since the Reverend Mother's allegation, was more fraught for being unexplained. Sofia told herself the old woman was nothing but a lying troublemaker, but her accusation remained horribly plausible, and it was hard to meet the Doctor's eye with the burning memory of Isabella's family tower as a great chimney. Was he truly capable of such deeds?

Giovanni examined the miniature stage before them. 'What is this?'

'Don't you have the Marionette Theatre in Concord?' Sofia shouted in his ear. 'Poor thing! They take a story everybody knows, from History. This is, let me see—'

Draped in a shabby gown, a bulky puppet bounded on stage, precariously balanced on the edge of a narrow bridge and cried, *'None shall pass!'* to the mass of soldiers on the other side.

'Horatius on the bridge?' Giovanni ventured. 'In our version, he betrayed Rome to the Etruscans.'

'Ours too – but in these shows the roles are played by locals.'

'Ah, I see,' said Giovanni, 'and Horatius is – the Doctor?'

On the other side of the audience, Sofia noticed Quintus Morello and his sons. They'd chosen a spot where they could keep an eye on the show, and the Doctor.

Much to the crowd's amusement, the 'Etruscans' wore Concordian uniforms. A tall, slender one pranced up to Horatius and cried,

'Good knight, wouldst thou make way
Please. Tell me what I have to pay.'

The ambassador puppet did a double-take as he noticed his stump. 'AAhhh!'

'I swear, by Jove, that Rome will last,
Eternally for none shall pass!'

289

Horatius waved his black banner bombastically.

'But nothing lasts so well as Gold

So best be rich before you're old!'

Horatius caught the oversized soldi and stood aside as the ambassador and troops hopped across the bridge.

'Some shall pass I meant to say.

Welcome to Rome, enjoy your stay!'

Sofia watched the Doctor smile and raise a glass to Quintus. 'Most generous, Gonfaloniere!' he shouted over the hoots.

The children in the crowd laughed, all but one; Sofia's former sparring partner was holding a little girl's hand. Isabella had grown as pale as Lucia during her stay in the convent, and she had lost her freckles. Sofia wasn't surprised at Lucia's stony demeanour – the novice never smiled – but it was odd behaviour for a little girl. She followed Isabella's gaze to the Morello; Valentino was laughing, delighted with his caricature.

The Doctor leaned over to Sofia. 'Why have you stopped going to the Baptistery?'

'You've been spying on me?'

'The information came unsolicited. Don't trust that woman.'

'I don't. Answer my question. Who told you?'

He pretended to watch the show.

'Valerius,' she said.

He laughed loudly, then whispered, 'He's taken an interest in Bardini fortunes. You seem to have lost yours. I'm not angry. After tonight, it won't matter anyway.'

Horatius laughed villainously:

'Would it turn new friendship sour

If I asked for just a little more?'

The ambassador threw an oversized treasure chest.

'Traitors are insatiable, that I know

If you want more money, here you go!'

Horatius wailed as the bridge began to collapse.

'Lend me a hand! It weighs a ton!'

'Alas, Horatius, I have but one.'

Horatius sank under a wave of coins, and the ambassador addressed the audience with mock solemnity.

'Alas, the Roman could not swim.

Betraying traitors is no sin!'

The curtain dropped with a cymbal crash. The Doctor and the gonfaloniere applauded with the crowd, toasting each other. He suddenly turned to Sofia and embraced her.

'Sofia, obey me – this once,' he whispered urgently. 'Slip away quietly, get to the tower. It's not safe out tonight.'

She pushed him away. 'Doc, you promised! What have you done?'

The Doctor's eyes glazed over as he transformed into a smiling reveller. 'Speak up! I can't hear you.'

'What's wrong?' said Giovanni.

'Nothing, nothing,' she said quickly, backing off and forcing a smile.

This was serious; normally, the Doctor wouldn't say anything until afterwards. If the target was Giovanni she was there to protect him.

The evening drew on and music took over. A drummer beat out the proud, strutting rhythms of old Rasenna, and the puppeteer revealed another talent when he took up the accordion. He started with a joke song, about an old womaniser cuckolded by his pious wife.

When the laughter finished, the Doctor tapped his goblet for silence. 'Friends, join me in a toast to the Morello, and our continuing partnership in government.'

The crowd cheered, and cried, '*Salute!*'

'To healthy profit margins,' Fabbro said to Vettori, winking.

'Eh, look who it is.'

Vettori turned to see Hog Galati standing, nervously sweating and looking awkward in the midst of smiling faces. When Vettori extended a friendly hand, he took it quickly, obviously relieved.

'Signore Vanzetti, I— Well, I just wanted to congratulate you on this day. Oh, this is my youngest son, Uggeri.'

The boy wore an ugly cambellotto tilted low on his head so that his eyes were hidden. When he removed it, Fabbro could see he had father's black curls but little else: he had dark, cold eyes that looked straight ahead.

Vettori shook hands. 'And what will you be when you grow up? A mason, like your father?'

Hog blushed. 'A bandieratoro like his older brother, I fear.'

'Well, don't force them to be something you want them to be. You know, I always thought that Pedro would—'

'Nobody forces me,' Uggeri interrupted bluntly. 'I want to be bandieratoro.'

'All right, son, all right,' said Vettori quickly, disturbed by the boy's intensity. He was close to Pedro's age, but he had the composure of someone older. The tension of the moment diffused in the sudden hush as Gaetano Morello climbed the stage and called for attention.

'Signorina Scaligeri, would you sing for us? We must live together now.'

Sofia gave Gaetano a look he couldn't decipher. 'So we must,' she said, then turned to the musicians. 'You know "The River's Song"? Just follow my voice.'

It was the only song the Doctor had ever taught her, an old lament built around an eccentric conceit: the words were the Wave's thoughts as it raced towards Rasenna, cursing Man for making it party to its wars.

As the Contessa sang, each man retreated into his secret thoughts; dreams that comforted, memories that taunted. Giovanni's eyes too were downcast; Rasenneisi melodies were shrill and strange to him, but he felt the song was sung for him alone.

'I'd like to say your bride-to-be only has eyes for you, but—'

Gaetano shoved Valentino away. The song ended with an instrumental crescendo; when Gaetano looked back,

Sofia was walking towards him. As the music peaked, she touched his cheek.

'Sofia, I need to warn you—' He leaned forward and whispered, 'You should get to your tower—'

Sofia put her finger on his lips. '*Shhhh.*'

The crowd looked on pruriently as her hand touched Gaetano's chest, the other moving to the back of his neck. His eyes widened as her fingers reached the scar, but she reached his knife before him.

'Doctor!' Quintus protested.

'It was you, Tano. You butchered the Vaccarelli, didn't you?'

'Sofia, stop!' the Doctor said.

A line of blood appeared where she pressed the knife to Gaetano's throat.

'Do it then. You know what happens next,' he said coolly.

Giovanni touched her shoulder. 'Don't.'

She spat on the ground then dropped the knife; Gaetano glared at the engineer.

'You did this!'

'Blame yourself, Gaetano!' Sofia hissed.

He knocked Giovanni to the ground.

Sofia put her hand on her dagger. 'Back up!'

People were unsure whether to watch the drama unfold or run. With effort, Giovanni sat up. 'Sofia, don't let this happen.'

Bandieratori of every colour looked on, waiting for the order. She helped Giovanni up, then turned to the gonfaloniere and the Doctor. 'If either of you hurt another Rasenneisi family when I'm Contessa, I'll cut you out like cancer!'

When she pushed her way through the crowd, Quintus remarked, 'So, that's my new daughter-in-law.'

Relieved to see her going towards the bridge, the Doctor slapped his back with nonchalance. 'Lovers' quarrels defy logic, Gonfaloniere.'

Quintus laughed, equally tolerant. 'We're old enough to know they rarely last.'

Halfway across the bridge, Sofia grabbed the balustrade and looked down at the water, nauseated. There was no escaping the spreading blood.

'Sofia.'

'*Madonna*, look at you. Tano got you a good one.' She laughed despite her tears. 'Here, let me see.'

She wiped the blood from Giovanni's face with her sleeves, then touched his nose tenderly. 'It's not broken.'

'What's happening tonight?'

'I don't know, but it's not safe.'

'If the bridge brings more blood, I'll never— Sofia, my hands are dirty already!'

She smiled sadly; he imagined he had blackened his soul by following orders, but it took far more than that. 'You're no killer,' she said, thinking of Gaetano. Killers travelled light, guilt didn't slow them down.

'You don't know me.'

'I know enough; you're the first person I can drop my flag with.'

'That's only because I can't use one.'

'Giovanni! I want you to stay – stay for ever. That's what I wished for!'

She tore the Herod's Sword from around her neck and pressed in it into his hands, then kissed him suddenly. 'Take it. I need you to promise me something.'

'Anything,' he whispered.

'Go to Tower Vanzetti. Stay inside.'

'Are you involved?'

'Of course not! They'll blame each other for Marcus' murder, but General Luparelli won't listen to conflicting versions. He needs someone to hang, or he'll raze all Rasenna.'

'What can you do?'

'Find the murderer. Now go. You promised.'

'Wait, I—'

But she was gone, swallowed by the night's darkness.

Dancing only stopped when fog rose from the river to invade the piazza. The crowd thinned as children were sent to bed and couples stole away. Finally, only drunken old men and their maudlin songs remained.

The Doctor toasted Valentino and Quintus. 'I leave the night to better and younger men,' he said, draining his glass. 'It has defeated me.'

'Golden dreams,' said Quintus.

The Doctor stumbled by Giovanni on the bridge and wagged a finger. 'Get to bed, Captain. Haven't you heard? There are ghosts roaming tonight.'

It surprised Giovanni that Bardini had let himself get so drunk; perhaps the bridge *had* changed things.

Once over the bridge, the Doctor looked befuddled by the labyrinth of narrow, twisty streets before him and randomly tumbled into an alley.

Gaetano silently dropped from a rooftop and crouched in shadow as the Doctor staggered by. Instead of following, he waited, held his breath and listened. He could hear only the erratic rhythm of a drunkard's footsteps. Good. He signalled, and three bandieratori dropped down and drew in on the target. At the intersection of four alleys, the Doctor stopped to urinate.

Gaetano heard the blades drawn; did the Doctor? Unlikely, he was cheerfully singing of the cuckolding cuckold. But when Gaetano crept closer, the Doctor stumbled, pushing Gaetano into the wall, and a sharp elbow cracked his rib. Where were the others? Why didn't they help?

'First time north, Tano?'

He tried to get up and got kicked in the jaw.

'No, I think not. You've visited regularly, haven't you?'

Gaetano saw the others held at knifepoint by Bardini men.

'That reminds me; you owe one of my boys some flesh.'

As the tall bandieratoro sauntered over, the Doctor held Gaetano's head still.

'Remember me?' Mule grabbed an ear and pulled.

'*Ahhhhhhh!*'

'Don't look away,' the Doctor whispered in the bloody hole in Gaetano's head, 'this is the good bit.'

The blood loss was making him groggy, but still the voice kept talking. 'Your wedding's cancelled – but don't be disappointed. The good news is I'm promoting you. By tomorrow, you'll be the eldest Morello. Don't thank me, just remember when you wake up who owns Rasenna, to whom you pay rent. That's thanks enough for me.'

Standing by the resurrected statue, Quintus Morello waited for them to return, their knives wet with Bardini's blood, the deed done. He looked up impatiently at the sombre Lion. 'Oh, cheer up, would you?'

Footsteps in the fog.

'Who's that? Did you get him?'

'Got him.'

Quintus tried to hold himself up against the Lion, but for some reason his legs didn't work. Secondo pulled the knife out, listened to the gasping for a while, then knelt down and used the gonfaloniere's long sleeves to wipe clean the blade. 'Go to sleep, old man. Dream golden dreams.'

CHAPTER 37

At dawn the towers remained encased in lingering fog, rearing out of the mist like ancient tombstones. Rumour alighted from tower to tower, whispering to sleepers within of some great crime accomplished, and Rasenna awoke, groggy from the night's revelry and just beginning to remember that they had been foolish, disgraced themselves, received insults cravenly or given them boorishly. The memories of hearty laughter echoed with hypocrisy, deception ineptly masking hatred, disgust still vital.

Any souls with business that morning scurried between the towers like beetles caught in the light. Rasenneisi senses, honed by twenty years of hate, scented fresh blood on the streets.

Only Workshop Bardini was undisturbed by the whispers. It was silent but for the patient respiration of a hundred students, waiting and ready.

A little later than usual the Doctor came down from his tower and smiled to see them sitting there, flags at their sides: his army ready for war, if he said the word. 'We have cut off the dragon's head, but its body is twitching yet,' he announced. 'Show me your loyalty today. Do nothing. Before the sun sets, the Morello will destroy themselves.'

He looked around. 'Where's Sofia?'

'Nobody's seen her,' said Mule.

'Or Valerius,' Secondo added.

'*Porca vacca!* Nothing's easy. All right, goddamn it, I'm going over. Stay put!'

Valerius ran through the sloping streets, his gaze on the space between the rooftops. Someone was following him, but this time he had his flag. He was still scared, though; the Morello would love to drop his body on the Bardini doorstep and let the Doc share their troubles. He turned a corner and hugged the wall, listening. The shadow dropped behind him and he turned with a showy banner-swipe. The shadow dodged the blow with ease, snatched his flag and threw it away.

'Sofia!' Valerius laughed. 'Where have you been? You're supposed to protect me from the Rasenneisi who want me dead.'

'I'm one of them,' she said coldly. 'I know it was you, Valerius.'

He laughed again, but took a step back. 'What are you talking about?

'You murdered Marcus.'

'Who?'

'That was his name, the boy you killed. You're really blooded now. How's it feel?'

'I preferred you before you started acting like a nun. How did you know?'

'Fabbro Bombelli saw a northerner crossing the bridge that night. Then the Doc told me you'd been spying on me, trying to act like a Bardini bandieratoro.'

'That's what I am!'

She slapped Valerius with an open hand.

'You don't raise your hands to me! The Doc—'

'Won't be in charge after tomorrow. I'm done taking orders from all of you.'

'So what if I killed him? It helped the Bardini, didn't it?'

'You murdered a paesani in cold blood.'

The cherub's face creased into a sneer. 'That's funny coming from a Rasenneisi. At least Concordians require a reason to kill each other.'

'Reason? Marcus was a boy – an innocent!' she said and slapped him again.

He fell against the wall, bursting his nose open, and screamed, 'I did it for you! *You!* I love you! You were too busy with the engineer or praying to your pig *Madonna* to notice that the Morello were winning.'

'You don't know *anything*. You're a civilian.'

He grabbed his banner. 'I'm more of a Rasenneisi than you!' he cried, and lunged at her. Though Sofia hadn't expected it, she easily avoided his attack – but Valerius didn't want to connect, he wanted space. He bolted into the fog.

Sofia raced after the receding footsteps. His confession

was the only thing which could prevent war. The beast was breaking its shackles. The blood was spreading.

The Palazzo della Signoria's damp heart looked empty, yet the notary was scribbling as if an especially busy session were underway.

'I thought you'd be here.'

'Try to be more punctual next time, Doctor,' said Valentino summarily. 'Let's not spend all day at it, Notary.' He sat in his father's chair, wearing the gonfaloniere's chain and gown, still stained with last night's blood.

The notary cleared his throat and read with a quivering voice, 'The House now votes on a motion to commence hostilities against the Concordian Empire. All in favour?'

'Aye,' said Valentino.

'All against?'

'Are you mad, boy?'

'The Doctor's abstaining. Notary?'

'The Ayes have it. Motion carries.'

The Doctor kept his composure. 'Only the head of a Family has a vote.'

'You would enter our towers now, tyrant? I am the rightful head of the Morello. My brother will not contest me.'

'Rasenna would not survive a war, fool.'

'What matter is that?' Valentino said pleasantly.

'You,' the Doctor growled at the notary, 'leave. It's time for a closed session.'

The notary scrambled towards the door, scattering scrolls like a moulting lizard.

'Here, take this fool's bauble!' The mace smashed against the door as it closed.

'The People have spoken, Doctor.'

The Doctor cracked his knuckles. 'You want war, boy? I'll give you a taste.'

Devious bastard, Sofia thought, realising Valerius had calculated that he'd be safest on the side of the river where everyone wanted to kill him. She caught up to him on the bridge. In desperation, he turned to fight. She knocked his flag into the river and rapped his ankle with precision. It went *pop* and he fell with a bleating cry.

'You've got to confess!'

Face down, Valerius snorted. 'General Luparelli will want more than contrition. I know my dear father, and the people he answers to. The Apprentices will want blood!'

'The Guild will go easier on you.'

'You know that's untrue.' He sat up and wiped his nose, laughing strangely. 'You never cared for me at all, did you? The funny thing is, I thought you loved Gaetano. I told myself you wouldn't look at me because you'd never love a Concordian. Shall I tell you his name? It's an unsuitable match.'

'Blood's not important when you love someone!' She turned away from Valerius in disgust. And standing there—

'Sofia, look out!' Giovanni pushed her out of the way,

catching the knife Valerius was thrusting, and they toppled backwards together. There was a shrill cry as the knife sank into flesh.

Valerius' body was the first to move.

'No!' screamed Sofia.

Giovanni pushed him off with a grunt and went to Sofia and held her.

'I thought you were— Oh, Giovanni!'

'Sofia, I love you too!'

Valerius gripped the balustrade. Whimpering, one hand on the knife in his gut, he pulled himself up. 'Look what you did to me, Contessa!' He tore the blade out and flung it down in front of her. 'I can't hurt you, not with that, anyway.'

He leaned against the balustrade and tumbled over.

'No!' Sofia heard the splash before she reached the balustrade. She saw his smiling cherub's face just before the buio pulled him under: a boy happily dying for revenge, a real Rasenneisi, just like he had always wanted.

'They'll burn Rasenna for this,' she whispered, watching the half-realised forms of buio swarming beneath the river's surface. She didn't cry. All she felt was relief that Giovanni was alive.

'We'll face it together,' he lied, knowing he must do alone what needed to be done.

In Palazzo Morello the students sat facing the Dragon crest, flags ready and waiting, a mirror of the Bardini

AIDAN HARTE

workshop, but the reflection was warped: they were no longer an army, just leaderless boys facing death.

Earlier that morning, Gaetano had woken in a pool of his own blood. Bardini's men had dragged Gaetano halfway across the bridge before abandoning him and he'd staggered home, too delirious to notice the other trail of blood leading to the doorstep. Servants bandaged his wounds and let him rest.

It was only when he stumbled out of bed at noon that he learned of the night's other events: the wounded gonfaloniere being found on his own doorstep, and Valentino, after putting him to bed, leaving the palazzo dressed in his father's robes of office. Gaetano went to investigate, and found his mother spread-eagled on the floor in front of the bedroom door. She was sharing her goblet with the dog. 'Gaetano, where *were* you?' she asked. 'Valentino's just come back. He's a good boy, such a good boy . . .' Her voice trailed off.

Gaetano found Valentino standing over their father's bed, clasping his hand. 'What happened to you?' he asked.

'Doctor Bardini and I had a vigorous exchange of views,' Valentino mumbled through a swollen jaw. He threw down Quintus' hand. 'Congratulate me, Brother. Father has just named me Head of the Family. Will you follow me?'

Gaetano saw his father's petrified attempt at an

305

approving smile and guessed how Valentino had made his case. It didn't matter – nothing mattered any more.

'Where?'

'To War.'

Gaetano kissed his brother's hand. 'My Lord.'

CHAPTER 38

The decina posted on Rasenna's walls was as pointless a gesture as the decrepit battlements. They heard before they saw the solitary horse race out of the mist.

The Herald pointedly halted within arrow-range and proclaimed: 'Burghers of Rasenna, Concord approaches. Prepare Tribute.'

As there was only one possible answer, he scorned to wait, turning immediately and returning to the mist. Rasenna held its breath as the double gates were raised. There was a long silence, worse than a scream. Mothers in every tower prayed and hushed their fractious babes. The Wave's thunder still sounded in the town's nightmares, and now they were coming: the Flood Makers.

Proudly wearing the gonfaloniere's chains of office, the Doctor left the Signoria. He found them on the bridge.

'Bracing morning, Captain! Sofia, I've been waiting to tell you the good news. The wedding's off!'

'Valerius is dead.'

The Doctor smiled as if it might be a joke, then took a step back. '*Madonna!* What have you done?'

'Valerius killed Marcus,' said Sofia.

'No, no – that was Valentino Morello.'

'Why would he?' Giovanni asked.

'Because he's mad, because he hates Concord. When the bridge came under my protection the boy was a convenient alternative.'

Giovanni shook his head. 'Concord's just an excuse. The Morello only want to rule Rasenna, like you, Doctor. You knew from the start the bridge could help you consolidate your power and contrived a strategy of tension to make me seek your protection.'

'Nobody made you do anything.'

'The Morello had nothing to do with Frog's murder.'

Sofia looked at Giovanni, then the Doctor. 'Say it's not true!'

'It was necessary,' the Doctor said, walking towards her. 'I wanted to protect you from all this.'

'By murdering your own? *Burning families?* Protect me from *what?*'

'People like me, I suppose,' he said softly. 'What now, Captain?'

'If Concord don't have a culprit for both murders, they'll take Rasenna apart, brick by brick. You can blame the Morello for Marcus' death, but not for Valerius too.' He took a breath. 'Take me.'

'What are you saying?' Sofia cried.

'Say Valerius' blood is on my hands – mine alone.'

The Doctor rubbed his chin thoughtfully and looked at the engineer. 'Could work, I suppose. You'll confess to Luparelli?'

'Giovanni, no!'

'Yes, I will.'

'Good boy!' The Doctor laughed and grabbed him. 'That makes everything so much easier. Sofia, return to the workshop.'

'They'll kill you!'

'Do as he says, Sofia,' said Giovanni. 'I know what I'm doing.'

He was certain now why he'd been sent to Rasenna: only he could prevent war. The rest were either powerless to stop it or mad enough to want it.

As their steps echoed across the empty piazza the Doctor tried explaining himself to his silent prisoner. 'I only want to protect her.'

'As do I, Doctor.'

'If you mean that, you'll confirm every word of my story. Trouble is, that little bastard was General Luparelli's son, so there's no telling what he'll do. Play your part and there might still be a town for her to inherit tomorrow.'

Looking down at the Herod's Sword she had given him, Giovanni said, 'I won't contradict you.'

In the bloody aftermath of the celebrations the players fled Rasenna, abandoning their stage and props. The Doctor picked up the Morello puppet and deftly made it dance a tarantella. He laughed and threw it aside when he heard the distant rumble. 'Here they come!'

While the first wave of infantry were still squeezing through the north gate, the cavalry rode ahead though the streets and thundered across the bridge without ceremony.

The Doctor glanced at Giovanni. 'It's done its work, Captain. Congratulations.'

The cavalry passed unchecked though Piazza Luna to the single straight road that led to the southern gate. Though the legion sent to confront the Hawk's Company was Concord's smallest, it was vast beyond the Doctor's comprehension. He thanked the Virgin that he was not John Acuto.

The Doctor ordered Sofia to return to the workshop, so she did exactly that.

'Bandieratori, flags up!'

The students looked at her uncertainly.

Secondo said, 'Doc ordered us to stay put.'

'Get up, or they'll burn Rasenna down around us!'

'But the Doc said—'

'Your loyalty is to the Scaligeri,' Sofia snapped, struggling to sound imperious and not desperate. 'If you love Rasenna, follow me.'

Mule stood. 'Let's go!'

Secondo held onto his brother's sleeve. 'His orders were explicit. The first rule is obedience, remember?'

Mule turned to Sofia. 'Maybe we should—?'

'Secondo was the one who did Frog,' she said loudly. 'Weren't you?'

Secondo looked around. Now the students were focused on him. 'Shut up, Sofia!'

'Make me.' She glared at him – and Secondo keeled over suddenly, whacked in the back of the head by his twin.

'How's that for explicit? Bandieratori, you heard the Contessa. Let's move!'

The last cavalry squadron halted in the piazza and divided to form a guard as the infantry crossed the bridge.

'Doctor Bardini, it's been a long time.'

The Doctor smiled solemnly. 'General Luparelli.'

A dozen years had passed, but the Doctor easily recognised the boy he had taught in the man. Another cherub, like Valerius, but grown large, with scrubbed pink skin bulging between joints of polished armour.

'That's what these swine call me, Doc, but you can always call me Luparino!'

'Yes, I remember.'

'*Madonna*, I remember it like yesterday. I remember I didn't want to leave at the end of it.'

'You wanted to be a Rasenneisi.'

'The things that matter to young men! I became worried that Concord wasn't on the side of the angels. Now I'm certain it isn't, and it doesn't bother me a bit, ha! Ah, wonderful time for me, wonderful. Expect Valerius is just the same?'

'Well . . .'

'Of course he is. We'll let the infantry pass before we get down to it, shall we?'

The Doctor smiled fixedly.

The din of the legion's passage disturbed even the Baptistery's silence.

The water in the glass trembled. Knowing her end was close, the Reverend Mother had expected the final vision – but not its violence. It had her now and she understood, at last, how great the power flowing through Rasenna was; so much larger than the squabbles of the Families, more important than the coming war. With an effort of will she put her imminent death aside: ego's huge powers of distortion could prevent her *seeing*, and one life was a small matter, after all. The water began to boil. The vision clarified, and fell

The engineer

The horse

The arrow falling

Water

Sofia screaming

Two men hanging

Dreams are not to be commanded by dreamers, but she must be sure who was hanging here . . . She'd expected resistance, but the vision shifted easily enough. It was something Water needed her to see.

She saw Quintus Morello and Doctor Bardini before the glass shattered.

After a moment, she turned to her acolyte. 'Lucia, I'm relying on you now. The Virgin will give you grace.'

'Don't leave!'

The nun leapt up. 'I must – it wouldn't do to keep Death waiting.'

CHAPTER 39

After the extensive supply train came the archers and gunners. Two units broke off and assembled beside the general.

'Now, Doctor! I recognise a man with a problem, so let's see if we can fix it, once we get business out of the way. I have Tribute and two Concordian lads to collect, one of whom I'm rather attached to, ha ha!'

'General, the Tribute is here in full.'

Luparelli gestured to an aide to take the chest. 'Received with thanks. It's no small amount for a small town – business must be good. Perhaps we should raise it next year, ha ha! And the boys? So sorry to rush – I'd love to catch up, but you know, the situation down south with these damn condottieri. It's like trying to delouse a whole country! You understand.'

'Perfectly,' the Doctor said. 'The boys, it grieves me to say . . .'

Finally Luparelli began to realise that something was seriously amiss. 'Bardini, *where* is my son?'

'He is dead, General. Both of them are dead.'

Luparelli staggered and looked around dazedly, then back at the Doctor, as if he had misheard. After a long moment he shook his head and bellowed, 'But this is treachery! Gunners!'

As the soldiers leapt to surround them, the Doctor pulled Giovanni to his side and started speaking quickly. 'General, please! Let me explain! This is the man – this traitor – he is the one who murdered Valerius.'

'Impossible!' he scowled. '*We* sent this engineer—'

'The boys discovered that he planned to betray Concord,' the Doctor said, and as the general started to look even more confused, added, 'He intended to collapse the bridge with you and your troops on it, and I'm ashamed to say our gonfaloniere colluded. The boys came to me for help; I was sceptical, but I knew if Valerius said it, it must be true. I begged him to let me confront the engineer, but he was too brave, General, and his bravery's reward was this traitor's dagger. Ask him: he bears the Empire no love. I'd have hung the dog myself if I had the right to execute citizens. General, the Bardini are—'

'Shut up,' Luparelli snapped, and turned to Giovanni. 'Captain, is any of this true?'

'I am responsible for Valerius' death,' he said evenly.

Luparelli calmly removed his iron-coated glove and struck Giovanni with it.

'*Uggh!*' he cried involuntarily as the metal cut his cheek.

'Damn you!' Luparelli shouted, 'my little angel never harmed anyone! Why would you do such a thing?'

The Doctor, hugely relieved that Giovanni did not respond, gave a hopeless shrug. 'I've heard rumours, General. A quarrel – a girl.'

'*Madonna!* It doesn't take long to go native, does it? Like father, like son, I suppose. What of the other boy?'

Feigning reluctance, the Doctor solemnly pointed to Palazzo Morello. 'My student was murdered by a traitor. The Morello murdered their own.'

'How many?' Gaetano asked from the darkness.

The palazzo's door was opened a crack and Valentino peered out of it.

'I see a cavalry squadron, archers, gunners – and the Doctor, pointing this way. I told you he would blame us. Still with me, Brother?'

'Till death.'

Seeing General Luparelli's indecision, the Doctor chose his words carefully. Much depended on them. 'The engineer will tell you how I defended your bridge with my men' – he held up his four-fingered hand – 'with my own blood. Think how the Morello hate you, General! To murder a student under their supervision, in their territory.'

Luparelli said. 'No doubt you've some recommendation.'

The Doctor bowed his head sorrowfully. 'Rasenna can know no peace while such crimes go unpunished.' He looked up suddenly with gleaming eyes. 'Exile them!'

'It was me,' said Giovanni.

'What did you say?' said Luparelli.

'I killed them both.'

'Shut up!' the Doctor hissed. 'Pay no mind, General. It's a lie.'

'No Rasenneisi shed Concordian blood,' the engineer repeated.

'I said shut up!'

The General looked at the Doctor with suspicion and was about to speak when a soldier called his attention to the crowds filling the side-streets around the piazza.

'This begins to resemble an ambush, Doctor. Who are these men?'

'The bridge crew,' the Doctor said incredulously.

General Luparelli glared at him and grabbed his chains of office. 'I don't remember Rasenna so democratic! You're gonfaloniere now, aren't you? So talk to them, before I do something you'll regret for the rest of your very short life.'

In all the Doctor's calculations, the Small People had never been a factor. 'Go home,' he said, but his voice barely carried. 'Rasenneisi, this is Signoria business. Return to your towers.'

Pedro, bearing the Vanzetti banner as their Standard, had never felt so proud of his father. He knew what it had cost Vettori, that it might still break him, yet he took the risk.

Fabbro, seeing the Concordian guns up close, was less sanguine. 'This is crazy!' he muttered.

'Think of all he's done for us,' Vettori said. 'We can't abandon him.'

'But Vettori, they'll kill us!'

'If we stay frightened, we're slaves.'

'That's business. There's calculated risk and there's suicide.'

'I'm not a slave any more. Decide for yourself, my friend.'

Fabbro looked again at the Concordians and pushed his way back though the crowd to the prudent ignominy of safety.

The door of Palazzo Morello widened just enough for a slender figure to step out. Draped in his old ambassador's cloak, Valentino Morello trotted across the piazza as if oblivious to the commotion, as if today was any other day.

The Doctor grabbed the general's arm and hissed, 'Here is your enemy!'

Irritated, Luparelli pulled his arm free and struck the Doctor with his glove. 'That's *enough*! You think I'm here to fight your battles, you weak fool? You don't change – I remember it all, your petty conspiracies, your feuding Rasenneisi . . . To think I once thought you wise.'

'General Luparelli?' said Valentino, 'it's been too long.' He gave a gracious bow.

'Lord Morello? Have we met?'

Though his face was alarmingly swollen, Valentino smiled charmingly. 'Don't you recall?'

'You have me at a loss.' The General proffered his

unarmoured hand but grasped empty air.

Valentino's cloak fell back, revealing a long sword, which he raised and swung.

Hot blood struck the Doctor's stunned face and he tripped on the stage, pulling Giovanni with him as he fell. The engineer struck his head on a step.

The general's hand fell onto the cobblestones and the fingers began twitching, like an overturned insect trying to right itself.

'*Forza Rasenna!*' Valentino screamed, thrusting the sword aloft, and there was an explosion of gold as bandieratori burst from Palazzo Morello. Valentino slashed away at the gunners, left and right, and was about to dispatch the general when he caught sight of the Doctor. 'You stumbled, Gonfaloniere Bardini—?'

The general, stunned and hyperventilating but seeing his last chance of survival, scrambled for a fallen gunner's arquebus.

Valentino said with a manic grin, 'Allow me to right that—'

Gore rained over the Doctor as Valentino's chest exploded.

'*Forza Rasenna!*'

The Woolsmen took up the cry as they advanced into the piazza. Vettori was trying to reach Giovanni, but nothing was clear in the mingling gunsmoke and fog.

The archers on the other side of the piazza launched

a barrage into the confusion, and as their deadly hail sliced the air, the front row, as one, dropped. Vettori was struck down with the rest. The crowd buckled, then sundered; one moment there was order and unity; the next, every man was alone, screaming and pushing for his life. Pedro dropped the Standard to protect Vettori from being trampled as Woolsmen tried to flee.

Hog Galati tried pulling him away. 'You can't say here!'

Pedro snapped his arm away. 'I'm not leaving him!'

'Let me pull him out of the piazza at least.' And he got Vettori back to the alley before the second barrage fell. Then Hog coughed strangely and said, 'Say goodbye now. Say goodbye—'

He stumbled back into the piazza and Pedro saw the arrows sticking in his back as he lifted the Standard.

'*Forza Rasenna!*' Hog cried as more arrows found their mark.

'Pedro, it's us!' Vettori was gagging on blood.

'Papa?'

'It's not them, it's *us*,' he whispered. 'The Signoria – the Small People. Don't be afraid, promise me.'

Pedro didn't understand, but he repeated, 'I promise.'

He closed Vettori's eyes, then stood, ready to take up the Standard, when he felt a firm hand on his shoulder.

'You're coming with me now,' Fabbro said.

The Doctor left Giovanni where he lay and ran to the general, avoiding swords, arrows and banners. In the thick of the mêlée, Luparelli was sitting in a shallow pool of blood, patiently trying to reconnect his hand to his wrist. The Doctor tore up a Morello banner and bandaged his wound, then dragged him to the Signoria's loggia, where the fighting was less intense.

The mist burning off as the sun rose higher revealed the true disparity between Morello and Concordian. The Concordians had regrouped after the initial surprise attack and had now taken the offensive. Their victory was certain; disorganised bandieratori, no matter how athletic, could not leap walls of pikes or dodge arrows or arquebus fire. Gaetano held them back outside the palazzo until the bombardment became too intense, when he ordered the Morello to retreat and had the door closed and barred.

Once Luparelli was on his feet again he marched unsteadily to the palazzo to take charge himself. The Doctor trailed him obediently, smiling contentedly – in spite of all that had gone wrong, he *had* succeeded! – but his grin faltered when he spotted the dark line of Bardini flags assembling across the river. Luparelli saw them too, and pushed him towards the bridge.

'Keep them back, or I promise you, when I leave Rasenna the only thing I will leave standing is my bridge.'

Sofia led the Bardini though the northern streets, gathering men from other towers as they marched. Reaching the river, she saw the commotion in Piazza Luna and broke into a run, crying, 'Follow me!'

The Doctor was dashing towards her, waving her back frantically. Realising the only steps she could hear on the bridge were her own, Sofia turned. The borgata had stalled on the northside.

'Bardini, hold!' the Doctor shouted.

'Traitors!' Sofia screamed, 'I am Contessa Scaligeri; follow me!'

The Doctor reached Sofia. 'They're traitors *if* they follow you – can't you see? Our enemies are being killed for us!'

Giovanni came to with the general's horse nuzzling him. He stood unsteadily and tried to take in the mayhem: Woolsmen slain, the piazza strewn with golden flags, blood running freely between the stones. He was covered in blood – somebody else's, once more . . . once more back in the pit . . .

Was this what the Doctor had wanted all along, to clear the field of his rivals? Including the Contessa? Nothing else made sense any more. He had been positive that he was *meant* to sacrifice himself for Rasenna, but somehow war came on regardless. That didn't matter now. To save Sofia would be enough – he could do that even if the world was intent on destroying itself.

Luparelli was overseeing the palazzo siege, but he recognised his horse as it went by – and its rider. 'A thousand soldi to whoever hits the traitor!' he bellowed.

'Count Scaligeri ordered me to keep Rasenna safe, for you,' the Doctor repeated.

'Your only loyalty is to yourself,' Sofia said, and threw her banner down.

'Don't make me hurt you, Sofia.'

'You think you're capable?' Before the Doctor could lift his flag, Sofia attacked: a series of chest kicks doubling him over, then a knee to the chin. He used his flag to stop his fall, pushed himself up with a grunt and charged at her, his flag elegantly masking a flurry of sudden jabs.

Sofia sidestepped, clawing his face as he went by. She looked back at the northsiders. 'Come on, you cowards!'

'Stay!' the Doctor shouted, then touched the bloody cuts on his face. 'Impressive. *I* didn't teach you that.'

'That's nothing. Watch this!'

The Bardini students couldn't advance and they wouldn't retreat, so they did what Rasenna had taught them: they waited. The fight would decide.

The Doctor defended himself against another onslaught of Water Style, knowing he couldn't do more and hoping it might be enough: he only had to stall long enough for the Concordians to do their work.

Sofia jabbed his shoulder. It didn't hurt but his arm went dead and she snatched his banner away.

He jumped back and risked a glance south. 'Look! Palazzo Morello's burning – we've won!'

'You never understood what my grandfather meant,' Sofia said.

Secondo arrived from the workshop and joined the borgata. 'What's going on?'

'See for yourself,' said Mule coldly.

'Doc, behind you!' Secondo shouted.

'Sofia!'

Sofia and the Doctor turned together to see Giovanni thundering towards them on horseback.

'Giovanni, look out!' she screamed as a black swarm of arrows rained down in his wake.

When one sank into his shoulder he jerked left and obediently the horse crashed through the balustrade and they tumbled together towards the river.

'No!' Sofia screamed.

The Doctor recognised the moment to strike. He dropped her with a neat punch to the chin. He picked her up and looked defiantly at his bandieratori. A hostile army stared back.

'It was for her own protection,' he said calmly.

By the time Palazzo Morello's doors had been blown in, most of the students had abandoned their flags. The rain of debris which had knocked Gaetano unconscious now concealed him as the Concordians rushed in. Those servants too loyal or too stupid to flee were swiftly struck down on the stairs. Donna Morello, standing beside her husband, had been prepared to kill herself in classic style but when the soldiers broke in she entirely forgot her purpose and rushed at them, screaming a war-cry.

Quintus Morello was dragged from his comfortable deathbed to witness his wife being hurled from the balcony.

The Reverend Mother arrived at the river and found her way blocked by a tall, surly bandieratoro.

'We have orders, Sister.'

'As do I, *amore*.' She tapped his chest lightly and Secondo landed several braccia away, unconscious once more.

Having dealt with the uprising's point of origin, Luparelli ordered the Palazzo della Signoria to be burned as well and then made his way onto the bridge, gunners in tow.

The Doctor looked at the swirling water enviously. The engineer had won himself a good death: it was best it happened here, and quickly. In Concord they'd have made him suffer.

Luparelli was enraged to be robbed of his revenge. 'See that smoke, Bardini? When you fail to keep peace, Concord forces peace on you. Your parliament burns!'

He bowed. 'Yes, General.'

'Don't look so pleased. Rebellion must be punished. If the Signoria is guilty, the Families that ruled it are guilty too, and you *are* the Head of the Bardini.'

As the ragged form of Quintus Morello was dragged towards them the Doctor looked around to see the soldiers forming a line in front of his borgata. He suppressed the instinct to fight his way out – if the general was denied justice, vengeance, call it what you will, he would level

Rasenna and go on his way. Dying might not have been part of the plan but a warrior was always ready. What matter, if Morello was executed too? The Contessa's reign would be that much more secure.

'I'll come quietly,' he said. He handed Sofia to a soldier and submitted to be bound. He called out, 'What I do now I do willingly, for the Contessa. Mule, take her to the tower. It's hers now.'

'Keep your place,' Luparelli said. 'The Contessa is coming with us.'

'General, I saved your life today!'

'And your instruction has saved it many more times. I'd return the favour gladly, but you give me no option. Your own circuitous policy has led you here.'

'I don't care what you do to me, but spare her!'

'That will be the Apprentices' decision. I have already said: if you fail to keep peace, we *will* force it on you.'

As Morello, barely conscious, was led to the section of shattered balustrade, the general saw his gunners backing away from the old woman implacably advancing towards them.

'Excuse me, General?'

'This isn't the time for prayers, Sister.'

'You're quite right. I am here to hang.'

The Doctor looked around. 'Sister?'

'The Doctor is not the eldest Bardini,' she announced. 'I am.'

'Is this true?' Luparelli said quickly, relieved for an excuse not to execute his old master. 'Very well, set him free. I repay my debts, Doctor.'

'He's taking Sofia!' the Doctor said as the Reverend Mother removed his noose herself.

'You've earned a traitor's death, little brother,' she said quietly, 'but you must live a little longer.'

She put the noose around her own neck, tightened it. 'Until Sofia returns, Rasenna needs you. I've *seen* it.'

Luparelli mounted up. 'My God, what a sorry mess. Let's get on with it. Take the prisoner.'

Sofia regained consciousness as she was being slung onto a horse.

The Doctor had to be restrained as he cried out, 'You can't do this!'

Sofia screamed at him, 'This is what you wanted, isn't it? Damn you!'

'Sofia, I *never* meant for this to happen – everything I did, I did for you, *everything*! Bardini, flags up!'

The northsiders stayed frozen. The fight had decided for them.

As Luparelli rode over to the Doctor and knocked him out with a heavy boot to the jaw, the Reverend Mother, standing beside Quintus Morello, said softly, 'Don't be afraid, child.'

Behind them, two solders awaited the order.

'Sister!'

'You only need faith,' the nun said, taking Morello's hand.

'No!' Sofia screamed.

The Concordians mounted up.

'Thus perish the enemies of Concord.' The general stopped to spit into the river. 'Waste of a damn good horse.'

Sofia watched the black flags fade as she was led through the carnage of Piazza Luna, and the Lion watched her go as impassively as it had watched the last disaster fall on Rasenna.

PART II:

CONCEPTION

Verily, verily, I say unto thee, except a man be born of water and of the spirit, he cannot enter the kingdom of God.

Saul 58:15

CHAPTER 40

As the Guild grew, so did the Curia's concern at its influence. Seeing a rival church in the Guild, and in Natural Philosophy a rival faith, the Cardinals reviewed the *Discourse* for evidence of Heresy, composing their treacherous arguments even as the Guild's foremost minds developed the Wave at their behest. The Wave's remarkable success confirmed that the time had come to act. In the cold autumn of Forty-Six, Bernoulli was called before the Holy Inquisition and charged with *Deifying Reason*. They accused him with his own words: his impious presumption that nothing was unknowable[21].

The fashionable consensus that the Curia were tools of an aristocracy who saw the Guild as a rival élite is not only cynical but simplistic. This philosophical clash was genuine. Before Bernoulli,

---

[21] With such hypocrisy was the revolution nourished. Consider: the same Curia that commanded Bernoulli to make the Wave subsequently characterised it as an usurpation of God. The same Curia employed Natural Philosophy when it suited them. The same Curia's theologians were pleased to use Pythagoras' description of the flawed Third dimension as a mathematical explanation of Man's fall, a practice that Bernoulli gently reproves in the *Discourse* as 'unsound'.

most of what the Curia was pleased to call Natural Philosophy was superstition buttressed with feeble mathematics. Though Bernoulli cast much aside, there was much that he kept. For example, he found Johannes of Palermo's *Laws of Attraction* correct, up to a point. Difficult as it is to see from our luminous present, it was this idea of conditional truth that was truly iconoclastic, truly insidious.

When Bernoulli's devoted Apprentices urged him to flee, he refused, believing it was his duty as a Natural Philosopher as much as a Citizen to speak what he knew to be true. Clergy and Nobility packed the Senate, eager to see this upstart Engineer brought low. Bernoulli was harangued by a parade of Cardinals who charged that Philosophical Relativism led inexorably to Blasphemy. If Truth is not a constant, what then is Good? What is Evil? Variables too?[22] Finally Bernoulli was asked to affirm Divine Authority and replied:

> *The Lord is omnipotent and infinite and the Destiny He has writ is immutable. Up to a point.*

It was a trap, of course, for the Inquisition. Bernoulli knew that his trial would gather all his enemies. The coup began in an orgy of explicable but perhaps immoderate violence. While belated Noble resistance was crushed in the city, praetorians stormed the Senate.

> *Senators, Necessity may be the Mother of Invention but she is also the Mother of War. I listen to her voice most intently.*

So began the last, somewhat rambling, address the Senate heard,

---

[22] Choice examples of the Scholastic category-mistakes that impeded philosophical progress for centuries.

punctuated by screams and cheers from the streets. The climax revealed a hitherto private mysticism:

Hear me, Senators and know History's certainty. History has no allies. History requires no preparation, no tact, no caution. It needs none. Its will is Law, that you think it Right or Wrong matters not. None of you know what is necessary. I know it. I do it. Stand against me, you stand against a flood. Necessity and I, together we'll drown all. I tell you I am Time's Executor. I am History's end. Yield to me!

Shaking and sweating, pale and overwrought, the Senate's new Master collapsed into fever. The Revolution was complete, the Re-Formation just beginning[23].

---

[23] When the first proscription list began with Senator Tremellius' name, speculation began that he was manipulated from the start. Right or wrong, the truth is the Re-Formation consumed its Author.

CHAPTER 41

Tap

Tap

Tap

She woke, shivering on metal, into dark silence disturbed only by the ceaseless drip. It smelled like . . . *nothing.* In place of Rasenna's noisome blend of spice and sweat and blood was a sterile absence: a ghost-trace of iron, bitter at the throat. She began to explore the darkness, but soon stopped. It was a cold world, and greasy to the touch.

She couldn't much remember recent events except one, and that one was impossible, a poisoned whisper from a bad dream: *he could not be dead.* She could not have been here long: her jaw still ached where the Doc had punched it, and there was another, fresher, pain at the back of her head. She was still too weak to stand, so she lay back and listened to the drip, as the journey from Rasenna came back in fragments . . .

*

. . . of rock fell into the sea, knocked lose by the carriage wheels. She watched their escape with envy through a small vent in her mobile creaking cage.

After the Twelfth left Rasenna, Sofia was sent north in a small convoy – either General Luparelli found prisoners burdensome, or this particular prisoner was wanted in the capital. Most of the journey was by narrow winding roads along the coast, avoiding Rasenna and other towns. It was late autumn and the rolling Etrurian landscape was frozen into austerity. They travelled north until they came to a place with leafless trees covered in thick dust, the land stripped of life by something more permanent than winter. Sickened by it, Sofia concentrated on keeping warm inside.

It was snowing when she caught her first glimpse of Concord. It was really two cities, the new built on the corpse of the old. Sandstone walls and the towers on the periphery were all that remained of the city defeated by Rasenna at Montaperti, and they were left behind as the carriage crossed an immense bridge lined with flags and torches. It was recognisably from the same architectural school as Giovanni's, but where his had elegant human proportions, this had been built for titans. They approached a wall of steel-blue plates overlapping like fish-scales; they rippled open with the crunching chime of a phalanx, an echo of the many legions that had marched through it over the decades.

They were woodsmen once, so Giovanni had told her,

and she could see how they had replaced forests with soaring columns capped with steel branching into coiled limbs. Narrow, endless stairs connected the old city of earth and wood to the dark white city of steel and marble. She counted scores of aqueducts, wide as rivers, all flowing from the same source: the mountain that dominated the city centre like a decapitated giant, looming black and baleful. Looking irrelevant amidst its jagged peaks were the networked towers of the Engineers' Guild, minute parasites on an indifferent behemoth. From the mountain's summit there rose up an awful black cathedral, a fell idol looking down on its wretched worshippers without love, without pity, as if it was not the interloper, as if it had always been here and Man himself were the aberration. She had never seen anything like it – but like any Etrurian, she knew its name, for it could only be *that* tower, more ambitious even than Nimrod's: this was the Beast itself, the Molè Bernoulliana.

Only the mountain on which it stood rivalled the Molè's spiralling height. Its smoky-green triple-dome was capped by a savagely tapering needle stabbing the sky. Its array of buttresses was festooned with entangled wires: the web of an army of blind spiders, toiling away for mad centuries . . .

. . . and here, memory became confused as the carriage door opened and a hood was thrown at her. She had been transported somewhere else, this time by boat, then she was led up steps and into a large open space – she could tell that by the way her footsteps sounded. The only voices were hushed – guards conferring, she supposed. Though her hands had been bound together, they were otherwise free, and she'd begun to lift the hood when the blow came from behind.

Then darkness. Then silence . . .

Tap

Tap

Tap

Tap

And now she was here, wherever *here* was. She could feel no seams in the rough stone walls, so either the individual bricks were huge, or the whole cell had been carved from rock. As her eyes became more accustomed to the darkness she thought she discerned light coming weakly from one wall. Crawling closer, she found a large metal door with a window that might have been large enough to squeeze through, but for the thick iron bar bisecting it. She grabbed the bar and pulled herself up. As she looked out, she sneezed, and it echoed in the space above and below. She cursed the unaccustomed length of her hair – it would never dry in this place. Already it had taken moisture from the air till it could absorb no more, and now it straggled lankly round her neck and down her back.

She thudded her head on the bar.

'Guess not,' she whispered to herself.

Before she could inspect the exterior, her legs gave out. The ground was damp, but she was too exhausted to care. She fell again into darkness . . .

. . . and was woken by an agonised groan of metal. The only machines she had ever heard were those Giovanni had used on the bridge, but they had sounded nothing like this, mountains of rust scraping together, like animals in pain, too tired to scream. She lifted herself to the window again, stooping, because of the low roof, and peered into the darkness.

Outside, above and below, there was nothing, but in the centre of this empty space was a glass column, thick as an old oak, and beyond that an endless curved wall, dotted with other cells like hers, hundreds of them, all set in a great spiral in an inverted conical pit. As her eyes grew used to the twilight gloom she could see the pit was not bottomless, as it had first appeared. It ended about thirty rows below in a dark lake.

She studied the wall across the void, and after a while she realised that the rows of cells were moving – very slowly – and that was most likely the cause of the groaning. That mystery solved, Sofia started to wonder if she was alone, but that question was answered quickly enough when the groaning stopped and the screaming started. Peering across the void, she caught a glimpse of a bearded, skeletal figure, dancing around his cell. There were other people too, and they were all running to their cell windows, thrusting out bony arms as if to grasp something. Listening closely, she could make out a variety of dialects, some prayers, some blasphemies, but mostly gibberish.

Strange, she thought. The movement wasn't terrible, merely disconcerting.

Another noise, like a bee's hum, came from the lake below, and she saw a light beneath the water, like a long blue-glowing worm, writhing with spastic motion. The volume and pitch of the hum rose till it sounded like swarming wasps, and the screaming correspondingly erupted into frenzy. Sofia could see the occupant of a cell in the row just below hers: his head was bleeding, but still he kept beating at it with his fists.

The light broke the surface, like the sparks Giovanni had used to repel buio with, but engorged to lightning bolts, and circled the bottom row, then the next row, then the next. Some cells it skipped over, others it briefly illuminated; Sofia could see no discernible pattern to its erratic movements, other than that it was moving up the spiral of cells, and coming ever-closer to her row.

As it got nearer, she could smell burning hair and ozone intermingled.

The light shot though the row below her, skipped the bleeding man's cell and stopped at his neighbour's before shooting on to the next row. Sofia had only a moment to witness his rapturous relief before her cell was flooded with light—

—and *pain*. There was no heat, yet her body burned, and she clenched her teeth together so she could not scream; she would not given them that satisfaction—

—and it was gone, as suddenly as it had come.

For a while there was numbness, then, as heartless as a sunrise, pain returned, this time coming from inside, from the space between her bones, growing until gums and scalp and eyes *screamed* . . .

Inside her cell there was only the drip, but outside there were two distinct sounds: the ecstasy of those the light had spared, and the sobbing of those it had chosen. Before long they merged unintelligibly. Sofia cried because the pain was too real for a nightmare. She was in the belly of the Beast, and Giovanni – there was no hiding from it – had drowned in the Irenicon. She had pinned her foolish wish, that he would stay in Rasenna forever, to the Madonna. It had been granted.

CHAPTER 42

'Come down!'

He recognised the expectant note in Cat's whine: the stupid creature was waiting for him up there. He stumbled over a pile of dirty plates to get to the ladder. His steps became slower the higher he mounted, and at the last rung, he stopped altogether. He looked up warily as snow floated through the square of cold, cloudless sky. What else was up there?

Rasenna. If he could see it, it could see him. He was naked and exposed, his hand no longer hidden. They'd taken Sofia, and with her his excuse for his crimes, and without that his past loomed, a monstrous reflection.

'Starve for all I care,' he mumbled, retreated down the ladder and crawled back under his bedsheets.

The Doctor had abandoned his perch for so long that many assumed he was dead. No one took to mourning: the quarrel with Sofia and the truth of Little Frog's murder had sent fissures though the workshop; younger students stayed away and older bandieratori deserted. He avoided mirrors. His shabby appearance had once been affectation; it was no longer.

'Go away,' he growled to the knock at his chamber door.

'I *need* a doctor.' The girl's tone told him that she wouldn't leave this time.

He swore, crawled out of bed and opened the door. 'Good morning, Sister.'

'Morning was a couple of hours ago,' said Lucia.

'What can I do for you?'

'You *are* a doctor, aren't you? As well as a murderer, I mean.'

'Sister, look—'

'You look!' Lucia jabbed a finger to his chest. 'The Reverend Mother died to save your worthless neck. She must have had a reason – maybe it was so you could save a life *worth* saving.'

'Whose?'

The novice lost some of her assurance as she answered, 'Someone who isn't ready to die yet.'

Gaetano was woken by the angry hiss of snow falling on smouldering wood. He crawled out from the debris and saw the blackened shell that was all that remained of Palazzo Morello: the Dragon that consumed itself. He had been abandoned by all, but he would stay – let the snow fall as it might; he would keep a fire burning.

While clearing the fallen timbers from the workshop floor he came upon a mirror, cracked and buckled. He wiped off the ash and set it against a wall where he could see its warped reflection when practising. When he was resting, he spent silent hours studying his new face. The scars were the climax of a career of low deeds, a liberating confirmation: finally the outside matched the inside. He would share his epiphany with Rasenna. She would see her true reflection and know her true name was Hell.

He recovered old strength with a new clarity. The weight of doubt and guilt died with his family, burned away with his home. The succession was clear. The last Scaligeri was gone, so the last Morello would rule Rasenna. He had obeyed for too long. It was time to be obeyed.

Mulling on fortune's caprices, the Doctor walked out of the shade of the Baptistery into the bright snow-covered garden. Owning this part of Rasenna would have given him immense satisfaction once; before he'd been shown his miniature empire for the illusion it was. He'd thought himself strong, yet he had proved incapable of keeping the one promise worth keeping.

Lucia came from the chapel. 'Doctor.' She had become somewhat less hostile when she saw the effect of his ministrations. The Doctor didn't blame her for being hard on him; the Reverend Mother was the only mother Lucia had known, and in the passage of a day her whole world changed. His sister's death had dropped all responsibility for the Order on this slight girl's shoulders. That might explain her obsession with saving this patient; if they could wrestle just one innocent from Death's grasp, then the world was not completely unjust.

'How is he today?'

'Little better, still feverish, babbling all the time. He wants to make his confession.'

The Doctor rubbed his freshly shaved chin. 'It'll do him good. When the mind's at ease, the body follows.'

'You don't understand: he wants to confess to you.'

The Doctor frowned. 'Delirious—?'

'Clearly!' Lucia snapped, then continued more calmly, 'but whatever miracle saved him from the buio, if this fever doesn't break soon . . .'

'It'll break. I'll talk to him.'

The Doctor gave dietary instructions and reminded her to rest too. More than once he had glimpsed her shedding tears over her sleeping patient, when she thought she was alone. Perhaps it was more than ordinary compassion.

In the chapel, a young novice was patting the patient's brow with a damp cloth. The Doctor recognised the daughter of his old ally.

'He keeps asking for Sofia. I didn't tell him she was—'

'We don't know she is, child. Hostages are most useful when they're alive, you know.'

'I hadn't thought of that,' said Isabella, brightening for a moment, before remembering her duties. 'He's still burning. I try to cool him down, but he soaks the water up like a sponge.'

'You're doing a good job. Leave him with me for a while.'

He watched her go. It was good to see youth bearing

tragedies that broke their elders. If they were Rasenna's future, perhaps there *was* hope – for this patient at least.

'Giovanni, wake up!' he commanded.

After the Concordians left, the bridge was not empty for long. Fabbro ventured south to visit his deceased partner's son. They left Rasenna together on what Pedro at least considered a fool's errand.

'Maybe it is,' Fabbro said equably, 'but what have we to lose?'

Pedro couldn't argue with that and, when they found Giovanni washed up on a bank downstream, Fabbro took it as Divine Providence.

And perhaps he was right, for that first crossing was the beginning of a flood. Under the Signoria's watch, Rasenneisi might – *would* – have been more circumspect, but both Families were underground, so the Small People found reasons to cross each day, and almost immediately partnerships sprang up, both conjugal and financial, and though the results were sometimes chaotic, they were, often as not, profitable too.

It was the giddy optimism of a world starting over, and it felt wrong to hide away from it, but if nothing else, Pedro owed his father a period of mourning. He tried to find meaning in Vettori's last words as he sat in the window of Tower Vanzetti – more cramped than he remembered – and focused his old magnifier on Fabbro. The merchant was overseeing the unloading of another shipment of wool as if nothing had changed, as if he still had a partner to weave it. Of course, Fabbro would soon find a replacement.

Some might think it strange that his father's old partner – his old friend – just kept working, but Pedro knew it was the merchant's way of dealing with grief. He looked around at his father's silent looms and, suddenly, snapped the scope shut. Why *should* Fabbro find a replacement?

That morning, Pedro visited the towers of every Vanzetti worker and asked them why they had not returned to work. They told him the same thing: they had assumed there was no work to go to.

Giovanni's eyes took a long time to focus and his voice came from a distant place. 'Doctor,' he croaked, 'I need to confess.'

The Doctor laughed softly. 'For what grave sin, Captain?'

'Sofia thought I was good, but I've blood on my hands, Doctor. That's why the buio didn't take me, they recognised what I am. And now she's—' He tried to rouse himself but fell back.

'Sofia's alive! You're the one who'll die if you don't start eating. You're delirious, that's what's making you say these things.' The Doctor firmly held him down. 'Listen, boy, I've known killers. You're not one.'

Giovanni's eyes fluttered, sinking under again.

The Doctor grabbed him and shook until he became lucid. 'You build bridges for soldiers to march over, that makes you an accomplice, at most. Sofia knew you better than you know yourself. You failed trying to do the right thing. I failed doing all the wrong things; be grateful you don't live with shame like that. And remember, Luparelli saw you drown – to Concord, you *are* dead. I'd give anything for a fresh start like that. I've heard your confession. Here's your penance: Live and help Rasenna. Are you man enough to accept?'

When Giovanni next woke, Lucia was lighting candles around the room.

He coughed. 'He thinks she's alive.'

'He's right.'

'It's not possible. How can you have faith after all that's happened?'

There was a candle in front of the window and its flame trembled in the breeze.

'Did you know the Virgin wasn't special, not at least in the way the Curia imagined?' Lucia said. 'Her conception was soiled with Humanity, just like ours. The Lord chose her because she was strong enough to bear the responsibility – that *grace* made her special.'

Lucia went to the window and moved the candle. 'Sofia's strong too, Giovanni.'

When she looked at him again, he had sunk back into unconscious. '*Madonna*, give us grace,' she whispered. We need it so badly.'

CHAPTER 43

The half-light never changed, so there was no way to tell how long she'd slept, or if it was morning or evening, but she woke to a sound that was becoming familiar: the screaming told her the light had returned. Too weak to move, she lay on the damp floor and watched the drip hard at work, envying its purpose. Was this how the Scaligeri line ended, its last scion's body and mind worn away until nothing was left?

It was just below her row now. She could hear the sudden wails of the chosen. Her eyes shut tight and—

—nothing. The hum moved on. Yesterday and today, the Angel of Death had passed over. The Doc said death should find a warrior ready, but when it came for her, she would either be insensible or too insane to notice.

She looked at the bar in the window. How long had the drip taken to wear that groove in the floor? How long would it take to penetrate metal? She turned her back on the pit and focused on the drip, feeling each drop as it fell, its weight, its speed, its surface tension.

Tap

Tap

Whooooomp KRAK!

Tap

'*Uhhhh—*'

Sofia wasn't sitting where she had been a moment ago. An invisible hand had batted her against the wall. So to move even a single drop, she had to open herself to all its latent force – *impossible* – and yet she had seen the Reverend Mother control an entire glass full without suffering the same fate. It wasn't possible.

ShuuuuDUNK.

The door slowly opened. That seemed impossible too.

She tentatively poked her head out into the void. There was nowhere to go – was it an unsubtle invitation to end it all? Looking down at the lake, she wondered which would kill her first: the cold or the buio.

Her attention was drawn upwards by a screeching sound and she saw a falling star, gleaming inside the glass column. A moment later it was by followed by a scream of torn air. She followed its descent, expecting a splash, but instead, the lake water became agitated, with tremors racing to the centre. The jet shot up to meet the capsule and lifted it, with another surge of power, to Sofia's row.

349

The metallic capsule, like a coffin, but larger, hovered tantalisingly close, though a gap remained.

There was another tremor from the lake and a long metallic panel emerged, pivoting around the glass column. The walkway stopped at the same point, forming a path to the coffin.

With a silent prayer, she stepped out and waited.

Nothing happened. She took a few more steps and the coffin door cracked open like a seed-pod. She decided it might be wiser to observe for a while from her cell, but before she could do anything, the walkway began dropping. There was no time, no option. She had to leap.

When she reached the coffin, its door clamped shut behind her. From inside she saw it was not metal, but thick glass, like the column, almost opaque with scum.

The coffin sank abruptly, pushing gut to gullet, and after a moment, the water rose again to shoot her into darkness. She peered up and saw, falling towards her, a pale body, but as it came closer she realised the scale had deceived her; it wasn't a person but a colossal statue emerging from the blackness as she drew closer. There was no time to study it before the coffin passed by. After a few moments there was light enough to discern a blur of masonry in front of the glass, as if the coffin were ascending some impossibly deep well. The light grew until she was forced to squint; she realised she had grown used to darkness.

The first thing that drew her attention in this new vast

space she was emerging into was, again, the angel – it was the same statue, but this time rising with sword aloft in triumph. There was something comforting about its confident smile. But there was no time for study.

This time when she looked up she saw the approaching interior of a dome, broad as the sky. The roof was decorated by a mural of the Last Judgement; an unusual rendition in that there was an apeish beast consuming sinners at its centre rather than a Madonna rewarding saints. Sofia looked down through the glass at her feet, comprehension dawning. Just as the statues appeared to reflect each other, the pit was *under* the Molè Bernoulliana, inside the black mountain where the aqueducts flowed. The conclusion was impossible, yet inescapable – the Molè had been built twice, first, proudly spiralling skywards, visible to the whole world, and then again as a dark reflection, hidden from all but its architect.

The coffin passed through the mural, swallowed by the devil, and emerged into another, smaller, dome. Her speed was diminishing, so now there was time to see its curved walls were lined with books beyond counting, so many that even the dome had insufficient shelf-space. More books were scattered across the floor and stacked in tall heaps. In the midst of this forest of words stood a plump little man. He waved eagerly as the coffin flew by. Sofia didn't wave back – her attention was fixed on an old-fashioned banner hanging from a tall narrow bookshelf behind him.

Then she was gone, into the third and final dome. Here the journey ended.

A port closed beneath and when the coffin had settled, its door hissed open. In front of her there was a space between two great stone tables to the left and right, and beyond that a great pendulum made long bisecting sweeps of the room, flushing dead air towards her. She stepped out and stumbled – she was dizzy, but it was more than that: the surface was rhythmically moving, shifting both up and down and from side to side. She was inside a boundless clock; the walls were not really walls but moving parts of an engine. Man-dwarfing cogs made slow revolutions, bleeding black grease and cracking into each other with explosive violence.

Behind the pendulum, at the summit of a short set of steps and standing in front of a vast slate board, were three figures, all dressed in the flowing robes and mitres of the Curia they had overthrown, identical but for colour. The boy wore yellow; the youth, orange; and the young man on the left wore a red so vivid he seemed to be ablaze. He was writing numbers rapidly on the slate while the others watched respectfully.

These were Bernoulli's three wise men: the Third, Second and First Apprentices.

She took a step away from the coffin and rested her hand against one of the tables. When she was sure she wasn't going to be sick, she announced herself. 'My Lords.'

Her voice sounded a small thing against the cacophony,

yet with a screech of murdered chalk, the scribbling stopped. The man in red stood back with his colleagues to examine the work. In the ensuing silence, Sofia glanced down and saw on the table a large map of Etruria and the surrounding Tyrrhenian Sea. Reverse the colours and the peninsula would look like a single long river flowing into the ocean of Europa. She was unused to maps, accurate ones at least, but Concord's location was obvious: all roads led to it, all rivers from it. The smoky green of Concord dominated the north; the south was of varied colours. Painted markers like chess pieces dotted the map. On the other table, there was a more detailed map of the south.

Presently, the man in red nodded. He remained while the boy and the adolescent ascended. They didn't slow their pace as they crossed the pendulum's path, assured that they commanded Time even as they commanded Etruria.

They circled her silently for a moment.

The boy spoke first. 'Sofia Scaligeri.'

Before she could respond, a sarcastic voice behind her added, 'The "Contessa" of Rasenna. Do you know where you are?'

The Beast. They wanted to hear her say it. She replied simply, 'Yes.'

The boy continued, 'Cooperate, Contessa, and within a month you will be fighting. Rasenneisi rise quickly in the legion ranks. You'd prefer that to dying in a cell, surely?'

'What do you want?' she asked.

'The truth – your version. The engineer who built Rasenna's bridge. Who was he?'

Sofia turned to face the adolescent. 'You sent him, you should know.'

'We know what we know. We want to know what he told you.'

'He told the truth,' Sofia said. Her voice was unexpectedly loud and the last word echoed around the chamber.

The adolescent chuckled. 'What do Rasenneisi know of Truth? Have you heard rumours?'

'His name was Captain Giovanni.'

'We know that. What was his surname?'

'*SenzaChiama*, like the rest of you. He had none.'

'Think, Contessa,' the boy said.

'He's dead, so what does it matter?'

'What's the point of protecting a dead man?'

Sofia bowed her head, clenched her fists. *What should I say, Giovanni?*

Why did he confide about his father's execution? She knew how feuds worked. Any surviving relatives would be endangered if she revealed anything.

'He said engineers have no name. The Guild was his family.'

The adolescent laughed outright at this, a grotesque sound. 'Was he angry about that?'

It hurt to remember at all, and to remember like this,

in this place, was torture. Was that their aim, another turn of the screw?

The boy asked seriously, 'Why did he kill the Concordian boys?'

'He didn't.'

'He confessed to General Luparelli.'

'That was a lie.'

'You said he told the truth,' the adolescent interrupted. 'Were they interfering with his work?'

'He wasn't like that.'

'Like what?'

'Like you. He was ashamed of Concord, if you must know.'

'Of Concord, or of himself?'

'He had nothing to be ashamed of. He was *good*.'

'Good? He killed no one?'

'He— There was an accident.'

Before Sofia could say more, the boy asked, 'Why did he dredge up the Lion statue?'

The heat and noise made it impossible to concentrate. She stopped trying to face her questioner, focused instead on answering the question. 'To stop the fighting.'

'And did it?'

'It became worse, didn't it?' the adolescent sneered.

'You're trying to confuse me. Go to Hell!'

'He lied, he murdered his countrymen. Why?'

'Because he loved me!' Sofia screamed.

Her outburst echoed around the engine-room while the

pendulum swung back and forth indifferently. The Apprentices paused a while.

'You can't treat me like this. I am the Contessa Scaligeri!'

'We don't make such distinctions here. So, murder is a romantic gesture in Rasenna?'

'You can't understand,' she said.

'Why?'

'Because Natural Philosophy can't help you here! Giovanni was *good*. He died doing right – or trying to. You can try to scare me, confuse me, hurt me if you want; it won't change the truth. He died a Rasenneisi!'

She turned her back to them. 'Lock me back up. I'm through with your questions.'

'You think he loved you?' a voice like an ill-tuned instrument asked.

Sofia turned and saw the man in red coming down the stairs.

'What if he lied?'

As he came closer, she began backing away.

He leaned in and whispered, 'You must have considered the possibility?'

With a scream, she threw a fist. He did not block the punch; he was simply elsewhere when it came. She tried again, and again the First Apprentice avoided her, then he tapped her chest with a rigid palm and she flew backwards and slammed into the coffin. Before the doors shut, she heard them conversing. It was like a person talking to himself.

'She knows nothing,' said the boy.

'*He* knew nothing! His death has no consequences, just as his life had none. As I told you, First Apprentice,' the adolescent said irritably.

'Be not complacent,' the tuneless voice said, 'Consequence is the final mystery.'

The porthole opened beneath the coffin; a star fell into darkness.

That night, the blue light returned. There was no mark on her door; it simply deigned to pass over. Tomorrow it might not; an inconsistent torturer was worse than one who followed rules, however harsh.

She dragged herself to the door. The pit-bottom lake was getting closer day by day. This was a more subtle torture; with every turn of this giant screw those chosen were robbed of strength and those spared, of hope. It must have another purpose – just using it to petrify doomed men was too petty a reason for this remarkable engine, Sofia thought; logically, its effect on individual prisoners must be secondary. And yet sometimes logic was a poor tool. Her senses had become keener since her training, and this amount of fear and despair *was* powerful. The very air quivered with it.

She looked back at the wall she'd been thrown against in her last attempt to control the drip. The nun was not only able to feel the current, she could control it. She'd said it took years of mediation. Sofia didn't have that kind of time, but she wasn't resigned to being a cog for what little of it she had left. She sat down cross-legged, as if she were back in the Baptistery, and let her breath mirror the drip's slow rhythm. She gathered focus and asked the stillness, *Where do I go now?* She already knew the answer was

Down

into the Pit, where something pale, ancient and dark writhed in slow anticipation. A tentacle uncoiled. It was more powerful in this place. The Beast was where the Darkness incubated, the loci of all misery, where the buio were churned and remade.

This is Fear.

She wrenched open her eyes with a scream. There was no escape, within or without. All doors were locked.

CHAPTER 44

Better to be caged, she thought when her door remained shut the next time the coffin appeared. This time, however, when the grimy capsule opened a fat little man – maybe the bearded creature she had seen surrounded by book-stacks in the second dome – leapt gingerly onto the plat-form and looked around with the curiosity of a newborn, a queer impression enhanced by the rosy gloss of his skin which looked soft as undercooked meat.

In age he looked close to sixty, and although he was dressed too expensively to be a notary, he looked like one to Sofia. Beneath squinting eyes his neat beard circled a small mouth bent up into a nervous smile around which his fingers played; his hands were neither a fighter's or worker's – a scholar then.

He glanced at his solemn escort from time to time as if seeking approval. The youngest Apprentice was more accustomed to the pit and his attention didn't wander as he led the way to her cell. Sofia instinctively took a step back on seeing the boy in yellow approach. The boy's large hands and sure strength reminded Sofia powerfully of the

Doc: he took his time, but was confident in his power. He had a pallor strange to see on one in such obvious rude health. This period of his education was evidentially conducted indoors, far from the kindly eye of the sun.

Sofia couldn't help but think of an oversized infant accompanied by a diminutive adult.

'Has it revolved today?' the little man asked.

'Probably not,' said the boy wearily.

'I wonder,' he began with a nervous titter, 'would it be possible, do you suppose, to see it?'

'The current's activated by a random algorithm.'

The fat man blinked innocently.

'I can't turn it off,' the boy said slowly. 'If we're here, we'll be shocked too.'

'Oh, I so wanted to see it!'

'Well, there's a manual switch for each cell.'

He clapped his hands. 'Really? May I? They – I mean, *you* – wouldn't mind, would you?'

The boy sighed. 'Why not question her first?'

'Oh! Yes, capital idea! Hello, hello in there?'

Sofia looked at the little face peering in the window.

'Do I have the great honour of greeting the Contessa Sofia Scaligeri?'

'What do you want?'

'Ha! Direct, isn't she, Third Apprentice! In a word, Contessa, to be as forthright as you manage to be without apparently trying, what I want is a thing, a very small thing, useless to you, but most precious to—'

'Names,' said the boy.

'I didn't have any for you. I don't have any for him.'

The little man chuckled, a sound like a blasphemy in this hopeless place.

'Not that kind of information, Contessa, oh no! What did the Apprentices want to know, secret battle plans? Troop positions and such? Oh no, I leave war to the experts. Wars start to interest me only when the contestants have been dead for a couple of decades. Which is to say, I am merely a humble historian. Though perhaps, ha ha, I should say, with all modesty, that "merely" does not do my status full justice; I am, you see, rather well known in Concord – I dare say in all Etruria.'

He drew himself up to his full height, though the difference was hardly noticeable. 'I am Count Titus Tremellius Pomptinus,' he announced, 'Knight of the Order of Saint Jorge, Laureate of the Empire, and Librarian of the Imperial Record.'

He leaned closer, his voice dropping to a confidential whisper as he went on, 'I should add that several Tremellius generations were Concordian gonfaloniere – of course, that was when the office still existed!'

Sofia backed away to escape the historian's breath. She suspected his performance was not only for her benefit.

The historian's eyes bulged dramatically and he turned to the boy. 'I mention that only as historical record.'

'Fine.'

Tremellius' pudgy fingers played with his beard. 'It is

relevant, you see: she's a noble too, so this will make her at ease with me.'

He didn't seem to notice or care that she could hear every word. He turned back with an unctuous smile.

'Forgive my manners; we've become very proletarian these days. This is Torbidda, our current Third Apprentice!'

'We've met,' the boy said.

'Ah, well then, you know already what a tremendously bright young fellow he is. Someday he'll be First Apprentice, captaining our great ship of state, and you'll remember my kindness then, won't you?' He reached out as if to grab a cheek, then thought better of it.

'He helps me to hold back the deluge. Ceaselessly! It pours ceaselessly in from the world's every corner – Europa too, some of them write, you know – so much information: tax forms, geographical and mineralogical surveys, political reports, census and books, so many books – in so many languages! The babble of the Hebrews I learned, the dusty tongues of Aegyptus, Grecia and Etrusca, I exhumed, unwrapped and conjured life into. Then came the hard bit, wrestling sense from them! My masters need information on so many subjects, and Contessa—'

Sofia drew back as he leaned in confidentially and whispered, 'They are *so* impatient!' Crossly, he added, 'I do it all alone! Well, perhaps not *all* alone.' Again he reached out to scruff the Apprentice's hair, and again, he changed his mind.

'As I mentioned, I am also a historian, and it is History

that brings me here. And you to me, Contessa, in a manner
of speaking, ha ha! We are all moved by its current; our
tragedy is that we only become aware of it after its passage.
Just like the Wave over Rasenna – you never saw it coming,
did you? Ha ha! There's still so much to understand about
Concord's rebirth, how it came to be, who drove it and
why. I of course have coursing blue blood in my veins,
Contessa, like you, so you will assume I am, like you,
biased against engineers . . .' He glanced at the boy.

'Well, you would be wrong! Quite wrong! Knowledge
enlightens me, gives me the perspective to cast off the
shackles of class consciousness and rejoice at liberation.
The true value of the Concordian Empire is not land or
slaves or new towns to tax, no, no, no! It is the Empire of
Knowledge we have built. What was dark, Girolamo
Bernoulli illuminated; that which was mystery, Nature
and the Elements, we now understand, and in understanding, we control. The World, from Rasenna to Gubbio,
has been flooded with our knowledge.'

'What do you want, fat man?'

'The proverbial blunt Rasenneisi. Is this the switch, Third
Apprentice?'

The boy nodded. Tremellius turned the lever and Sofia's
cell was suddenly flooded with blue light. She fell, immobile, to the ground.

Tremellius giggled uncontrollably as he looked in.
'Contessa, the Apprentices don't need you. *I* do. You'll die
soon without me. I can give you food and, if you cooperate

– think of this! – I can get you transferred to another prison!' His innocent face was free of malice, simply happy.

'I ask only for names, dear child: sons, fathers, grand-fathers. I am writing a history of Etruria and you are the Scaligeri heir. I expect that you know all the branches of Rasenna's family trees; I simply require a guide, to help me navigate that tangled forest. It's not going to hurt anyone. The people I'm interested in are long past harm. What say you, Contessa?'

Sofia tried to answer but only succeeded in drooling. '*Guhsplurl*.'

'She'll be like this for an hour or so,' said the Third Apprentice.

'Really? Oh *merda* – you might have warned me! I wanted to begin today!' Tremellius leaned into the window. 'I can see you're tired. Sleep on it, dear child. Dream dreams of gold and freedom.'

Next day, he came alone.

'Eat slowly,' he said as he handed a plate of dry chicken and hard bread to her.

Sofia placed the food on the floor. 'Aren't you going to hit the switch?'

'Oh, an accident, my dear! This old place just needs main-tenance. Bernoulli said the body is the perfect machine, and you need maintenance too, ha ha! You must recover your strength. Let's start over. Look! I brought a gift.'

He handed a rolled-up cloth though the barred window.

'Now, I'm not silly enough to give a Rasenneisi a stick to go with a banner, but look, Contessa! The black and gold! Don't you recognise Scaligeri colours? You see, I understand that blood matters. I knew it would give you some comfort to have it back, finally. Aren't you going to unroll it?'

'A pillow. Thanks.' She threw it, still rolled up, in the corner. 'You want information? So do I. How is it that the Apprentices know Water Style?'

The historian looked around cautiously as if expecting to find an Apprentice at his shoulder. 'Well, they don't call it *that* any more, but I understand that Bernoulli taught it to his First Apprentice, the First Apprentice taught the Second, and so on.'

'But how did *Bernoulli* learn it?'

'You could say he taught himself. After the Re-Formation, the clergy weren't exactly cooperative. You see, it's said that men were originally taught by angels—'

'I've heard that one,' she said, crunching on the bread.

'Like so many old stories, once freed of religious trappings it was explicable by Natural Philosophy. Bernoulli speculated these angels were pseudonaiades.'

'But the Wave *made* the buio.'

'Or perhaps it only brought them to our attention. In any case, in controlling rivers, Bernoulli also controlled the pseudonaiades.'

'Tortured them, you mean.' Sofia felt a strange foreboding. 'You're saying all engineers know it?'

The historian smiled. 'Dear, silly child, of course not. Only the very gifted are even capable of learning it, and no one ever mastered it like Bernoulli. It's taught in some elementary form to all cadets who become Apprenticeship candidates, which, I suppose, isn't many.' He sighed wistfully. 'Everything's less romantic these days, isn't it?'

Sofia looked up from the food. 'If the body's the perfect machine, why build a machine to ruin it? That's what this is, right?'

'Only the Apprentices know the Molè's purpose,' he said grudgingly, then smiled. 'Besides, Bernoulli also said, "To know man, dissect man," which I've always taken to mean that you never truly appreciate something until you've taken it apart, ha ha, rather like History.'

'Don't you ever think for yourself? What makes Bernoulli so special?'

Tremellius took the question as a great joke; his jowls started wobbling as he chuckled. 'Ha ha! Where to begin? Bernoulli cast off the superstition that previously shackled us. I speak of Man, you understand, not merely Concordians. When the Molè falls and Time grinds the mountains to sand, Bernoulli's proofs will remain inviolate.'

Sofia let him drone on until she had emptied the plate. She was still ravenous, but the food had given her a clearer head. 'All right, what do you want to know?' she asked.

*

Days ground by. The drip still fell into its groove, but Sofia had given up trying to stop it. The Apprentices had given up on her too; they probably assumed she was dead, Tremellius joked. Most prisoners didn't last to the water.

That was for the best. If there was to be any chance of escape, the Apprentices' attentions had to be elsewhere. Nobody was coming to rescue her, certainly not the Doc; without Quintus Morello or the Reverend Mother to restrain him, Rasenna was his, as he had planned all along. Giovanni would have come for her, but he was dead.

Tremellius visited daily, feeding her in return for information. After Sofia ran out of Rasenneisi genealogies, she began to invent obscure dynasties, until Tremellius finally became suspicious. In desperation, Sofia asked about his writing.

It was like a dam breaking.

Gurgling with pride, the fat little man told Sofia his book would be *unique*. 'Bernoulli is naturally the central figure of my History, but mark me, Contessa, mine will be a realistic and sober portrait, with dark strokes when necessary.'

Feigning enthusiasm was unnecessary; Tremellius was enthusiastic enough for both of them. 'We live in a new age because of him, Contessa! Think of the strength it took for a mediaeval mind to thrust us into this future. How he lifted us onto his giant shoulders is the subject of my tale. Most men are shaped by History's current. Girolamo Bernoulli was a man who stood outside it.'

CHAPTER 45

The ill-fated attempt of Thirteen and Fifty-two to reverse our glorious revolution was once too controversial to pronounce upon. No longer[24].

The years spent perfecting Wave technology[25], preparing for the next test, were years in which Bernoulli neglected his family, but it is churlish to ask if things might have turned out differently if he had been less remote a father; a lesser man could not have been father to his city. Responsibility for his son's fate is his son's alone.

---

[24] Which makes the current generation of Historians' willingness to repeat old myths and Imperial propaganda doubly disappointing. Our vocation is to doubt, to fearlessly probe and dig, however unsettling what we unearth may be to earthly power. Our first duty is to Truth.

[25] Concord had been locked in a mortal struggle with Rasenna, so while Rasenneisi bewailed their fate in Fourth-seven, they understood it had been earned. Gubbio, an unimportant backwater, had maintained neutrality throughtout the conflict, however, it was

Jacopo Bernoulli was a weak man, lacking talent but overburdened with ambition. His father was surrounded by the first generation of great Engineers, but Jacopo, raised in the shadow of power, had more in common with the first generation of disenfranchised nobles. It is true that a clique of opportunists exploited his credulity, but we may justly condemn him for taking up the dagger. And Justice was watching, for another family member betrayed Jacopo in turn.

Thus is treachery repaid with treachery.

Might things have turned out differently? Bernoulli thought so. His philosophy, harshly cynical in the bloom of youth, took on even darker cast after the scandal, trial, execution and attendant purge:

You seek Truth? Look not to Love nor to Art nor to Philosophy. Look to the tragedy in which we are bit players. Look to Nature. Look to beasts tearing the flesh of their young. Our bodies vying with themselves. War is the

deemed to be a perfect site for the second test of the Wave. Without any formal declaration of war, Concord sent a Wave substantially more destructive than that which divided Rasenna thirteen years before. It incurred universal censure and, more seriously, created the Frank-Anglo pact that has so protracted our current Europan war. Filippo Argenti, the second First Apprentice, criticised it as 'a callous failure, technically and politically'. The drain of resources halted Imperial expansion at a crucial period, and though Gubbio was extensively studied, the after-effects remain mysterious.

perpetual truth of Nature. Nature is War. War is natural.
Its fruits are beauty, grace and harmony.

Here we detect the important philosophical shift where a war of expansion is recast as a crusade[26].

---

[26] Taken from Bernoulli's address on the Re-Formation's fifth anniversary. This subtle revision of the meaning of *Re-Formation*, the expansion of Concordian society rather than its perfection, became more pronounced over the decade. By Fifty-nine it had transmuted into the bellicosity that made the second test possible. That is not to give credence to the theory that Gubbio's purpose *was* Gubbio; personally, the present Author finds trite the fashion of describing the *test* as a *demonstration*. That Concord has not since employed the Wave proves nothing.

CHAPTER 46

The Bardini workshop was an empty battleground. There was no longer violence, but neither were there scenes of chivalry and courage. The Doctor practised flag-sets. He was rusty and distracted, and everything was harder when one needed to think, but the old senses were still sharp enough to know when he was being watched.

'Good to see you vertical for a change, Captain,' he said when he'd finished the set.

'Thanks to you, Doctor.'

'Thank Lucia, she—'

'No – I wouldn't have recovered if you hadn't told me Sofia was alive.'

'It wasn't a trick. There's no reason to stop hoping.'

'Concord takes hostages. No matter how well towns behave, it doesn't return them. They keep prisoners alive if they're useful, but Sofia has nothing to interest them. Concord no longer needs hostages, it needs only—' He stopped, his face white.

'Go on.'

'Energy. They'll have put her into the belly of the Beast.'

'What are you going to do?'

'I came to say goodbye. I'm going home.'

'Going to get yourself killed, you mean.'

'Doctor, I *loved* her! Without her—' He paused to collect himself. 'Anyway, I'm going.'

The Doctor studied him for a while. The young man was much changed. He was emaciated, and his skin was pale as a weather-faded fresco, but there was something more. There was no longer that distance; whatever else he was, he was all here, for better or worse.

'You know why my sister took my place in that noose? She told me that Sofia would return to Rasenna some day, and she would need me. That's why the river gave you back. She'll need you too, just like Rasenna needs you now.'

'The Reverend Mother told me things too,' he admitted, 'but after what's happened I don't believe in Destiny. Things just happen. Sofia's not coming back.'

'Come with me, Captain. I want to show you something.'

Cat was waiting on the tower rooftop, whining triumphantly.

'*Madonna, tranquillo,*' the Doctor muttered. He went to the side of the tower and looked down on Rasenna; Giovanni did likewise. The winding streets led his eye to the river, and the bridge bestriding it.

'Looks good, doesn't it?'

'Seems like pride to agree.' There was wonder in

Giovanni's voice. 'It still looks like my plan from here. I didn't think it would. So many details changed in the making.'

'Up here, you see the important things.'

After a moment, the Doctor went on, 'I've seen hundreds of boys become men over the years, seen all grades of talent, all types of character in the workshop. And I've learned that it's not talent or character that makes a real artist, but the *combination*. You've got to have a vision, but the greatest vision's useless without the will to execute it. I know you're brave. I'm no engineer but I recognise talent when I see it.'

'Runs in the family,' Giovanni said quietly.

'I'm not finished. You've got both, but you've also got this guilt to get over if you're going to be any damn use.'

'You wouldn't ask me to stay if you knew the things I'd done.'

'I keep my ears open. I know how Concordian engineers learn their trade.'

'Then how can you possibly—?'

'Same reason I don't throw myself off the tower and be done with it.' The Doctor laughed. '*Everyone*'s guilty in Rasenna. If we can't have proper angels, we'll make do with fallen ones. The question is: will you help or won't you? Don't think I'm going to let you back down those stairs without an answer. Sofia believed in you.'

'She didn't know me!' Giovanni shouted, angrier than the Doctor had ever seen him.

'She knew enough.' The older man looked away, remembering broken promises.

Giovanni watched the work on the river. 'Town's getting busy.'

Some difference in his voice made the Doctor look up at him. 'Yes, it is. I hadn't the courage to come up here before today. So, which is it? Stand up and fight or lie back down and get it over with?'

'Concord doesn't even let its forests grow. Subject towns making money is as provocative as building new walls.'

'We'll need better walls before they hear about it.'

'We'd better get started,' said Giovanni, and turned towards the stairs. The Doctor stood out of his way.

He began to climb down, then paused. 'Doctor, I'll work for Rasenna, but not for you, understood?'

The Doctor nodded and turned back to the town and the river that was part of it. The sun hit the water, a band of white pulsing through the old town, bringing new life, bleaching everything pure until old stains faded; for the first time, it seemed to belong.

Cat whined contentedly.

'What are you laughing at?' he said.

Down on the embankment, Fabbro saw the silhouette up on Tower Bardini and swore. He preferred Rasenna without great men.

'In Rasenna, we're all saving to buy boats before the next flood,' he said to the man walking beside him. It had been a good meeting so far; the Ariminumese merchant had that combination of blunt speech and sharp thinking he respected.

'So, can you fill the order? And don't answer quickly, Bombelli, it makes me nervous. I don't think you know Rasenna's reputation in my city. People said I was crazy just coming here.'

'Why *did* you come here?'

'I keep my eyes open: I've seen quality goods from Rasenna in the markets, but not the important ones. You need distribution partners,' he said, looking around at the towers.

'I do, and I know what you're thinking.' said Fabbro. 'We've no soldiers but those we hire, and yes, they steal. Shipments regularly arrive with a tenth of the cargo missing.'

'Fallen overboard?' the other said wryly, 'Well, some predation is normal but that's a high price to do business with Rasenna.'

'Not for you. It's my cost to bear as a citizen – if we partner up.'

'How do you meet costs? These boats—'

'I don't own them – I've arranged leases from Ariminumese bankers, if you must know. Your paesani will tell you I'm a good bet.'

'Or tell me you're a *minchia*! Don't trust bankers, Fabbro. Surely your Signoria can protect you from these bandits?'

Fabbro laughed. 'Believe me, if our Signoria hadn't burned down, none of this would even be possible.'

'But with fighters at a loose end, aren't there hijackings?'

'We've hired enough flags to prevent outright looting. The Families are both underground, so it might go either way yet. Me, I see it as a time of great prospect.'

'Before the flood comes, right?'

'Exactly! Come to my tower, we'll eat and discuss the details.' As he spoke, Fabbro caught sight of Pedro coming across the bridge.

He excused himself for a moment and ran to meet him. 'Get the net, Pedro! I'm about to land a big fish.'

'Well, you might want to reconsider me as your fishing partner. I can't stick to the price you agreed with my father.'

'We have a deal!'

'What do you want me to do?' Pedro looked over his shoulder and dropped his voice. 'My employees get robbed so much it's better to work for someone who pays less.'

'Business costs,' said Fabbro with a chuckle. 'You remind me of your father when you're like this. *Tranquillo*, Pedro, we're in this together. How's this? I'll up what I'm paying and your workers can take home the same.'

'That would help short-term, but Morello's putting people on the streets again. He's testing the wind before he raises his flag.'

'Well, we don't have to wait around. With no Signoria draining us, we can afford to hire flags of our own.'

377

Pedro was uneasy. 'Signore Bombelli, you sound like one of them. We're Small People, we're not fighters.'

'You think I like it? But that's what we've got to do to stay in business. Look behind me.'

'I don't see anything.'

'Look up, at Tower Bardini.'

'*Dio Impestato!* I heard he'd hung himself.'

'I heard a nicer story, that someone cut his throat, but no such luck. If the Doc's back, pretty soon he's going to start making moves again too. Men like Bardini can't stop themselves. We've got to show the Families that they don't have the monopoly on flags any more.'

Pedro was becoming calmer. 'It could work. I'll take a smaller percentage. You don't have to hurt yourself because of who my father was.'

'Forget it, the cut's the same. Getting rich makes me a target. I need all the friends I can afford.'

Pedro laughed. 'Go and land your fish. I think the natives make him nervous.'

All day the Doctor watched the comings and goings around Tower Bombelli. It was as busy now as Tower Bardini used to be. It was late when the stranger left, sliding down the ladder a sight easier than the laboured steps that had carried him up. So he'd cut a good bargain – but Fabbro's friendly wave was no sham. A fair deal for everyone then. The Doctor guessed the man was a merchant; he dressed well enough to advertise success, but practically enough to travel.

The Doctor watched the merchant as he made his way to the northern gate. These days that was much busier too, with trade coming in and goods leaving the town. Visitors to Vanzetti's and Bombelli's Towers crossed paths on the bridge and often arranged to meet there again, one with wares to sell, the other with money to buy . . . And a fair was held, the first Saturday of the month, then, as word spread, the same Saturday the next month, and then every Saturday – all his to tax, yet he let them be.

He rubbed Cat's ears, asking, 'Where's this fool civilian going?'

The merchant, contemplating future profits instead of his present route, had wandered into the back streets.

Cat jumped down, sensing a change in the Doctor's mood. Three masked bandieratori were creeping along the rooftops. The one wearing a hood was much taller than the others, probably the oldest. He gave a signal and the other two went forward, the smallest boy with the cambellotto leading the way. The one who hung back was familiar to the Doctor, as was the dodge underway. The hood was going to 'rescue' the foreigner from the bandits; a 'reward' would then be demanded.

What surprised him was to see it done in the shadow of Tower Bardini – but then, he *had* hid himself away lately; in Rasenna, that too was a signal.

'Well, I'm back now,' he said to Cat, picked a rooftop and leapt. Air howling in his ears as it passed, the stone streets hurtling towards him, to be still as the world moves: he'd missed it. Calmly he reached out and grabbed the flagpole at the side of his tower and turned with it, landing against the neighbouring tower and pushing himself off, into air again. It wasn't like old times. The rooftop he landed on wasn't the one he'd picked, and he smashed into it instead of lightly landing. Catching his breath, he scrambled along the gable.

All of the pair's intention was on the mark. *Amateurs*, thought the Doctor, *always have a look-out.* He leapt and landed in the alley, along with a rain of loosened slates. *Merda! He* was the amateur.

The bigger boy fumbled with his flag while the smaller boy wearing the cambellotto took his time. With the lightest of pulls the Doctor took the bigger boy's stick and with it nudged him into his partner's swinging flag. He went down without a sound. The smaller boy wasn't fazed and swung again. *Not bad.* The Doctor ducked and grabbed the boy's flag. The strong grip was surprising too, but it couldn't make up for a lack of training, and a well-aimed punch dropped the boy just as the merchant rounded the corner.

'Good day, Signore.' The Doctor bowed. 'Your quickest route to the north gate is that way.'

The merchant stuttered his thanks and bolted.

The Doctor waited for the hooded boy to come to the 'rescue'.

'Mule.'

'Doc? I thought you retired!'

Mule went to embrace the Doctor and got slammed into the wall instead.

'Where's your brother?'

'What brother's that?'

The Doctor pushed a little harder.

'Ugh! Working for Morello.'

'What about you? Working *my* streets, under *my* tower? Who do you work for?'

'I'm freelance.' Mule smiled. 'Doc! These civilians, they all bring heavy purses. Don't worry, you'll get a taste.'

'I'll only say this once, so listen: these merchants with their juicy purses bring money to Rasenna. Rob them, and they won't come back.'

When Mule blinked dumbly, the Doctor sighed. 'Look on it as an investment if I can't appeal to patriotism. Rasenna's back in business. We leave them alone and we all get rich. Got it?'

Mule didn't look back at his erstwhile partners. 'Not really, but I'm Bardini, so what you say goes.'

The night had descended on the deserted backstreet when the younger boy regained consciousness. He was disgusted that Mule had deserted them, and at the wasted day. He picked up his cambellotto, settled it on his head and kicked the other boy awake, then set off. The boy followed him down to the bridge calling, 'Uggeri, wait up!' Piazza Luna was deserted and dark. They tentatively approached the ruined Palazzo Morello, pushing and daring each other forward.

'I don't think no one's here.'

'I saw him,' said the younger boy firmly. He was the one who had impressed the Doctor with his coolness.

Scorched planks had been propped in the Palazzo doorway but the boys were small enough to squeeze though.

'Anyone here? Tano? Aw, there's no one here. Let's go.'

Gaetano stepped out of darkness. 'You will address me as Lord Morello. What do you want?'

They saw others in the shadows. The smaller boy, undaunted, spoke up. 'We want to join the new Morello borgata.'

'You can get paid to protect Bombelli's shipments. Don't you like money?' said Gaetano.

'It's not like that, Lord Morello,' the big one said nervously. 'We're bandieratori, so—'

'You want to fight?'

He nodded in relief, uncomfortable beneath the heat of Gaetano's gaze.

'That's not enough any more. You didn't lose anyone in the uprising.' Gaetano turned to the smaller boy. 'But you did.'

'Yes, my Lord.'

'You're a Galati – Hog's boy?'

'Uggeri is my name.' The boy had always been serious but something had changed. There was a silence about him now, tense as a storm's eye.

'Your father wasn't much, but your brother was. He stood with me to the end.'

'I know. I'm on my own now.'

'We all are. Who gave you that eye?'

'The Doc.'

'Bardini flag's flying again?' said one of Gaetano's bandieratori, a tall flat-faced boy.

'Dangerous time to have the wrong partners,' said Gaetano.

Secondo shrugged. 'Just curious, Lord Morello.'

Gaetano turned back to Uggeri. 'Well, is he?'

The boy met his stare. 'Maybe. It was a hijack. He let the mark go.'

'Do you know why?'

Uggeri shook his head.

Gaetano said sadly, 'Does this town never learn?' He turned to the others, focusing particularly on those, like Secondo, who'd once been Bardini affiliates. 'He's playing the patriot since my father's not around to play it. He'll let everyone get comfortable, earn a little, then make a loud noise and those shopkeepers on the bridge will beg him to take their money. Rasenna will sleepwalk into tyranny if *we* let it, Uggeri.'

'That mean we're in?' the bigger boy said.

'Show me what you're capable of,' he said, throwing Uggeri a flag. 'Things have changed. I only want killers.'

CHAPTER 47

Sofia swore when she saw the coffin drop. The historian had already brought food that day; she hoped that he hadn't come back for seconds.

Over the week she had negotiated a new bargain: he fed her in return for an audience – the problem was that Tremellius often tried out several drafts a day. Sofia, knowing she was finished as soon as the text was, tried keeping him distracted with irrelevant questions. Luckily, he liked to talk about himself.

But instead of the fat little man, the Third Apprentice emerged with a tall, dark-skinned prisoner. The scarecrow of a man was shackled and hooded, but his rapidly moving jaw was working fine: 'Kid, don't be naïve,' Sofia heard him say. 'Every prison I've been in the guards did favours.'

She went to the window. The voice was familiar.

'Look, we can do business – you have something I need, and I've got disposable income.'

'But not at your disposal,' the Third Apprentice said equably. 'Why should I believe you?'

'Every condottiere has a stash, in case he's taken hostage.'

'We don't trade hostages,' the boy said, removing the hood.

'And is that really economically responsible?'

The last time she saw him he had been in armour. That was gone, but he wore the same green neckerchief, and he had the same cajoling manner as when he visited Workshop Bardini a year ago. His patter had not persuaded the Doctor then, and it did not seem to be working on the boy now.

Colonel Levi, close to panic, was talking fast. 'Look, the market's big enough for everyone. Your engines give you an edge, you exploit it: I respect that. But war's an expensive business. When Concord stopped returning hostages, it overturned the right of the Etrurian market to regulate itself. That's barbaric.'

'Not to mention all the people they kill,' Sofia hollered.

'That's bad too,' Levi agreed. 'Hey, I know you! Rasenna, right?'

The Third Apprentice searched for the cell key, not really listening. When he opened the door, the body of the previous owner slumped against his feet.

'*Cavolo!* Was he shocked to death?' Levi asked.

The boy examined the corpse briefly. 'No, looks like cardiac arrest. Stress-aggravated, I imagine.'

'Stressed? Here?'

Apparently impervious to bribery *and* sarcasm, the boy hauled the corpse over the railings. The splash's echo in the darkness galvanised the condottiere. *This* was his last chance. He lunged, but the boy just stood aside and let him hit the railing, then dropped low with a sweeping kick. Levi landed face-down and gave no further trouble.

Sofia was staring up at the disappearing coffin when Levi's befuddled face came to his cell window.

'Contessa!' he shouted over, 'nice to see you again. Shame about the circumstances. Doc Bardini was wise not to team up with us after all. *Madonna*, the Company took a hiding at Tagliacozzo!'

'I'm here too. Didn't make much difference.'

'I guess not. Hey! My wall moved. What's that sound?'

'Get ready for lights out.'

'Isn't it early for that?'

Tap

Levi groggily stumbled to his window. Across the void he found Sofia looking back. 'Contessa? Oh, I forgot where I was.' He pulled on the window bar. 'Unfortunate. Dying's not part of my five-year plan.'

'Didn't you say you'd escaped from lots of prisons?'

'I've been *in* lots of prisons. I got out the civilised way,' he said, rubbing his thumb and two fingers. 'This is the Beast, kid. Even if you get out of your cell, there's nowhere to go. I don't know how to call that thing down. Far as I can see, there's only one way out of here.'

'You don't seem too worried.'

'Well, what's the point in getting upset? Not everyone

in Etruria is as emotional as Rasenneisi. Occasional imprisonment is just the cost of doing business as a condottiere. We accept that. The problem, as I tried explaining to the little fellow, is when the competition changes the rules. It's killing us. They just march in and take over!'

'As opposed to?'

'As opposed to marching in and *threatening* to take over, like civilised people.'

'Contractors profit from war more than anyone. You don't have much to complain about.'

'I'm not doing much profiting over here, you know.'

'So how *did* you find yourself in the position of a lowly soldier?'

'Don't ask,' Levi sighed.

'Come on. I'm curious; I thought that condottieri drop flags at the first sign of trouble?'

'That's a classic small-town misunderstanding. Yes, we have been known, on occasion, to make tactical retreats. And what's wrong with that? We're paid to win, not to get killed or taken prisoner. One ransom can eat a condottiere's whole season pay-packet.'

'The horrors of war.'

'Some of my bills are horrifying! Armour, mail, squires, horses, repairs – I could go on—'

'No thank you. Don't you just steal from civilians?'

'Nothing to steal these days,' Levi said slowly, 'and by the way, go easy! This hasn't been a great week so far and we just met!'

'How long does it usually take?'

'I get it: you don't like condottieri.'

'No matter who suffers, *you* prosper. You bleed towns of their last soldi, then leave them to Concord. What's to like?'

'Well, I wish life was as simple as Doc Bardini explained it. You think he became boss of Rasenna though eloquent oratory?'

'No, I suppose not.'

'Sorry, kid,' Levi said quickly, 'didn't mean to bring up a sore spot.'

'Just for that, when I break out I'm leaving you here.'

'Come on. We're neighbours. We should be making friends.'

'Right. So how *did* you end up here, Colonel?'

'Call me Levi. Seriously? I think we were betrayed.'

'I know the feeling.'

Levi told her about the Hawk's Company's defeat at Tagliacozzo. John Acuto had attempted to meet Concord on its own terms, and though he'd conscientiously prepared his alliance and strategy, everything had come undone in a moment. Sofia listened with an odd sense of déjà vu.

Before she could tell him about it, Levi cut himself off. 'Oh *Madonna*, what's that sound? Not a visit of the blue fairy?'

'Relax,' Sofia said, 'this is my own private torture: the death of a thousand footnotes.'

Levi sank back into the darkness of his cell as the historian pulled himself free from the coffin.

'Now, I hope you don't mind, but I've brought some more Chapters of my book,' he said as he saw her. 'It's so rare to find a good listener!'

CHAPTER 48

In the same year the Guild was founded, Bernoulli began the Molè. Over a quarter of a century, growing from the first simple structure to the colossus that now overshadows our capital, the Molè proved to be the other constant of his career. Following the triumphant bridge, young Bernoulli had persuaded the Curia that a true temple must resound and echo the perfection of God's system. He redrew century-old plans with curious proportions to ensure that very harmony.

In this land so partial to conspiracy, there are naturally rumours of hidden wings, secret purposes. Bernoulli's successors inherit the

---

[27] Is one of these secrets the answer to the *Dialogue's* last question? I enquired of my Masters what such a proof would prove. Pythagoras describes two-dimensional perfection as $X^2 + Y^2 = Z^2$. The rumored proof proving that $X^3 + Y^3 = Z^3$ is mathematically absurd. Perfection and reality are incompatible.

title First Apprentice, together with certain secrets of state[27]. It was not simple misfortune that so many Apprentices died during construction; it was a cull, for only the best may wear the red - or so at least the more fanciful of my predecessors theorised.

Indifferent to these fevered rumours the Cathedral[28] climbed ever closer to Heaven, but as it grew taller, its architect grew weaker. Three days after its consecration he died.

[28] It was Concord's awed citizenry who dubbed it the Molè, usually translated as *Miracle*, although I find the secular *Wonder* renders it more accurately. Bernoulli himself gave its less reverent handle.

CHAPTER 49

'We need new samples. If buyers don't see our product, they won't know they want it.' In Tower Bombelli, Fabbro was finishing his morning briefing. 'That's it. *Avanti!*'

'Someone to see you, Pop.'

Fabbro's daughter Maddalena showed in a dark-haired boy wearing a combellotto. The dark-haired boy had never seen anything like it – the counting room was the eye of the mercantile storm brewing in Rasenna. Nothing had its own place, so everything vied for space on every available shelf or flat surface, in every chest and basket; even the ceiling was hung with camphor pomades. There was a gleaming mound in one corner: the crests of bank-rupted families, silver and gold beaten into strange shapes: pyramids and stars, whales and worms. They would soon be melted down to something more univer-sally appreciated.

The merchant himself, getting stouter, was squashed behind a desk buttressed with a collection of scales; Etruria was as incontinent with currencies as dialects and a town needed someone who could accurately and cheaply change concordi to soldi to grosso to fisoli, to keep the money flowing in all directions. Bombelli's integrity was unquestioned – after all, he gained most from Rasenna's new reputation for trade.

'Young man, how can I help you?' he asked, looking the boy over.

Uggeri waited for Fabbro's children to leave, then dropped a large purse on the desk.

Fabbro didn't blink. 'What's this?'

Uggeri's deep furrowed brow was odd in a boy of his age. 'Sample of *our* wares. Lord Morello knows you're investing in boats and equipment. He wants you to know who to come to if you need extra capital.'

When the merchant frowned and went back to writing, Uggeri thought he had blundered somehow. Lord Morello had given him this job so that he could show his range, show he was more than a brawler. He spread his arms wide, smiling this time. 'It is a gift, Signore Bombelli. No interest, understand?'

Fabbro looked up. 'I keep track of everything in this book, you see? One line for sales and one for purchases, so I know how I earn money.'

'He doesn't want anything in return,' Uggeri repeated, more hesitantly.

'He steals his from southsiders, people like Pedro Vanzetti's employees, doesn't he?'

'Why should that concern you?' Uggeri said, with just a touch of menace.

Fabbro put down his quill. 'I understand now. It's a token of *friendship*. And if I ever need a silent partner, the door is open.' He smiled, his restless hands at rest.

The boy sighed with relief. 'Signore, you understand everything.'

Fabbro stood up. 'Just business.'

It was noon, and the bridge was packed with tradesmen and merchants. Pedro was haggling over crushed lapis when the old dye-trader broke off and asked, 'That boy's a southsider, isn't he?'

The crowd parted for Fabbro's sons. They threw Uggeri to the ground at Pedro's feet.

'This thief stole from you,' said Fabbro, throwing him the purse. 'Check it.'

Business casually stopped to watch the scene play out; some variety of fracas was a daily diversion. In the silence, the coins' jingle was painfully audible.

'Now get off our bridge!' Fabbro shouted. 'It's for Rasenneisi.'

'Fake Rasenneisi,' the boy said, dusting himself off and giving Pedro a parting look. '*I'm* real.'

Fabbro watched the boy saunter away. After the uprising, when anger had outstripped fear, the Small People had turned away from the Families. Now, to keep them from turning back, he ensured money flowed to both sides of the river. Morello's attempt to bribe him with his neighbour's wealth undermined the very meaning of the bridge, so it was easy for him to rebuff. But Rasenneisi were so used to deferring to the Families that slipping back would be easy.

He addressed the crowd. 'Sorry for the upset. Please go about your business.'

'Don't be a traitor, Bombelli,' a southsider said. 'You're siding with one of them.'

Fabbro pushed the man away. 'Young Vanzetti is one of us, *idiota*. Morello stole from my partner. That means he stole from me.'

'You're only loyal to money,' a voice jeered.

The old dye-trader shuffled over. 'You think it's just northsiders suffering? We get raided too!'

'Workshop Bardini's defunct,' the northsider disputed.

'Exactly – and left to their own devices, Doc's bandieratori cause more trouble than before.'

'Oh, for the good old days,' a northsider jeered.

'Well, at least no one tower cast its shadow on the rest,' the southsider returned. 'It was better than anarchy!'

As arguments flared around them, Fabbro studied Pedro carefully. 'You thought he was working for me, didn't you? I hire bandieratori to protect my stock, not extort from my partners.'

'How could I know that?'

'Because I paid you more so you could keep your workers – why would I steal it back?'

'It's what the Families have always done.'

'You insult me; your father—'

'Died on these streets! I know how Rasenna works. The Small People get pushed around, and you're growing bigger.'

'This is ridiculous.' Fabbro looked around the bridge. 'If we can't trust each other, we can't do business. I was crazy to think it could work.'

As the intermingled Rasenneisi separated, the foreign traders belatedly realised that today's squabble wasn't one to watch safely from the margin.

'People, quiet!' The voice cut through the squabbling. Fabbro, most of all, was surprised at the sudden authority in Pedro's voice. 'If we can't agree, we can take our problems to the Signoria.'

There was a scatter of laughter. 'They burned it down, remember?'

'They burned a palazzo. Before he died, my father told me something that I didn't understand until just now, when we started arguing like the Families used to. *We* are the Signoria.'

Pedro looked around the faces, all listening now. 'We can't blame the Families for Rasenna's problems any more. If it needs fixing, we're going to have to fix it. We can't buy security by hiring more flags – that's what the Families did. The Small People *are* Rasenna, so if anything's wrong with Rasenna, it's wrong with us. And if we can change, then Rasenna can too. My father also told me that the Empire installed a Concordian as head of the Signoria after the Wave.'

'A podesta – my town still has one,' said a bearish Tarquinian trader.

'I remember that unfortunate fellow,' said the old dye-trader gruffly. 'Maybe Vettori's bedtime story had a happy ending, but the podesta was assassinated within a year.'

'By persons unknown,' his neighbour chuckled.

Pedro said, 'Yes, and do you know why Concord let us rule ourselves afterwards?'

When no one spoke, he continued, 'Because our feuding made a garrison unnecessary. I don't say it was wrong to kill him – a partisan leader's worse than none. I say we need someone who doesn't have a side to take.'

'So who do you suggest?' the old man interrupted. 'Nobody's innocent in Rasenna.'

Pedro looked at the sceptical crowd, northsiders, south-siders and foreigners, all together on the bridge. 'The reason you're standing where you're standing. Captain Giovanni.'

Pedro expected accusations of betrayal and outrage, but instead there was only a thoughtful silence. People looked for each other's reactions, not necessarily trusting their own: that it seemed right, natural.

'The Concordian?' the dye-trader said doubtfully.

'I never saw Rasenneisi work as well together as here,' said Fabbro.

People murmured agreement.

'I'm too old and too poor to chase dreams,' the dye-trader said irritably. 'He's a good man, certainly, but is it

practical? Would a Signoria led by the Captain have legitimacy? Hell, I'll say it straight – without strong men, would
anyone listen to us?'

'Where does authority come from,' said Pedro, 'if not
us? Our fear gives the Families power. If we reject both
banners, we take that power away. That's what Giovanni
showed us: it wasn't the bridge that brought us together,
it was fear that kept us apart.'

'If it were true . . .' the old man said with a wondering
whisper.

Fabbro clapped his hands together. 'Right then! All in
favour, say Aye.'

The shout of approval, heard from Tower Bardini to Palazzo
Morello, relit hope in the Doctor's heart.

It kindled Gaetano's into a blaze. Deciding that it was
time to remind the Small People of their vulnerability, he
gave his crew a list of names. Once more Pedro found his
workforce not showing up to work and once more he went
knocking on doors. He returned despondently home hours
later, wondering what to tell Fabbro tomorrow. Behind
the few doors that had opened he saw frightened employees
with fresh bruises and broken bones. The doors that
remained closed were most ominous of all.

Pedro realised something was wrong when his own door
swung open. A flag struck the back of his legs.

'Pick him up,' said Gaetano.

Secondo and Uggeri yanked him up by his shoulders.

'Shopkeepers form a parliament? Is it a joke?'

No answer was expected; the question was followed by a gut-punch.

'You make me laugh. You've got some money now so you think you own Rasenna? You think I'd let you take it?'

'It's our decision,' Pedro mumbled.

'Small People are too witless to appreciate how Concordians work. Don't you see he planned this? That bridge is cancer, destroying us from inside. All you see is the money it makes you!'

Another punch, this time to the face.

'You're a relic,' Pedro said.

Gaetano laughed. 'You've got more salt than your father, I'll give you that. Here's how it is: you don't go to work tomorrow – you wait for my permission. If you want a new Signoria, you petition me to form it. Got it?'

Pedro spat out a tooth. 'No, come again?'

When Pedro woke, he sat up too fast and had to wait for his eyes to clear. It was evening. The workshop was thrashed. There was wool everywhere, fabric shredded and, worst of all, his father's looms broken apart. He lay back down and groaned. 'Business costs.'

CHAPTER 50

Sofia was close enough to the water now to hear the last gasps of prisoners as their cells went under. And she was close enough to see that the surface was alive with buio, driven mad by the vortex of churning water. All Nature was imprisoned here.

Sometimes the rotation took Levi's cell far away but often they were near enough to talk. Levi was noticeably less animated than when he had arrived – and thinner too, though that hadn't seemed possible. While she was fed daily, Levi was stoically suffering starvation and the lottery of the blue light.

After one of the historian's morning visits, Levi asked, 'Are you really that interested in his book?'

'I'm defenceless, and he's a frustrated sadist who loves the sound of his voice. The longer I keep him happy, the longer I stay alive. Hungry?' She threw him the loaf she'd kept from her breakfast. 'Catch!'

'Damn, I thought you'd woven a rope from your hair.'

'I'll work on it. So what *is* your five-year plan, Levi?'

'It's more of a target really: me, captain of my own company, and enough gold to take a bath in.'

'Well, good luck with that. Listen, I was thinking about Tagliacozzo. You *were* betrayed.'

'How can you be sure?'

'I was here when the battle took place, but what you described was familiar. Levi, I saw the plans in the engine-room when the Apprentices questioned me. They knew your strategy before the battle.'

'*Madonna!*' said Levi and went back to eating.

'What, that's it? Doesn't it make you burn for revenge?'

'I want to live. Revenge won't fill my belly.'

'You'd make a lousy Rasenneisi.'

'I'll take that as a compliment, Contessa.'

That night the collective tension was churned into frenzy until the pit resounded with mad cries. Sofia woke with water dropping on her face. She went to the door and peered out: another revolution and they would be under the water.

'Levi, are you awake?'

There was no answer, just an echo, answered by the moans and creaking of the pit. He might be dead already, and she would have done nothing to help him. Sofia looked up in desperation as the coffin descended for what might very well be the last time.

CHAPTER 51

The tale rehearsed thus far is well-known,[29] but the present Author's privileged access to State Archives has allowed him to uncover a more disconcerting narrative. Close reading of Bernoulli's notes from the period before the Guild's formation show that even as he planned his bridge, even as he sketched the *Discourses*, he secretly researched another subject: Miracles.

If it seems ironic to the Reader that the tyranny of priests was overthrown by one so devout, he will do well to remember that Natural Philosophy was not as rigidly defined then as now;[30] if we acclaim Bernoulli as the first Modern, we must remember he hailed from a mediaeval world as distant from ours as the Etruscan was

---

[29] Though it must be obvious to the Reader that such thorough research has as seldom been tempered with such rare insight as it has been so eloquently expressed.

[30] Too rigidly defined now, some argue. The *Empiricist* school and the more generous vision of the *Naturalists* continue to find their adherents within the Guild. The second First Apprentice, himself an aggressive *Empiricist*, did much to foster the materialism of our contemporary Guild. Our current First Apprentice takes a more embracing view; like Bernoulli, Guglielmo Bonaccio is a bridge-builder.

to his. If we never learn why such a mind entertained such fantasy (indeed, there may be no explanation), his real achievements must always stay our censure.

Young Bernoulli wasted months researching esoteric subjects we have today dismissed as the grossest superstition. Regretfully, only a summary is possible[31]. He believed that the myths of Virgin birth[32] and Transubstantiation[33] were linked in more than a Scriptural sense. His ambition, it appears, was to give them some mathematical explanation.

Bernoulli abandoned these blind alleys from the tumult of the Thirties through the repeated crises of the Forties, but the reprieve was temporary. In the early Fifties the Molè's final ascent mirrored its architect's descent into senility, an unravelling that began soon after he began dissecting pseudonaiades by means electrical. Perhaps he pried out other secrets with their liquid anatomy. More likely he was already mad.

---

[31] Owing to the dearth of records. If Bernoulli was secretive in his public works, imagine, Reader, how jealously he concealed his researches alchemical.

[32] He investigated folktales of auto-conception with credulity marvellous to our age of reason.

The archives contain accounts of ewes producing lambs without rams, frogs changing sex, fish inseminating themselves and reptiles dying to be reborn with new skin, new youth.

[33] Metamorphosis is a recurring theme. As the Virgin made water become wine, so he theorised that water and man were interchangeable states.

While the Molè occupied his days, the Etruscan Scriptures[34] consumed his nights. He reread their so-called *Books of Fate*, and, coming to believe the old story that our ancestors had success-fully predicted the hour of their Empire's collapse, he sought to fix the date of Concord's[35].

The present Author takes no pride revealing the pathetic last chapters of Bernoulli's life nor does he believe that these revela-tions diminish our great debt to him[36]. That his secret half was unknown till now is some small reassurance that however deep this madness went, it never impinged upon his real duty. The Curia

---

[34] The first two books of the *Disciplina Etrusca* concern Divination and Interpretation. But judging by dog-ears and annotations, the last book, concerning Ritual, is the volume that most preoccupied Bernoulli.

It too trisects: the first book concerns *Lifespan*, of everything from People to Empires. The second, those *Worlds* we visit in meditation and death. The last book, on *Reading*, purports to be a key to hidden truths in Scripture; imagine a lock that is key to itself!

[35] Why he assumed Concord's end and the Second Coming would occur concurrently is unknown. The date, he speculated, corresponded to the relationship of the Golden Number to its conjugate, approxi-mately -0.618. 'The first describes all that is Perfect. Its Dark Twin (the absolute value of the length ratio in reverse order) must then describe all that is Wrong. The perfection of an anti-God.' An elegant hypothesis, but what the Devil he meant by it, we have no idea.

[36] What it says that we, who live surrounded by his monuments, have remained ignorant of this, his shadow, is a question for Philosophers more than Historians. If nothing else it reveals the slip-shod scholarship of the present Author's colleagues.

was unworthy to govern because it allowed itself to be governed by superstition, but Bernoulli suppressed that irrationality and, rising above it, he showed his true worth.

It is the most signal victory of an uncommon life: before he conquered the World, Bernoulli conquered his soul. Reader, pass on in respectful silence. Who but genius knows the dark countries genius must traverse?

CHAPTER 52

Tremellius finished with a sigh that contained years. 'The end.'

Sofia leapt to her cell window with wide-eyed interest. 'It can't be! What happened next?'

'You can stop now – the act. It's the end for you, Contessa. Not my book – that'll never be finished. I know what you've been doing these last few weeks. I know how wretched it is to live without hope.'

Sofia's smile faded.

'And I know I'm just a slave with useful talents – nobody studies the Humanities these days. This place feeds on hope. Call me sentimental, but I wanted to deny it yours.'

'Why?'

'Because it's stolen mine. Because you are the last Contessa of Rasenna. Because blood matters.'

'You don't believe anything you write, do you?' she said sadly.

'Of course not!' Tremellius shouted, 'it's not History, it's a creation-myth – it's all obfuscation and mystery when really it couldn't be simpler: an exceptional generation of engineers sought a king. One got lucky – King Bernoulli, though of course none may call him such. The Engineers insist that they came to liberate, that our religion and aristocracy were shackles. Well, maybe they were, but they just took our place! I write this story and weave a pattern into it, confidently explain the reasons why this followed that, but nobody really knows how we were made small. A power came into the world and swept us all away. My family were gonfalonieres! I know what we lost.' His voice tailed off. 'I just don't know how.'

'You have to help me!' Sofa cried. 'I need more time.'

'Dear child, I'm just a noble – nobody listens to me.' He sighed and composed himself. 'Best that you're weak when the end comes.'

'What are you doing?' she screamed. 'No, don't—!'

He pulled the lever calmly and blue light flooded her cell. Sofia fell and her head hit the ground and the sound it made was

T

   A

       p

Her body sank into the cold water like the star falling. All the pain, the anger, she left them behind on the surface.

Behind the darkness was the infinity of what might have been and might yet be.

But first she had to face the Darkness – or go back to the cell, to the drip, to a slow death. No. She swore that she'd drown before that. She swam

Down

Fear, the Dark Ancient, boiled furiously, a black sun being born. A tentacle shot out of the darkness and another. It pulled her in. She didn't fight it. She prayed:

Madonna, be my shepherd.

And suddenly it was the moment before dawn, an electric hum in the air, nothing was different, but everything had changed completely. The tentacles loosened, the Darkness fled. And then there was

L I G H T

And Sofia beheld Her: the Handmaid, adrift in timeless space, incubating salvation as She waited patiently. Then Sofia heard an insistent sound like becalmed thunder. A heart fiercely beating – Her sacred heart! – beating in the darkness most silent and terrible, waiting to synchronise with History's slow pulse once more. Then eyes that were old as the stars opened and beheld Sofia at last. Heaven roared in joy but the world did not hear it. The voice that spoke was kind and whispered not in words but in music.

Do not be afraid. Years beyond counting, I waited for you. I see you now.

'I'm nothing!'

No, you are strong enough to break through fear, strong enough for what lies ahead.

'I'm not ready!'

Lies and all your fear, all your grief.

Giovanni fell again, slowly tumbling into nothing, into the black water.

Sofia closed her eyes to block out the vision and when she realised she saw it still, she knew that She too saw. Those eyes that had looked upon the most terrible grief now looked on hers. A rumble then, like a storm brewing in the distance, and once more She spoke:

Changed but stronger, it will return.

'I'm not strong like you.'

I am not strong. Only my love was strong. That is what sustained me then, sustains me now, and no other power but Love can sustain you in the coming darkness. Only Love.

Love.

Sofia opened her eyes. The next drop fell, but it did not land. She had it now. Control did not feel like something she had *learned*, it felt like something *recalled*.

Tremellius talked on, obliviously. 'The Heavens revolved around us until King Bernoulli taught us there's no scheme to History, no Music around the Spheres, only a bloody vacuum. Man's triumphs and failures, his laws, his crimes, they're nothing but dust – just stories for children. God's breath does not warm us, nor inspire men to prophesy, nor virgins to conceive.'

Tap

The water didn't drop because it had to. It dropped because Sofia let it. She focused on the next drop and instead of catching it, made it change direction. It splashed against the door.

Tap

'If there is no pattern, there are no constraints. We're free of Commandments. Free of God. *Madonna* help us, we're *free.*'

Anger rose up, but she didn't release it. She let the drop hang in space as another fell into it, and another, until it was trembling under the growing weight . . . just a few seconds more . . .

She grabbed the banner she'd used as a pillow.

Tremellius sighed again and made his way back to the coffin. 'Farewell, Contessa. Dream golden dreams.'

It blasted through the window and out across the void, and Sofia dived though the gap, rolling as she landed on the walkway.

Levi woke to see the fist-sized hole blasted in his door.

'Ungrateful *troia*, get back in your box!' Tremellius screamed.

Feeble as they were, Sofia couldn't block his kicks.

'After all I've done for you, you'll get me in trouble! I should drown you right here!'

Water had pushed back, and Sofia could hardly move her arms, let alone fight. As she fell back on the walkway her hand touched the lake surface. Seeing how weak she was, Tremellius was emboldened to catch her in a choke-hold, using his weight to push her head down. She saw buio rising from the depths towards her.

Suddenly, Tremellius slumped over. Behind him stood Levi, brandishing the window bar from his cell. He pulled her up as the buio lunged.

'Thanks,' she coughed.

'Thank *you*, Contessa! Technically, this is your break-out.'

'I thought you were dead.'

'Takes more than a few days' fast to kill me. I've endured army food.' He laughed.

A metallic groan heralded a new revolution of the pit.

'Help me!' Sofia shouted, and together they dragged Tremellius into the coffin with them.

'Didn't he just try to kill you?' said Levi, conversationally.

'He kept me alive first. Besides, we might need help up there.'

'It's going to be awfully tight. How do you make this thing go up?'

'I don't know, someone up there always operated it. Wake him up!'

'I shouldn't have hit him so hard,' Levi lamented. 'There's got to be a button!'

'Is it this?'

'How the hell do I know? Just hit it!'

The coffin stopped in front of the second colossus. Levi jumped out, ready to fight, but the great hall was empty. The darkness was barely dinted by scattered candles and the last faint rose glow of sunset spilling in misty wisps through the open doorway.

Sofia looked up at the statue, wondering if it was the original or the shadow. Whichever it was, there was something about it that made her heart glow despite the circumstances.

'Getting dark. Well, that's lucky.' Levi was talking to himself nervously as he looked around for another weapon.

She walked towards the base of the colossus until she was standing in front of the carved letters, each a braccia tall: *Although changed, I shall arise the same.*

She realised suddenly *why* the angel's smile was comforting; the statue's idealised portrait was familiar. Horribly familiar.

She went to the coffin and dragged Tremellius to his feet. He was groggy, but conscious.

'The statue,' she demanded, 'who is it?'

'The angel?' he said dazedly, trying to keep up, 't— that is Saint Michael triumphant, he who cast out the Serpent.

An allegory of the Re-Formation, I suppose. The artist was, let me see—'

'Whose *face* does it have?'

'Oh, I see, well, naturally the portrait is he who cast out Superstition.'

It hit her like a blow. Choking back tears, she asked, 'What was Giovanni's surname?'

'Oh, no need to be coy with me, Contessa. I'm not an Apprentice.'

'What was it?' she screamed.

'Bernoulli—'

Sofia pushed him against the glass. 'You lying *cazzo!*'

'Giovanni was his grandson – I can prove it,' he gurgled.

'The darkness will help, but we need some kind of distraction,' Levi said, prying an antique sword from the wall and oblivious to what was happening in the coffin. He turned to see Sofia, getting back into the coffin. 'Hey! Where are you going?' Tremellius was still with her.

'I have to see something. I'll be back,' she promised, and before Levi could protest, the coffin door hissed shut.

'If you're not back in five, I'm leaving!'

Tremellius led the way from the coffin to his desk between the towering stacks of books, babbling nervously, 'I just *assumed* he would have told you – it's only natural to be proud of *that* lineage. But having proved himself unworthy, perhaps it was natural to be ashamed—'

This last finally penetrated Sofia's stupor and she mumbled, 'It's certainly a name to be ashamed of.'

'Well, you are not Concordian,' he said, reasonably. He pushed some heavy volumes out of the way and fished out a scroll. 'Look, this is Girolamo Bernoulli's family tree.'

'What about those stories of him floating down the river?' Sofia said as she took it from him.

His fat little fingers scrambled for a paper cutter under the books. 'Oh, more nonsense: the Bernoulli were just common masons. He *appeared* to come from nowhere because Small People *were* invisible to the Curia.'

Seeing her staring at the family tree, totally absorbed, he lunged.

Almost without looking up Sofia caught his wrist, took the knife away and slapped him hard across the face. '*Don't.*'

As he raised his hand to his cheek she said, as if nothing had happened, 'He proved unworthy, you said.'

'At first, he *did* live up to expectations,' he gibbered. 'This was a boy expected to be the youngest First Apprentice ever. He had his grandfather's intelligence, and not just that, he had his ambition and ferocity too – it was he who revealed his father's plot.'

'No!' she cried, 'Giovanni wasn't a traitor!'

'Technically, Jacopo Bernoulli was the traitor. But yes, the Giovanni you knew was very different. Something went wrong in his third year at the Guild Halls.'

Sofia looked at the scroll. The tree narrowed to Girolamo

Bernoulli, his son Jacopo and grandson Giovanni. The truth had been staring her in the face all along.

Tremellius' eyes darted to the waiting coffin – this might be his last opportunity. He leapt up.

She slammed the knife into his hand.

'*Ahhhh! Ah ah ahhh!*'

'What went wrong?'

He squealed, 'I don't know! No one does. He was – how to put it? – *active* at Gubbio.' He glanced timidly at Sofia's face. 'In the aftermath of the Wave he was engaged in fieldwork with the pseudonaiades, continuing his grandfather's research. All was going well until he was attacked by one, or so he said. Most people just thought he lost his nerve – burnout's common among young engineers – but whatever happened, he returned to Concord different, though at first he seemed just the same. Before, well, everyone knows about Gubbio – he had no qualms, he was willing to do *anything*, but when he came back—'

Tremellius wiped sweat from his brow. 'Dissection's nasty work by all accounts, and I can see that most people don't have the stomach for it, but with his lineage – and after such a promising start – you can imagine the disappointment. Gradually the Apprentices lost confidence in him, and interest, until the, um, incident that brought you here. The last Chapter, you know, a disappointing career ending in the disgrace of mutiny.'

Sofia cocked her head to the ceiling. 'Why did they care if he'd told me his name?'

'Hard to say. The current First Apprentice has taken a rather mystical turn. He's convinced that the second meeting of Scaligeri and Bernoulli was more than coincidence. I assume he wanted to know if Giovanni was simply a traitor like his father, or if it was more than that.

'Certain secrets are not written in books, Contessa, but whispered over the years. The First Apprentice believes that a new age is dawning. More than that, I cannot say.'

Sofia twisted the knife handle.

'*Ahhh!* I can't say because I don't *know*! That's all I know, I *swear*!' He looked shifty for a moment. 'Why do you *care*, Contessa? The boy's dead, his history's of no consequence. All that lives of Bernoulli is this temple.'

'I loved him,' Sofia said, more to herself than the historian.

'You – *aha ha*—'

She could feel it, even as she stood there: the Darkness was regenerating, more powerfully this time. Anger is stronger meat than grief. She was angry at herself, angry at the nun for keeping the truth from her, but most of all angry at *him* – she would not say his name – angry for making her love him, for making her grieve him.

She held the paper to the candle.

'What are you doing?'

'Blood matters,' she whispered as she walked back to the coffin, dragging the burning scroll behind her.

The historian watched as scraps of paper lit up in her

wake. He tentatively touched the dagger's handle, but the pain was too great. As the hungry flames climbed the book shelves, as the towers tumbled, he wept.

Levi breathed a sigh of relief as the star ascended once more.

'We should leave,' he said quickly.

'This is Bernoulli's tower, Levi.' When he looked at her blankly, she shouted, 'We have to burn it!'

'Are you all right? You seem—'

'Just help me!'

The angel watched impassively as they took torches to the tapestries of the great hall.

As the library became an inferno, Tremellius' fear of death routed his fear of pain. The Apprentices would save him. He wrestled the blade out and scrambled to the glass column. The engine-room was empty but for the Third Apprentice, serenely cleaning the slate.

'Scoundrels! They have left us to burn!' the historian cried.

'Be calm,' the boy said, 'the others are in the lantern.'

Sofia rammed the glass column with a candelabrum until great cracks splintered up the shaft.

Levi had to pull her away before she hurt herself. 'That's enough, Contessa. The heat will do the rest.'

Scraps of burning paper were falling from the distant

dome. They pushed the massive doors closed as they left. Sofia gave the angel no final glance. It would not see her cry.

Tremellius was unconvinced. The 'lantern' was the Grecian mausoleum crowning the Molè's triple dome. 'Perhaps we'd be better off going down?'

Far below, the water shot up though the pit. When it reached the great hall, the pressure was enough to finally shatter the fissured glass.

Tremellius toggled the coffin's handle ineffectually. 'It's not working. We're trapped!'

'Just follow me,' the boy said, walking to one of the walls. He turned and watched the pendulum as the historian waddled over to join him. The wall parted for a moment, a piston lowered, and the boy stepped into the darkness. The historian scampered after him. They ascended from piston to piston in the space between the inner and outer dome. The noise was deafening and the light was dim, but the boy, comfortable as a sewer-rat, led the way confidently.

Finally he threw open a trapdoor to a breathtaking night. Tremellius was gasping already from the climb, but the sky was so fretted with stars he fancied he could pry his fingers into them and tear night aside for day. He felt he could breathe freely for the first time in decades, that he had escaped Girolamo Bernoulli's mind. Red and orange, the First and Second Apprentices stood in the open door of the mausoleum, watching.

'My Lords, what are you thinking?' he asked. 'That is Bernoulli's tomb.'

The First Apprentice answered, 'I'm surprised there are rumours you haven't heard. The tomb is empty. It will be our refuge from the fire.'

'Calm yourself,' the Second Apprentice added. 'He has not returned; he waits where he always has, in his real tomb. In the real Molè.'

'This is not the Molè?'

'The Beast is the real wonder of our age. This imperfect reflection shall burn.'

'You knew this was coming?'

'Bernoulli told us the Signs that would herald his return. The destruction of his greatest lie was one. His monument is concealed, just as his secrets are revealed only to initiates.'

Tremellius' eyes widened. 'I am an initiate?'

'You are redundant. There is no need for historians at History's end.'

'Then – what shall I do?' he said with a nervous laugh.

The man in red gave a smile worthy of a wolf. 'You shall be free.'

They picked at random one of many long stairways winding from the mountain's summit to the canals and were lucky. At the bottom, Levi untied one of the boats while admiring the layout from a soldierly perspective. 'It's a citadel. Even if you took the city, you couldn't hold it without the Molè.'

Sofia couldn't bring herself to look back at it, still less praise it.

Levi soon discovered the canals had parallel currents, leading to and from the mountain, and once he got the boat into the right one, they speedily crossed over the new city.

'They made it so hard to get in,' Levi said. 'Getting out will be easy!'

He glanced back nervously at Sofia, who was staring at the water passing by them, clutching her banner tight. Once they reached garrisoned city walls they could no longer count on mere luck. They'd have to fight their way out. Was she up to it?

Through a sea of thick fog below, Sofia finally saw the great city again. Its smooth streets were set in a perfect grid, the few curves allowed graceful and restrained. Marble columns gleamed, their cold beauty illuminated by orbs of blue fire. Everywhere there was proportion and order, balance and harmony. It was an alien beauty, and her soul shrank from it. There were no citizens abroad, only soldiers. It was a city remade as a prison for its population, and for a terrifying moment she saw the world from Girolamo Bernoulli's remote perspective, a beautiful sphere infested by swarming pests, perfection riddled with human maggots, with all their corrosive lies and hopes.

She risked a look back at the Molè and was startled to see the sky empty, washed white by fog, and tall columns fading into nothingness like tired brushstrokes. The Molè's upturned whale's belly left no impression on a sky it should have dominated.

'Levi, where—?' she began.

'Should be a big enough distraction,' he chuckled as the dome became suddenly illuminated by flames.

'Look, the lantern,' she said, pointing at the summit of the third dome.

A man slid and rolled and bounced and finally shot though the wall of flames at the base of the last dome, emerging into the empty air, burning like a falling star. They were too far away to hear his scream. All over the city, bells rang out.

The city walls emerged from mist.

'Get down, Sofia,' said Levi in an undertone.

A sentry called out a challenge, 'Hey, who goes there?'

Levi saluted casually. 'Me. Tie this off, will you?' he said, preparing to throw the rope.

When the sentry reached out for it, a noose fell around him and he yelped as he landed in the water. The cold would finish him before the buio could get there.

Levi helped Sofia out of the boat. 'What happened up there, Contessa?'

'Nothing. I'm all right,' she said.

'You don't look all right. I don't know how you did that trick with the water, but it obviously costs something.

We're going to have to get down and out as fast as possible.
I need you to keep up. Got it?'

Sofia rubbed her arms, trying to get warm. 'Is it the
only way? How many men are down there? I'm weak and
you're half-starved.'

'Just the odds I like. Just stay behind me, kid.'

Levi opened the door, and then closed it just as quickly.
'Hmm, this could get ugly.' He made the sign of the Sword,
and said, '*Madonna*, help us out and I swear I will live a
better life. Contessa?'

'What?'

'Swear!'

'Oh, right. I swear.'

He opened it again and leapt in with a yell. A guard
coming up the stairs got kicked in the chest, brawler
fashion.

'You weren't kidding – that *was* ugly.'

'You going to be this helpful all through this escape?'

'Look behind you!'

Levi gave an involuntary cry as two more guards bundled
up from the landing. He slipped, luckily, as the first guard
swung. He kicked and the guard fell to the ground,
clutching his groin. His helmet came off when he landed.
Levi scrambled to his feet, just avoiding the second soldier's
sword. The blade sparked on stone with a clang. Before
the swordsman recovered, Levi had grabbed up the helmet
and whacked him.

He rubbed his hands with satisfaction and winked at

Sofia as he reached for the door at the end of the corridor. 'And that's how condottieri do it.'

His smile faded. The room was full of guards, drinking and playing cards. Levi stood there as the laughter stopped. Behind him, Sofia quickly sized up the situation. Levi was doing well, for a civilian. But they were both weak, and now outnumbered. If even a single guard escaped to raise the alarm, they were done for.

'Catch,' she said, throwing Levi her bundle.

Before any of the guards had moved Sofia was inside, striking with precision, bouncing between pre-selected targets. She knew where every blow landed, what effect it had. A moment later, all the guards were on the floor and Sofia was filling a satchel with food from the table. She threw Levi a chicken drumstick.

'And *that* is how Rasenneisi do it,' she said with a grin. 'What's the matter? Not hungry?'

Levi lost the dazed look, cleared his throat. 'All right, I'll admit you've got some skills, but stay behind me next time! I don't need you hurt before I break us out.'

'Sure thing.' She was glowing; it was good to be in a straight fight again. 'What are you looking for?'

'Someone you haven't concussed. This fine fellow will do!' Levi threw a mug of beer in the moaning soldier's face. When he started struggling, Levi held a sword to his neck and brought him to the window. A red glow lit up the night.

'See that? That's not the sun coming up early, that's

the Molè. This nice young Signorina did that. You don't want her angry. We need fast rides out of town.'

'Heralds get the best horses. Their stable's on the other side of the Ponte Bernoulliana.'

'How do we open the gate?'

The solider explained, and Levi thanked him with a whack of the tankard.

Before they got to the bridge, Levi had several more opportunities to admire Sofia's skills. Only when they reached it did she hesitate. Like the statue, it was a reflection: a dark mirror of Giovanni's bridge. She remembered talk of a Rasenneisi Engineers' Guild with a shudder.

'Sofia, we can't wait for sun up,' Levi said urgently. 'Come on!'

They galloped away from the dark white city, swift hoofs echoing in the night, not stopping to rest until they'd had an hour's hard riding. Dawn broke, but the air was still frigid with winter sparseness and snow blew down from the northern mountains. They didn't notice; they were too glad to have left that unnatural desert surrounding Concord behind.

'We made it!' said Levi with a savage whoop, 'can you believe it? The only man to ever escape from the Beast! Levi, you are an immortal!'

Sofia slumped in the saddle, more tired than she had ever been.

'Going home, Contessa?'

'Where are you going?'

'Southeast. The Hawk's Company's rendezvous was in the Ariminumese contato – they might not have got there in one piece after Tagliacozzo, but that's where I'll start looking. If there's truly a traitor in the Company, I'd be partly responsible if I didn't warn John Acuto.'

Sofia gave no indication of having heard. The emotional rush of the escape was fading, leaving her with a host of truths she'd sooner not face.

Giovanni had lied to her. He had hidden his name, his past and who knows what else— He was capable of betraying his own father to the engineers. What else had he done – what else had he planned? She had accused the Doctor of betraying her, but how much worse was her own betrayal? Whatever Doc's methods, at least he always fought for Rasenna.

She had never before questioned if she was worthy to be Contessa. Now the answer was unavoidable.

'I can't go back,' she whispered.

Levi pretended not to notice her tears. She'd been strong for him, so he'd be strong for her.

'You want to keep fighting? Come with me.'

'I've nothing worth fighting for.'

'Don't they have money where you come from? There's a home for anyone who can fight in the Hawk's Company, and Contessa, you can fight!'

'I don't want to be a condottiere,' Sofia said, wavering.

'You get to fight Concord,'

That settled it.

'Send your horse south anyway. Two tracks will slow them up if they try tracking us.'

She did it, and then begged a favour: 'Never call me Contessa again. It's Sofia, just Sofia.'

CHAPTER 53

Mad-dog winds chased each other through the dusky streets. Lucia had retired to the chapel, to meditate, she said. Instead she was spying on the three men though the broken stained-glass window. Giovanni was trying to fend off Fabbro's and Pedro's arguments; the more insistent they became, the more reluctant he got.

'I'm just not the right person.'

'You're the only person!' Pedro insisted. He was still sore from his beating, and he wanted to press the question, but Fabbro, the more experienced salesman, knew when to give a customer time to consider.

Lucia's vision had come suddenly, and told her much – too much. But what dreams she had prayed for were dust now; only the Virgin's will mattered. Seeing Giovanni walking towards the chapel, she returned to a serene pose of meditation: that was what History expected of her.

'They asked me—'

'—to be podesta. You must accept,' she said.

'It can't be me.'

'It can only be you, Giovanni.'

He saw her trembling. 'Why are you crying?'

'Because I have seen my death!' she said, her breath escaping in sobs. The truth was a lie; her vision was not the reason she cried – but she must now be as selfless as the Reverend Mother had been. History made no allowances for foolish girls who fell in love.

Giovanni was silent for a moment. 'I thought I would die when I went into the river. Yet I didn't. Maybe it's the same—'

'Giovanni, listen—' Lucia took a breath and composed herself. 'The Virgin's will is manifest in us all, but in you, Time's river divides.'

'That's what the Reverend Mother said, but what does it mean? That I have two destinies?'

'I cannot tell you in words, but I can show you.'

'Sister, stop!' Giovanni cried. 'I *cannot* be taken into any more confidences! I am not who you think I am – I told Sofia that I came to build the bridge for Rasenna, but I built it for *myself*, to salve my conscience, never thinking of the bloody consequences. Sofia died for me, and now they want me as podesta. I don't deserve this trust. 'Lucia, I must tell you who I am or be damned for it, if I'm not already.'

Lucia said, 'The Contessa lives.'

Giovanni slowly sat down in front of her. 'I wish it were possible, but I know, better than anyone, what Concord does to its prisoners. My name is—'

'Giovanni Bernoulli *was* your name. You are something else now.'

'How—? How do you know who I am?'

'One cannot understand water without faith. Now you must begin to believe. Sofia will return, and she will be changed. And when she does return, you will have to make a choice yourself, to save yourself, or save her' – she held up the glass of water – 'but to make that choice you have to know—'

'What?'

'That you are the contents of this glass. You are trying to make sense of it,' she said, 'don't. You *are* water, and unless you believe that, Rasenna is doomed. Imagine a world where you are not heir to the beast but simply the contents of the glass. *Imagine.*'

She released the glass and it shattered against the stone floor. For a moment there were no other sounds but the tinkle of the glass shards coming to rest. Slowly Lucia breathed out and then said briskly, 'Good.'

Giovanni said nothing, only staring at the water floating in a slow-shifting column in front of him.

'You're here for a reason, Giovanni. The buio were pure, and we spoiled them, as we will spoil everything, given time. You're coming to see how we are connected to them. The buio have lived with that knowledge since the beginning. It defines them. In our Salvation is theirs; in theirs, ours.'

At the door, she looked back. 'Contemplate water for a while. I will keep watch for you.'

*

Night fell on Rasenna, but the Doctor could not sleep. A scent in the air, auguring something awful and imminent, kept him awake. He took to the roof, hoping fresh air would clear his senses, knowing it would make no difference. There would be blood tonight.

The moon's reflection on the river quivered with the same anticipation.

Movement on the bridge caught his eye – two figures running south, chased by a bandieratoro with a Bombelli banner. The first was a boy with a head-start; the second was a tall man, limping and carrying a torch.

The boy made it to the safety of Piazza Luna and disappeared into the night without a glance back at his lagging partner. The bandieratoro caught up with the limper. There was a moment's struggle. The limper dropped his torch, but knocked down the bandieratoro before hopping away. When the bandieratoro recovered, he picked up the torch and took the time to aim carefully.

The torch stuck the limper's back squarely and in the moments he lay prone the flames caught. He might have screamed, but the sound did not reach Tower Bardini. He crawled to the balustrade and pulled himself onto it, then lay still.

The bandieratoro approached the smouldering carcase, poked it, then turned back north. The Doctor's gaze followed. Bombelli's tower was obscured by smoke.

He landed by the tower's Madonna. There was a lot of smoke, but the fire had been contained.

Fabbro was surveying the damage with his wife. He greeted him casually. 'Not as quick as the old days, Doc.'

The Doctor caught his breath. 'Your family?'

Fabbro looked sceptical at the Doctor's concern, but Donna Bombelli said quickly, 'All safe. Thank you, Doctor.'

'Morello,' he grunted.

'After Vanzetti's was hit, I figured we'd be next. We were ready.'

'You could have sent for me.'

'I have flags of my own now,' Fabbro said proudly.

One of his older sons, Salvatore, came back; the Doctor recognised the bandieratoro from the bridge.

'Got one, Pop,' he said.

The Doctor looked around. 'It doesn't make sense.'

'Small People standing up for themselves? Get used to it.'

'If Morello wanted to burn you out, he would have. He has plenty of experience, believe me. He knows you've hired flags too. He knew you'd expect this after he trashed Vanzetti's.'

Fabbro was worried now. 'You think it's a warning?'

The Doctor shook his head. 'Vanzetti's was the warning. This is a distraction.'

'From what?'

But the Doctor was already scrambling up the walls. Realising the answer, Fabbro glanced up at the icon and prayed that the Doc would be as quick as the old days, for Giovanni's sake.

*

The wind was dying down and a faint rose blush on the clouds heralded approaching dawn. Lucia walked out into the garden, clasping her hands tightly to prevent them shaking.

'*Madonna*,' she prayed, 'give me grace. I would have made an obedient handmaid. I do not question Your will, I simply ask that You give us both the strength to bear what we must bear.' She entered the Baptistery and blessed herself in the font. The water was ice-cold but her hand no longer trembled. Grace.

'There is no need to hide,' she said quietly. 'I know you are here.'

From the shadows the Morello bandieratori emerged. In the half-light, their flags were glistening sheets of burning gold.

'The door was open, so we took the liberty,' said Gaetano. 'Stand aside and you can go free.'

'I *am* free. Here is where I am meant to be. So come and take him, if you can.'

Giovanni woke gasping for air, with a memory that didn't make sense. He *remembered* the Wave that struck Rasenna. It was a dream where past and present merged, for he was on the new bridge, not in the old town centre, as the earth trembled and a shadow fell over Rasenna. The glass was broken. The water was spilled on the ground: obviously making it float had been part of the dream.

Dawn was breaking as he stepped into the garden. He

stopped to look at the sun and stretched and yawned. Strange, he thought; the pigeons were usually so noisy in the mornings. He entered the Baptistery.

There was blood everywhere. Broken bodies were strewn around the floor, heads smashed open, torsos impaled on flagpoles and legs sticking out of the baptismal font.

'Lucia!' He pulled her broken body out of the water.

'If it's any consolation,' Gaetano slurred through a swollen lip, 'she sold her life dearly. You really have something that turns girls' heads.'

He pushed Giovanni over and knelt on top of him, pinning his arms and holding a knife in front of his face.

'I'll tell you what else you're good at: failing. You could have saved my brother in Concord, but you didn't. You could have saved Sofia, but you didn't. And you could have saved that novice if you'd stayed dead, but you didn't. So let's try it again, one last time. Where should I start, Captain? Your ears? I'm short one, see? Your hand, for my brother? Your neck, for my father? Or perhaps that Concordian nose, for sticking it where it's not wanted. Will they still adore you*UH!*'

A smear of black and white. A foot smashed into Gaetano's jaw. The knife went spinning.

Gaetano shambled after Isabella, but the young novice avoided him easily. 'Come here, *amore mio*,' he said drunkenly. 'Look how I baptised your friend – you can be reborn too.'

Giovanni grabbed his leg and shouted, 'Run!'

Gaetano kicked Giovanni's hand away and stomped on his chest, then turned just as Isabella ran at him; she skidded between his legs then spun on the ground, giving a sharp kick to the back of the knee. As he fell, he lunged and grabbed the hem of her habit.

'Little pest! You should have died with your misbegotten family,' said Gaetano, pulling her towards him.

'You too, Tano.' The Doctor held a knife to his throat and, with a steady pressure, brought him to his feet. Isabella pulled her habit free and stood behind Giovanni.

'Shall I do him right now, Podesta? He's earned it.'

Giovanni looked down at Isabella. She shook her head gravely. 'Thou shall not kill.'

'Doctor,' he said, 'take him to the bridge.'

The crowd, summoned by the chiming bells, formed a circle and pushed the prisoner into the centre of the bridge. Death hung in the air, as eager to fall as a sharpened axe.

'Hang him, Podesta!'

The violence of Rasenna was palpable, as material as the towers, the river, and Giovanni felt as powerless to stop it as he would be to stop a second Wave. The beginning and end of Rasenna's law was the right to revenge, yet somehow a little girl had found the strength to push back at it. And, somehow, Lucia had seen her death coming and gone to meet it unafraid. To be podesta he would have to find that same strength . . .

Lucia knew his name and still said he must be podesta.

The Reverend Mother must have known his name too. Did they really see *his* crimes, or were they obscured by his grandfather's shadow?

Leaving his place by the Doctor's side, Mule went to the balustrade and turned over the burned corpse. He pushed Secondo's body into the river, spitting a hopeless curse along with his verdict – 'Traitor!' – then turned back, both eyes red now and streaming tears.

And Giovanni knew the moment he heard the lonely splash *why* it had to end.

'Rasenneisi,' he shouted, 'if I be your podesta, will you accept my judgement?'

'Yes!' they roared.

'This man came to assassinate me. He killed my friend. Shall we hang him?'

The mob howled for blood, louder than before.

'And what if, tomorrow, this man comes for me?' Giovanni pointed at the Doctor. 'Do I hang him too?'

His finger moved to Fabbro. 'Or this man? Or you, Pedro? Or you? As long as Rasenneisi follow separate banners, any of you may one day be strong enough to *be* the law. If the Contessa was here, things would be simpler.'

'She will return,' said the Doctor.

'Perhaps, but to what? If we don't change this, she'll have nothing to return to. As long as Rasenneisi follow separate banners, strength is the only law that matters, and I cannot be your podesta. Twenty years ago a Concordian army occupied Rasenna after the Wave struck.

They pillaged nothing but the Scaligeri banner, and by that one act, made a strong town weak by setting it against itself. But by Rasenneisi law, because they were strong, they were right to do it. So hang Morello – but not because he's a schismatic, hang him because he's in our power and we are strong. Why deliberate? This is *Rasenna*. We need no other reason.'

He grabbed Gaetano and pushed him towards the gap.

'Who will give me rope? I cannot be your podesta, so let me be your hangman!'

The crowd was silent. The Doctor cleared his throat. 'What would you have us do?'

'Throw down your banners! Throw down your banners, or give me rope!'

The sun was up now, and the wide river beneath was beautiful as gold. It felt as if they were awaking, all together, from a long, fevered sleep. The Doctor dropped his flag. After a moment, Fabbro dropped his. His sons and men followed. Woolsmen dropped their Guild colours.

Giovanni removed Gaetano's gag.

'Lord Morello, will you throw down your banner?'

Gaetano ignored him and unsteadily walked over to the Doctor. Glaring at his enemy, he spat on the Bardini flag. Fabbro quickly put a restraining hand on the Doctor.

'I'll be hanged first,' Gaetano said, 'and the last true Rasenneisi will curse you all for traitors with his dying breath. Traitors and *fools*. Why are you listening to this Concordian's lies? He tricked you before, remember? He said you were building a bridge. It was a scaffold for your paesani!'

'So be it,' said Giovanni. 'My first act as podesta is to banish you for life.'

'You don't have that authority. I exile myself.'

When Gaetano was returned his banner he defiantly proclaimed, 'One day soon this flag will return, and with it the honour today lost.'

The crowd watched the Morello heir ride from Rasenna with the awe reserved for miracles, then turned to Giovanni with the same expression.

'My second act as podesta is to propose this: we have expelled faction from within, and we will do so in future. Any man who usurps the Signoria will be banished. From without, the threat comes from Concord. We lost our last battle, to be ready for the one to come. We need warriors, an army of northsiders and southsiders, and weapons and walls, and wealth to pay for them. Doctor Bardini, will you train our army?'

'I will, Podesta.'

'War's a creature that eats from both ends and a growing prosperity affords greater protection than any wall. With better machines and faster ships we can compete with cities like Ariminum and, in time, Concord. Signore Bombelli, will you counsel us?'

'I will, Podesta.'

'Neither walls nor wealth will stop Concord's engineers. Nothing can cancel that power but the *same* power. I therefore propose that Rasenna form an Engineers' Guild of its own.'

A sudden disquiet went through the crowd. The wrinkled brows of older citizens were troubled with a dark memory.

Giovanni paused for protest that never came.

'Hear hear,' said the Doctor, a little too loudly.

'Signore Vanzetti, will you help me form it?'

'I will, Podesta,' Pedro said quietly.

And they were a mob no longer but citizens, united by hope and a question.

Fabbro voiced it: 'Can we win?'

'United, we can do anything.'

'Then,' said Fabbro, with a wink to the Doctor, 'who shall divide us?'

He led the cheer. *'Forza Rasenna!'*

CHAPTER 54

'It's unnecessary, First Apprentice.'

Snow drifted down through the charred skeleton of the triple dome. The winds that assaulted the black mountain now roamed the ruins of the Molè's great hall. The cold air and darkness leached every colour to grey but the First Apprentice's red gown. His face was as tragic as ever as he lovingly caressed the individual letters spelling *resurgo* at the base of the colossus. The angel had come through the fire intact, though the gilt decorating its breastplate and sword had been scorched away. All was changed.

'Bernoulli's heir must be true to his legacy.'

'Oh, you are,' said the Second Apprentice, with a bitterness that belied his youthful face. He was breaking off shards of glass from the shattered column and dropping them into the empty darkness of the Pit. 'He was delusional towards the end too.'

'Are not the signs he left us borne out?' said the man in red with passion. 'He told us that after his blood betrayed him, one would be born to overturn the power of this world. *Our* power.'

'His blood *already* betrayed him – his son – and yet we remain. You look for signs where you should seek facts. Yes, you should have killed her; just accept that you made a mistake, and move on,' he said with empathy. 'You're insecure because the generation of Forty-seven wanted a Bernoulli instead of you; there is nothing you can do to change that. You'll always be judged against him.'

There was a faint *krinch* of crushed glass. The First Apprentice spun around and knocked the shard out of the young man's hand with a chop, then kicked him in the chest.

'*Uuggh!*' the Second Apprentice gasped. He staggered towards the shattered column and would have tumbled into the pit had not the First Apprentice grabbed his collar.

'And you would love to wear the red, boy, so *you* must just accept that you will have to wait your turn.'

He was defiant. 'We have enough problems in Europa without wasting more time on foolishness.'

'Granted, the Captain was a weak vessel without talent, but don't you find it odd Bernoulli's grandson turned against us *there*, of all places? You *were* right. I should have killed her while I had the chance.'

'Our scouts say they went southeast. She could be in Oltremare for all we know.'

'She's a Scaligeri. She'll return to Rasenna. We must finish her, and it, for good.'

'But we've already set the target.'

'There are other ways to deal with Ariminum. Are you blind? *Something* happened in Rasenna to turn Bernoulli's own flesh against him – what other power could it be?'

'Logic worthy of a Cardinal! We're Philosophers. How do you know these are not just coincidences?'

'Faith.' He smiled. 'You'll need to acquire some if you're ever going to wear the red. Until then, your agreement will suffice. Do I have it?' He let the Apprentice's collar slip a little in his grasp. A cold charnel wind came up from the darkness.

The man in red showed his teeth. 'Feel that, boy? Be assured that it feels you, and it smells your fear.'

The Second Apprentice was pale, but struggling to keep his composure. 'I'm not going to bow to superstition, but there are perfectly valid strategic reasons to target Rasenna. It's proved itself incapable of obedience once too often. We can't let that stand.'

'Good enough,' said the man in red, with a laugh that was soft and without music, as he pulled the Second Apprentice up. He walked to what was left of the doorway and looked beyond the snow falling on the dark white city.

'Run to the world's edge, Contessa. We'll catch you.'

CHAPTER 55

She would never return to Rasenna, but it was instinct to compare its rolling hills with the flat fields of the Ariminumese contato. The calm sea was as flat as the land, but she could sense its power; the salt-sharp coastal air was edged with it. The last time she had seen it she was peering through a cage. Now, looking at its world-spanning expanse without constraints, she swore that she'd never return to confinement, whether it was a cell's walls or Rasenna's towers. This was *freedom* – from strictures, from the burden of a name – and she would embrace it. She *must*.

Levi studied the landscape for other reasons. Although they had crossed some land scarred by troop tracks, there was no evidence of outright pillaging.

'This field is newly sowed,' said Levi.

'So?'

'*Madonna*, Rasenneisi are a slow breed. So the farmer expects to be around for the harvest. So the Company isn't besieging Ariminum, it's negotiating a Contract.'

'The city is buying an army?'

'The Hawk's Company is not for sale,' Levi said proudly, and then coughed. 'Besides, it's a renting culture.'

They rode until they spied the camp in a valley a few miles from the city walls. Even at a distance, Ariminum's wealth was obvious. An extensive port dominated one half of the city, while the inland half had burst its limits, with new towers being built outside the walls, spurning their shelter.

'Didn't we promise the Virgin we'd live better lives if she helped us escape?'

'Being a condottiere is the best life there is. Oh! It'll be good to see some friendly faces again,' said Levi happily. 'Hey, watch out!'

An arrow landed a braccia away. The horse bucked, but Levi got it under control.

'Dismount, Sofia. Make it slow.'

'Your friends don't seem too friendly.'

Five heavily armoured soldiers rode towards them. Another arrow landed beside the first.

Sofia reached for her dagger.

'Don't . . .' said Levi.

'Are we just going to let them ride us down? I'll be damned if—'

'*Tranquillo!* It's too late to run. They fired to show us we're covered.'

The leader of the advance party rode forward then stopped and lifted his visor. '*Porca Madonna!*' he said reverently, 'it can't be!' He pulled off his helmet altogether and laughed heartily.

Sofia recognised his monkish hair and stiffened.

'Scarpelli? I thought you were dead!' said Levi.

'We thought *you* were dead!' exclaimed the broad-shouldered condottiere, leaping down. 'Come here, you slippery dog!'

They embraced like brothers. 'Where have you been lying low? Salerno? Veii?'

Levi cocked his head and said casually, 'Concord.'

'Tell me another one, Levi. They're not in the hostage game any more.'

'I didn't *buy* my way out. I broke out!'

'You escaped from the belly of the Beast?' Scarpelli failed to conceal his scepticism. 'That's a first! And this pretty young lady?'

'You remember Sofia?'

'No, I don't believe I've had the— Hold on, the Rasenneisi?'

Scarpelli took a step back with a hand protectively to his neck and laughed nervously. 'How could I forget Doctor Bardini's prize student? You're quite a fighter, Signorina.'

'Thought we could use another one, so I took her along,' Levi said expansively.

'Well, welcome both. It's damn good timing – we're about to begin negotiations with Ariminum.'

'I figured. For a campaign?'

'I'll tell you all about it in camp. Let's just say it's been an uneasy courtship so far.'

Levi and Sofia followed Scarpelli down into the valley.

When he was out of earshot, Sofia slapped Levi on the head.

'Ow!'

'Took me along?'

'Sorry! Listen, just follow my lead until I know who we can trust. And, technically, I did take you with me—

'Ow!'

The old priest opened the cage and selected one of the older doves. He covered its head and cooed softly. When it stopped struggling, he snapped its neck with an efficient twist.

A man stood at the flap of the tent, impatiently watching the procedure. He was a little younger than the priest, though his square beard was greyer and his face more lined by years of worry. He was a big man, and the armour on his upper torso and the bulbous general's cap on his head made him look even larger. If the old bull had passed his prime, it wasn't obvious.

'I want a name. I want to know what he's planning next.' It wasn't a request. The general expected obedience.

The priest ignored him, and continued studying a diagram in a tattered book. His old eyes were shadowed by greyly blossoming cataracts, and they wept constantly. He threw the book to one side angrily and turned to an old chest stocked with vials of powder, various roots and dried plants, and a variety of rusted cutting tools.

'I've told you before, John Acuto: guts tell no names.

Keep the questions broad and you'll get useful answers. Don't, you won't.'

The general bristled, but did not retort. Only the priest dared speak to him this way. The general wasn't the type to seek, cultivate or keep friends, but if he still had one, it was the priest. They were rocks moulded by the same river: both old, where every other face in the Company was young and trusting – young and trusting enough to still believe that Fortune truly did favour the brave. It was a relief to be around someone burdened with the same bitter knowledge: that Fortune was fickle, and favoured cowards and champions, saints and scoundrels, as the fancy took her. In fact, she favoured all but her most devoted suitor, John Acuto – and now it appeared she chose even traitors above him.

'Fine. Should I worry?'

'No point. The dog stalking old men is not outrun.'

'Don't riddle me, Priest. Is there treachery in my Company?'

The priest wiped away the snail-trails pouring down his cheeks, grunted, and set to work.

It began well. It usually did. He deftly ripped out handfuls of chest feathers, then cut away the skin and fat of the breast. Snapping the bones away, he pulled out the irrelevant organs and placed them separately in trays sitting ready.

And then the familiar cloud came over him, and the usual confusion arose to spoil the work. A breeze disturbed the tent flap and smoke got in his eyes and John Acuto's massive shadow covered the light as he paced. The priest rubbed his red-wet hand across his brow and thumbed through the pages of his weathered Etruscan Scripture. The pages concerning divination had been torn, and sewn back together, torn again, stained with dried blood . . .

'What do you see?'

'I see . . .' He pulled the entrails out and picked off the small feathers sticking to them. His heart pounded. He laid them out and tried to dispel the cloud with a distracted wave. Was that blob of flesh the bird's heart, or just meat? He looked at the beaker, at the water swirling in a maelstrom of blood. He swore and tipped the tray's contents into the fire. They bubbled and spat, filling the tent with noxious air.

'Nothing. I see nothing, John Acuto.'

'Never mind, never mind.' The general put his hand on the priest's sunken shoulder. 'Sometimes Fortune prefers us to stumble in darkness.'

As the general went to leave, the priest raised his head. 'General, I may be a blind old fool but you don't need augury to know there's a traitor in the Company. You can smell it.'

Acuto narrowed his eyes; was the priest just telling him what he wanted to hear? No, it was the truth. His own intuition had prompted the question. 'Aye,' he said after a moment. 'I hoped to be told I was mistaken.'

*

They rode down into the valley. While Scarpelli brought Levi up to date on the developments since the Tagliacozzo débâcle, Sofia took in the camp. She'd been expecting the carousing usual in Rasenna before and after raids – drinking, gambling and fighting – but the place was as serious and neat as Fabbro Bombelli's account book. The tents were arranged in straight rows, like a Concordian camp. She was amused that the only army in Etruria to challenge the Empire in the last decade did so while imitating its mechanistic efficiency.

'*Madonna*, is John Acuto Concordian?'

Levi laughed. 'The general's from the Anglish Isles, but we've all sorts here – Teutons, Franks, Ibericans, some Russ, Welshmen, even some Hibernian brutes. We condottieri take business seriously.'

Sofia smiled to see how merry Levi was and how proud he was of the Company. He was right, too: no one was idle. Soldiers were tending their horses, sharpening swords, polishing armour, repairing, cleaning – or training as if battle was imminent. In Rasenna, violence was unplanned, coming on like a convulsion. It was intense, irrational and transient. It was queer to be amongst men who treated war as profession, not vocation.

She stared at a man sewing up an arm wound with a bored look on his face. He was almost four braccia tall, with broad ox-like shoulders and a thick neck. He caught her stare as he bit through the thread and threw her a wry half-salute and wink. Saluting back, Sofia saw the giant's smile broaden when he spotted Levi at the horse's reins.

'Hey, pedlar boy!' he called in a thick accent.

'Yuri?'

'We thought maybe you were promoted to Heaven.'

Levi leapt down and embraced the giant. 'Not yet, my friend.'

Sofia noticed how Yuri's easy smile faded when he saw Scarpelli. He embraced Levi again and whispered, 'We talk later maybe.'

Levi remounted, telling Scarpelli that the Russ owed him money before changing the subject. 'Speaking of money, shock me: who's been appointed treasurer in my absence?'

Scarpelli gave him a look. 'The Dwarf.'

'Oh. Didn't know he could count,' Levi said mildly.

Scarpelli laughed. 'We're lucky you're back in time for the negotiations.'

'The Ariminumese are wary about the Contract?'

'The Contract, the campaign, the venue, seating arrangements, just about everything!'

'They've never used condottieri before, so they think we're criminals.' Levi turned around to give Sofia a preemptive look of reproach.

She politely feigned astonishment.

'That's the trouble,' said Scarpelli, 'they've never *had* to use condottieri. And you know what these burghers are like: insufferably proud of their puny militias in peace time, but when war comes they start to have visions of their precious walls tumbling like Jericho's.'

'Towns protecting their walls? Shouldn't it be the other way round?' Sofia asked.

Scarpelli smiled at her, a little more naturally this time. 'It's absurd, Signorina, but that's how we humble contractors make a living. When burghers get anxious about their property, they pay whatever we demand. Rich towns think it's the height of sophistication to hire an army to fight for them – they think they're better and smarter than everyone, nobles, Concordians and us. Especially us.'

'Well, they can think what they like,' said Levi.

'Because in the end you'll bleed them dry and move on.'

'Sorry about her, Scarpelli. Anything more complicated than flag-waving makes Rasenneisi suspicious.'

Scarpelli just laughed. 'She's right, isn't she? That's how it *should* work. But wait till you meet these Ariminumese, Levi. They're practically holding *us* hostage.'

'Times are changing.'

'Try telling John Acuto,' Scarpelli said with sudden bitterness.

Levi raised his eyebrows. 'He's not involved in negotiations, is he?'

'He was always a better soldier than politician, but since Tagliacozzo he's been as paranoid as Herod. I'm sure he'll share his theories with you.'

'Acuto suspects treachery?' Levi said guardedly.

Scarpelli was blasé. 'Ever know a general who lost who didn't? The panic started when the Standard fell and they found the Standard-bearer with a dagger in his back.'

'But the carroccio was behind the front line.'

'So they say, but you know how chaotic it was. We lost, simple as that. But since then, the old man's been consulting Father Blood-and-guts on strategy and checking for assassins under his pillow, so you'd better get your escape story straight before he questions you.'

'*Questions* me?' Levi stopped his horse. 'Last I checked, I'm a colonel, not a prisoner. It's not a *story—*'

Scarpelli clapped him on the back. '*Tranquillo*, Levi, I'm just telling you what to expect. Follow me.'

At the centre of the camp was a large tent flying the Hawk's banner. On Etrurian crests, hawks were depicted as plump-plumaged patricians; this foreign bird-of-prey was a clinical killer, sharp and lean, drawn with straight decisive lines.

The tent flap was suddenly thrown aside and a short man, dark-skinned like a Moor, scurried out between the two guards. He was followed by a large, angry man brandishing a scroll like a general's baton.

'Tell your Signoria that if that's all they have to offer, they'd better swallow their pride and make terms with Concord. This is the Hawk's Company!' He threw the scroll at the notary. 'This isn't a Contract, it's an *insult*!'

'You're not the only contractor in the peninsula, John Acuto.'

Acuto slapped the notary's hat off and grabbed him by the collar. 'Then hire *them*! Throw your money away. Just don't be surprised if you wake up one morning with your palazzi burning around you.'

Scarpelli leapt down to pry the notary from the general's grip. 'What the general means is that we need a few days to digest this and prepare a counter-offer,' he said, picking the Contract out of the mud.

'Take your time,' the notary said, 'we're in no hurry.'

Scarpelli helped the notary mount his sumptuously decorated mule and escorted him out of camp.

Acuto glowered after them. 'What's wrong with cities these days? Used to be we only had to show up outside their walls and bang a drum to get cooperation.' Finally noticing Levi, the general cut short his rant and glared at him.

Levi dismounted, gesturing to Sofia to follow his lead. 'General,' said Levi warmly, extending his hand.

The general looked at Levi with much the same hostility he'd shown the notary. 'How did you secure your release?'

'I escaped, General,' said Levi, awkwardly dropping his hand.

'Escaped. Not the first time you've left a Concordian prison in one piece. Not many are so fortunate. Come in, Colonel. I wish to congratulate you privately.'

Levi swallowed. Telling Sofia he'd be back in a minute, he turned and entered the tent just as an old man shuffled out. Distracted, hugging a book to his body, he stumbled. Sofia caught the book and held his arm as he regained his balance.

'Good catch, Sister!'

'I'm not a nun, Father,' she said quickly as she handed him the book, but he barely heard as he hurried on his way. Sofia remained outside the tent for an hour. She wasn't eavesdropping – the general's roaring was impossible *not* to hear. She was pleased to hear Levi defend himself at last.

'*Concord* killed Harry, General, not me – and not you, though I see you're still intent on blaming us both.'

When Levi came out with a red face and set mouth, Acuto called after him, 'Colonel! You're coming to the negotiations tomorrow. I need that clever tongue for once.'

Levi saluted frostily.

John Acuto's glare fell on Sofia.

'What are you looking at?' she said.

'Colonel, who's this?'

'My name is Sofia Sca—'

'Nobody. She escaped with me.'

'Another spy then? Nice to know I'm important enough to merit two.'

'Say that again, Methuselah—' Sofia put her hand on her dagger.

Levi rested a restraining hand on her shoulder. 'I can vouch for her.'

'That's supposed to comfort me?' said Acuto. He looked down at Sofia. 'What can you do?'

'I'm good with a knife. I'll show you, if you like.'

Levi saw the guards watching Sofia; she hadn't taken her hand off her dagger.

'She means she's a cook, General.'

Acuto snorted. 'Fine, fine. But you taste everything she prepares first. If I'm to be poisoned I want to take my assassin with me. Best teach her manners too.'

As Sofia and Levi made their way to the mess-tent, she saw the soldiers weren't in the same condition as their neatly arrayed and polished equipment. Every man bore scars from past campaigns as well as wounds still fresh from Tagliacozzo.

'I'd like to teach *him* some manners,' she fumed.

'I hope you *can* cook,' said Levi.

'Don't worry, I grew up looking after myself. But why not tell him who I am?'

'Sofia, if you wanted to be that person, you would have gone back to Rasenna.'

She was only stung for a moment. 'Answer the question.'

'Condottieri aren't knights, they're businessmen,' said Levi, still tense. 'Your name could make you a commodity.'

They found the giant hard at work in front of a range of boiling pots.

'Yuri, got you a new assistant. Sofia, everybody's sick of Russky food. Maybe you can mix it up a little.'

Yuri wagged a spoon in Levi's face. 'The peoples are loving my cookerys. I get many compliments to it.'

'I thought you were a soldier,' said Sofia.

'Why do you think this?'

She pointed to an old scar on his neck. 'That's an arrow wound, so is that, and you didn't get those' – looking at the fresh stitches – 'from peeling vegetables,' she said.

'You have smarts like Levi,' said Yuri, 'but not to be so sure of vegetables, especially asparagus, very sneaky!'

'Everyone's a soldier here,' said Levi, 'cooks, surgeons, even priests. John Acuto runs a tight ship.'

'I am hearing he's giving you some welcomes.'

'The old man's gone crazy!' Levi exploded, 'he's seeing conspiracies everywhere—'

'But maybe there is one?'

'I *know* there's one – but I also know the real problem: times are changing; things are getting harder.'

The giant nodded. 'Maybe.'

'Acuto said you'd escaped Concord before,' said Sofia.

'He's just being sarcastic. I was a hostage for a time, about five years ago, when the Hawk's Company still worked for Concord, when Concord still returned hostages.'

'Back home, they said John Acuto betrayed Concord.'

Yuri slammed a tomato into mush. 'This is big lie!'

'Relax, Yuri,' said Levi, 'that's what all Etruria thinks. It wasn't like that, Sofia. Concord double-crossed us. We had a Contract with them, so at the start of each season, we'd provide hostages – pretty standard; contractors don't have great reputations for fealty, after all.'

'You don't say?'

'Anyway, that year, I was one, and so was Harry.'

'That's an Anglish name.'

'Harry Acuto. John Acuto's son.'

'Brave fighter,' said Yuri.

'And a good friend,' said Levi quietly. 'I was released. Harry wasn't – Concord's way of cancelling our Contract, I guess. Since then, the Hawk's Company only takes Contracts from Concord's enemies.'

'Was good policy, for a while,' said Yuri.

'I bet. Dying men spend freely,' said Sofia.

'Now everyone's broke, and the general's still wary of me just because I lived and Harry died. I told him that Concord had known of our plans, and it just made him more suspicious.'

'That's how condottieri think, all twisty like noodle.' Yuri dangled a string of pasta.

'Concord wants you to fight amongst yourselves. That's how the swine work,' Sofia said.

'Well, it's working,' said Levi. 'I'm beginning to think we should have stayed and taken our chances with the buio.'

CHAPTER 56

The first *official* day of Contract negotiation was something all condottieri looked forward to. Most towns, relieved to have secured champions, would hold celebrations, where the Contract brokers could play at being chivalrous knights to the rescue. The company could also expect lavish quarters for the duration of negotiations.

Strange then, said Levi, to find Ariminum's gates closed that morning, and stranger still, after they were grudgingly opened, to ride through streets that were empty but for barking strays – empty, though Ariminum was a busy, wealthy town. The reason for this shabby reception was obvious, and disconcerting – their hosts were telling them they were unwelcome.

The Sala dei Notari, a lofty chamber of wood-carved dignity, had been built on an inhuman scale, with everything a few inches too high, all a little too large for the stony-faced Signoria, men who faded beside the decorative banners, shields and ribbons covering the walls. John Acuto and his colleagues felt, as was intended, out of place and inferior, like petitioners begging for debt-relief rather than the city's saviours.

Before the session came to order, Acuto glanced over his negotiating team, appraising his three wise men's loyalty, a game he played with everyone these days.

Scarpelli's face was, as usual, a mask, polite and blank. The Dwarf, now treasurer, was innocent and guilty both at once – he owed his inglorious title to his obvious ambition as much as his strange proportions. He always did what was asked of him, but still Acuto distrusted him – maybe it was the covetous way he stroked a banner that hung within reach, or the way his yellow skin shone like old fruit? Hardly good reasons not to trust the man.

That left Levi, whom Acuto had once considered a protégé. Since Harry's death the distance between them had been insurmountable, though Levi had attempted to bridge it. Acuto followed his gaze, and saw Levi was studying the carved town mascot looming over the proceedings; the griffin looked about as sympathetic as the beak-nosed Doge of Ariminum glowering down at them beneath.

The general's massive frame perched awkwardly on a small stool. He assumed his discomfort, like the other slights, was intentional. Well, let them play their games. The foundation townsmen built their courage upon was ignorance – ignorance of how easily buildings burned, how little strength it took to tumble walls and how much could be lost in a moment. So let them have their pride, so long as in the end he had their money.

The Moorish notary brusquely called the session to order and the general rose to speak. 'My Lords, long has Ariminum been famous for pride and prudence and wealth; I must now add hospitality to that list. Today, the urgent need of Ariminum and the talents of my famous Company meet harmoniously. Let us make haste then to sign our Contract and begin what will undoubtedly be a bond of mutual advantage.'

Levi caught the general's eye as he sat down. If they had been on winking terms, he was certain he would have got one now. The old bull had been negotiating Contracts for decades. Whether the townsmen were deaf to sarcasm remained to be seen.

After a protracted silence, long enough to be rude, the doge glared with bare hostility at the condottieri. 'We deigned invite you inside our walls, John Acuto, but you were *not* invited to speak. Ariminum has traditions that were old long before you stole into this country. We begin Signoria meetings with prayer, not vacuous pleasantries.' He made the sign of the sword and stood. 'On this, the day of Saint Francis, we pray he will protect us as he protected the people of Gubbio.'

The doge suddenly interrupted his pious drone to ask, 'You've heard of this miracle, John Acuto?'

Acuto's smile didn't falter. 'I know the town.'

The doge continued, 'Oh? Perhaps you are familiar with its recent history, but once, long ago, it was terrorised by a Wolf. The Saint came and called the Wolf from the forest. "Brother Wolf," he said, "if these townsmen feed you, will you promise not to kill them?" Naturally, the townsmen's lives were incomprehensible to the beast, but it understood a free meal. Without the gift of speech, it could only twist its emaciated body – it was starving too – in such an unnatural way that everyone understood it agreed to the Contract. Saint Francis piously went on his way and the Wolf lived in peace with the townsfolk ever after.'

'Charming story,' Acuto said, hiding his impatience.

'You were not invited to speak!' the doge shouted.

'When the Wolf died, the townsfolk mourned it and buried it in holy ground, just like a citizen. You see, they'd forgotten that it was a beast. But a beast remains a beast, no matter how it learns to twist. You will *not* be given quarters inside our walls, John Acuto. You will remain outside with your mercenaries. Expect a lengthy stay. All Etruria knows the only language condottieri speak well is Contract-law, so we will *not* make haste; we will deliberate, we will parse, and if you don't like it—'

'My Lord, this hostility is—'

'—all you can expect! If it does not please you, break camp, and we will find a company with less vanity and more respect. The scavengers that remain in Etruria would be happy for the work. This marriage of convenience will be brief, so speak of no "shared interests" – you would not be here if your private war with Concord had not beggared you, and we would not be reduced to hiring *you*, the cancer of Etruria, if Concord did not covet our wealth.'

'You speak candidly, my Lord,' said John Acuto.

'If you prefer the dung of hypocrisy, leave our contato, Brother Wolf. Go to the poor wretched towns that are left, if you haven't already raped them of every soldi.'

John Acuto stood. 'Candour suits me entirely, Doge. You talk of war and drape your walls with ribbons, but they are not combat banners and you are not soldiers. You think you have me at a disadvantage because bargaining is your profession? I advise you to remember *my* profession. If the Contract is not signed within a month and a day, I will break camp, but first I'll break your walls and burn your towers. Then you'll be the starving dogs!'

He kicked aside his stool and strode out. The three wise men looked aghast, then scrambled to follow.

The negotiators passed through the town gates attended by barking dogs. Levi studied the famous triple walls. They would be difficult to breach if it came down to it. He broke the silence. 'Well, they hate us.'

'Expect friendship and you're in for disappointment,' said John Acuto wearily. 'This wretched country's climate doesn't suit it. Aye, they hate us. Lucky for us, they love their money more.'

The evening meal was simple, with the emphasis on nourishment and quantity over taste, but Sofia had added a feminine touch the soldiers were grateful for.

'Look, Yuri – the general's joining us.'

'Why would he not?'

'In my town, the Families keep a distance from the Small People.'

'Do I look *small* to you? Company is not like towns is. If general don't eat with men, men don't elect general.'

Sofia was ladling out the stew when Acuto's turn came.

'I apologise for my earlier rudeness, Signorina. Old soldiers see enemies where there are none.'

She shrugged. 'Levi's the one you owe the apology.'

Yuri winced, expecting an eruption, but the general just took his plate with a grunt and sat down with his officers. After the majority of the men were served, Yuri told Sofia to eat. She sat beside the fire with Levi. He and the Dwarf were already arguing. The Hawk's Company was small enough that the Dwarf was needed for both fighting and brokering, but Levi, knowing enough about both to know the Dwarf was incompetent, could never disguise his scepticism.

The general smacked his lips. 'You prepared this *l'ampra dotto*, Signorina?'

'Yes,' said Sofia coolly, not to be won over by compliments to her cooking either.

But flattery was not his aim. 'Rasenneisi dish, is it not? If you originate there too, perhaps you weren't lying about your knifework.'

'I don't lie!' said Sofia hotly.

'Look!' The Dwarf wheezed a laugh. 'The Rasenneisi Dish's blushing!'

'I wouldn't—' said Scarpelli.

'Oh, relax, I'm just being friendly. Anything else on the menu tonight, *amore*?'

Acuto said, 'Dwarf, you may not be a knight, but try to be a gentleman.'

Yuri lifted the Dwarf by the collar until his feet dangled. 'You have complainings, you come to me.'

'Let's see if she can fight her own battles,' said Acuto.

'Suits me,' Sofia said, putting down her plate and cracking her knuckles.

Scarpelli and Levi exchanged a knowing glance. The Dwarf was embarrassed to suddenly be the centre of attention.

'General, I'm not going to hit a girl—'

He came to with Sofia kneeling over him.

'Don't try to talk. Your jaw's dislocated.' She braced his head and pushed his chin to one side.

He screamed.

'Next time, I set it crooked.'

The Dwarf whimpered and passed out again.

John Acuto cocked an eyebrow at Levi. 'Tell me again, Colonel, who rescued whom?'

'Well, she didn't slow me down,' said Levi breezily, glad to be civilly addressed again.

Yuri sat down beside Sofia. 'You teach me this moves?'

*

After the meal, the officers discussed the difficulties with the Ariminumese.

'The month you gave might not be enough, General,' Levi said.

'An empty threat. That overdressed griffin was right; we've bled every town in the Peninsula dry, those Concord didn't get to first. We need this Contract more than Ariminum does and they know it. I'm going to turn in. I have to write home and tell my wife I'll be delayed another season.'

He stood and announced, 'I suggest those of you with loved ones do likewise. We camp here for spring. Golden dreams, gentlemen.'

Levi watched the general lumber into the darkness. 'He's still writing those letters?'

'Still—' said Yuri wearily.

When that subject was exhausted, Levi discussed Tagliacozzo with the other captains. Everyone had a different version of the battle, but the unspoken consensus was that the Hawk's fortune had simply run out. Their loyalty was intact, but even a stranger like Sofia could see it was shaken.

As it got dark, damp winds heavy with the last chill of winter blew in from the sea. The men sang songs of distant homes in distant lands, melancholy airs that Sofia understood, though the words were strange. Before her turn came, she stole away. She had no loved ones to write to, nor home to sing of.

CHAPTER 57

No screaming. No groaning metal. No sound in the pit not

even

the

drip

She walked to the door. Her cell had almost reached the water. The surface churned as the platform rose up and stopped at her row. She looked up for the coffin, but the darkness was empty. The lake's surface began to churn once more and the coffin rose slowly *from* the water.

'Who's there?'

The coffin door opened with a sibilant hiss. Black water oozed, sloshing, out. She saw fingers, white maggots with black fingernails, curl around the door. She backed against her cell wall. She heard a rasping wet noise, drowned lungs breathing. The sodden steps came nearer. The bolt shot back, her cell door moved slightly on its hinge. Tired of waiting, the Darkness had come to her.

She woke screaming.

'*Porca miseria!*' Sofia struck the flint again, but got not even a spark. Spring had arrived, stubbornly inclement, and the rain was unrelenting. Getting warm was more pressing this morning than cooking, but the straw was damp and the wind was howling; it was never going to light. Until the Contract was signed the Dwarf had stopped paying salaries, a policy that worried Levi. Bored soldiers need money, because if they can't gamble or whore, they find amusement in ways that cause discipline problems. He advised Sofia to stay close to Yuri, and to wear her hair in a bob. Sofia cut it. She'd hated it long anyway.

'Can I help?'

Sofia looked up with a scowl. 'What do you want? I'm still not a nun, before you ask.'

'It was not my intention to offend, Signorina. My name is—'

'I know who you are: John Acuto's pet fortune-teller. And you can't help unless you fart fireballs.'

'Rarely – but if you are trying to boil that water . . .' The priest held his hand out and the water shuddered and abruptly started bubbling.

'You know Water Style?' she gasped.

He smiled. It was a strange sight with his piteous weeping eyes. 'I believe I'm not alone.'

'I don't know what you mean,' she said, regretting opening her mouth.

'You mean to say, you're *really* not a nun?'

Sofia searched his clouded grey eyes and saw he was genuinely puzzled. 'I studied with one. She's dead now.'

'I'm sorry to hear that, and sorry for not believing you – traditionally, we don't make initiations lightly. For most people it's a lifetime's commitment.'

'She had her reasons, I suppose.'

'Maybe she saw her end coming.' The priest was thoughtful. 'The water's stopped boiling. Why don't you try?'

Sofia looked into the cauldron. As before, the water was perfectly still, with only a few wisps of vapour to show it really had been boiling. She had avoided meditation since she'd learned who the engineer really was – the Reverend Mother had told her to have faith, but it had been a mistake to trust her: if she hadn't realised Giovanni was blood to the devil who sent the Wave, then what good was Water Style? And if she did know who he was— Well, the Doc was right, blind faith in *anyone* was foolish. Even the Doc, even the Virgin – they were all liars, manipulating her for their own ends.

The Hawk's Company was different; here everyone was anonymous, all violence impersonal. Here she could do the only thing that made sense any more: fight Concord.

'Look, I just want to be normal,' she started.

'You needn't be afraid of the dreams, you know. That's

how the Virgin shows us the future in motion. It's ours to accept or change.'

'Damn it, I said no!' she shouted.

'There, that wasn't so hard, was it? Better get those vegetables in.'

The water was boiling again.

'I don't believe it – you're doing that.'

'You've almost given up on yourself, haven't you?'

'I already told you, I'm not interested in fortune-telling.' She stirred the pot aggressively. After a moment she glanced up.

'Boiling is easy,' he said patiently. 'It's much harder to cool it down. Whoever you are, you're not a cook.'

'You want to hear my confession? I'm a traitor, all right? Happy?'

The priest tutted quietly. 'Well, you'll fit in if you stay. Everyone is guilty to one degree or another.'

Sofia changed tack. 'You want me gone? You're threatened by someone that knows your tricks.'

'I could sense your power even before I saw you. It's as big as the sea out there! Whoever taught you recognised that you're special. But if you stay here, sooner or later, special or not, you'll make choices that will tarnish you for ever.' He turned and began to walk away.

'What did you choose?' Sofia said.

He turned. 'You're afraid of what you might see. For me, the water's always clouded.'

'You don't know me!'

He was gone and the pot was still boiling. It *was* her. Could she stop it too? Sofia held out her hand and concentrated.

It was waiting, suckling on anger, swollen like a louse, the Darkness that had a name now: Giovanni Bernoulli the liar.

She came up gasping to find the water boiling furiously, spilling over the top, and tears pouring down her face. She was exiled; there was no going back. It was worse than any torture she'd endured in the Beast, because then she had believed her punishment unjust. Now she knew better.

In the Sala dei Notari, Levi studied the town's mascot. You know where you stand with griffins – they show their teeth from the start. The Ariminumese were infuriating. After weeks of offer and counter-offer they said they were ready to sign, but the terms were still insulting.

Or, Levi thought with another glance at the griffin, perhaps they were as good as the Company could expect in a world where only Concordians paid top prices. If they accepted that, it would be only a matter of time before condottieri questioned the logic of perpetual war against Etruria's top payer. Would Acuto have an answer? In the accounts, Harry was just another written-off solider. The Company's purpose was to make money, not to make Etruria a better place.

The doge pushed the counter-offer away like a meal

without salt. 'No,' he said without ceremony. He walked out, followed by the Signoria.

The notary cleared his throat. 'The Signoria reconvenes in a fortnight. In the interim, there is the matter of your camp supplies . . .'

CHAPTER 58

'We're back to the start if we pay.'

'And if we refuse, it's war. We knew it was coming, but we're not ready. In a few months, maybe, but now? Whether we consent or refuse, we doom ourselves.'

Couched in congratulations for Rasenna's growing wealth, the letter was the clearest threat yet.

'There's another option,' said Giovanni.

'What?'

'I'll tell you tomorrow.'

'You want me in on a Signoria meeting? Bad idea, Podesta. Sends the wrong signal to southsiders.'

'The right signal. If towns can change, people can.'

The new Palazzo della Signoria echoed with lively discussion. The notary, straining to keep up, wondered if perhaps the old days were better, before deciding no, nothing could be better than having a say in what one wrote.

Conjuring up visions of burning towers and empty

471

purses, Fabbro advocated paying the larger tribute, and Pedro agreed that there was no other option.

'What's the alternative, Podesta?' asked Fabbro impatiently.

'Dally.'

Fabbro was nonplussed, but the Doctor laughed.

Giovanni explained, 'Paying *without* procrastinating would draw Concord's attention. We allay suspicion by doing exactly what they expect of paupers. We write as grovelling a letter as we can compose, quibbling with the amount, asking for another extension, begging to pay in instalments. They will reply sternly. We will equivocate. They will insist. We will plead and then—'

'They will demand another ambassador to send back mutilated!' said Fabbro.

'Only if we send one, and we will not. We will say we have to elect a new ambassador.'

'But what does it give us?' said Pedro.

'Time!' the Doctor answered, clapping his hands together, 'After Tagliacozzo, Concord has turned from Etruria to Europa. When someone forgets to watch their back, that's an opportunity.'

Giovanni held up the letter. 'This isn't a tax, it's a declaration of war. A war we cannot avoid, only delay. To pay would be to drop our shield even as the blow falls. We must use the money and time we have left wisely. The stronger our walls, the sounder our defences, the fitter our bandieratori, the better our chances when

Concord realises we mean to defy them. Before the giant moves, we must grow large enough to defend ourselves.'

'Or,' the Doctor remarked, 'make friends with other giants.'

Afterwards, Giovanni walked the Doctor to the bridge. 'It isn't the stuff of Homer.'

The Doctor shrugged. 'Whatever works, that's the best strategy. If you can't be Achilles, be Odysseus.' He caught the direction of Giovanni's wary glance. 'You didn't expect everyone to behave just because some shopkeepers agree they like money, did you?'

Since Gaetano's banishment, the burned-out shell of Palazzo Morello was like a slumbering monster in their midst. Around the dragon's cave, groups of boys loitered. Instead of Morello gold, there were a dozen different banners: a dog pack that only watched, but that was enough; people coming and going from the bridge felt their hungry stares.

'That's cynical, Doctor. I thought that after we exiled Morello—'

'I'm telling how I saw it a year ago.'

'How can they still stand apart? Even if we delay, Concord will be at the gate before the year is out.'

'Children don't think about tomorrow.'

'Can't you reason with them?'

The Doctor laughed. 'The only thing a pack understands is strength. It's not just this side of the river; every day, a different bandieratoro whispers in my ear about what an opportunity this is.'

'What do you tell them?'

'I tell them to shut up, and I keep Bardini banners north.'

A boy pushed his way through the group in the doorway. The Doctor recognised Uggeri and noticed that even the older boys showed deference. Calmly, Uggeri watched them walk by.

'Isn't that Hog Galati's son?'

'He's the last of Morello's crew of killers,' the Doctor said. 'Got some salt too.'

Uggeri spat, and turned his back on the Doctor to enter the ruined Palazzo. Most of the other boys followed.

'A Rasenneisi needs something to love so he can fight for it,' the Doctor said. 'They don't remember the Wave. They hate each other more than Concord.'

A balmy evening swaggered on and the bridge stalls closed up as merchants went to waste money in Rasenna's hostels, taverns, houses of gambling and other activities.

'Unity can't wait until Concord's at the wall. By then—'

'Like I said, children don't think about tomorrow. The Bardini banner can't unite them either. Now that Morello's gone, hating me is the only thing southsiders have in common.'

'So what do we do? Exile the ringleaders? That boy—'

'Stick a crow's head on a stick?' The Doctor laughed. 'A show of force would unify them, but against us. The Scaligeri flag was the last thing that unified all Rasenna.

For a long time that was the only choice – to be slave or master. They don't have a leader any more, but it's only a matter of time before one of them raises colours. Still, we'll figure out something. Coming up?'

'Not tonight. Work. Golden dreams, Doctor.'

Giovanni had opened his floor in Tower Vanzetti to Rasenna's young engineers. They called it the studiola, and even this late he knew they would be working. Delaying Concord was only logical if every hour was used to prepare for the inevitable confrontation.

Doctor Bardini climbed the steps, brooding on the violence promised in Uggeri's stare, not afraid, but unsettled by the boy's resemblance to the young man he himself had been.

The Doctor hadn't dreamed in years, but that night he was immersed in a twenty-year-old memory:

In Tower Scaligeri, a serious young man takes dictation. Count Scaligeri stands by a long narrow window watching the black and gold banner blowing in the wind. The Count's study is on the tower's top floor, so the winds are always fierce. It has been especially gusty that day, which makes it all the more disconcerting when the flag abruptly goes limp.

The boy's penmanship is good, but the word he is writing, Concord, comes out illegible. The table, the tower, Rasenna itself is shaking. The ink and water swirling in the jar beside him begins to separate, small drops rising to the surface and floating in space.

'My Lord, look at the water!'

'So they have done it, Madonna help us.'

The boy looks up and sees the Count leaning out of the window to tear down the banner.

'Bardini, the hour has come. Where is my son?'

'With my sister, in my father's workshop.'

'Something is coming,' the Count says, 'and I must wait for it. Take my banner, protect my son – whatever happens, the Scaligeri must survive.'

'I should stay with you!' the boy says stubbornly.

The Count slaps him. The boy is speechless: he has never seen his master angry.

'Never start a fight you cannot win.' The Count touches his cheek. 'If you learn nothing else from me, learn that. Obey me one last time. Get to high ground. Do not look back.'

The boy takes the banner and goes to the door. He looks back one last time. The Count sits at the desk to complete the letter. Only the ink remains in the jar beside him; the water floats in the air. Frozen rain.

He looks up suddenly and roars, 'Fly!'

Down and down and down the steps the boy runs. He passes noblemen and women panicking in the piazza. He passes the Lions, silently roaring defiance at the spreading darkness, up the north steps to the old town and the 'healthy' hills, to Tower Bardini. He does not look back. The thunder grows louder until the shadow covers everything and the

rumble drowns out the screaming. Morning birds fall silent.
Night falls on Rasenna.

The air in the Doctor's chamber was stifling, reeking of guilt and disappointment. Why did his youth come back to him now? After Count Scaligeri, he never sought another leader. And what had he achieved? Nothing. He'd failed to keep any promise he'd ever made – his career, a record of things lost: banners, battles, and a daughter in all but name. And now, after all this time, he'd put his trust in another leader – what chance that he'd chose wisely this time? What chance he'd picked a fight he could win?

He slowly lay back down on his sweat-damp mattress, and cursed himself – sleeping without a banner to hand was apprentice stuff. As his hand silently searched the floor beside his bed, he spoke to the darkness:

'What are you waiting for, an invitation?'

The boy stepped into a shaft of moonlight. His skin was ghostly-blue, the knife he held a purer white. It burned with the same intensity as his eyes.

'Not surprised, old man?'

'It's what I would do.'

The Doctor waited, but the boy just held his knife ready.

'Uggeri, isn't it? Why did you really come?'

'You're fake, aren't you?'

He sighed in the darkness. 'Not any more.'

'You used the Contessa. Now you're using the engineer.

This fake Signoria thinks it's in charge, but you're whispering in the ears that matter, aren't you?'

'You won't believe me, but no.' Even as his hand touched his banner, he kept talking. 'I wouldn't if I was in your position, but then, in your position, I'd be dead by now!'

He rolled out of the bed. Uggeri threw the dagger, but it struck his banner. He kicked the bed, slamming it into Uggeri's shins. The Doctor pried the blade out of his stick and advanced. Uggeri watched calmly as the Doctor aimed. The knife landed in the floor beside him.

'Take it and go.'

'What's the matter?' Uggeri said casually, 'no wind in your flag?'

'I said get the hell out.'

The boy left through the window he'd entered. The Doctor watched the shadow scramble over the rooftops, knowing what would come next as well as he knew himself. Uggeri would raise his flag. He couldn't let that happen. He'd failed Count Scaligeri; if blood needed spilling to keep his promise to Giovanni, well then, blood would spill.

CHAPTER 59

'Important order,' Pedro explained, shutting the door in Giovanni's face.

Later, as Giovanni drafted the response to Concord with Fabbro, he mentioned the incident, only to learn there was no new order.

He returned in the evening to Tower Vanzetti to investigate – but Pedro wasn't home. He went down to the studiola, a bad feeling in his gut.

'What the hell?'

It was still bright enough to see the bridge from the window. Giovanni watched as Pedro handed Doctor Bardini a bundle. The Doctor put the banners on his shoulder and marched into the piazza.

Obviously he had changed his mind about that show of force: he was carrying a Bardini banner south. If Giovanni had seen it, other towers had seen it too. Southsiders might be dispirited and leaderless, but they wouldn't surrender without a fight. He reached the piazza too late. The Doctor had entered the dragon's cave.

*

A bonfire burned in the centre of what was once the work-shop. Its flames reflected in the warped mirror, throwing up strange shadows in the charred ruins. In the dancing light, the boys surrounding the Doctor looked large as men, and more dangerous. They carried Galati's blue banner, but that wasn't the real change. There was a difference between a pack of bandieratori and a borgata. A borgata needed someone to obey.

Uggeri sat on a pile of rubble which had once been a staircase; now it was a throne. When he spoke the others listened. 'You think your bandieratori hiding in the shadows have us surrounded? *They're* surrounded, by Rasenna.'

'I came alone.'

'So that's what this is.' Uggeri leapt down. 'It won't do you any good. When you kill me, someone takes my place. That's how Rasenna works, old man.'

The Doctor looked back to the doorway. The leaders of other southside borgati were blocking the way, should either think to flee. They'd come to see which dog won the fight.

The Doctor thrust his banner into the bonfire. He let the cloth catch, and then held it up and let them see it burn. 'How Rasenna works is what I came to talk about.' He threw the charred stick into the fire. 'I'm at your mercy.'

There was a long silence in which they studied each other. 'So talk,' the boy said.

Uggeri's soldiers looked to him. The fire popped and cracked, goading them to act.

'Hear that, *bambini*? Concord's coming. Kill me tonight, we're all dead tomorrow. Concord won't need to knock down our walls and towers – they'll fall on their own.'

As the Doctor spoke he looked around the hostile faces of Uggeri's army. It was early evening, and dark clouds enshrouded a pale distant sun. The wind stirred up the bonfire and the Doctor's voice with it.

'I wish I could blame Concord for it, but I remember life before the Wave – faction had already slithered into paradise, though it was under Count Scaligeri's boot. If that's the type of unity we want, we can have it. You only have to follow one tower's banner.'

'Yours, Bardini?' Uggeri sneered.

'I don't deserve loyalty: the Families that replaced the Scaligeri set the serpent loose. I take no pride that my flag's still flying. I know my methods. I made a weak man my enemy to make my tower strong, and Morello used me. Well, look at our reward.' He gestured to the blackened stones. 'Our separate towers don't protect us, they enfeeble us. Where there was a river between us we bridged it, and as a result we have grown, in wealth and unity, choking the serpent till it's almost dead. We must go further. We must make bridges between our *towers* – make *them* one. Whether you hear or not, *bambini*, Concord is coming. We die tomorrow unless we cast out the serpent today. Our new Signoria needs an army, not more borgati. United, Rasenna may survive, but that means you, not the merchants or engineers, must exile the real enemy: faction!'

He untied the bundle and a dozen new flags fell to the ground. He took one and untied it. As it fell open, a wind caught it. It was blood-red, with a Lion's silhouette embroidered in gold.

'Here is a banner belonging to no tower. It belongs to Rasenna. If I carry it and my enemy carries it, we are enemies no longer. We are brothers!' He picked up another. 'Who will take it up?' he roared. 'Who dares?'

His voice echoed in the palazzo and throughout the piazza outside. Southsiders nervously eyed one another, unsure how to take this challenge. The boy threw his banner on the fire, took a new banner from the Doctor and unfurled it. They stood watching each other.

'You better be real, old man,' Uggeri said.

After a minute's doubtful silence, others came forward and added their flags to the flames. The sparks flew up and the glow could be seen from every tower of Rasenna.

PART III:

ADVENT

Therefore the Lord Himself shall give you a sign;
Behold, a virgin shall conceive.

Jeremiah 7:14

CHAPTER 60

Every venture has its own risk. Betrayal attends love, death attends war; ruin attends commerce; but the penalty for avoiding risk is always the same: nothing happens. For Rasenna's merchants that had been the worst penalty: years of self-imposed stagnation.

Now they were bold, and boldness made them rich.

Rasenna's new affluence showed in a wealth of different ways, from elaborate weathervanes on her tower-tops to expensive clothes on her citizens below. Colour used to be reserved for essentials like banners, but now black, grey and tan retreated before vivid yellow, brilliant scarlet, lush Cambria green.

Both rivers seemed to flow faster – who could deny that the steady pulse of people to market was a river too – and as wealth breathed in new life, it brought new people; there was novelty everywhere. Strangers stopped to marvel at the engines used to construct the riverside towers or the mills, and passing through the new walls, admired the engineering skill their design revealed: octagonal – eminently defensible – towers projecting from each corner;

the slope, to turn aside the impact of bombardments. If the stranger understood such things, he saw the builders' chief concern was imminent siege, but he could not pause for long, as others pushed behind him, eager to see the miracle of Etruria. After all, it was not aesthetics that drew the pilgrims, but commerce.

Stepping onto the bridge, our stranger might rub one of the Lions' paws and pray for good bargains that day. Although one of the northside plinths remained empty, the other three Lions, intact and virile, were now back in their traditional perches – dragging the remaining two sentinels from the riverbed had been the first task for Rasenna's growing Engineers' Guild and its visionary podesta.

The bridge lured them all with the clamour of wares advertised and sold. Bombelli's currency-changing stall was set up beside the broken balustrade – just as one Lion was left broken in memory of the Wave, so the gap remained, as tribute to the fallen of the uprising. The clinking of coins was a constant heady accompaniment to the din of bargaining. Thieves attracted by the sound of easy money soon learned the risk of working the markets far outweighed the putative rewards. And just as Rasenna changed, so the bridge changed daily, with different stalls selling different goods, each taking their turn.

Bandieratori no longer loitered at street corners; like everyone else they had business to attend to. While some were on duty, patrolling walls, manning towers and policing the markets, the rest were drilled in new tactics and weapons.

'*Salute*,' Pedro said without looking up from his work. 'Sorry about the dust.' It was late, and Giovanni had sent the other apprentices home. They were young and enthusiastic, but they'd been going without sleep to get Rasenna's defences ready, and he needed alert minds.

'What's that you're working on, Pedro?'

'Just a distraction. The Doc gave me the parts, asked me if I could put them back together.'

'It's the annunciator I gave—' Giovanni was quiet for a moment, then, 'He still thinks she's coming back.' Without its cover, the angel looked undressed, its gown's elaborate whalebone showing. 'You've changed it?'

'Not really, the old design's sound but for a few redundancies.' Pedro held up a discarded part. 'These gears were sparking off each other.'

Giovanni held it up appraisingly. 'Lighter, easier to reproduce.'

Pedro was embarrassed. 'Too bad we need weapons, not toys. I just needed a break.'

They'd both been coordinating other work with defensive engineering – Giovanni rehearsed battle plans with the Doctor, while Pedro kept busy overseeing workshops across town.

'You think we've got a chance?' It wasn't a question

Pedro would have asked around the others. Giovanni understood by now that he'd taken on much more than authority when he became Rasenna's podesta.

'Last time Concord didn't have to beat us; they just had to show up.'

'We're still one town against an Empire.'

'That's the thinking that let Concord build that Empire. True, we're only a town, but we won't have to defeat an Empire.'

Pedro gave a careless Rasenneisi shrug. 'Oh, just a legion. No problem then.'

Giovanni smiled. 'If we can bloody their nose, every town in Etruria under the Concordian boot will join us. And that's a fight we have a chance of winning. Our mistake was trying to overpower them. Rasenna's got the greatest fighters in Etruria, but against disciplined troops holding a line – well, you saw what the Twelfth did. Our particular skills, we need to get close, and to get close, we need to change the rules. Look here—'

There were four powder piles on his desk: 'Charcoal, saltpetre and sulphur.' He carefully held up the forth saucer. 'Together, it's called serpentine. Bernoulli found the recipe in an Ebionite alchemical text.'

'How do you—?' Pedro began, then, 'What does it do?'

'Give me that that gear you took out of the angel.'

He watched as Giovanni crouched and poured a small pile with a trail to it.

'Stand back and cover your ears.'

Giovanni struck the gear. There was a sudden hiss as the trail lit up, then, as it reached the pile, there was a loud '*Pop!*' that sent a cloud of dirty yellow smoke spiralling into the air.

Pedro laughed when Giovanni looked up coughing, his face blackened.

'It's used for propulsion, in cannons and such.'

'Pity we can't lob a cauldron of it at them. That would even the odds quickly.'

Giovanni shook his head. 'Thank the Virgin it's too unstable for that. Our new walls can withstand arquebuses, and cannonballs, but not direct explosions. Any large amount is liable to explode prematurely, killing the wrong person.'

'Then what's it good for?'

'Changing the rules. Concord will try to make our walls our prison – they'll want to starve us, bomb us and burn us, then roll up their siege-towers and spit out an invasion. With serpentine, we can decapitate their towers when they approach. They'll have to approach on foot, between rows of burning toppling stacks.'

'We need to cast cannons then?'

'Small ones, with tempered iron. I already have smiths working on prototypes.'

Pedro tried to conceal his misgivings on finding the engineer so adept at the art of war. 'This isn't just for Rasenna, is it?'

Giovanni wasn't listening. He rubbed tired eyes, feeling

the chemical sting. 'When I came here, I'd lost faith in myself; she believed in me.'

Pedro saw his discomfort and changed the subject. 'What do you suppose Bernoulli was looking for in alchemists' recipe books?'

'I don't have to guess,' Giovanni said, suddenly angry. 'Power. In whatever form he could harness it. That's all he was ever looking for and—' he stopped himself, then went on more calmly, 'in any case, it gives Concord's legions tactical advantage in battle, just as hydro-engineering gives them strategic advantage. The Ebionites didn't know how to use it safely.'

'They kept blowing themselves up?'

'It's prone to accidental combustion when dusty. Bernoulli found a solution: just add water. It makes a better weapon, too. The flame spreads evenly before exploding. You can change the ratio depending on whether you want noise, light or power. I haven't perfected the mixture, but I'll make sure it's loud and smoky. Legions are used to winning, so anything we can do to puncture their complacency is to our advantage.'

Pedro looked serious. 'We can't win a war by avoiding battle. Sooner or later, we'll have to make contact.'

'Superior discipline beat us, not technology. Up until now, our bandieratori have been expending too much energy on noise and colour. The Doctor is training them to coordinate like a Concordian phalanx.'

Pedro interrupted abruptly, 'Can you increase the speed serpentine burns?'

'Yes, but increased pressure explodes cannon.'

'We need many small explosions, not one big one.'

'Then we'd have to get close, give up the advantage of our walls. We can't plant them like caltrops either. It's impossible to keep the fuse and powder dry.'

'I know how we can get close *and* keep our distance.'

Giovanni smiled. 'Tell me more, Maestro.'

CHAPTER 61

As the Doctor studied the letter, Giovanni told him Pedro's scheme in broad strokes.

He chuckled. 'Won't even the odds, but it'll give them a scare. I hope the legion they send *is* the Twelfth. Luparino never did have much salt.'

The letter that had brought Giovanni to the Tower Bardini that evening was the latest of the exchange which had been carried out over the summer. In contrast to previous missives, its language was polite, almost timid.

Giovanni was optimistic. 'Perhaps we'll have more time than expected before they grasp our intentions.'

The Doctor rolled up the letter and handed it back. 'Podesta, I've got a nose for this type of thing. They *know*. We'd better be ready, stocked up and locked up, within a month.'

Giovanni descended the northern slope less complacently than he'd climbed it. Concord was coming. He had overlooked some crucial factor. The place where he had first met Sofia was now a building site, transubstantiated into valuable real estate by other currents. The bridge was deserted. He stopped by a Lion, looking down at the water, thinking of the old saw about rivers always changing. Perhaps men seemed equally inconsistent to buio.

'Giovanni!'

He looked over to the embankment. 'Pedro! You gave me a fright!

Pedro came up. 'One of the eggs malfunctioned. How was the Doc?'

'More illuminating than usual. We've got to step up preparations.'

'I suppose we can fix this later. There hasn't been much buio activity.'

Halfway across the bridge, they stopped. Something was standing at the far end, waiting.

'Turn around slowly, Pedro.'

They turned to find several buio blocking the way north also. Turning again, more buio had joined the first. They began slowly advancing.

'What do we do, Giovanni?'

Jump? No. Surviving the river again was as unlikely as lighting striking twice. Giovanni looked up at Tower Bardini, hoping to see the Doctor's silhouette against the moon. For once he wasn't there.

The watery columns seeped closer until they were surrounded.

Giovanni knew that judgement had finally come.

'Pedro, you'll have to run when they attack me.'

Water must be water.

'Who said that?' Giovanni cried.

We. Our souls hear your soul.

'Who said what?' Pedro asked.

'You can't hear them?'

'Hear what?'

Many voices spoke at once in his mind. The columns were immobile and indistinguishable. Small ripples passed over and leapt the space between them.

Something has changed, he thought. The Reverend Mother said all water was one – if she was right, then Lucia had accidentally doomed him by having him 'contemplate Water'. Now they knew he was a Bernoulli, and knew too about Gubbio. Every day he paid a little more, but it didn't matter. Some debts are too large to pay. However they knew, they'd come for revenge.

Thou shall not kill.

Giovanni looked around at the faceless pillars.

'You drown men!'

Not murder. Water must be water.

'If you didn't come to kill me—'

You must feel Wind.

The night was still and peaceful.

'. . . no.'

'Giovanni, what are they saying?'

Forgotten much. Wind blows in wet world, not dry world.

'The river?'

We will be part of it. Stop us.

'I don't understand!'

Water must be water. Stop us.

The buio were sinking away, into puddles.

'From doing what?'

Forgotten much.

The puddles flowed over the edge.

'Answer me!' he shouted.

They were alone on the bridge, unchanged, as if the visitation had not happened.

'You didn't hear anything, Pedro?'

'No, I saw but— What did they say?'

Giovanni looked down into the dark rushing water. What sounded like riddles was obviously much more than that.

'They kept saying "Thou shall not kill" and "Water must be water".'

Pedro could see the Concordian was too upset to reason. 'If buio have language, perhaps they have morality of a sort.'

'You don't consider drowning murder?' Giovanni snapped.

'I'm just trying to be logical! It's not air that kills fish but fishermen, right? So drowning isn't murder because it's natural. What else?'

'They kept talking about a wind in wet world.'

Both were silent then, at the same moment. 'A current?'

'*Madonna!*' said Pedro.

'Something's going to make them kill, and they want us to stop it,' said Giovanni. 'They didn't come for revenge. They came for help.'

Later still, Pedro was sombrely studying the calculations scribbled on the studiola wall. '*Can* we stop it? I mean, power to create a forced Wave, once it's formed, the energy has to be used. That's Bernoulli's Second Law, right?'

'That's why we can't let the Wave form. If it forms, we're sunk – literally. The technology's moved on since Gubbio, and there's been time to store enough energy for a Wave five times as large.'

'That would wipe Rasenna off the map! Why not just send an army?'

'I have no idea.'

'Don't you?' Pedro said with sudden hostility. 'Why did you think the buio came to punish you?'

Giovanni shook his head, blankly.

Pedro stood up. 'Captain, what's your father's name?

'. . . Jacopo.'

'His surname.'

'An engineer's father is Concord,' he began in a confident voice that faded to nothing. 'I knew if anyone figured it out, it would be you.'

Pedro pushed Giovanni over in his chair. 'We made you podesta!'

'I told you not to!' Giovanni cried.

Pedro picked the only weapon to hand, a chisel. 'My father trusted you. I should kill you.'

Giovanni stood up and faced him. 'It's your right.'

'It's the right of *every* Rasenneisi, Concordian!'

Giovanni doubled over with the punch.

'You're lucky that we need your native cunning.'

Giovanni saw the chisel drop and heard the door slam.

CHAPTER 62

The weeks had blurred into drawn-out months and hope of the Ariminumese ever signing the Contract was ebbing daily.

Tents clustering in cliques redrew the camp's lines crooked. Fights broke out every day – over equipment, over gambling, over Ariminumese women, over many things, and ultimately all over nothing. Faction thrives on hopelessness. With no prospect of fighting Concord, the enemy became Ariminumese merchants, who took advantage, John Acuto, who did not pay advances, and each other, who were available. The Company sank into chaotic equilibrium all too familiar to Sofia. It was like being sober amongst drunks.

Even waning, John Acuto's star still shone: it was easy to fight and get dirty, harder to keep one's armour polished. Levi said Acuto liked her because she stood up to him, but the past had moulded them to fit – she was a tomboy raised by a fighter, and Acuto was a father without a son. But the more they talked, the more of a contradiction he was: a man who excelled at war but hated it. He fought for profit like a man doing penance. *What sin is absolved by blood?* she wondered.

'I never understand race who build Molè but cannot queue.' Yuri had sprained his wrist breaking up one of the daily mealtime fights. Sofia made a splint and brought him to the priest, who doubled as camp-surgeon.

He examined her work. 'Nicely done, Signorina.'

'I knew a doctor once.'

'He taught you well. I couldn't do better. Yuri, just avoid punching anyone for the next few days.'

'I no promise, Father. These Etrurians, they crazies,' said Yuri darkly, leaving the tent.

'Keep him out of trouble,' the priest said.

'I wouldn't have to if you told John Acuto to leave Ariminum. He listens to you, Father. Tell him – tell him the guts recommend it.'

The priest smiled as he lit the fire. 'You think augury is sham too?'

Sofia didn't blush. 'All that matters is that the old man believes it. You have a responsibility. He asks your advice. Maybe you don't see it, but every passing day undercuts his authority.'

'So you think someone's planning mutiny too?'

'Mutiny doesn't need planning any more than weeds need planting.'

The priest moved a pile of books and dropped a cushion

on the tent floor. 'Sit down, Sofia,' he said, seating himself amongst the litter of feathers and small bones.

'Are you going to tell my future?'

'Don't patronise an old man. Even now you could see more than I ever have, if you'd let yourself.'

'Yuri said you've correctly predicted the outcomes of battles.'

'Two parts experience to one part luck. But once – ah, once, my Sight was *keen*. The Virgin's turned her back on me since Gubbio.'

Sofia drew back. 'Gubbio? But– That was Concord!'

The priest picked up a bone. He breathed out heavily, and said clearly, 'Concord sent the Wave. We sacked the town.'

Sofia just looked at him.

'The Company had just come down from Europa. Etruria was a great feast waiting to be eaten. The Concordians saw us for what we were, savages with just enough discipline to be useful.' While the priest spoke, his fingers moved the bones around as if trying to reassemble some long-dead beast.

'They sent us there in the aftermath. What happened, happened. We don't talk about it. I'm not saying we became saints after Gubbio but . . . It didn't matter, no matter what we did; it hung about us like a smell. I suppose Concord realised Acuto had lost his appetite and that's why it terminated his Contract. Those who joined later, Levi and the rest, still think this life is a great adventure.

They're too young to know the cost, too young even to consider it. I think Harry's become another casualty of Gubbio in Acuto's mind, another body thrown on the heap. I told you, Sofia, everyone in a Company is a soldier: smiths, grooms, cooks—'

'And priests.'

'You too, if you stay. Go home, before this becomes home.'

'I have no home!' she shouted, kicking the bones away, then, more calmly, 'So since then you've been rattling bones and gutting birds for show?'

'The price of blood is always too high.'

Sofia looked into the smouldering fire. 'You give yourself too much credit. You're guilty because you were weak, but you're not responsible. The general wears the laurels.'

She ran past drunken soldiers carousing by campfires. They weren't men – they were wolves in human pelts, like the old story. Outside the camp, there was a large weathered rock overlooking the valley. The old bull stood on it, studying Ariminum in the night.

'That sentry's not too sharp, Rasenna. Good thing Concord doesn't think we're worth spying on.'

'Is it true?'

'No. Luigi's a decent watch. I doubt you make much noise and I've been sneaking around for years—'

'I said, is it true!'

'Why are you crying, girl?'

'The sack of Gubbio. Who's responsible?'

The general slumped. 'Who told you?'

'Answer me!'

A long time passed. Sofia prayed he would scoff and deny, but a decade of excuses no longer held up.

'I am.'

'Bastard.'

'I didn't plan it, but I let it happen. If I'd known my destiny was to go down to Gubbio—'

'I've heard that excuse before. No one made you take that choice.'

'I'm guilty, no argument there, but I would have ended there no matter which road I chose. I was caught up in History. The war's been going on in Europa since my father's time. The Concordians think they'll end it, but I doubt it. The Anglish and Franks quarrel like brothers, growing strong in the struggle. My family were the people Etrurians call Small – poor. My ambition was to be a knight, until I saw how knights show fealty. I wanted to be rich, not dead, so I sought a new fortune. I decided the wisest course in a violent world was to fight for profit. Ha! The idiocy young men call wisdom. In Etruria, every town was a kingdom and any man could be king, if they were strong. A place where the midday sun is hot, the women are beautiful and towns are willing to pay others to fight for them – sounds a better place to be a knight, doesn't it?' He smiled, tasting the dream afresh.

'The Etrurians called us condottieri instead of knights.

We didn't care what they called us, so long as they paid. We hitched our carroccio to the Empire's expansion, all the while still thinking we were forging our own destiny, even as we fled from what we knew was right. That naïveté made us ideal. The Concordians put us in the right place, knowing our nature. After what was left of the town was—'

He stopped and searched for the word. '—subdued, the Concordian engineers came and did worse things.'

'Don't you dare shift the blame!'

'You misunderstand – we stood by. That was worst thing Concord did. They left us no one else to blame.'

'You expect pity?'

'No. I know this debt will never be paid. There were plenty ready to hire us after we chased the Moor's Company out of Etruria, and we became rich. It didn't help drown out the screaming. Look, Sofia, I'm a soldier of Fortune abandoned by Fortune!'

She turned away. 'I can't.'

Ariminum's port never slept. Fleets of loutish fat-bellied ships waited to be unloaded and loaded, to come and go between the numberless trading partners of the Republic. In a town so busy making money, a girl, beautiful or not, tearful or not, running by the street-sellers' stalls, was sure to be ignored.

The gauntlet of islands protecting the harbour from the sea's temper also stopped wind dispelling the accumulated stench. The sea's conquest of the decaying land was a slow march by stealth, a mist that suited those who wanted to be lost.

Sofia only stopped when she reached the end of the dock. It was quieter here, where the ships were bound for more obscure ports. At the end of a long narrow pier an elderly yet resolutely undignified boat was moored. At first sight it looked long-abandoned, but on closer examination, its sails were neatly rigged.

The old sailor who'd been charily studying the horizon noticed the girl emerge from the mist. Like his boat, he'd seen better days. His skin was cracked leather, like an old turtle's, and burned bright red by a life on the water. Even on a day when the sun was a diffused blush in the mist, he squinted as if looking directly at it. 'Ahoy, Signorina! Come to me, kiss me and say you'll miss me?'

Sofia wiped her eyes and examined him with hostility. Another wolf, probably.

'If you're here to accuse me of besmirching your honour, I must warn you that I smirch only when invited.'

'Where do you sail?'

'Further than you want to go, I'll wager. Oltremare, once known as the Holy Land, if you believe that.'

'I can cook.'

The sailor disappeared. A moment later, the end of a thick corded rope hit the dock with a thump. As she reached for it, it suddenly pulled back up.

'What's the purpose of your pilgrimage? Business or pleasure? There's a war there, you know.'

'War's everywhere.'

'That's true,' he said thoughtfully, waiting for more.

'I don't want to go there especially. I want to leave here.'

'Then perhaps you're not a pilgrim but a fugitive.'

'I'm neither.'

'Perhaps you are and don't know it. You *are* running from something. What is it?' He pulled up the rope fully.

She couldn't go back. 'Liars,' she said.

'A common complaint, but I cannot help you. There are liars in Oltremare, some of the best. Plenty on board too. Alas, Signorina, you picked the wrong boat.'

Nevertheless, he dropped the rope. 'But perhaps you're running from a particular liar?'

'What does it matter?' Sofia reached for the rope, only to have it pulled away again.

'Well, I need to know what kind of shipmate is on the end of my line.'

'If I don't like liars, I'm honest.'

'*Ack!* Whatever else you might be, you are a weak logician. Even liars hate to be lied to. But my question is whether you are escaping a dishonest world, in which case you are a philosopher like myself, and are welcome.'

The rope lowered, then was quickly yanked up again.

'Or you're running away from someone who fooled you, or helped you fool yourself, in which case you're a coward.'

'I'm not a coward!' Sofia's voice sounded small next to the sea's grand and indifferent silence.

The rope finally dropped to the boardwalk and the sailor said, 'As it happens, I'm both. The sea's got enough salt already. You're welcome aboard, but hurry – tide's changing.'

Levi found her sitting by a dying fire, keeping warm, wrapped in the Scaligeri banner. If there was no country far enough to escape the past, at least the Hawk's Company was a place she could lose herself. This time there was no one else to blame for deception. Of course war entailed murder, rapine and massacre. What else could it be?

'The Company's part in Gubbio,' she started. 'Did you know?'

He sat down by the fire. 'That wasn't the Hawk's Company I joined. After I heard, I thought about leaving, but—' He sat down with a sigh. 'What will you do?'

'He should retire,' Sofia muttered, 'go home to his wife.'

'He couldn't disband the Company if he wanted to. All these men are far from home – what would they do? Take up farming? Even if they wanted to, they'd be killed before they picked up a pitchfork.'

'By who?

'By Etruria! Do you think we are welcome guests? Feuds turn to wars when towns can hire help. We're fuel on a burning fire. We're pests, and individually we'd be exterminated like pests.'

Levi mimed squashing bugs – *splat*, *splurge*, *splug* – then grinned. 'Together, that's something different. Forgive me, I know Rasenneisi don't go in much for unity.'

Sofia punched Levi in the arm. 'Illuminate me.'

'*Ow!* Together, we get paid to make and *not* to make war. Together, kings pay us money *and* respect – that's the real reason we fight our unwinnable war.'

'You told the Doc it was Etruria's war. You said Concord had to be stopped, for everyone's sake.'

'I did?' He laughed. '*Madonna*, I'll say anything when I'm selling.'

'You're a bunch of chicken-hearts.'

'Don't judge us so harshly. Most of us weren't lucky enough to be born with names like yours, and the few who were are bastards, or second sons left out of their father's estates.'

'Which were you, a second son or a bastard?' Sofia snapped. Condottieri were only one link in the chain shackling Etruria. War paid for itself; peace brought mass unemployment, so war's purpose became self-perpetration. 'Sorry,' she mumbled.

'Well, it *is* more glamorous than ploughing. Not many homeless thieves get to play at being knights.'

She poked the fire. Was this nobility? An overflowing pot, pouring disenfranchised rejects into other lands, spreading disorder and war. In Rasenna, there was a river of blood. In Concord, a different type of aristocracy, a brood of monsters. Everywhere, the noble gave birth to the bestial.

The title she'd been so jealous of, the system she'd been a part of – it forged the chains.

'Stay,' Levi said.

'What choice have I? I've nowhere to go.'

CHAPTER 63

'Thought I'd find you here. Sure it's safe down there?'

Pedro didn't look up. 'I borrowed your tools to repair the malfunction. Hope that's all right.'

He was crouching on the narrow shelf where Piazza Luna abruptly terminated. 'I don't understand it. I've been taking depth samples. There's no deviation from what's normal at this time of year.'

'That's because *it* hasn't happened yet. The individual partials of a Wave don't need to move to transfer energy. For buio, the past, present and future don't come in any sequence. They're just different states of existence, permeable states.'

'Oh,' Pedro said frowning, 'that explains this then.'

He scooped up some water in a beaker and held it still until tiny globules began breaking free. They hovered above the surface until the wind took them or they ran out of energy and fell.

'That's right,' said Giovanni, 'whatever's causing this is weak because it's in the future. It's growing stronger as we get closer.'

They both looked at the river gloomily until Giovanni said, 'I'm the same person I was.'

'No, Captain, you're not. If the truth got out, it would tear Rasenna apart again. They'd fight for the privilege of hanging you. Does the Doc know?'

'No one knows. Sofia didn't either.'

Pedro laughed suddenly. 'I know *that*. The Contessa would have cut your heart out. If by some miracle Rasenna survives this, you have to go.'

'I know.'

'So, can we survive it?'

'I don't know. I've been working on it but—' Giovanni struggled to maintain a philosophical distance. 'Only another Wave, out of sync by half a pulse, can cancel a Wave. But it must be as strong or stronger.'

Pedro looked back at the river. 'What's stronger than that?'

'No power in the world – none that I know.'

Pedro threw down the beaker. 'Where's your salt, Captain? Before I knew anything about Natural Philosophy, I used to figure out things by hearing what they did. Show me how the Wave works . . .'

Sketches and scribbled-out calculations were strewn all over the studiola's floor.

Working alone, Giovanni hadn't made much progress. He tried to explain the impasse. 'Thinking the Wave is something than can be unleashed overnight keeps Etruria terrified, but it can't: it takes huge amounts of energy.'

'From where?'

'The Curia's Architects were obsessed by acoustics. That's how my grandfather won the competition to build the Molè: his design was a great spiral based on Euclid's extreme and mean ratio, a number that the Curia believed revealed the name of God. My grandfather wasn't that superstitious, but he *did* believe it was a power he could harness.'

Giovanni took out the main lens of Pedro's magnifier. He extended the segments and said, 'The engineers secretly built another building under the Molè with that same spiral reversed.' He flicked his wrist and the magnifier inverted. 'An anti-Molè, if you will. Together they amplify whatever power is generated within. The Curia wanted a cathedral filled with songs of praise. My grandfather had other plans. After the Revolution, the Beast became a prison for men and water, the perfect place to collect, distill and perfect fear. Over time, the Water comes to associate Man with this torture, so when it's finally set loose on a town—'

'—the Wave is triggered by the town's own population. Elegant,' Pedro said with uneasy admiration. 'What was he like, Giovanni?'

'I barely remember. Always busy. I saw even less of him than my father. What I did see was that everyone respected him. I was different then; I would have done *anything* to impress him.'

'Sorry, I shouldn't have asked.'

Giovanni shook his head angrily, then looked up. 'So. Any ideas?'

Pedro was doodling. 'Maybe. You?'

'Maybe. Remember the day I came here? Sofia told me signalling was your primitive way of communicating. I found it ingenious, though I didn't contradict her.'

Pedro smiled. 'Fast learner.'

'It's an efficient means of communication if you have limited power. We can't hope to match the Molè's power – unless we steal some.'

He showed Pedro a sketch of something like a church spire, connected to an engine. 'A machine that transmits a signal with a pulse frequency of 1.6 will resonate with the Molè.'

'Allowing their magnifier to magnify our own signal.'

'That's the idea – like the signals the eggs emit, but over a longer distance. If the buio hear it as they approach Rasenna, the Wave won't form. But it'll take time to build, and this isn't something we can afford to mess up. What's your idea?'

Pedro held up Giovanni's Whistler. 'This thing works by listening for the echo, right? Can you teach it a new tune?' He handed Giovanni a sheet on which he had matched a sequence of numbers and musical notes. 'Something with a progression that occurs at the inter-vals equal to the ratio—'

Giovanni read, '1-2-3-5-8—'

'And so on. We can play it at the bridge, so if anything gets past your transmitter, or we miscalculate, it's a fail-safe.'

'It's an elegant solution. An engineer's solution. Vettori would be proud.'

Pedro reddened as he adjusted the rod's dial. 'Wonder what a golden spiral sounds like?'

'Don't underestimate them again,' the Doctor cautioned, 'it won't be long before they figure out the Wave signal is blocked. That's if your plan works.'

'It'll work.'

The Doctor shrugged. 'If it doesn't, we won't be around to worry about it. Assuming it does, Podesta, I think we need to start making friends with other giants. You're looking down at your bridge, as usual. Try looking beyond.'

'South?'

'A year ago all those towns exhausted by war or bankrupted by condottieri were resigned to vassalage. Now we've reminded them that Rasenna once led a Southern League against Concord.'

Giovanni looked at the land south of Rasenna, cooling as night drew on, and he imagined the wild possibility of Tarquinia, Salerno, Ariminum, Caere, Vulci and Veii, not as rivals but allies. Some would be suspicious of any gesture of friendship, some would wait and let rivals risk the wrath of Concord. But might some raise a flag?

'You think we can bring the south together?'

The Doctor showed the letter he'd drafted. 'Podesta, we *have* to. I don't know why Concord is willing to waste another Wave on us, but that willingness tells me they won't back down easily.'

'We'll bring it to the Signoria tomorrow.' Giovanni stopped on his way down the ladder. 'That lament Sofia sang, on the night the bridge opened—'

'"The River's Song".'

'Where did she learn it?'

'From me. It was something my sister taught me – a strange lullaby, but then, my sister was a strange woman. Why do you ask?'

'No reason. Golden dreams, Doctor.'

The Doctor grabbed an orange, looked south and whistled. A grand alliance was optimistic but the inescapable fact was only with a miracle, or combination of miracles, could Rasenna survive.

'What do you think, ugly? We got a prayer?'

Cat moaned sceptically.

He threw an orange peel. 'Bah. All cats are pessimists.'

CHAPTER 64

The three wise men fought on two fronts, redrafting the Contract night after night, battling Ariminumese intransigence on one side and John Acuto's temper on the other.

Sofia missed Levi, and was glad to see him approach the mess-tent.

'Yuri, I'm taking your little helper. Watch out, Sofia, I think Acuto sees a protégée in you. He wants you to see the business side of Contracting, not just the glamour.'

Sofia threw a wet dishcloth. 'I'd prefer to kill Concordians, if that's still on the menu?'

'By the legion! But not until we get this damned Contract signed. Come on, you'll enjoy the cut and thrust of negotiation.'

'Do I get to talk?' Sofia said, leaping into the saddle.

'Certainly not,' he laughed.

'Why *is* this Contract taking so long? Doesn't Acuto want to get home to his wife?'

'Acuto's been saying that for the last decade.'

'Maybe he's afraid of going home.'

Levi glanced over his shoulder. 'You can relate?'

'Go to hell.'

'Well anyway, he has no choice. Contracts take time and I can tell you, I've seen tough negotiators, but these take the prize. For example, we'd usually be sold supplies cost-price—'

'To prevent you raiding the contato.'

'It's the done thing. But word's out that Acuto will fight Concord, regardless of price.'

'Last I looked you were condottieri. Why don't you throw your weight around?'

'Time was, we would. But Acuto's taking this shining knight business more seriously the older he gets. Scarpelli thinks you're a bad influence. I'm inclined to agree.'

'I know you're a mercenary, Levi, but since when are you *such* a mercenary?'

He laughed. 'I just don't think we need to advertise our good deeds. We should be taking advantage of townsfolk, not the other way around.'

As the notary brought the session to order, Levi whispered, 'Remember, you're here to watch, listen and learn from the professionals. The trick is never to lose your temper.'

He stood. 'My Lords, we think we've finally found a payment schedule that will suit—'

The doge interrupted, 'Colonel, new information has emerged that will change the terms of agreement.'

Levi's smile faltered. 'My Lord, at this late hour—'

'In fact, the situation has so changed that it remains to be seen if we need you at all.' The doge held up a letter. 'Do you recognise this seal?'

Levi and Scarpelli looked at each other blankly, but Sofia spoke up. 'It's Rasenna's seal.'

Scarpelli threw her a look that said *be quiet or be gone*.

'Correct, young lady. Your friends are only concerned with our country's military landscape, but Rasenna returns to the map of Etruria at last – and she returns rich. Soon they will have bankers giving loans.'

This suggestion prompted nervous smiles from the Signoria – most were scions of banking families.

Levi took the chance to interrupt. 'I fail to see what relevance—'

'Precisely,' the doge snapped, '*you* fail to see, but Rasenna's new podesta does not. He sees Ariminum's pre-eminence and invites us to lead a reformed Southern League. It remains to be seen what scraps are left in this alliance for the dogs of war.'

Struggling to maintain his composure, Levi stood. 'With respect, Doge, it is naïve to—'

'Be seated! This house will not be lectured to!'

'But you will lecture us and waste *our* time.'

'Levi,' Scarpelli cautioned.

But Levi was beyond caring. 'My Lords, it may amuse you to imagine yourselves empire-builders, but such fantasies can be fatal. War's not something to play at. You risk the wrath of John Acuto and Concord both. While you daydream, one will knock your walls and the other will burn your towers.'

'You threaten us, Colonel?'

'Consider it augury. Rich enough to buy an army is rich enough to tempt Concord. Hiring the Hawk's Company is a logical deterrent; joining this League would be a sense-less provocation. Concord's aims are in Europa – all it wants from southern Etruria is peace. Ariminum is rich enough to rent an army – but you must be realistic. You are bankers and merchants, not fighters.'

'Perhaps not, but the men of Rasenna are.'

Scarpelli stood, pulling Levi up with him. 'We should adjourn. We've all got some rethinking to do.'

'My Lord?'

The doge had been so busy glowering at Levi that he'd forgotten Sofia's presence.

'Yes, my child?' he said pleasantly.

'What is the new podesta's name?'

He lifted the scroll close to his face. 'A Bardini or a Morello, I suppose. Who's in charge these days? Hmm, unusual: no family game given, just an initial. It must be a Bardini. It's signed Giovanni B.'

As they left the city with yapping dogs at their heels, the Dwarf admonished Sofia for interrupting.

She was in a dark, cold place, where a storm was kindling. Even his death was a lie! To think, if she'd never discovered his true identity, what joy she'd be feeling. The dagger was barbed every way, she couldn't let it be and she couldn't pull it out.

'You were told to keep your mouth shut!' the Dwarf fumed.

Sofia ignored him. 'Levi, this League is a trap. Rasenna's new podesta is a Concordian spy.'

Levi shook his head slowly. 'That wouldn't make sense. Concord has always ruled by division.'

'Just like condottieri,' she muttered.

'Not quite,' Scarpelli said. 'Concord has long-term goals.'

'And we do it for money,' the Dwarf laughed.

'Maybe the League's *designed* to fail. If Rasenna brings all the towns together only to betray them, it'll finish the cause of unity for good.'

'Too subtle,' Levi said dismissively, 'but it *is* surprising that Ariminum is even considering this alliance. They've always exploited the other southern cities; they've that much in common with Concord. If Rasenna's growing rich by trade, it's as big a threat to Ariminum as Concord.'

'But don't forget,' said Scarpelli, 'Ariminum's got the fear!'

'You see that doge standing up to Concord?'

'He stood up to Acuto,' said the Dwarf.

'That's different. Concord may be overstretched, but it's not weak. If Tagliacozzo taught us anything, it's that Guild technology trumps every alliance. Paying homage to Concord would be easier and cheaper than starting a war Ariminum can't win.'

Sofia remembered the day Giovanni said he'd blood on his hands. She hadn't believed him. Nobody told her love made one deaf as well as blind. What was he planning now?

'It doesn't make sense,' they announced together.

John Acuto crouched awkwardly at the tent flap. His shadow fell across her. 'Don't go.'

'I'm leaving at dawn. Of all people, I thought you would understand.' As Bernoulli was engineering Rasenna's destruction, from the inside this time, and she was the only one who knew it. She had no choice. 'You were a knight, John Acuto, but you ran from your destiny. You recommend that course?'

'No,' he said quietly.

'General, Levi said you couldn't disband the Company if you wanted to. What if the Company had a home?'

'All Europa is our home.'

'I mean a permanent home.'

'Find me a town where violent men are welcome.'

She waited.

'Bah! Rasenna had its chance to join me at Tagliacozzo. It turned me down.'

'All Etruria refused you.'

'Concord would grind us to dust together.'

'You could win this time.'

'Win? Have you been paying attention? Tagliacozzo was

a rout, and you told me yourself how Rasenna's little rebellion was squashed before it started.'

'You lost because you were betrayed. We lost because we were borgati facing an army. United, it would be different.'

'Walls are for knocking down, not hiding behind. I'm glad you've stopped running from whatever chased you here, but don't try to rope my Company in on a doomed mission.'

'It's already on a doomed mission. Times are changing – everyone knows it but you. Every town's bankrupted or in vassalage to Concord, and Etruria's just the start. If you really want to fight the Empire, this is your last chance.'

He saw she wasn't giving up and sat down with a heavy sigh. 'Businessmen deal in Contracts. By what authority do you speak for Rasenna, girl?'

Sofia said nothing.

'That's what I thought. Besides, what can Rasenna offer that Ariminum can't? I'll fight Concord for Ariminum and get paid. The future is here, not on a doomed crusade for a doomed town,' he said and walked away.

'You're a rare fool, John Acuto, to have lived so long and found nothing worth fighting for but money.'

Soldiers in neighbouring tents stopped to watch. Acuto turned around slowly. 'Remember yourself!'

Sofia stood in front of him. 'Remember *yourself*! They say your son died a hero. *Madonna*, he'd be disgusted to see you now.'

The general growled and grabbed her by the arm. She hit him in the jaw. The blow would have felled an ordinary man. John Acuto wiped the blood from his nose and ordered the soldiers who came running to stay back.

'You had *better* be gone tomorrow. There's no place for you here any more.'

CHAPTER 65

The sickly incense wafting out of the priest's tent was an effective warning he was not to be disturbed. He set the cauldron on the fire; messy work demanded warm water.

The blade went in easily. The sleeping dove did not struggle.

He prayed, 'Virgin, you see everything. You see a blind and worthless and faithless priest with but one friend left. I beg you, let me help him. Leave me in darkness for ever more, but give me Sight one last time!'

As the bird's life spilled out in warm blood, its viscera did not have the familiar stench; they were tart as new ploughed earth. He spread them out amongst the dust and the bones, and whispered, 'Sweet Virgin, let me See!'

He shook epileptically as the vision crashed upon him with the power of an ocean. When it passed over, he cried out, 'You are betrayed, John Acuto!'

He ran to the tent flap, pulled it back – and found a smiling Scarpelli standing there.

'Going somewhere, Father Blood-and-guts?'

The priest stepped back, coughed and looked down at

the blade stuck in his belly. Scarpelli pushed him onto the ground.

'*Madonna!* This place stinks!' he said. Disgust turned to sudden anger and he knelt on the priest's chest, holding him down in the dust, which was sodden with fresh blood.

'Sorry, Father. The Company's going through a period of restructuring.'

'Traitor! You'll die like a dog, with a leash for a noose.'

'Another prediction, blind man? Please – you couldn't foresee the one death that mattered.'

Scarpelli slid the knife sideways across the priest's abdomen. It went in easily. The cauldron water began to boil.

Sofia was trapped in a deep slumber. The pit was waiting for her, as real as ever.

Tap

       Tap

Tap

She heard the hum, but as the cells' revolution began, there was no one to scream but her. Great stones ground against each other. The lake water churned and the coffin emerged, changed, aged as if submerged for centuries. It hissed putrid gas when it cracked open, and a hand emerged, not white and bony, but flesh: live and bloody.

The priest stumbled out, frightened and bewildered, viscera dangling and weeping blood.

His voice was strangled, distant. 'Sofia, it's you, it always has been. He's searching for you. Return to Rasenna! Every river overlaps there.'

A bolt of blue light dropped from the sky. When it hit the water, everything shook. Heaven and Hell broke open.

'It's you, Sofiaaaaaaaaaaaaaaaa!'

She woke in darkness, gasping for air, covered in sweat. Her pillow was damp with tears. The vision did not take wing like a normal nightmare but sat gloating on her chest. She'd nursed the anger since learning who Giovanni was; now she knew he was alive it didn't need nursing; it grew like a tumour until it seeped from the pit into her dreams: a bloated maggot feeding on cancerous meat and spiced with tears of betrayal, grief and suffering, just as the Virgin had promised her. The Virgin had promised love stronger than all three, yet of that she felt nothing.

She turned over. The dawn's light cast a shadow against her tent. She held onto the banner as her other hand reached for her dagger.

'Sofia?'

'Levi?'

By the crazy gleam in his eye she knew he hadn't slept either. 'Something's wrong. Yuri just saw the Dwarf and John Acuto leave with an Ariminumese escort, going to sign the Contract.'

'That's good, isn't it?'

'It's impossible. There hasn't been a new draft in weeks. It doesn't smell right. I need help.'

'All right, first we need to get the priest.'

'Prayer won't stop mutiny.'

'I can't explain right now, Levi. Just trust me.'

The Dwarf reigned in his horse. 'We'll wait here, General.'

He drew a deep breath and blew a feeble whimper on a hunting horn. He threw the horn at the Ariminumese soldier. 'You blow it.'

The horn sounded lonely and strange on the empty plane. They were half a mile yet from Ariminum's walls.

John Acuto took off his helmet and wiped his brow. 'What's that for?'

'Signalling, General.'

'I realise that, but *why*? Are we being denied access to the city now? If they make us negotiate from the saddle, I'll make them pay for it.'

'No, General. Treachery is afoot.'

'Levi, that viper!' Acuto swore, 'I knew it!'

'I dare say Levi's dead by now,' the Dwarf said. The Ariminumese soldier stayed behind the general.

'Good work. Was he alone?'

'Extraordinary! You still don't understand.' The Dwarf pointed to the party of knights riding from the town gates. 'They come for you, old man.'

It took him a moment to comprehend that he had not been rescued but kidnapped, but by then a pommel had slammed into his skull. By then it was dark.

Steam from the cauldron filled the priest's tent. He lay beside a dove, cut open in the same way.

Levi looked at her forcefully. 'Be honest: you *saw* this, didn't you?'

'No! I have dreams— I can't control it.'

'But you knew he was in danger. Sofia, you asked me to trust you. I do. You have a power; I don't know why you're fighting it, but I'm asking for help.'

'What can I do?'

'Just think about John Acuto. Where is he?'

'It doesn't work like that. Something's blocking it. Levi, I'm afraid.'

Levi knelt beside the body. 'You know, back when business was good, we'd all get paid handsomely. Some hoarded, others spent freely. Next campaign, Fortune treated the misers and profligates the same. If your time's up, it doesn't matter how rich or poor you are.'

He closed the old man's wet staring eyes. 'Sofia, life's only worth something if you live it. If you hide away from danger, you rob yourself twice, of life, and of the prize that's behind the fear.'

'Prize? What prize?'

'The only thing money can't buy in my experience: freedom.'

Sofia looked at the steam swirling from the cauldron. She whispered, 'I'm not afraid.' She watching the steam vapours snake through her fingers. Bubbles burst and spat scalding water. She closed her eyes and plunged her hand in.

'NooooSofiaaaaaaaaaaaaaaaaaa—'

She heard Levi from far away. She floated there and waited, and looking down, she saw the dark sky and though it, a battlefield – but it was a battle fought and lost many years ago. The vision shifted and now it was just an ordinary field where the general waited with two others.

The brooding sky pressed down and the vision rose up again, repainted with more detail: John Acuto's hoarse bellow, manly and sorrowful, a bull cut down, and blood pumping through rough hands vainly trying to halt the leak as the rivulets cascaded over fingers like ruby rings. She saw Acuto, unconscious in his saddle, and two horsemen waiting beside him, looking at the east and waiting. The earth was shaking.

The vision shifted once more. She couldn't control it; there was something it wanted her to see.

Below, where the water ran cold, something old and hateful shifted and uncoiled. It smelled her fear and was hungry.

She was in Rasenna, and the earth was still shaking. Giovanni was alone on the bridge. He was looking *at her*, and behind him night was falling as the Wave rose up.

A tentacle grazed her leg and she flinched into *Daylight*.

'—*fiaaaaa, don't!*' Levi screamed, but suddenly the water wasn't boiling. Levi cautiously dipped a finger in. It was chilly.

'How in the name of—?'

'There's no time – Acuto's in trouble, outside Ariminum.'

'Figures. If it's outside their walls they can claim ignorance,' said Levi. 'You should go.'

'Me?'

'They'll send knights. It pains me to say it, but you're a better fighter than me. I'll stay here.'

'Why?'

'Because I'm a better soldier.'

'Who's that?' said the Ariminumese soldier.

The Dwarf squinted. A lone rider was coming from the west.

'I'll tell you who it's not: Scarpelli. He said he'd fly an Ariminumese banner.'

The soldier dismounted and loaded his crossbow.

'Someone's about to get a surprise,' he said.

John Acuto's horse reared, and kicked the soldier into the mud. His arrow shot off into the sky and narrowly missed the rider.

The general unsheathed his broad sword with a groggy roar as the Dwarf swung. He didn't parry, but let himself fall from his saddle, and landing next to the fallen soldier, he rolled over in time to see the Dwarf spurring his horse to trample him.

Acuto flung his sword at the horse's front legs, and there was a whinny of pain and its head met the earth with a sudden sharp crack. Momentum kept the body rolling and it was Acuto's turn to roar as his legs were pinned.

The Dwarf picked himself up and walked over unsteadily, panting and wheezing.

'How much,' Acuto spat, bile and blood, 'did Concord pay you?'

'The deal was with Ariminum. Part of the deal was you.'

'Levi was right: you're a lousy businessman. You should've cut out the middleman. Concord would've paid more.'

The Dwarf paused to ponder. 'You think so?'

Acuto suddenly sat up, pushed an arrow into the Dwarf's stomach and yanked it out again, the barbs ripping a mess of entrails with them. The Dwarf gurgled for a while, then fell face-down in the dirt.

'That's for the priest, you dog.' He fell back, exhausted, and waited for the lone horseman, praying Fortune had sent a friend, and knowing he had few left.

Several mounted soldiers were waiting when Levi returned to his tent. 'Scarpelli,' he shouted, 'I think the Dwarf's going to betray Acuto.'

'There's still time.'

'Yes, if we hurry we—'

'There's still time to join us. I wanted to involve you, but the Dwarf thought you couldn't be trusted.'

'A compliment of sorts.'

'Acuto betrayed us, Levi. *I* didn't sign up for a Crusade, did you? We're here to get rich, not change the world.'

'And the priest?'

'He'd never have agreed to what needs to be done,' Scarpelli said impatiently.

'What's that?'

'Ariminum want to deliver the Hawk with their tribute to Concord. A goodwill token.'

'With their tribute? They never intended to do business?'

'Oh, they did – just not with John Acuto. Come on, Levi! It's the obvious choice. Concord's winning.'

'Just tell me one thing: who betrayed us at Tagliacozzo?'

Scarpelli shifted in his saddle.

'They killed Harry!' Levi cried. 'You were his friend too.'

Scarpelli laughed bitterly. 'That's funny. Harry was a condottiere born, and if he were still alive, he would be sitting with me. It's you who betrays his memory if you don't join us.' He laid his hand on his sword.

'Like you said, the choice is obvious.'

Yuri and a company of archers emerged from the surrounding tents. Some of Scarpelli's men tried to flee, some tried to fight; they were all cut down. Stunned, Scarpelli dropped the sword he had not even had the chance to raise.

'You were always a better politician than a soldier,' Levi said with contempt. 'Take him. John Acuto can judge him.'

'Levi! Help me, please – for old time's sake!'

'You betrayed the Hawk. *This* is for old time's sake.'

Pushing with her legs, Sofia managed to move the horse's body enough for the general to roll free.

'Where's Levi?' he groaned.

'I got the easy job, saving your ungrateful hide. Levi's saving your Company.'

Acuto touched the wound on his head tenderly. 'I'm done for, girl. Get out of here.'

Sofia tore an Ariminumese banner into strips and did not answer.

Acuto continued, 'I know Rasenneisi can handle themselves in a fight, but no one survives a cavalry charge. Do an old man one last favour and go.'

He doubled over, coughing. Sofia quickly counted the approaching horsemen. The knights rode in a body, the wet earth sinking under the weight of their armour.

'I'm staying.'

'Today's youth worry me. In my day, we only made selfless gestures when there was someone around who'd live to sing about them.'

'You'll live.'

Acuto grinned, showing bloodstained teeth. 'You're a doctor too? It's worse than you know. Listen—' He held his nose and blew.

Sofia heard a hissing wind, and congealing blood popping.

'Skull fracture,' she said quietly.

'Aye. Not something I'll shake off with chicken soup.'

'Then die well – not in this mud over a petty money squabble.'

'That's my profession you are slandering. Sadly, there's no demand for heroism these days.'

'I know a place.' She bandaged the general's wound quickly.

'Even if you could persuade an old brain-damaged general, why would his Company follow? No, my story ends here.'

'Damn you then!' She turned angrily, calculating her chances. There were twelve knights in heavy armour. The horses made it harder. An advance body of four broke off and spurred their mounts into a full gallop.

'I've waited a long time to see my son again . . .'

Sofia didn't look away from the approaching knights as she answered. 'I thought you were a fighter, John Acuto, but you're just a weak old fool. Rasenna's got too many of those already. Maybe I was wrong to invite you.'

'Damn *you*, Sofia. I know what you're trying to do, but it's too late. Go, before they're upon us!'

She readied herself.

The lead knight drew closer; he tilted his lance and charged. She sidestepped and tapped his lance as it passed. It dug into the earth, vaulting the knight into the air. He landed hard, metal breaking on bone.

When the next two riders came, Sofia leapt for the first, swinging around his horse's neck with a kick to the chin. She took his place in the saddle just as he crashed to the ground. He got up, dazed, but lucid enough to unsheathe his sword. She pulled hard on the warhorse's reins; it reared and came back to earth, crushing its master into the mud.

The next knight was already charging. '*Yaaah!*'

Sofia charged too, but before they passed she leapt from the saddle onto the knight's lowered lance, sprang off and kicked – not his breastplate, but the body encased within.

The armour bent like paper. Metal is the weakest element, no match for water.

He was unconscious before he landed.

Sofia picked up a lance and broke off the handle. With one eye on the horizon, she took a banner from her satchel and unrolled it; black and gold gleamed darkly. She fastened it to the stick then closed her eyes, testing the weapon with a combination, listening for the snap – and hearing it. Vanzetti made their banners to last.

She waited calmly. The other knights had seen their colleagues attacking individually, and falling one after the other, and now they charged together and it made no difference. As John Acuto watched eight experienced knights fall to a slip of a girl, he decided that, Contract or no, he must see Rasenna before he died. It would be a fitting last pilgrimage for a warrior.

Sofia drove the banner into the ground and pulled the old man to his feet. 'General. I offer the Hawk's Company a Contract.'

'We've been over this. Who are you to offer Contracts?'

'I am Sofia Scaligeri, Contessa of Rasenna.'

CHAPTER 66

The walls of Rasenna emerged from a slow-churning white sea, and the morning mist advanced until the fiery banners of besieging and besieged were the same neutral grey. As yet there had been no assault. The Twelfth Legion had arrived a week ago, and now the town and the river together were blockaded. The forests nearby were besieged too, for wood to make siege-towers, ladders and other tools.

The tumult outside Rasenna prompted none within; her walls and towers were silent. To Concordians, accustomed to inspiring panic and hate with their war-machine, this pure indifference was strangely disquieting.

General Luparelli contemplated the empty walls with rueful curses: he cursed his previous clemency, and he cursed Rasenna for all it had stolen from him – his hand, his son, and worst of all, his laurels. After Tagliacozzo, did he not deserve plaudits? Had he not deserved a Triumph? But as usual, he got nothing; it was a noble's lot.

Unusually, all three Apprentices had come to watch the siege unfold. For some reason, they had become suddenly fixated on Rasenna. Luparelli did not know why, nor did he care to know; he just welcomed the opportunity to make Rasenna pay.

So it seemed especially cruel when the First Apprentice showed him the terms of surrender.

'My Lord!' he spluttered, 'these terms are absurd – we will lift the siege if they surrender the engineer? That's impossible, I saw him die!'

'He lives,' the man in red said simply. The front line separated to make way before him and General Luparelli followed dutifully.

'I don't question your orders, but can you be sure your information is accurate?'

The Apprentice came to a stop by the legion's carroccio. 'Bring him out!'

An aide led out the prisoner. His pale, malnourished body was a ruin, a patchwork of bruises and scars. His eyes darted around like a snared animal.

'You recognise the Morello heir, General?'

Luparelli held up his stump. 'I remember his brother, my Lord, and if this *boccalone* told you Captain Bernoulli lives, don't believe it. Rasenneisi are liars!' The general grabbed Gaetano by the arm. 'What's your game, boy?'

The prisoner said nothing.

'We too thought he was lying, at first. When he finally understood our intention, to make Rasenna our final example to Etruria, he became somewhat less cooperative.'

'You cut out his tongue?'

'We remained sceptical until our Wave signal was disrupted – only a very gifted engineer could manage that. His tongue is no longer necessary; these walls suffice to tell us a Concordian engineer schools Rasenneisi in our hard-won secrets.'

The general recovered his composure and growled, 'They'll be less impressive as rubble.'

'Well, we shall see,' the Apprentice said. 'The traitor will deliver our terms, General. Before you send him home, collect what's owed; the heir inherits everything, including family debts.'

Fabbro, Pedro and the Doctor crouched behind the walls, waiting.

'This fog is a godsend,' whispered the Doctor. 'The Virgin hasn't abandoned us, even if Ariminum has.'

'Is everything ready?' Fabbro asked. He was accustomed to being the one supplying all the answers, and now he felt redundant. The last month of anxious preparation had taught him the stark truth: that Rasenna's fate once more depended on her warriors.

The Doctor kept his eyes on the Concordians. 'All's done that can be. War isn't any more predictable than business.'

'Where's Giovanni? Shouldn't he be here? Surely they'll want to talk first?'

'We're done talking.'

'He's on the bridge, Signore Bombelli,' said Pedro, 'monitoring the Wave frequency. It's been building for a month and now it's peaking. If we can hold it back for a couple of days more it'll dissipate.'

'If we don't?'

'We wake up tomorrow dead.'

'That's not funny, Doctor. What are these water buckets for, in case of fire?'

'Look, it's going to get dangerous soon,' Pedro said. 'You should get to a safe tower.'

'No. I failed your father when he needed me, I'm staying.'

'Your family need you now, and Rasenna will need you in the aftermath.'

'What if there is none?' he said reluctantly.

'Then it won't matter,' the Doctor said.

But when Fabbro finally got up, there was a sudden loud crack and he dived back under the battlements.

'Has it started?'

The catapult's *whip-snap* echoed in the silence and a golden missile flew over their heads.

'Not yet,' said the Doctor, leaping up, 'but that's our ultimatum.'

The golden bundle landed in Piazza Luna and blood started seeping almost immediately from it, running towards the river. As the Doctor knelt beside it, he saw Uggeri coming across the bridge.

'Stay in position, damn it! You don't need to see this.'

'Yes, I do.'

He didn't argue any more. The boy did have the right to know his old Master's fate. The Doctor unrolled the Morello banner. Inside, gold had turned red. If the fall hadn't already killed Gaetano, blood loss would have. His arms were bound together and severed at the wrists: a disgraceful death. The Doctor tore away the scroll fastened to the stumps.

'Uggeri, I need you to follow the plan. If everybody does their part, we'll avenge all our fallen soldiers. Is every-thing ready?'

'That's what I came to report.'

'All right. Keep your flag up, bandieratoro.'

'You too, old man.'

The Doctor watched him go and ripped up the scroll. As he covered Gaetano's face with the Morello banner, he thought on his own death, doubting it would be much better. He'd lived life thinking that the only good fight was one that was winnable, but reason and experience, those two dry sages, assured him he would not see tomorrow. And yet the fight was good – the best.

Giovanni called from the bridge, 'What did it say, Doc?'

'Nothing – surrender or die – all good?'

'So far.'

As General Luparelli rode closer to the walls, he could see the rows of stakes planted in the surrounding embankment. His horse grew skittish and he failed to calm it; he couldn't master himself, let alone another.

He cleared his throat and shouted, 'Men of Rasenna! You have seen how we treat collaborators. Think how we shall treat enemies. Your walls, your towers and your leaders' lives are forfeit, but you can save your women and children. Accept our terms. This is your final warning. Give us the—'

Out of the silent mist, a solitary dab of gold floated towards him with the patter of mechanical wings. The General swore; he'd been looking forward to taking revenge on Rasenna, and taking it nice and bloody; but it looked like the quailing burghers were prepared to give up the engineer. He should have known Doc Bardini would do anything to save his skin.

ticktickticktickticktickticktick

The annunciator's wings beat like a terrified bird's as it ascended and the general had to spur his horse forward to catch it. He took the paper from its grasp and read:

'Luparino! Still wondering if you are on the side of the Angels? Look to heaven, Dr B.'

The wings slowed. 'Is this a joke?' he shouted up at the walls.

And then he saw them, lighting up like stars, as another and then another angel emerged from the mist until a thousand annunciators were floating from the walls over the neat line of his siege-towers, over his head.

Ticktick tick tick tick
　　tick

General Luparelli stared at the angel in his hand, a single thought exploding in his mind.

tick

Beeeeeeeeeeeeeeeeeb!

'Oh sweet mother of Go—!'

The soldiers saw the general shatter before they heard the blast. His blood-spattered horse bolted and trampled the soldier who ran to catch it, but the ruckus was ignored as every eye stared in horror at the hovering swarms now descending.

Wings beat slower, then stopped, and first one angel, then dozens, dropped to the ground. The first wave hit behind the front line, in the midst of ranks packed too densely to flee. They landed in clusters, causing stampedes and wreaking even more carnage, wave after wave of them, until the legion's handsome face was spoiled and the irregular *crump!* of the explosions was joined by the shrill screams of the dying.

Rasenna's walls remained gallingly empty, indifferent to the suffering. When the panic subsided, the Second Apprentice sniffed and gave an amused snort, recognising the bitter smell of serpentine.

The First Apprentice tapped an aide on the shoulder.

'Fetch me the general's baton, there's a good boy,' he said, and when the aide returned, snatched it from him, looked about for a moment and then handed it back. 'I suppose you'll do.'

'Oh—! Thank you, my Lord – I really don't know what to say—'

'Say "attack", General.'

'Yes, my Lord, of course – Concordians, attack!'

The order was an incantation. At once sleeping engines shuddered into life. Catapults sent hails of fiery comets over the still-silent walls and where they struck the towers, the burning cages burst open and spilled fire in the streets. The fog meant targeting was arbitrary, but terror and confusion were the real aim of these opening moves: a panicking town defeated itself, so the best military theory advised.

But from Rasenna there was nothing.

Fire rained uselessly on empty streets, and no screams or cries were heard over the muffled explosions. Concord's war-engines were the terror of Etruria; for their onslaught to be simply ignored was unprecedented. Lurking behind the soldiers' professional concern came a more atavistic fear: if panic found no purchase in Rasenneisi hearts, it needs must prey on others.

Swallowing their own fear, they advanced, dragging and pushing their engines closer to the walls. The siege might be progressing unusually but they took reassurance in the knowledge that there was another front, and another army, advancing beneath their feet.

In silence and darkness the subterranean siege had begun days ago, when the sappers began burrowing like black worms, ignoring the constant threat of collapse and suffocation. Unlike their brothers overhead, the sappers never lost heart – for men already in graves, there is no retreat; their only way out was to dig, stopping only when they reached the walls, where they would kindle fires with pig-fat hot enough to crack stones. When the walls fell, some would be buried and some would see daylight, and either fate was freedom.

Overhead, the infantry waited patiently, ready to rush headlong into any breach created. This dual offensive was how the Concordian Army won sieges; there was no reason for disquiet, for with an army so well-drilled, so experienced, there really was only one question: how long Rasenna would hold out?

Pedro made the rounds, checking in at every wall-tower. Since the Twelfth had arrived Rasenna's engineers had been monitoring the sappers' progress. The Concordian belief that their machines' speed made countermining ineffective was correct – unless countermining had begun weeks ago. Studying the landscape over the last months, Giovanni had predicted where tunnels would most likely be dug; now they waited for their early-warning system to reveal which route they'd taken.

They watched the water bucket together. The tremors were regular.

'Getting close?' the engineer asked.

'Too close,' said Pedro, and gave the command.

The walls shook as the water passed under and, a moment later, deep behind the Concordian ranks' front line, the tunnel's concealed entrance exploded. Sappers' bodies rained down with the water and mud and rock.

Just as Concord's underground advance was parried, its more conventional assault stalled too. Before the first row of siege-engines could get close enough to the walls to cast their grapping hooks, the top-heavy beasts toppled ignominiously into the concealed pits everyone had failed to spot.

As Concord's own power over machines and water turned back on them, even veteran courage wavered.

The Apprentices, discerning a designer's hand everywhere, marvelled. Their soldiers were no more free than livestock herded to slaughter. Like an architect, the Captain had known where pressure would bear fruit, and their army's rote-learned tactics, efficiency and speed were liabilities against the rare – the *very* rare – opponent who could exploit them.

'And you said he lacked imagination,' the Second Apprentice observed.

The First Apprentice was serene. 'He learned something at his grandfather's knee, but he cannot understand what is happening. Our privilege, gentlemen, is not only to witness the moment when God moves His hand in the world again, but to have the power to slap It away!'

The Third Apprentice laughed like a boy.

The first wave of infantry, concentrated at Rasenna's north gate, fell without a blow as rusted caltrops planted weeks earlier pierced boots, leaving the slow-moving incapacitated to be crushed under their own machines which followed so close on their heels.

'Loose the Sows!' ordered the Twelfth Legion's new and increasingly apprehensive general.

The crews were protected by the hide roofs of the battering rams as they blundered to the embankment and its rows of waiting stakes. Those who escaped the crush at the wall were swiftly cut down by unseen archers, but they had done their job and cleared paths for the siege-towers, which spat flaming arrows at the walls as they followed. Soon the towers themselves became targets. The most effective firebrands were mallets wrapped with rags and studded with nails, all dowsed in burning pitch; they stuck fast wherever they hit.

Catapults were too unwieldy to effectively cover the towers, so smaller ballistae were wheeled up and their practised crews quickly gauged trajectories to concentrate their loads on one target, the northern barbican. This too was routine; the gates were naturally the weakest part of any wall.

Under the unyielding barrage the first gate broke and the infantry, frenzied for revenge, trampled injured comrades to be first to the breach. They paused only to flay a fallen siege-tower of its protective skin. They used the hide-covered wattle to bridge the embankment, but no sooner had they entered the barbican than a second gate dropped behind them. Trapped inside the tower, immobilised by their own numbers, all they could do was scream when the long pikes came thrusting out of the murder holes overhead.

Every normally successful Concordian advance was undone with such strange ease that each unit was more cautious than the last. But still the odds were weighted heavily in Concord's favour – and then blind luck lent a hand. A burning siege-tower managed to reach the wall and drop its drawbridge. Though most of the crew were struck down, some survived to run along the wall to the northern gate, the focus of the battle. At the same moment another tower to the east fell into a concealed trench, tottered, creaking, like an old tree in a forest, then crashed against the wall; though its crew were crushed to death, soldiers behind quickly clambered up the accidental bridge to join the struggle at the gate.

The hidden pike-men vanished suddenly, and sensing weakness, more infantry rushed the barbican and managed to lift the portcullis – it jammed less than halfway up, but left space enough for the Concord men to squeeze into the town in ones and twos. 'Now by God, now! Show no mercy!' the new general whooped. 'To the breach!'

Strangely, no Rasenneisi attempted to stop them.

They rushed into the streets, bawling challenges, howling like wolves. By tradition, when Concord soldiers first breached a besieged town, they abandoned their normal strict military order for a short carnival of brutality. After a taste of anarchy, the unfortunate town's population would beg for martial law to be imposed. From a commander's point of view, the worse the soldiers behaved, the better; it was that wilding-hour that veterans reminisced over, bragged about and prayed for.

The pack spread out, prowling for townsfolk and found . . .

Nothing.

Just like Rasenna's walls, the streets ignored them. The men's great excitement and the narrowness of the steep alleys made orderly advancement impossible. On every street corner, a Madonna glared down, not a Mother of Mercy but a vengeful She-Devil, reproachfully displaying the slain babe at her breast. Under that pitiless, omnipresent gaze, penned into the restricted streets and isolated by the impenetrable mist and an imperious silence, wolves became sheep.

*

The town must be abandoned, the young soldier concluded. *The gate had been defended just long enough for the rest to escape. Clever ploy.*

Something came out of the mist; he swiped his sword but missed—

Just a pigeon. He laughed nervously, thankful that the mist hid his blushes from the others.

Then he realised there were no others.

He retraced his steps, holding his blade up to the whiteness. He wasn't lost; that was something: he recognised this particular four-alley intersection. He looked down each for his colleagues.

Nothing, nothing, nothing, nothing.

He listened – was that something? There was a fluttering sound, then silence. More pigeons?

Too late, he thought to look up.

The bandieratori were patient. They let the Concordians get drawn out before picking them off; Uggeri's decina were especially effective at this. Occasional screams were *allowed* to be heard, which made them all the more chilling. The streets, the fog and the silence were the Rasenneisi's allies in this battle. Some soldiers, scared into witlessness, dropped their swords and waited for the end; others roared challenges into the mist and ran, slashing at the fearful emptiness. Concordian fell on Concordian crying *Mercy*, crying *Traitor*, just crying.

Others ran, more terrified than ever in their lives.

*

The wheezing soldier turned corner after corner until, quite by accident, he reached the river. He was a veteran of Gubbio, of Veii; to die in Rasenna of all places – it didn't make sense! In the middle of the bridge, a hooded figure crouched over a curious device. The soldier uttered a despairing oath, finally beginning to understand: Rasenna had *engineers*! Why hadn't the Apprentices warned them?

He turned around and saw what was impossible to see in between the clustered towers: each of the towers was connected in a great web of rope-bridges, and they were all manned by bandieratori-turned-archers, shooting deadly darts into the mist below.

He made an especially easy target.

CHAPTER 67

A week passed before the Ariminumese dared venture from their walls. Where the condottieri camp had been, they found a newly erected gallows, and under a wooden sign with the word 'Traitors' burned into it, was Captain Scarpelli, and a dog, both hanged by the neck.

The doge understood the dog was his proxy and trembled. The only question was how long before the condottiere returned for justice?

The Hawk's Company, justly famed throughout the peninsula for its speed, moved quickly, but for once John Acuto did not lead the march. In the last carriage of the baggage train Sofia watched helplessly as the old bull deteriorated by the hour. He demanded water but could not drink; he demanded paper to write, but could not hold a quill steady. Finally, sinking in and out of delerium, he lay back and surrendered to fevered memory.

'She asked me what I hoped to earn, Sofia, and when I said I'd be rich, she accused me of abandoning her for Fortune. I told her I'd write, but she turned her back on me. You know women – Fortune's jealous, brooks no rival lovers. She stopped answering my letters!'

'You're tiring yourself, General,' Sofia said. 'Hush.'

'My boy, Harry, came to me – that was later. He followed me to Etruria to tell me that after I left, Plague made a cuckold of me. Or was it Fortune? She stole her, then tired of me . . . she stopped answering my letters . . .'

Yuri rode with Levi up to the carriage. 'Thought you'd want to know, Sofia. We're in sight,' Levi told her.

She heard the strange note in Levi's voice. 'What is it?'

'It's not how I remember.'

'You tolded me it was poor!' said Yuri, reproachfully.

She leapt down from the cart. 'I want to see.'

The First Apprentice placidly studied the battle though his magnifier. 'General, it's time to pull your men back.'

'But my Lord, we've breached – I mean to say, we're *winning*!'

'The opening round goes to Rasenna. It's just that nobody's escaped to tell you yet. Here – look east.' He thrust the scope at the general. '*East*, I said!'

'Why— It's an army!' the general said.

'Well deduced, General! You certainly *are* earning that promotion.'

'Perhaps it is our allies, come to lend aid?'

'The Ariminumese don't fight their own battles – they're certainly not going to fight ours. Look at the Standard.'

'Ah.' The new general paled noticeably and unconsciously

took a step back. 'Perhaps we *should* retreat to a better position? Of course we can defeat the Hawk's Company again, but if they meet us here—'

'Yes, we will be under siege ourselves, rather ironic. But there's nothing for it. My colleagues shall deal with Rasenna; you deal with John Acuto.'

The general saluted. 'Yes, my Lord.'

'Keep our horses ready. We will need a quick exit.'

And the three Apprentices marched into the fray and their colours were soon obscured by the mist and smoke.

Only the towers were the same. Sofia didn't know which she felt more, dread or elation. Rasenna's walls were standing proud and strong, and keeping a Concordian legion at bay. If this was the engineer's work, what was its end? What was the point of further subterfuge if he was in league with the Apprentices? Perhaps Rasenna was only a pawn in a larger game and this was about reclaiming his Family title from the Apprentices.

She knew only one thing for certain. When the Darkness touched her, she realised that her heart was a traitor. Her choice now was whether to betray her heart, or Rasenna.

'I have to get in there,' she said.

'Impossible.' Levi pointed. 'Look, they're turning. They've seen us.'

The forces that had not yet been committed were manoeuvring away from the walls; the rest were pulling back slowly.

'Attacking their rear is all we can do for Rasenna now.'

'That's plenty,' said Yuri.

'I'm surprised Rasenna's withstood this long – most towns would've surrendered already.'

'Not Rasenna. I need to get in!'

'Sofia, we can't just charge at them. Our best tactic is to draw them away.'

'It can't wait that long. I have to get in there or there won't be a Rasenna to help. I've *seen* it, Levi! Another Wave is coming and I've got to stop it!'

Clad in his hauberk, John Acuto climbed from the carriage. 'How?' he growled.

'I don't know yet, but I know I have to get in there to do it. Please believe me, General!'

'Sofia, we're outnumbered three to one. Unless there are men in there to fight, men who'll leave the safety of their walls to help us, we'll be riding to our doom.'

'They'll fight, Levi! Even if it's just women and children left, Rasenna will fight.'

'So be it. I'll clear you a path, Contessa.'

Levi dismounted. 'This is madness. General, you are in no condition to ride.'

'I'm in no condition to be living at all. Let me leave life as I should have lived it, as a knight!'

'You're fortunate to still be alive.'

'Damn it, Fortune has nothing to do with it! We make our own fortunes, for good or ill. All the excuses we use – Concord, money, kings – it's nonsense. Nothing stops a man but himself. We can be *knights*, Levi! Knights!'

Levi didn't argue and Yuri gave a shrug. 'Why not?' They both saw the strength it took the old bull to keep standing.

'Then let me help you, General.'

Once in full armour and heaved into the saddle, Acuto said quietly, 'This needn't be pure folly. A nice rain of arrowheads will puncture their confidence, so get the Welsh lads out first. I'll lead the cavalry and we'll smash their lines wide open.'

Levi passed the order on and then rode up to the line to get a better look at the Concordians. Sofia rode up behind him.

'Was a doomed charge in the five-year plan?'

Levi shrugged. 'Don't underestimate condottieri pride. Treachery beat us at Tagliacozzo. You're going to see how we do in a fair fight.'

'Why are *you* doing this, Levi? For the money?'

Levi laughed. 'Not this time. This *is* Etruria's fight. Scarpelli might have been right, chivalry may be a myth, but look at the old bull: half-dead already and still ready to fight. If it's a myth, then what a myth! If there's nowhere left in Etruria for condottieri, I suppose I'll be a knight, fighting for lost causes.' Levi rabbit-punched her arm. 'And fair damsels like you.'

Sofia smiled thinly and said nothing.

'Are you afraid we won't break through?'

'I'm afraid of what I'll find in there.'

Levi touched her shoulder, gently this time. 'Whatever it is, Contessa, you're equal to it.'

In the shadow of the walls the press of dying men was bitter. Their cries did not distract the Apprentices. Nothing distracted them.

Morning retreated before noon and dark clouds gathered in the north, blown in on the same wind that had begun to scatter the mist.

Arrows flew by from both directions as they climbed up a fallen siege-tower and leapt down onto the walls. For the first time, Bernoulli's heirs looked upon Rasenna.

'Handsome bridge,' said the Second Apprentice.

'That's where the Captain will be,' said the man in red. 'I must congratulate him. The Contessa's sure to be protecting the failsafe. Remember, destroying her is more important than destroying it. It'll be on a tall building somewhere.'

'There,' said the Second Apprentice, pointing, 'that tower on the northside slope, with the orange trees.'

As Sofia rode back to the line, John Acuto spurred his horse forward, winking at her as he passed. The men watched as he stopped to look down at the Concordian Army.

After a moment, he turned back and unsheathed his sword. 'Impressed?'

'No!' the Company roared mightily.

'Then look again!' he roared back and waited, letting an uneasy silence spread over the line.

'Look: see their famous discipline, their numbers and their engines. That is what you face. If you are afraid, this is what you fear. So look again. Are you impressed?'

There was no answering roar this time and the general spat. 'I'm not impressed. Concord's strength is drills, numbers, machines, and I'm not impressed because I know the quality of the men they face. You may have forgotten; look at the man next to you. Thank the Virgin that you will not face *that* man in battle! Look at the ranks of knights behind you! Thank the Virgin that you will not face *them*! You, my men, *you* impress me. If you faced that knight, these ranks, this company, you would be wise to fear. *But you do not!*'

He pointed his sword down at the Concordians. 'These are slaves! They know condottieri who surrender and retreat. They have never faced knights who fight and win! Do they even remember what a charge sounds like? By God, we'll show them!'

The Company's roar was like thunder, thunder soon joined by the rumble of a thousand horses advancing.

CHAPTER 68

The bandieratori capos went to the northern wall to discover why the Concordians were not attacking.

'They're retreating,' Pedro explained morosely.

'*Porca Madonna!*' Uggeri said.

'What's the problem? We got them on the run.'

Uggeri looked at Mule scathingly. 'It's disastrous.' He too had been party to the Doctor's planning; stalling the Concordian Army's machinery was only half of a plan relying on attrition and terror: Giovanni and his engineers would repulse forays during the day, and decini would 'raid' the Concordian lines by night. This sudden withdrawal was more than a surprise; it might be a fatal setback.

'Doc thought we could sap their strength for days. What do we do now?'

'Listen,' said Pedro.

On the walls, the ripples in the buckets grew until they tipped over.

'Sappers?' shouted Mule.

Pedro turned the magnifier east. 'I don't think so.'

A wall of gleaming silver filled and then spilled over

the horizon. The legion turned to meet it, but the manoeuvre wasn't executed with typical precision – it was impossible to assemble a unified line under fire from Rasenna's walls. By the time they turned, the approaching condottieri were under ballista and archer range.

He focused on the cavalry's first row. The rider in front looked like a charging bull, but something behind him had caught Pedro's eye – a banner, black and gold. He knew it well. It was the banner depicted in the Vanzetti crest, their finest piece of work.

He searched amongst the debris on the wall until he found what he was looking for, dragged loose the discarded grappling-hook, hurled it over the wall and pulled the attached rope taut round a merlon.

'Contessa!' he cried, but his voice was lost in the growing clamour. The hook had landed in front of the embankment just as the first riders reached it.

There was no way she could hear him, unless —

'Hey!' Mule exclaimed as Pedro snatched his banner.

The cavalry crashed into the Concordian lines, spears snapping, pikes driving into breasts of horse and man, hoofs crushing helmets and punching through armour. The wave of beast, man and steel broke the line and poured through the breach.

Following in its wake, Sofia saw someone on the walls waving a banner. She read the signal and saw the lifeline. Ahead, the tumult of hacking, screaming bodies was fast approaching. She took her feet out of the stirrups and pulled herself up until she stood crouched on the saddle, holding the reigns loosely. As her horse leapt into the fray, she leapt too.

She caught the rope and hung there for a moment, looking down at the ground, churning with dying men. In the centre, John Acuto was slaughtering prodigiously before the Concordian pikemen took courage. And she watched, hot tears pouring unnoticed down her face, as the old bull dropped, skewered from all sides and blood pouring from his lips like a stricken bull. Looking up, he caught her eye. His face was ecstatic. 'See what I earned!' he bellowed, and then had done with the world, declining payment like a king.

Pedro helped Sofia over the top and she bent down to catch her breath and wipe her face.

Then she looked up, and she saw the bandieratori lining the wall were southsiders and northsiders, and they were all carrying the same flag, and understood, as only a Rasenneisi could, that all had changed.

But there was no time to wait. 'Pedro, there's a Wave coming.'

'No, we're blocking it.' Pedro handed her his spyglass. 'Doc's protecting the first transmitter, but Giovanni's alone on the bridge.'

Now she looked more closely Sofia could see that Tower Bardini was the hub of the rope-bridges, and that two black ink-stains were fighting their way towards it. The mist was blowing away and with it the Rasenneisi's advantage. With nowhere to hide, bandieratori became embroiled in fatally brief duels with the black spectres.

She looked down at the bridge and saw a hooded figure. Her heart skipped a beat, and then skipped again when, in Piazza Luna she saw another ink-stain, red like blood, marching calmly towards the bridge. A familiar cold chill crept over her.

'The Doc can take care of himself,' Pedro said quietly.

Mule took back his flag from Pedro. 'I'm coming with you, Contessa.'

She flinched; she had not expected to be addressed that way again. The bandieratori were looking at her, familiar faces like Mule's, new ones like Uggeri's, but all with the same expectation and the same loyalty. She was their Contessa still, whatever flag they now carried.

'I'll need a new banner. This one's too old,' she said, and threw down her family colours.

In the silence, a boy stepped forward. 'Take mine.'

'The Hawk's Company fights for Rasenna now,' Sofia said. 'They need our help.'

'We know what to do,' said Uggeri.

'Good.' She turned to Pedro. 'Keep attacking the Concordian rear, throw everything you've got at them. There'll be no second chances.'

She was right. This was the type of fight Concordians excelled at, and it wasn't long before they were presenting the condottieri with a closely packed line of impermeable advancing steel.

After John Acuto fell, Levi took up the Standard and rallied the Company. The Concordians made a renewed effort, and pushed them back from the wall. In the chaos, Levi was thrown from his rearing horse. He left the Standard where it fell, remounted and turned tail, and the majority of the Hawk's cavalry followed in disarray.

Sensing rout, the Concordians broke their newly formed lines to pursue. General Luparelli would have recognised the old ploy, but his replacement, leading the charge, did not.

The condottieri suddenly spun around and recharged their pursuers, riding them down in a maelstrom of mud and blood and flailing hooves. The manoeuvre gave them space, but the advantage could only be temporary: in a grinding competition of strength, inevitably numbers would tell.

The Doctor, studying the inexorable approach of the two Apprentices, began to cut the ropes leading to Tower Bardini. There were archers stationed in the surrounding towers, but the Apprentices' speed and their billowing robes, yellow and orange, made them impossible targets.

The Third Apprentice was getting closer. The boy, fast as a wharf rat, climbed along the rope to get to the bandier-atoro firing on him from a nearby tower, advancing fearlessly in the face of the onslaught of arrows. He reached the tower and snatched the bandieratoro's bow away and the Doctor watched, lips tight, as the Rasenneisi fell screaming from the tower. When he looked back, the boy had vanished behind the slanted roof.

He turned and scanned in all directions for the yellow, recognising the distraction for what it was too late. An orange shape crashed into his side and as he was sent sprawling his flag went over the edge. In the centre of swirling orange robes the Second Apprentice's face was inhumanly calm as he watched the Doctor get to his feet.

The Doctor didn't wait but leapt at the youth; a moment later, he went crashing down onto the table. As he got up, the Apprentice kicked him hard in the chest and sent him skidding to the tower's edge. He stopped himself in time and, in desperation, picked up an orange-tree pot, but before he could throw it, the Apprentice lunged forward and jabbed him in the neck. The Doctor gagged and released the pot. It smashed down on his own head.

The Apprentice drew a dagger, but instead of finishing off the unconscious Doctor, turned his attention to the transmitter. A white shape leapt from nowhere with an angry whine and there was a ripping sound as the Apprentice pried Cat off his face and flung it from the tower. Cat caught a banner hanging from a neighbour's tower and scrambled inside, its moment of heroism over.

But before the Apprentice had recovered his equanimity, the Doctor dived at him, and the young man sidestepped, just as the Doctor had hoped he would – he hadn't been going for the man. His precipitous fall over the edge of the tower was halted suddenly as the cape snapped taut and the Doctor climbed back up until he reached the strangling Apprentice, and then let himself fall again, still holding the cape. The Apprentice's face slammed into stone and the Doctor scrambled up over the unconscious body and sat down hard, breathing strenuously, and mumbled, 'Thanks, Cat.'

The Twelfth Legion pushed until they were out of range of Rasenna's wall. With that danger out of the way, it was easier to sustain order, though Pedro did all he could to disrupt it by flooding the remaining canals.

Levi's horse had been killed, and Yuri's too, and now they fought side by side, trying to hold the hard-pressed line together. Both were conscious what a disaster a true rout would be.

'Levi,' cried Yuri, 'look!'

And the bandieratori of Rasenna came marching from the gate, spinning their flags like reapers at harvest. This was no mad charge; instead they assembled three rows deep and advanced steadily, each row spinning flags in a different rhythm. The motion all together was like an approaching wave, unbreakable and unstoppable.

'*Madonna!*' Levi whooped, 'our Contessa came through!'

When the last rope he had to cut twitched, the Doctor leapt to his feet and shouted, 'Come on!'

A sudden tightness in his chest made him gasp and he

glanced down. An arrowhead stuck out from his chest and as he watched, it was joined by another. He turned just as the Third Apprentice fired again.

The Doctor caught the arrow and roared, 'Come and fight like a man!'

The boy shook his head and calmly nocked another arrow.

'You don't die easy, do you, Doctor Bardini?' said a strangled voice behind him.

The Doctor turned and watched helplessly as the Second Apprentice cut the cord, then cast the transmitter from the tower. He heard the impact it made just as another arrow struck his back. He lurched towards the side of the Tower.

When the boy drew closer to deliver the killing shot, the Second Apprentice hissed at him, 'Torbidda, why are you still here? It's coming! Go, I'll follow if I can. If I can't, it doesn't matter.'

'What about the First Apprentice? If the Contessa's not here, she must be on the bridge.'

'I'll help him, but don't worry about us. Our time is over. You know what to do.'

'Yes.'

'Say it!'

'We are but vessels,' said the boy, and without a backwards glance, scrambled away on the rope.

Giovanni double-checked the readings and realised that the transmitter had stopped. He looked over his shoulder at Tower Bardini.

'Captain Giovanni,' said a tuneless voice. The First Apprentice was leaning against the Lion, watching him with a smile.

'My Lord,' he said, manoeuvring himself in front of the machine as the man in red approached.

'I see you don't lack for conviction any more.'

'I'm a Rasenneisi now. They don't come lukewarm.' Giovanni swung a fist, but the man in red slapped it and him aside in one easy motion. Giovanni's head struck the balustrade. He didn't get up.

The First Apprentice examined the apparatus Giovanni had failed to conceal. Professional interest satisfied, he unplugged the Whistler and shattered it on the stones.

'Looks like rain,' he said wistfully.

Sofia and Mule raced towards the river, first topside and then twisting through the alleys. The sounds of battle outside the walls, the clash of metal and screams of the dying, filled the air, but the streets were eerily empty. Every man, woman and child of Rasenna was either defending the walls or outside them, having joined the battle.

Even as the Hawk's Company rallied, the legion's rear ranks were forced to turn once more and defend themselves against this second assault. Even veterans had never faced fighters or tactics like these: not men, but a wall of dancing colour, and the sounds attacking their ears were not war-cries, but a hypnotic *whoopwhoopwhoop* of spin-ning flags. Without warning the rhythm would get faster and a bandieratoro would burst though the red and gold to attack, then vanish behind the colour again, leaving only cries of agony as the flags slowed to a soothing *whoop-whoopwhoop*.

And for the first time in two decades, squeezed between condottieri and bandieratori, the strength of a Concordian legion broke.

On Tower Bardini, the Second Apprentice touched his cheek as a raindrop stuck. The water mingled with the bloody claw marks. 'Perfect. We'll all be wet soon. Can you hear the rumble, Doctor? Can you feel it?'

The Doctor groaned.

'I pray you will excuse me. I must assist my colleague.' The young man leaned his weight on the Doctor's neck and pressed down. 'But don't worry. You won't miss a thing. I'll leave you here, where you can see it coming.'

The Doctor looked down on the bridge and something familiar caught his eye, a banner he hadn't seen for twenty years.

Madonna, they could win this fight yet win!

He grabbed and twisted the Apprentice's foot until it cracked, then pushed himself up with a roar and wrapped his arms around the Apprentice. 'You won't steal her again!'

But it was like trying to grasp water: the Apprentice

twisted in his grasp until he had only a weak one-arm chokehold. It wasn't enough. Laughing as he did it, the Apprentice stabbed down, and stabbed again, but as the dagger sank into the Doctor's flank, as his blood spilled, still he held on. An Apprentice could fight, but the Doctor could suffer.

'You can't stop me, old fool. You can barely stand,' the youth said mockingly.

The Doctor took a step back into empty air, dragging the Apprentice with him. The air howled as it passed by and the workshop rooftop hurtled towards them, the Apprentice struggling like a demon while the Doctor held him tightly, eyes closed, still as the world moved. They crashed through slate and into the boards an army had trained upon, spilling blood together on the wood shavings, the Second Apprentice's robes turning red at last.

The Doctor smiled. It was an inelegant death, and yet a good one.

When Sofia and Mule reached Piazza Luna, the rain was falling more heavily. It was still early, but it was getting dark, and it wasn't the storm clouds. Sofia did not notice the body covered in a golden shroud; her attention was solely on the bridge, where *he* was waiting. And the question: if a Wave *was* coming, why was he here?

They reached the original Lion and stopped there. On the far side of the bridge, Giovanni lay prone while the

First Apprentice stood looking down at the gap, waiting.

'Stay back, Sofia,' said Mule, rushing forward.

'Mule, no!'

He went in swinging. The man in red waited calmly, and when Mule came near, ducked under his banner-swing, lunged forward, grabbed his head and turned it backwards.

Sophia heard, '*CracKKkkk!*' and Mule dropped without a cry.

'Mule!' she sobbed.

The First Apprentice turned to face her. 'You'll join him soon enough, Contessa.' He frowned. 'That's not the banner you stole from us.'

'Rasenna has a new banner.'

'Then we'll take that too. Why did you come back? To be reunited with your lover? Haven't you figured out yet that he lied?'

'I know.'

'You know nothing, child.' He laughed his off-key laugh. 'He fooled everyone, even himself. There are currents intersecting here that you can't possibly fathom.'

'You're afraid of it, aren't you?'

The man in red dropped all pretence of a smile. 'You think the *Art Banderia* can defeat our Water Style? It didn't help your friend.' He kicked Mule's corpse and glanced back towards Tower Bardini.

'The thunder you hear means it didn't help your Master either.'

She dropped her flag. 'I had more than one Master. Did you come to talk or to fight?'

Giovanni, woken by the rumble, hobbled over to the machine in a daze. He heard a crunch and looked down at the glass fragments beneath his feet.

Then he saw, on the far side of the bridge —

'Sofia?'

It was true then, everything Lucia had told him. Sofia was alive, and he could tell her all the things he'd been too afraid to: the truth, his name.

Iscanno

Giovanni looked down at the river and saw a buio standing there.

Wind is coming.

With a scream of hate, the First Apprentice attacked. Sofia did nothing. She saw the Darkness and the First Apprentice for what they were: one. She was tired of running, tired of fighting, tired of being afraid. The Reverend Mother said only faith was necessary, and she had been willing to die for it. Was she that strong?

Sofia let go of a lifetime's training that told her to strike first and watched him, and watched herself.

This is fear, this is hate. Regard it steadily.

Sofia could feel the adrenalin surging though her body, into her heart, her limbs, bone and muscle.

The surge slowed, her heartbeat slowed. Time melted away. She did not dodge or strike; she breathed. The Apprentice's scream and his body slowed in space together, and then

S t o p p e d.

In the pit, the Dark Ancient screamed as it was burned by a fire brighter than a thousand suns. Sofia saw the Source and was covered by

L i g h t.

She had never been this deep before. Measurements like seconds and centuries were meaningless in this place; here she was outside Time. The future became the past: both a grey memory to be observed with not too much interest; neither could ever be as important again. She felt as if she had been keeping one eye closed her whole life and now she had suddenly opened it.

And there was something else: the thing that the First Apprentice had spoken of with dread, that *something* was about to happen here, and it was something good. Nature was pregnant with a wonderful idea – it was so obvious. How had she ignored it her whole life?

Exhale. The last of the mist swirled lazily in the air, thicker in patches, catching the crisp golden light and turning into curious shapes, spirals, letters. Was this magic all around me all the time? Why did I never see it? *Inhale.*

The mist quickened and raindrops fell freely and the scream grew shrill once more and all again was movement—

Sofia was not where she had been a moment ago.

'How—?' the First Apprentice gasped.

'I told you I was through answering your questions.'

The answer was beyond words: the First Apprentice was a Student of Water Style and she, though only a moment had passed, was now a Master. The blows hurtling towards her were a distraction, easily parried. When he threw another punch, Sofia caught his hand and twisted it effort-lessly, and his wrist was broken.

He didn't pause, so Sofia batted his other hand away and then kicked him under the chin, knocking him back towards the gap. He would have fallen through, had she not caught his collar and held it.

'Sofia!' Giovanni shouted, limping towards them.

The Apprentice gagged and whispered, a manic gleam of hope in his eyes. 'Contessa, you know his name – why don't you kill him? He lied to you.'

'Not about love.'

'How can you be certain?'

'Faith,' she said.

'Ah,' he said, now understanding the battle was lost. 'I too have faith. I shall tell my Master your name.' He ripped his collar from her grip.

The river recognised the voice of the one it hated most of all and was waiting at the surface to drag him under.

Giovanni looked back and saw the buio seeping onto the bridge, following him.

'Stay away from her.'

Cannot stay in Dryworld. Must leave, Iscanno.

'Stop calling me that! My name's Bernoulli!'

'It can't be!' Sofia gasped.

Giovanni turned to face her. 'It is, Sofia. I'm so very sorry – I wanted to tell you so many times—'

'No. Giovanni, you don't understand: you're not a Bernoulli – you're one of them! A buio!'

'What? No, I'm as human as you.'

Sofia walked towards him. 'Give me your hand.'

Suddenly they were in another time, another place, immersed in the same vision.

'*Where are we, Giovanni?*'

'*. . . Gubbio . . .*'

A boy came out of a Concordian tent and looked about. His eyes were as sharp as knives. Snow drifted in the cold grey air as if reluctant to touch the earth of this awful place. The tent was pitched beside a steep bank leading to a rapidly flowing river, the water leaping and surging as it flowed up and over an incline.

In the midst of the rapids were towers, freshly smashed. There were other remnants, lying in piles and pits, and carrion birds and wild dogs squabbled lazily, though they had no need to fight. There was enough for all.

The boy's tent was more elaborate than the others, and stood apart.

His work was private.

He was and was not Giovanni – he was younger, of course; but the difference was more profound than that.

His apron was covered in blood, his hands and face too, and yet he looked as pleased as a well-fed cat. He even walked differently, with a self-confident strut. Shooing away a crow with a blood-caked beak, he crouched by a basin and washed himself. He cupped the water in his hands and frowned at the reflection he saw. Someone – something – was behind him and he turned to face it.

He had no time to scream. Enveloped in the buio, he struggled noiselessly, the blood washing off his skin as he drowned. Now moving more slowly, the buio faced the river again and the body was expelled with a gush of bloody water and rolled down the bank to the river.

'You killed him.'

'I don't know how to say it, I – we – were angry. I had forgotten it till now. I was reborn that day . . .'

The buio tried to get back to the river, but found each step heavier. Blood was in it now, filling it, finding the places where veins would be, where a heart would beat.

'I was changed, but I arose the same.'

'You were punished for it? Why? He was the same as his grandfather, a murderer.'

'They – we – do not kill in anger. Bernoulli made us kill. I remember it now. Our Law is Water will be Water, but shall not kill. My punishment – our punishment – was to live a murderer's life.'

*

574

Sofia let go and the vision ended. The buio surrounded them, waiting. The rumble was amplified to a teeth-rattling roar now. It was midday, but dark as late evening, and the rain was pelting down.

'Whoever – *whatever* – you are, I love you.'

The other buio were sinking into puddles and flowing back into the river.

Wind coming. Must join it, Iscanno.

'No!' Giovanni said.

Cannot fight it – *part* of it.

When they were gone, he felt it too: the pull of the Wave. It was like a thousand hooks pulling at the smallest part of his essence, and it was almost upon them.

'Why don't you run, Sofia?'

Sofia said, 'There's nowhere to go, and I'm not afraid any more.'

She kissed him.

'Why are you smiling?' he said.

'Because you can't die,' Sofia said.

'I won't live without you. I was put here to stop this. Time is different for us; we knew the Wave was coming even before Concord thought of sending it. Sofia, something wonderful is going to be born here, they've been waiting for it – all History has been waiting—'

'What?'

'It wasn't an accident that I became – this, who I am. I'm here for a reason.'

They looked to the west simultaneously. The Wave had

not yet peaked; when it reached the walls it would scatter them like straw. It was several times broader than the river, wide enough to flood the town and contato together. As it came closer to the bridge the Hate grew, a crescendoing scream.

On the walls and on the battlefield beyond them, they saw it too and knew it would sweep them all away – Concordians, condottieri and Rasenneisi – all together.

Every atom of Giovanni's being screamed to join it, but he did not. Now that he finally understood the cost, he knew what was necessary.

'Go, Giovanni. It's too late! It'll pull you apart.'

'I won't let Bernoulli win.'

'I can feel what you feel – and *Madonna*, it hurts! You can't fight it! You're part of it.'

The signal peaked and the Wave climbed to breaking point, swollen with loathing for Men and their weakness, their cruelty, their lies. The wind died and every flag dropped. The shadow covered the trembling towers of Rasenna. On the battlefield, Concordian and Rasenneisi alike cried out to the Virgin for succour.

Giovanni pulled away from Sofia and faced it. He raised his hand and pushed, *pushed*, against the river. Raindrops hung in the air, waiting to fall. The river did not flow. The Wave did not break. Love was stronger.

On the walls, outside them, everyone looked about in wonder, all asking the same question: how were they still alive?

Like a tower collapsing, the Wave fell back into the river, and the rain that hung waiting to fall dropped – all of it. The towers shook with the impact.

The Baptistery bells chimed and every Rasenneisi cheered, all but one. Giovanni had pushed the river. Sofia watched as that power pushed back, on him alone.

'I'll always be with you,' he said, reaching out.

Before her hand touched his, he was scattered into a cloud of mist.

'Giovanni!'

The mist hung in the air, holding a man's shape for a moment, and then passed away on the wind.

'No cause for tears, Contessa.' Isabella reached for her hand. 'He's with you for ever now.'

But Sofia picked up the Herod's Sword he had left behind and looked on the river and cried anyway. The rain, liberated now, danced on the surface of the Irenicon. Water was water.

EPILOGUE

To walk the streets on summer days listening to the towers babble was sweet. Returning from a Signoria meeting, Sofia reflected on the year that had passed since the Wave. The bridges between the towers were permanent now, and neighbours spent hours on them, gossiping and arguing and watching the world go by for the pleasure of criticising it. The pale flecks of cotton, blown in on a temperate breeze from the Rasenna contato, floated indolently through the streets and the sun poured down until the cobblestones rippled like water. She often imagined that she walked in the heart of old Rasenna, with her grandfather and father proudly watching over her.

Nobody guessed it at the time, but the siege inaugurated the third contest between Rasenna and Concord: the final and most terrible war. There was more than a year's respite before Concord regrouped, time enough for Rasenna to rebuild broken walls and grow still stronger.

Rasenna had withstood the most powerful weapon

Concord had. It was predictable that the cities of Etruria would believe that it had engineers equal to Concord's; they neither understood Natural Philosophy nor believed that anything could be stronger. Still, it was true that a miracle had come to pass, and the cities of Etruria lost no time forming a new Southern League for collective security, the chance of revenge and, most of all, a stake in the Empire's assets when it collapsed.

This was premature.

Though the First and Second Apprentices had perished, leaving a mere boy in charge of an Empire that would never again be seen as invincible, much remained unchanged. The Guild still ruled Concord, and Concord still ruled northern Etruria. The Twelfth Legion was lost, but eleven other legions continued to fight and win the war in Europa. At best, Rasenna had been given an opportunity; whether it used that opportunity wisely, or squandered it as before, depended on the men and women who led it.

Under Pedro Vanzetti, Rasenna's Engineers' Guild expanded as rapidly as Concord's had more than three decades ago – but there was no question of Rasenneisi engineers abandoning their names.

Family banners hung proudly from family towers, no longer cause for contention or rivalry; the only banner that would be carried into future battles was the city's, as both a weapon for her bandieratori and a standard for her knights.

The men of the Hawk's Company, tired of scratching a

living in a country that could no longer afford condottieri, petitioned to stay in Rasenna, and Colonel Levi was nominated podesta. Vowing never to become too respectable, he accepted the honour.

Sofia crossed the bridge and stopped at the gap to watch the river. Though she had thrown off her rank, she was still conspicuous amongst the crowds. Stall-owners whispered to civilians that this was the Contessa Scaligeri – the noblewoman who had returned to Rasenna with an army; she might have seized power, but in giving up her birthright, she had instead slain the serpent of faction forever.

There were certain bandieratori and certain towers who urged her to reconsider, but the Contessa – *Sofia* – insisted there would be no return to aristocracy in Rasenna; the chain was broken. Her only ambition was to sit in the Signoria as one respected voice amongst many, and to support Gonfaloniere Bombelli.

She turned away from the river and walked back to the workshop. In the months after the second Wave she'd struggled to come to terms with a grief that existed without death, though she knew that Isabella was right: Giovanni was not really gone. He was with her forever, like the Irenicon was one with Rasenna.

The Scaligeri banner had found a new home on what was once called Tower Bardini. The Doc had been faithful to her, so she in turn kept his workshop alive, and it was as thronged with students as ever. Now she briefly conferred with Uggeri before climbing up to the tower roof.

Up here, she felt as if she could call upon the Doctor's ghost for counsel. She peeled an orange as she looked down on the bridge and pondered the questions still unanswered since that terrible, wonderful day: the Reverend Mother and her own visions had spoken of a choice *she* would have to make, yet it was Giovanni who sacrificed everything.

Why had the Apprentices been so intent on destroying Rasenna, instead of simply re-conquering it?

What were they so afraid of?

She still felt that a terrible ghost was loose in the world, and a wonderful promise. Her recurring nightmare always started the same way:

At night, with wind and rain howling through the ruin of the Molè's great hall. Indifferent to Nature's agony, the charred angel looked down at the circle of torch-bearing engineers standing around the repaired glass column. In the centre, the Third Apprentice, now First, now wearing the red, looked balefully up at the statue.

'This is a great honour,' the boy said nervously, 'we are but vessels.'

'We are vessels,' came the engineers' response.

'Although changed I shall arise the same,' he intoned as he approached the waiting coffin with faltering steps.

When the door hissed closed and there was no one to hear, he whispered, '*Madonna*, preserve me. I am afraid.'

The star dropped into darkness. A storm that had been incubating for centuries attacked the dark white city, with bolt after bolt striking the lantern at the Molè's summit. The charges shot through the triple dome and lit up the great hall as they hit the angel's upraised sword. The engineers fell back in fear as their torches were snuffed out.

In the underworld, a moment later, the charge shot from the second angel's sword, through the void of the pit and into the lake.

The water's surface boiled with buio in agony.

When the coffin rose from the filthy black water, the boy inside was no longer crying.

The thunder that followed was the sound of Heaven cracking open.

Sofia awoke. It was just before dawn, and she realised she was not alone. The air was humid, as if an imperceptible mist hung in the air, and on her skin were droplets like morning dew.

The buio stood at the window, waiting for the morning light.

'Is it you?' she asked.

The sun came up over Rasenna and swept into the room. The light swam over Sofia, and she understood the responsibility offered.

'Behold the handmaid of the Lord,' she said, and felt at once the quickening.

ACKNOWLEDGEMENTS

Thanks to my readers: Ernesto Brosa, Matt Whelan, Ciaran Lawless, Sheena Murphy, Fergal Haran, Michael and Norah Harte for advice on various drafts.

Thanks to Nicola Budd and the Quercus staff who got us to the church on time. A big רבה תודה to Lavie Tidhar for assistance with Hebrew incantations.

Thanks to my intrepid agent Ian Drury for seeing the potential of *Irenicon*, and to my wise and wonderful editor Jo Fletcher for helping me realise it.

Aidan Harte 2011

most holy
the north sea
the anglish isles
francia major
the frankish isles
rhinelands
the western sea
francia minor
burgundy
the gulf of avignon
aragon
castile
grenada
N
W
E
S
fez
africa